*Take a thrill ride through the glamorous domain
of L.A.'s ultra-rich—where making a fortune
is a high-stakes game and where a killer stalks
the most decadent and daring players.*

# JACKIE COLLINS

**Heats up Hollywood in her national and
*New York Times* bestselling miniseries**

## L.A. CONNECTIONS

### POWER

In Hollywood, it's not who you know.
It's who can keep your secrets.

### OBSESSION

It takes more than ambition to make it
to the top.

### MURDER

There are some secrets worth killing for.

### REVENGE

Living well isn't the only payback.

# MEET THE MEN AND WOMEN CAUGHT UP IN THE SHATTERING SECRETS OF
# *L.A. CONNECTIONS*

**Madison Castelli:** The feisty, smart, sensual journalist is sent to L.A. to interview Hollywood superagent Freddie Leon for the magazine *Manhattan Style*. Instead she's swept into the biggest crime story of the year, and into a desire that may shatter her tough professionalism or her heart.

**Kristin Carr:** More Norma Jean than Marilyn, her wholesome, nubile looks are a titillating contrast to her talents—as a high-priced call girl, specializing in rich and famous clients. Risk is all part of her job, and so is servicing Max Steele *and* the dangerous and evil Mister X.

**Freddie Leon:** A driven, devious deal-maker who manipulates his celebrity clients like a puppet master, he has enormous power, a hidden agenda, and a star's erotic eight-by-ten glossies locked up in his safe . . . for insurance.

**Max Steele:** Still boyish looking at forty-two, in shape, and happiest behind the wheel of a shiny red Maserati or luring a lady into his bedroom, he is Freddie Leon's longtime partner . . . and the worst mistake he could make would be to become his enemy.

**Jake Sica:** Easy charm, laughing eyes, and sexual heat on sizzle, this freelance photographer holds a natural attraction for any SWF . . . but he has fallen hard, fast, and furiously for a blond beauty whose secrets mask a deadly double life.

**Natalie De Barge:** Like a five-foot-two case of dynamite, this black and beautiful, vivacious newscaster just needs some heat to ignite an explosive career. Now with her best friend Madison visiting, she's about to be cast into the fire of a breaking story.

**Cole De Barge:** Natalie's handsome, gay brother—a fitness trainer who *really* knows the secrets of the stars.

**Mister X:** The identity of the man who likes his sex strange, kinky, and dangerous is as hidden as his dark soul. His obsession is to experience ecstasy beyond the limits, where fear and death meet.

**Books by Jackie Collins**

Revenge
Murder
Obsession
Power
Thrill!
Vendetta: Lucky's Revenge
Hollywood Kids
American Star
Lady Boss
Rock Star
Hollywood Husbands
Lucky
Hollywood Wives
Chances
Lovers and Gamblers
The World Is Full of Divorced Women
The Love Killers
Sinners
The Bitch
The Stud
The World Is Full of Married Men

# JACKIE COLLINS

**POWER • OBSESSION • MURDER • REVENGE**

## L.A. Connections

**POCKET BOOKS**

New York   London   Toronto   Sydney   Tokyo   Singapore

This book consists of works of fiction. Names, characters, places and incidents are products of the author's imagination or are used fictitiously. Any resemblance to actual events or locales or persons, living or dead, is entirely coincidental.

These titles were previously published individually.

POCKET BOOKS, a division of Simon & Schuster Inc.
1230 Avenue of the Americas, New York, NY 10020

*Power* copyright © 1998 by Chances, Inc.
*Obsession* copyright © 1998 by Chances, Inc.
*Murder* copyright © 1998 by Chances, Inc.
*Revenge* copyright © 1998 by Chances, Inc.

ISBN: 0-671-03664-5

First Pocket Books printing of this omnibus edition June 1999

10  9  8  7  6  5  4  3  2  1

POCKET and colophon are registered trademarks of Simon & Schuster Inc.

Printed in the U.S.A.

# Contents

# Contents

# Power

# Prologue

# Los Angeles
## 1997

**I**T WAS NEAR MIDNIGHT WHEN the gleaming blue Mercedes limousine pulled up outside the closed bookstore in Farmers' Market, on Fairfax. A uniformed chauffeur—dressed all in black, including leather gloves and impenetrable sunglasses—stepped out of the car and glanced around.

Nearby, a pretty girl sitting in her parked Camaro hurriedly said goodbye to her girlfriend, with whom she had been chatting on her cell phone, and left her car, locking it behind her.

"Hi," she said, approaching the weird-looking chauffeur. "I'm Kimberly. Are you here for Mister X?"

He nodded and opened the rear door for her. She climbed in. He closed the door and got in the front seat.

"Mister X requires you to put on a blindfold," he said without turning around. "You will find it on the seat beside you."

*Okay,* Kimberly thought. *A kinky one. But that's nothing new.* Kimberly (real name Mary Ann Jones, formerly of Detroit) had been a Hollywood call girl for eighteen months, and during that time she'd seen plenty. Wearing a blindfold in the back of a limousine was nothing compared to some of the things she'd been asked to do.

She put on the soft velvet blindfold and settled back, almost falling asleep as the limo sped to its destination.

Twenty minutes later the car slowed, and she heard the clanking sound of heavy gates opening.

"Can I take the blindfold off now?" she asked, leaning forward.

"Kindly wait," the chauffeur replied.

A few moments later the limo pulled to a stop. Kimberly adjusted her dress, a skimpy designer number she'd picked up at Barney's warehouse sale. Then she fluffed out her hair, blond and curly.

The chauffeur opened the door. "Get out," he commanded.

She removed the blindfold without asking, and followed him to the entrance of a large mansion. He opened the door with a key and ushered her inside the dark entry hall.

"Wow!" Kimberly said, squinting at an enormous chandelier hanging above them. "Wouldn't want to be under *that* in an earthquake!"

"Here's your fee," the chauffeur said, handing her an envelope bulging with cash.

She took the envelope and stuffed it in her brown leather shoulder bag—a Coach original she'd purchased in Century City that same day. "Where's Mister X?" she asked. "In the bedroom?"

"No," the chauffeur replied. "Outside."

"Whatever," she said, thrusting out her size-36

C-cup breasts—purchased shortly after she'd first come to Hollywood, on the heels of winning a beauty contest back home.

"Whatever," the chauffeur mimicked, taking her arm and leading her through an ornate living room to French doors that took them out to a black-bottomed swimming pool.

The man had a firm grip on her arm—too firm for her liking. And how dare he mimic her, she thought. Where the hell was Mister X? She was ready to get this over and done with so she could get home to her live-in boyfriend—a sometime male-model-slash-porn-star with muscles of steel.

"Mister X would like to know if you can swim," the chauffeur said, stopping beside the pool.

"Nope," she replied, wondering why he didn't put on some lights—the place was downright gloomy. "Although I'm thinking of taking lessons."

"You'd better start now," the chauffeur said. And before she was aware of what was happening he had shoved her violently into the deep end of the pool.

She sank to the bottom, rising to the surface seconds later spluttering and choking, her arms flailing wildly in the air. "Help!" she screamed, gasping for air. "I told you—I . . . can't . . . swim."

The chauffeur stood by the edge of the pool, his member out, right hand working hard.

"Help me!" Kimberly yelled, struggling desperately before vanishing under the water for the second time.

The man continued to go about his business, climaxing over the girl's head as she surfaced again.

"You're *crazy!*" she screamed, before going down for the third time.

And after that, everything went black.

# One Year Later

# chapter 1

**M**ADISON CASTELLI DID
not particularly enjoy covering Hollywood stories.
Lifestyles of the rich and decadent was not her
thing—which is exactly why her editor, Victor Simons, had insisted she was the right person for the
assignment. "You're not into all that Hollywood
bullshit," he'd said. "You don't want anything from
the so-called power elite, which makes you the
perfect journalist to get me the real inside story on
Mr. Super-Power, Freddie Leon. Besides, you're
beautiful, so he'll pay attention."

*Ha!* Madison thought ruefully as she boarded an
American Airlines flight to L.A. *I'm so beautiful that
three months ago, David, my live-in love of two years,
went out for a pack of cigarettes and never came back.*

What he *did* do was leave her a cowardly note all
about how he couldn't deal with commitment and
would never be able to make her happy. Five weeks
later she'd found out he'd married his childhood

sweetheart—a vapid blonde with huge boobs and a serious overbite.

So much for avoiding commitment.

Madison was twenty-nine years old and extremely attractive, although she played her good looks down by wearing functional clothes and barely any make-up. But try as she might, nothing could disguise her almond-shaped eyes, sharply defined cheekbones, seductive lips, smooth olive skin, and black unruly hair she usually wore pulled back in a severe pony-tail. Not to mention her lithe, five-foot-eight-inch body, with full breasts, narrow waist and long dancer's legs.

Madison did not consider herself beautiful. Her idea of good looks was her mother, Stella—a statu-esque blonde whose dreamy eyes and quivering lips reminded most people of Marilyn Monroe.

Looks-wise, Madison took after her father, Michael, the best-looking fifty-eight-year-old in Connecticut. She'd also inherited his steely determi-nation and undeniable charm—two admirable qual-ities that had not hindered her rise to success as a well-respected writer of revealing profiles of the rich, notorious and powerful.

Madison loved what she did—going for the right angle, discovering the hidden secrets of people in the public eye. Politicians and super-rich business ty-coons were her favorite interviews. Movie stars, sports personalities and Hollywood moguls were low on her list. She didn't regard herself as a killer, although she did write with searing honesty, some-times upsetting the people she wrote about, who were usually sheltered in an all-enveloping cocoon of protective P.R.

Too bad if they didn't like it; she was merely telling the truth.

Settling into her first-class window seat, she glanced around the cabin, spotting Bo Deacon, a well-known TV host with an equally well-known drug habit. Bo did not look well; puffy-faced and slack-jawed, he still managed to come to life when the cameras rolled on his popular late-night talk show.

Madison hoped that the seat next to her would remain vacant, but it was not to be. At the last moment a breathy, busty blonde in a micro black leather dress was escorted aboard by two starstruck airline reps who practically carried her to her seat. Madison recognized the girl as Salli T. Turner, the current darling of the tabloids. Salli was the star of *Teach!,* a half-hour weekly TV sitcom in which she played a comely swimming teacher who visited a different glamorous mansion every week, causing havoc and saving lives—all the while dressed in a minuscule one-piece black rubber swimsuit, which only served to enhance her pneumatic breasts, twenty-inch waist and endless legs.

"Wow!" Salli exclaimed, collapsing into her seat and fluffing out her mane of blond curls. "Just made it!"

"Are you okay, Miss Turner?" asked anxious airline rep number one.

"What can I get you?" asked overeager airline rep number two.

Both men were bug-eyed, staring down her ample cleavage as if they'd never seen anything like it before. *And they probably haven't,* Madison thought.

"Everything's hunky-dory, guys," Salli said, favoring them with a toothy grin. "My husband's meeting me in L.A. If I'd missed the flight he would've been blue-assed pissed!"

"I can believe *that,*" said airline rep number one, eyes still bugging.

"Me, too!" agreed the other man.

Madison buried her head in *Newsweek*—the last thing she needed was a conversation with this airhead. She vaguely heard the flight attendant asking the men to leave so they could prepare for takeoff; then, shortly after, the big plane began taxiing down the runway.

Without warning, Salli suddenly clutched Madison's arm, causing her to almost drop her magazine.

"I *hate* flying," Salli squeaked, big blue eyes blinking rapidly. "I mean, it's not exactly *flying* I hate, more like *crashing.*"

Carefully Madison prised the girl's fingers off her arm. "Close your eyes, take a deep breath and slowly count to a hundred," she advised. "I'll let you know when we're airborne."

"Gee, thanks," Salli said gratefully. "Didn't think of doing that."

Madison frowned. Clearly this was going to be a long flight. Why couldn't she be stuck next to someone more *interesting?*

She folded her magazine and gazed out of the window as the plane took off. Unlike Salli, she loved flying. The sudden rush of speed, that exhilarating feeling of excitement when the wheels left the ground, the initial ascent—it always gave her a thrill, however many times she'd done it.

Salli sat silently beside her, eyes squeezed tightly shut, pouty lips slowly mouthing numbers.

By the time she opened her eyes they were in the air. "Radical shit!" Salli exclaimed, turning to Madison. "You're *amaz*ing!"

"Nothing to it," Madison murmured.

"No, *really,*" Salli insisted. "Your advice actually *worked!*"

"I'm glad," Madison said, wishing Miss Rubber Suit (she'd seen the show once—it was titillating trash) would keep her eyes closed for the entire trip.

Rescue arrived in the form of Bo Deacon, who came ambling over holding a glass of Scotch. "Salli, my darling!" he exclaimed. "You look absolutely edible."

"Oh, hi Bo," Salli said guilelessly. "Are you on this plane?"

*Smart question,* Madison thought wryly. *It's so nice to be traveling with intellectuals.*

"Yeah, honey, I'm sitting over there," he said, gesturing across the aisle. "Got some old bag next to me. Whyn't we try getting her to trade places?"

Salli fluttered her long fake eyelashes. "How are your ratings going?" she asked, as if that would be the deciding factor on whether she changed seats or not.

"Hardly as hot as yours, babe," he leered. "Whyn't I go back and ask the old bag to move?"

"I'm kinda comfortable where I am," Salli said.

"Don't be silly," Bo said. "We *should* sit together, that way we can talk about your next appearance on my show. Last time you were on we got better ratings than Howard."

Salli giggled, pleased with the compliment. "I did Howard's *E!* cable show in New York," she said, small pink tongue licking her jammy lips. "He's *sooo* rude, but cute with it."

"You're the first broad I've heard call Howard Stern cute," Bo said, shaking his head.

"Well, he is," Salli said. "He's kind of big and gangly, and he's always talking about his little dick. *My* guess is he's really got a whopper!"

Madison realized she was actually sitting next to a real live cliché—the definitive Hollywood blonde. If she recounted this exchange to any of her New York friends, they wouldn't believe her.

"You know what?" Madison said, leaning forward, speaking directly to Bo. "If it'll help out, I can change places with you."

Bo noticed her for the first time. "Hey, little lady, that's very sweet of you," he said, putting on his voice that said "I'm a big star, but I can actually be nice to real people."

"Little lady?" Was he kidding?

"On one condition," Salli interrupted.

"What's that, honey?" Bo said.

"I've *got* to sit next to this woman when we land. She's the greatest. She got me through takeoff. She's like some kind of, you know, magical medicine man."

Bo raised an eyebrow. "Really?" he said, taking another look at Madison. "You one of those broads with special powers, honey? Maybe *you* should come on my show."

"Thanks for the offer, Mr. Deacon," Madison answered coolly. "I have a hunch you should stick with Max the chimp."

Bo winked. "So you watch the show, huh?"

*When I can't sleep,* she wanted to say. *When I've*

*seen every old movie, and Letterman and Leno are in repeats, and I'm absolutely desperate.* "Sometimes," she said, with a pleasant smile, gathering her things, getting up and moving across the aisle to Bo's vacant seat.

The woman he'd referred to as an old bag was an attractive businesswoman in her forties diligently working on her laptop.

"Hi," Madison said. "I'm switching places with Mr. Deacon. Do you mind?"

The woman raised her eyes. "The pleasure is all mine," she said. "I actually thought I'd have to *talk* to him."

They both laughed.

Madison grinned. This was more her kind of traveling partner.

# chapter 2

"**I DON'T GIVE A FUCK,**" FREDdie Leon said, staring coldly at the short bearded man, who sat uncomfortably in a Biedermeier chair across the other side of Freddie's enormous steel and glass desk.

"I'm telling you, Freddie," the man said, somewhat agitated. "The bitch won't do it."

"Listen," Freddie repeated. "If *I* say she'll do it, it'll happen."

"Then you'd better speak to her."

"I intend to."

"And soon."

"Don't push it, Sam."

Freddie's demeanor was as cold as an Eskimo's dick. He did not appreciate anyone advising him. He had not become the most powerful superagent in Hollywood by listening to other people, especially a man such as Sam Lowski, a half-assed personal manager whose only real claim to fame was his one big client, Lucinda Bennett—major diva, major pain in the ass, major talent.

Freddie Leon was a poker-faced man of forty-six. He had cordial features, ordinary brown hair, matching eyes and a quick, bland smile which rarely reached his eyes. Head and part owner of the powerful I.A.A.—International Artists Agents—he was nicknamed "the snake" because he could skillfully slither in and out of any deal. Nobody ever dared call him "the snake" to his face. His wife, Diana, had done so once. It was the only time he'd raised his hand to her.

Sam got up to leave. Freddie didn't stop him—he had nothing else to say.

As soon as Sam was out the door, Freddie waited a beat and picked up the phone, speed-dialing Lucinda Bennett's private number. Lucinda answered, sounding sleepy.

"How's my favorite client?" Freddie asked, putting all the charm he could muster into his cold, flat voice.

"Asleep," Lucinda replied grumpily.

"Alone?" Freddie questioned.

An arch laugh. "None of your business."

Freddie cleared his throat. "What's all this I hear about you being a naughty girl?"

"Don't talk down to me, dear," Lucinda said, her voice languid. "I'm too old and too rich to take that kind of crapola."

"I'm not talking down to you," Freddie replied. "I'm merely reminding you that good behavior always wins in the end."

"I guess Sam crawled in to see you," Lucinda said, the lack of respect she felt for her personal manager coloring her tone.

"Exactly," Freddie replied. "He tells me you're planning on backing out of the Kevin Page movie."

"He's absolutely right."

Freddie checked his irritation. Remaining cool was a requisite of his profession. "Why would you want to do a thing like that when the deal is already in place, and you're getting twelve million dollars?" he asked.

"Because Kevin Page is too young for me," Lucinda responded crisply. "I hardly want to look like an old hag on screen."

"I told you three weeks ago, Lucinda, it's in your contract—they'll hire the cinematographer of your choice. You can look eighteen if you want to."

"I'm almost forty, Freddie," she snapped. "I have no desire to look eighteen."

He knew for a fact she was at least forty-five. "Okay," he said calmly. "Twenty-eight, thirty-eight—whatever age pleases you."

"Don't try to placate me. Kevin Page is your client. He's made two hit movies, and now you think you can cement his career by teaming him with me."

"Not true. This deal is about you. It's essential that you keep reaching that younger audience. Demographics count." He paused before continuing. "You're an enormous star, Lucinda, there's nobody bigger. But you've also got to realize that there're plenty of young people who've never heard of you."

"Screw you, Freddie," she responded furiously. "I can do what I want."

"No," Freddie said, his voice hardening. "You can't. You'll do what *I* say."

"And if I refuse?"

"Then I'll no longer be your agent."

"Freddie, dear, sometimes I think you don't get it," Lucinda said, her icy diva voice piercing his ear. "Agents should be kissing my left toe to represent me."

"If that's what you want, Lucinda," he said, his tone perfectly cool.

"Maybe it is," she said, challenging him.

"Let me know," he said. And then he played his ace card. "Oh, by the way—remember that time way, way back, when you asked me to get hold of some early photographs your first husband took of you, and I was able to do so?"

"Yes."

"Strange thing," he said slowly. "I was going through my safe the other day, and it seems I still have a set of negatives."

Her voice rose, hot with disbelief. "Are you *blackmailing* me, Freddie?"

"No," he said evenly. "Merely trying to get you to sign a contract which has been on your desk for over a week. A contract that'll pay you twelve million dollars, star you with the hottest young actor in the country, *and* keep your career at the top, exactly where it should be." He paused, allowing her to mull over what he'd said. "Think about it, Lucinda, and let me know before the end of the day." Before she could reply, he replaced the receiver.

Actresses! They'd had to suck so much dick on the way up that once they made it, all they wanted to do was cause trouble.

But nobody caused trouble for Freddie Leon.

He had the power, and he was not shy about using it.

# chapter 3

NATALIE DE BARGE CON-
sulted her Bulgari Swatch watch, a recent present to
herself, and swore softly under her breath. How
come time passed so quickly? She was running late
again, and it made her crazy. She had so much to do
before meeting her best friend and old college roommate, Madison, at the airport. *And,* on top of
everything else, after driving to LAX, she then had
to get back to the studio in time for her spot on the
six-o'clock news, where she was the show-biz news
person on a local TV station. And although she
enjoyed what she did, she certainly aspired to do
more than cover trivial gossip and even more trivial
show-biz events.

Natalie was an extremely vivacious twenty-nine-
year-old black woman, with glowing skin, wide
brown eyes and a curvaceous body. The bane of her
life was the fact that she was only five feet, two
inches tall, which really pissed her off, because she
would have loved to have been born long and lean

like Madison—whom she was genuinely excited about seeing. They spoke at least twice a week, but it wasn't as good as living in the same city. Recently Natalie had split with her out-of-work artist boyfriend, Denzl. Quite convenient, since Madison was no longer with David. Ah yes, Natalie thought, they would certainly have plenty to discuss.

Natalie had already convinced herself that she hardly missed Denzl at all, although he *had* possessed a truly beautiful body. The sad truth was that sometimes a beautiful body was not enough. Denzl had leeched off her for over a year, and when she'd stopped paying the bills, he'd disappeared in the middle of the night with her expensive stereo equipment and entire CD collection of soul classics. She missed Marvin Gaye and Al Green more than she missed him.

"Hey you," said Jimmy Sica, the nighttime news anchor recently hired out of Denver. "What's with the hairstyle?"

Natalie turned, checking Jimmy out. He was six feet tall and extraordinarily handsome, which didn't impress her at all, because she wasn't into perfect good looks—she preferred her men more on the edgy side. "I cut it," she said, casually touching her short, sleek do. "You like?"

"Makes you look about twelve."

She grinned. "Gee, thanks! I *think* that's a compliment in this town."

"Long hair, short hair—you always look great," Jimmy said, smiling. He had a gorgeous smile—and a gorgeous fair-haired wife whose picture he kept prominently displayed on his desk.

"Why, thank you, Jimmy," she said, putting on an

exaggerated Southern accent. "I never thought you noticed."

Jimmy flashed his best anchorman smile, revealing perfect teeth and a strong jawline. "All the guys around here notice you."

Was Jimmy Sica coming on to her? No way.

"I'm meeting my girlfriend later," Natalie said, quickly changing the subject. "She's flying in from New York to research a story on Freddie Leon."

Jimmy was suitably impressed. "The agent?"

"Is there another Freddie Leon?"

"Sounds like an interesting gig."

"Madison's an interesting woman."

Jimmy zeroed in for a long lingering look. "If she's *your* friend, I'm sure she is."

"Uh . . . maybe I'll bring her to the studio one day, give her the grand tour."

"I've got a better idea. My wife and I are having a small dinner on Saturday at the house—why don't you bring your friend over? My brother's in town, and a couple of old college buddies. We can make it a party."

"What kind of party did you have in mind, Jimmy?" she asked coyly.

"Not *that* kind of party, honey," he said with a quick laugh. "Sorry to disappoint you, but I'm the straightest guy in town."

"I *know*," she said, mildly flirting in spite of the fact that he wasn't her type. "That's what I like about you."

He raised an expressive eyebrow. "Really?"

"Yes, really."

They exchanged smiles. *Hmm,* she thought, *he's definitely coming on to me.* Which made her slightly uncomfortable because he was married. Besides, he was way too tall for her.

"I'll run it by Madison and let you know," she said.

"Great," he said.

*Yeah. Great.* Maybe his brother would turn out to be the big love of her life—the prince she was forever searching for. Black, white, multicolored—the right guy had to be out there *somewhere*.

*Sure. And John F. Kennedy, Jr., is gay.*

"I'm outta here," she said, giving him a little wave. "See you later."

Jimmy Sica smiled his brilliant smile. "You can bet I'll be looking forward to it."

# chapter 4

THE PHONE RANG IN KRIStin Carr's pale peach apartment. It was past noon and she was asleep. In a vague fog she heard the loud ringing and waited for Chiew to pick up. To her annoyance, her lazy maid didn't do so.

Hazily Kristin realized it must be her private line. *Shit!* She didn't feel great. Too much Dom Perignon and coke the previous night, and a couple of Halcion to help her sleep. *Shit!*

Her long white arm snaked out from under pale peach satin sheets, groping for the receiver. "Yes?" she murmured, husky-voiced.

"Mister X would like to see you," said a female voice.

"Oh, God, Darlene. Not again! I told you after the last time, I'm not interested."

"Would four thousand cash change your mind?"

"Why me?" she groaned.

"Because you're the best."

Kristin thought about her two previous encounters with Mister X. The first time she'd met him in an underground parking lot in Century City as instructed. He was driving a dark pickup truck with no visible plates and was dressed entirely in black—including opaque sunglasses and a pulled-down baseball cap. Without leaving the truck he'd requested that she strip naked in the parking structure—which fortunately was deserted—and while she circled bare-assed around his truck, he'd jacked off. When he was finished he'd silently handed her an envelope through the window containing two thousand dollars, then hurriedly driven off.

The second time she'd met him in the back row of a movie theater in Westwood at noon. The darkened cinema was deserted, an Eddie Murphy movie played on the big screen, and Mister X was once more in deep disguise. He'd sat next to her, told her to remove her panties and hand them to him, then he'd satisfied himself on the panties and handed them back to her with an envelope containing cash. When she got out of the theater he was long gone.

It was the easiest money she'd ever made and also the weirdest. Mister X gave her a bad feeling.

"He's a freak," she said.

"Force yourself," Darlene said.

"All right," she said grumpily, tempted by the exorbitant amount of money, although her instinct warned her to say no.

"It won't be so bad."

"How do *you* know?"

"It's not as if he beats you up or anything. In fact,

you told me that last time he didn't so much as touch you."

"I wish he had," Kristin said heatedly. "Then at least I'd know he was *human.*"

"His money says he's human. That should suffice."

"Okay, okay," Kristin said with a deep sigh. "What dump do I have to meet him at this time?"

"Hollywood Boulevard. A motel past La Brea. I'll fax you the exact address. He wants you there at seven. And wear white—including shoes, hose and sunglasses."

"Does that mean I get a clothes allowance too?" Kristin drawled sarcastically.

"Four thousand's not bad," Darlene pointed out. "That's a thousand up on last time."

"Big fucking deal."

"Have fun."

*Darlene's a great madam,* Kristin thought bitterly. *All she cares about is the almighty buck. Screw safety.*

She slid out of bed and into the shower. Kristin was the original golden girl—everything natural. A sweep of long blond hair; all-American features; a curvaceous body with large breasts; and a tangle of fluffy gold pubic hair that turned grown men into horny little boys.

She looked like an angel. But she had a heart of stone and a calculator for a brain.

Kristin had a plan. The moment she had accumulated half a million dollars cash in her safe-deposit box, she was out of the business. Every little four thousand dollars helped.

But still . . . Mister X again, the second time in a week. She shuddered at the thought.

Reaching for a soft pink bathrobe, she wrapped it around her glorious body.

Oh, well, another day. Another step toward her goal.

Eventually she'd be free.

# chapter 5

"**W**HAT A JERK!" SALLI T. Turner exclaimed, her heavily glossed shell pink lips turning down at the corners, signaling her disapproval.

"Excuse me?" said Madison. She had just settled back into her original seat and was busy thinking about her interview with Freddie Leon—an interview that, if all went smoothly, was due to take place very soon. Victor had promised to set it up through his connection with a mutual friend, even though Freddie Leon was famous for never speaking to the press. In the meantime, Madison planned on talking to his friends, acquaintances, clients and enemies. In fact, anyone who had anything to say about the man.

Salli leaned closer, allowing Madison a frightening close-up of her mascara-caked false lashes. *She's too pretty for that much makeup,* Madison thought. *Why doesn't someone tell her?*

"Bo," Salli said in a half whisper. "He's a real horny asshole."

31

"I, uh . . . don't know him," Madison said, wondering why Salli had decided to confide in her.

"You don't have to," Salli snorted derisively. "He's a man, isn't he? And a famous one at that." She wrinkled her snub nose. "All these famous guys think they can get anyone. Do you *know* what he asked me to do?"

"What?" Madison asked, her natural curiosity aroused.

"Invited me into the john so we could make out," Salli whispered. "Only he didn't put it that politely."

"Are you serious?"

"Girl Scout's honor," Salli said. "Ha! Like I'd do it with *him* again. I mean, just 'cause I've got big boobs, blond hair and the whole bimbo bit, men think I'm like *hanging* around, *waiting* for 'em."

"It must be a problem," Madison murmured sympathetically, wondering what Salli meant by "again."

"I can handle it," Salli said, summoning up attitude. "In fact, I get off on the attention." She shrugged, tugging at her short leather skirt. "Hey—I know I have the equipment, but it's not like I'm *dumb* or anything."

"I'm sure you're not," Madison said gently.

"No, I mean *really,*" Salli said, becoming quite heated. "I've used what I've got to get where I am today 'cause it's the only way I could get noticed. Clint Eastwood used what *he* had to become a star. We're just different, that's all."

Madison didn't think it was prudent to point out that Clint Eastwood had been in the business for over thirty years, and had produced and directed many movies. Plus he had his own company and an impeccable professional reputation. But who knew? Maybe thirty years down the line Salli would have the same—stranger things had happened.

"Here's the truth," Salli said, leaning even closer, so that Madison could smell her peppermint-tinged breath. "My boobs are silicone, 'cause I *know* big boobs turn guys on. I've had all the fat sucked out of my thighs, and some of it pumped back into my lips. I bleach my hair and wear sexy clothes. I'm the proof that it all works. It got me a TV series and a *sensational* husband. *Wait* till you meet Bobby, he'll be at the airport."

"I'd like to," Madison said.

"He's a stud!" Salli boasted. "He'd *kill* Bo Deacon if he heard how disrespectful he was to me."

"Then I suggest you don't tell him."

Salli widened her eyes. "I'm not *stupid.*"

"Did you know Bo before?" Madison asked.

"A long time ago . . . before I made it," Salli said. "Then after I got famous, I was on his show a few times and we like *flirted* on camera. Nothing unusual about *that,* I flirt with them all—Letterman, Leno, Howard. *Everyone* does—Pamela Anderson, Heather Locklear, even Julia Roberts. That's the deal. It's expected." She picked up her drink. "Now I'm *married,* so he shouldn't be coming on to me. It's not nice."

"You're right," Madison agreed.

"Anyway," Salli continued. "I'm sure you're bored with hearing all about me. What do *you* do?"

"You'll hate this," Madison said wryly, thinking that maybe she should have mentioned it before.

"What?"

"I'm a journalist."

Salli burst into peals of girlish laughter. "Oh, no! A snoop! And here I am spilling the goods. Now I suppose I'll be all over the cover of the *Star* or the *Enquirer*. True confessions of a sex queen. I'm *such* a ditz!"

"Not *that* kind of journalist," Madison said quickly. "I write for *Manhattan Style*."

"Wow!" Salli responded, her big blue eyes full of surprise. "That's classy stuff. They'd never write about someone like little old *me*." A short hopeful pause. "Would they?"

"Why not? You'd be an interesting interview."

"You think?" Salli said eagerly.

"If you're willing to get into the whole Hollywood sex machine deal. If you were *really* truthful, we could probably have an intriguing piece. I'm sure you've got lots of tales to tell."

"You should *hear* some of my stories," Salli said, rolling her eyes. "I could lay stuff on you that'd make your tonsils hurt! Guys in this town—ha! There's *nothing* I don't know."

"Maybe I should talk to my editor."

"Wow!" Salli said, wriggling in her seat. "Can I be on the cover?"

"We have twelve covers a year," Madison explained. "Only four of those are show-business-related. That's a tough prize to win."

"Every magazine wants me on the cover," Salli said guilelessly. "Truth is, I sell magazines."

"I'm sure. But my editor walks his own path."

"Remember those pictures of Demi Moore on the

front of *Vanity Fair*—all naked and pregnant?" Salli
said brightly. "I heard it *zoomed* their circulation.
How about *me* naked? Would your editor go for
that?"

Madison shook her head. "More *Playboy* than
us."

Salli giggled. "I *know*. Only joking. I've been on
*Playboy*'s cover three times. They adore me." She
giggled again. "Or rather, they adore my big boobs!"

"I can imagine you're very popular."

"Why are you coming to L.A.?" Salli asked.

"I'm interviewing Freddie Leon, the agent. You
don't happen to know him, do you?"

"Wow! Freddie Leon," Salli sighed. "He's the
man."

"I take it he's high on your list of important
people?"

"Freddie Leon is only the most powerful agent in
Hollywood," Salli said reverently, nodding as she
said it, her blond curls bouncing. "My ambition is
that one day he'll represent *me.*"

"Have you ever met him?" Madison asked curiously.

Salli hesitated before answering. "Well," she said
tentatively, "once . . . a while ago."

"Yes?" Madison encouraged, sensing a story.
"What happened?"

"I wasn't his type," Salli said flatly, as if the
memory didn't please her.

Madison sensed a story. "Sexually? Or as a potential client?" she asked.

Salli wriggled in her seat. "One day I kinda
tracked him in the underground parking of his office.

He gave me the big brush." She frowned. "Maybe he's not into sex, 'cause believe me—I do *not* get turndowns—I mean like *never!"*

"You went there to have sex with him?" Madison asked, surprised at her openness.

"No!" Salli answered indignantly. "I went there to get his attention. I wasn't married then, my career was going nowhere, so I was taking a shot."

Madison decided that Salli's honesty was quite refreshing. There was a certain girlish naïveté hidden beneath the bleached blond hair and outrageous boobs.

"Are we nearly there?" Salli inquired, beginning to get nervous.

"Yes," Madison said. "Time to prepare yourself. Remember what I told you—close your eyes, take a long, deep breath and slowly count to a hundred. I'll let you know when we're on the ground."

"You're the best!" Salli exclaimed. "Truth is, I don't have any girlfriends, they're all jealous." She gave a wan little smile. "Dunno why—they could have what I have for a price. Well, not *everything,"* she added thoughtfully. "They certainly couldn't have Bobby—he's totally yummy and all mine!"

"How long have you been married?"

"Exactly six months, two weeks, three days and, if I had a watch, I'd probably say thirty-three seconds." She laughed, slightly embarrassed. "I don't sound *too* much in love, do I?"

"What does Bobby do?"

"He's like a major danger adventure guy. Rides motorcycles and cars, stuff like that. Jumps over, like, forty-two buses. All the things someone called

Evel Knievel did years and years ago, in my grandma's day."

"Oh, yes, I've read about him. Bobby Skorch. The man who takes his life in his hands every day."

"That's my Bobby," Salli said proudly. "Are *you* married?"

Madison shook her head. "Too scary for me," she said, thinking briefly of David, who'd never asked. For two years they'd been inseparable; now they were total strangers.

"I was married before Bobby," Salli announced. "To a psycho freakazoid *asshole* actor."

Madison laughed. "Tell me how you *really* feel."

Salli frowned again, thinking about her ex. "He sued *me* for alimony. Can you believe it? He *still* thinks that one day I'll take him back. Moron *city!*"

"How long were you married to him?"

"Long enough for the bastard to break my arm a couple of times. Not to mention black eyes and bruises and all of that."

"Sounds like a charmer."

*"He* thought he was."

Salli didn't speak again until the plane landed. Then she opened her eyes and unbuckled her seat belt. "That was a cinch!" she exclaimed. "Want a job as my flying coach?"

Madison smiled. "Think I'll pass," she said, standing up and stretching.

"If you don't have anybody meeting you, we can give you a ride in our limo," Salli offered. "Bobby's into the extra extra stretch with the Jacuzzi in the back. It's *sooo* Hollywood, but since we're both from little towns, we get off on it!"

"That's okay," Madison said, still smiling. "My friend's picking me up."

"You've *got* to come visit me," Salli said, scribbling her number on a menu and handing it over. "You're *sooo* cool—and great-looking too, in a kind of like *normal* way."

Madison laughed. *"Thanks,* I think!"

"I mean it," Salli said enthusiastically. "Our house in the Palisades is *amazing."*

"I'm sure."

"Oh, God!" Salli groaned, with an exaggerated shudder. "Here comes the letch."

And Bo Deacon was upon them, all washed and brushed—and drenched in a heavy cologne. He attempted to take Salli's arm, but she was too quick for him, niftily backing into a burly businessman who couldn't be more delighted that he actually got to touch the delectable Salli T. Turner.

An airline rep pushed past, eager to reach his two stars. Madison heard Bo say to Salli in a nasty whisper, "What's the matter, bitch? Trying to forget the people who got you where you are today?"

Madison shook her head and exited the plane, walking briskly through the airport to the luggage carousel.

"Girlfriend!" Natalie yelled, appearing out of nowhere. "You're here!"

Madison was delighted to see her. *"Finally,"* she said with a big grin. "It was a long flight."

They exchanged warm hugs.

"The traffic was a monster," Natalie said. "I only just made it."

"You saved me a limo ride."

"How's that?"

Madison indicated Salli T. Turner and Bobby Skorch locked in a steamy embrace by the exit. "I could've hitched a ride with them."

"No way," Natalie said disbelievingly. "The delectable Salli T. Queen of the wet dream brigade."

"I certainly could've. Salli's my new best friend."

Natalie laughed. "Does that mean you've traded my fine black ass for a bountiful blonde?"

"Yeah, right," Madison said dryly. "Can't you imagine me and Salli T. palling out? We've got so much in common."

"Hmm . . ." Natalie said, staring over. "The husband's pretty damn cute."

Madison glanced at Salli and Bobby, who were still making out, in spite of—or maybe because of—several hovering paparazzi. "All I can see is black leather, long hair, and tattoos."

Natalie gave a dirty laugh. "Sometimes I like 'em rough and colorful."

*Oh, God,* Madison thought. *Shades of college. We've only been together two minutes and we're already discussing men.*

"Here comes my suitcase," she said, lugging it off the moving carousel. "Let's go."

"Before you succumb to the limo ride?" Natalie teased.

"Don't be ridiculous!" Madison replied, laughing.

Within minutes they were in Natalie's car, heading for the Hollywood Hills, where Natalie shared a small house with her brother, Cole, a personal trainer.

Madison gazed out the window. Sunshine, palm trees, fast food restaurants and gas stations. Ah, L.A., what a place!

In spite of her misgivings about Hollywood and its inhabitants, she was excited about her assignment. Freddie Leon was a high-profile power broker who'd managed to keep an exceptionally low profile in his private life. One wife. Two children. No scandal. And yet here was a man who controlled the most important talent in Hollywood. A man who had everyone's attention.

She was determined to find out everything—unearth the real man beneath the impenetrable image.

It was a challenge.

Madison always *had* relished a challenge.

# chapter 6

**"I**'M LEAVING NOW," FREDDIE Leon informed his executive assistant, Ria Santiago.

Ria glanced up from her desk as Freddie passed by. She was an attractive Hispanic woman in her mid-forties who'd worked for Freddie for just over ten years. She knew him as well as anyone—which didn't mean a lot, because Freddie was an intensely private person who was all business.

"Shall I phone Mrs. Leon and tell her you're on your way?" Ria inquired, tapping a sharp pencil on her desktop.

"No," Freddie said. "I have to make a stop. I'll call her myself from the car."

"Very well," Ria replied, knowing better than to ask where he was going.

Freddie stepped into the private elevator he shared with his partner in I.A.A., Max Steele, and pressed the button for underground parking. When he stepped off the elevator, his maroon Rolls was waiting, waxed and gleaming, which pleased him because he was very particular about his cars—the slightest scrape or blemish drove him insane.

Willie, the parking valet, jumped to attention. "Weatherman says it might rain, Mr. Leon," Willie said cheerfully, careful to breathe in the other direction lest the Scotch he'd just swigged from the bottle hit Freddie in the face.

"The weatherman is wrong, Willie. I can smell rain when it's on the way."

"Yessir, Mr. Leon," Willie said respectfully, backing away even further. He knew how to kiss ass better than anyone; it got him a five-hundred-buck cash tip every Christmas.

Freddie got in his car and drove carefully from the I.A.A. building—an architectural delight—his mind running over the events of the day, making sure he remembered every detail. The less committed to paper the better—that was Freddie's philosophy. It had worked well for him over the years.

He hoped Lucinda Bennett was not about to cause trouble. He'd negotiated a major contract for her—more money than she'd ever received before—and with Kevin Page as her costar, their movie together was bound to be a hit. Now Lucinda was attempting to give him a hard time, which wouldn't work—his little remark about the negatives in his safe had definitely given her something to think about.

What kind of Hollywood was it today when he had to talk an actress, whose career would be over in less than five years, into accepting twelve million dollars?

Talent. They were a breed unto themselves. Egotistical, ungrateful and predictable. Which is why Freddie was able to convince them he was always right. Deep down they were children who needed tough love and guidance. Freddie gave them exactly what they wanted. Max was his complete opposite. Max was Mr. Smoothie. Divorced and always on the lookout for fresh new talent, Max cultivated the playboy image—a racy Porsche, a wardrobe of Brioni suits, a penthouse apartment on Wilshire, and countless beautiful women. The difference between them worked. Freddie handled the major superstars, Max looked after the slightly lower-level luminaries.

Freddie smiled to himself, a smile that did not reach his lips. Max thought he was the smartest guy in town; in truth he was a joke—Freddie's own private source of amusement—for nobody fooled Freddie Leon. And Freddie knew for a fact that for the last three months Max had been involved in secret negotiations to land a high-powered studio job. And if he snagged it he'd leave I.A.A. and Freddie without a backward glance, selling his interest in I.A.A. to the highest bidder.

Freddie had his own future to watch out for. Max Steele was a traitor. And Freddie knew how to deal with traitors better than anyone.

Oblivious to Freddie Leon's knowledge of his negotiations, Max Steele wound up a long lunch at the Grill. His luncheon companion was a breathtakingly beautiful Swedish model who bore more than a passing resemblance to a young Grace Kelly.

Inga Cruelle wanted to make the difficult transition from supermodel to movie star.

Max Steele wanted to get into her Victoria's Secret lacy thong and fuck the life out of her.

They both had their agendas.

"So you see," Inga said, as they lingered over decaf cappuccinos, her long delicate fingers toying with the rim of her coffee cup, "I do not wish to do what Cindy did. A starring role will be too difficult for my first attempt."

The ego on these girls was astounding, Max thought. However beautiful she was, what made Inga Cruelle imagine she could cut it on the big screen when there were hundreds of actresses out there—girls who really knew their craft—who couldn't even get in for an audition?

"Very wise," he said. Max was not movie-star handsome, but at forty-two he had an abundance of boyish charm, a full head of curly brown hair, an in-shape body and plenty of style. Plus his reputation as a cocksman was legendary.

"Elle seems to be doing it the right way," Inga mused, her long tapered fingers now twirling her coffee spoon. "She was quite good in the Streisand movie."

This was their second lunch together, and Max had played his role perfectly. They were the agent and the potential client. Nothing more. By this time Inga—who was used to reducing most men to slobbering idiots—must be wondering why he hadn't made any kind of move.

"Elle's a smart girl," he said briskly. "She works hard."

*"I'll* work hard," Inga said, her exquisite unmade-up face painfully earnest. "I'll even take acting classes if you think it's necessary."

*No, sweetheart. Why would you want to do that? You're a successful model. Don't put yourself out.*

"Right," he said. "Good idea."

44

"You are so understanding, Max, so helpful," Inga said, placing a delicate hand on his arm.

*Good. She was making the first move.*

"Listen," he said as sincerely as he could manage. "I want to help you, Inga, so I'm sending you to see a director friend of mine. Maybe, if he likes you, I can persuade him to shoot a test."

"A screen test?"

"Yeah, get a feeling of how you are in front of the camera."

Inga laughed, as if it was the most ridiculous thing she'd ever heard. "You've seen my photographs, Max," she said immodestly. "You *know* the camera loves and adores me."

"Still photographs are different. The movie camera has a mind of its own," Max said, marveling at her conceit. *"You* brought up Cindy. Yeah, sure she's a knockout, and she *looked* fantastic in her movie. But the big problem was her emotions simply didn't translate. She came across as a blank canvas."

"That is *exactly* why I do not wish to *star* in my first film," Inga said, as if producers were lining up to hire her.

"I could also set something up on a social level," Max said casually, baiting the trap. "Maybe a dinner at the Leons'."

"Your partner?"

"Freddie's dinners are legendary."

"Very well," Inga said. "Should I bring my fiancé?"

What was with this fiancé crap? It was the first *he'd* heard of it.

"I didn't know you were engaged," he said, slightly irritated.

"My fiancé lives in Sweden," Inga said, her precise accent a definite detriment to a film career. "He is arriving tomorrow to spend two days with me at the Bel Air Hotel, then he will fly home."

"Really?" Max said, even more irritated. "What does he do?"

"He's a very successful businessman," Inga replied. "We have known each other since school."

Max was not interested in the details. "When are you returning to New York?" he asked, wondering if she gave great head.

"Perhaps next week," Inga said. "My agency is impatient. However, I told them how important it is that I stay here until I have made a decision about my movie commitments."

"Sounds good to me," Max said, deciding that she probably didn't. Beautiful girls were not as into it as their plainer sisters. "Only I should warn you," he added, "no fiancés at business meetings. Leave him at the hotel."

"This will not be a problem," Inga said coolly.

Max snapped his fingers for the check, which the waiter immediately brought to the table.

*So, she has a fiancé,* he thought. *Am I wasting my time or what?*

*No, she also has that hungry look. The look all these girls have when they want to be movie stars.*

"Time to get back to work," he said, signing the check and standing up.

Inga slid out of the booth. She had on white slacks and a pale pink angora sweater, which gently covered the swell of her small, perfect breasts. He knew they were perfect and not silicone-enhanced, because he'd seen the nude spread she'd done for

famed photographer Helmut Newton in *Vogue.*
Eight pages of Inga. Black stockings, matching garter
belt, stiletto heels, and a Great Dane sitting pas-
sively at her feet. Very classy. Very naked. Not at all
crude.

Max decided the time had come to nail this
delectable Swedish morsel. He wanted to go down
on her—his specialty—in the worst way.

And soon.

Fiancé or no fiancé, he had no doubt she was a
sure thing.

# chapter 7

KRISTIN DID NOT POSSESS white hose, which meant a trip to Neiman Marcus. Not such a hardship, as she enjoyed strolling around the luxurious store buying clothes she didn't need and perusing the tempting makeup counters. Shopping was therapeutic—it took her mind off everything, suspending her in a land of soft, sensual lingerie, Judith Leiber purses and Manolo Blahnik shoes.

Recently they'd installed a huge curved martini bar in the men's department. Kristin felt comfortable sitting at it, sipping a vodka martini, daydreaming that she was a perfect Hollywood wife with two darling little children and an important executive big-deal husband. A *faithful* big-deal husband—because all the ones she came across were lying whoremongers who cheated on their wives without giving their infidelities a second thought. And Kristin should know—she'd had most of them in the three years she'd been a call girl in Hollywood.

Kristin and her younger sister, Cherie, had arrived in L.A. four years ago, with aspirations to become movie stars. Kristin had been nineteen, Cherie eighteen, and like hundreds and thousands of teenage hopefuls before them, they'd saved their money, left the small town they'd lived in all their young lives, and made the trek west in a beat-up Volkswagen.

Cherie was the true beauty of the family—or so everyone always said. Kristin was merely the sister who paled in comparison. But the two of them were the closest of friends, and did everything together.

As soon as they arrived in L.A. they rented a cheap apartment and both got jobs waitressing in a busy Italian restaurant on Melrose. Cherie lasted exactly one week before being discovered by one of the customers—Howie Powers—the bad-boy son of a rich business executive.

From the start Kristin knew that Howie was not good news. She found out he was heavily into drugs, booze and gambling. She also discovered he was into taking his father's money and blowing it on fast cars and as many women as he could handle. That is, until he spotted Cherie, and fell in love.

Howie pursued Cherie relentlessly, taking her to the best restaurants and clubs, showering her with expensive presents, treating her like a queen. It wasn't long before he persuaded her to give up her job and move in with him. Kristin warned her not to, but Cherie wouldn't listen. "He wants to marry me," she said, all starry-eyed and in love. "We're doing it after I meet his parents."

"And when will that be?" Kristin asked.

"Soon," Cherie replied. "He's taking me to Palm Springs to see them."

Kristin didn't believe it for a moment. Howie wasn't the marrying kind. He'd string Cherie along with promises until he grew tired of her, and then he'd dump her. Kristin knew the type—she'd experienced the rich-boy syndrome in high school when she'd given up her virginity to the captain of the football team and he'd boasted to everyone about his conquest. When she'd complained, he'd refused to speak to her again. A sobering lesson about men.

Kristin saw Howie as the sleazy playboy he was—especially when one day he came on to *her* while Cherie was out shopping. She loathed him, but at the same time she was forced to put up with him because of her sister. Until the night she discovered that Howie had gotten Cherie hooked on cocaine. Then she went crazy, fighting with both of them. Cherie told her to back off and mind her own business. So she did.

And two weeks later she'd gotten a midnight call informing her that on their way to Palm Springs to meet his parents, Howie had fallen asleep at the wheel of his Porsche, crossed the dividing line of the highway and smashed head-on into another car. The driver of the other car was killed, Howie was only slightly injured, and Cherie was in a coma.

Now it was four years later, and Cherie lay in a nursing home—a virtual vegetable—while Kristin was one of the most successful call girls in town. She'd had no choice; somebody had to pay the hospital bills, and that somebody certainly wasn't Howie Powers—who'd instantly vanished out of their lives.

"Excuse me, do you mind if I sit here?"

Kristin glanced up. A man had settled on the stool next to her, in spite of the fact that there were many empty places. He was handsome in a rumpled way—not at all Beverly Hills or Bel Air. He had on a white T-shirt, brown leather flying jacket, khaki pants and well-worn sneakers.

"Not at all," she replied carefully, wondering if he'd ever been a customer. Highly unlikely; he didn't look like a man who had to pay for it.

"I'm not coming out with a line," he said in a deep husky voice. "But can I ask you a big favor?"

*No favors, honey. Cash up front. I have bills to pay.*

"What?" she said shortly.

"This'll *sound* like a line," he said, grinning. "Only believe me—it's not. You see, I gotta go to my father's wedding, and I haven't worn a tie in years, not to mention the fact that when it comes to clothes I have no taste. So . . ." He thrust two ties in front of her. "Whaddya think?"

"What do *I* think?" she said slowly.

"Yes. I need an opinion other than my own. And you look like a woman with an eye for the best."

"Why don't you ask a salesperson?" she suggested.

"'Cause they don't have your class and style," he said, his grin widening. *"You* will make me into the son my dad always wanted."

It was so long since she'd experienced a genuine pickup that she couldn't help smiling. "You're not from L.A., are you?" she said.

"Nope," he replied. "Arizona. Drove here yesterday. The wedding's on Sunday. What's your pick?"

She stared at the two ties, both boringly conservative. "Come with me," she said, standing up. "I'm

sure we can do better." And with that she led him
toward the tie department.

An hour later, with a purple Armani tie in his
shopping bag, they were still talking. She'd found
out his name was Jake and he was a professional
photographer—much to his banker father's disgust.
He was thirty, unmarried and had moved to L.A. to
pursue a new job with a magazine.

"The money's great," he said. "And it'll be a
challenge photographing real humans instead of
animals and landscapes."

"Real humans? *Here?*" Kristin drawled, sipping
her third martini. "You *do* know you're in L.A."

"Don't sound so jaded," he said, "it doesn't go
with your looks."

*What the hell are you doing?* she asked herself
crossly. *Sitting here flirting with a total stranger. And
actually liking it.*

"I have to go," she said abruptly, standing up.

"Why?" he asked, standing too. "Is there a husband I should know about?"

*No, honey. There's a career you wouldn't want to
know about. I'm for sale. Lock, stock and fine ass.*

"A . . . fiancé," she lied, pushing the door firmly
shut. "And he's *very* jealous."

"Don't blame him," Jake said, giving her a long
lingering look.

She felt a jolt of unexpected excitement and
wondered what it would be like to sleep with a man
who wasn't a paying client.

*Don't even think about it. You're a whore—making
money. And that's* all *you're interested in.*

"Uh . . . good luck with the wedding," she said.

"It's his fourth," Jake said. "He's sixty-two. The bride's twenty."

"I'm sure your tie'll look great."

"Why wouldn't it? You chose it."

They exchanged another long look, before she forced herself to move off toward the escalator.

Just as she was stepping on, he came after her. "I'm staying at the Sunset Marquis," he said. "I wish you'd call me. I'd really love to take your picture sometime."

She nodded. *No chance of that.*

"Goodbye, Jake," she said.

It wouldn't do to be late for Mister X.

# chapter 8

**M**ADISON WAS ON THE
phone. "So?" she said, holding the receiver away
from her ear because her editor, Victor, always
spoke in an overly loud, booming voice, one capable
of shattering eardrums. "When am I getting my
interview with Freddie Leon?"

"You just arrived, didn't you?"

"Stepped off the plane an hour ago."

"What's *wrong* with you?" Victor said loudly.
"Can't you settle down for a couple of days and relax
like everyone else?"

"I'm not in a relaxing frame of mind, Victor. I'm
here to work."

"All work and no play . . ."

"Don't give me that cliché bullshit," she said
crisply. "Besides, you should be thrilled I'm a total
workaholic." A short pause to let him think about
*that* for a moment. "Now," she continued crisply.
"When do I get to meet him?"

Victor sighed. "You're an impossible woman."

"Never said I wasn't."

"My contact's out of town until tomorrow."

"*Wonderful* timing."

"Nobody's perfect. Only you."

"Glad you realize it."

"Okay, okay, tomorrow I'll get it set. That's a promise."

"Good." She hesitated a moment before continuing. "Uh . . . by the way, Victor, this is a kind of off-the-wall suggestion . . ."

"Let me hear it."

"Well, on the plane I was sitting next to Salli T. Turner."

"Lucky you!" Victor boomed.

"I wasn't sure you'd know who I was talking about."

"My eleven-year-old son and I watch *Teach!* every Tuesday night. Kind of a male-bonding thing."

"How sweet."

"There's nothing *sweet* about Salli T. Turner," Victor chuckled, sounding uncharacteristically lecherous. "As my son would say—'she's the shit!'"

"Victor!"

"Sorry," he boomed. "Did I just get carried away?"

"You certainly did," Madison said, laughing. "Totally unlike you."

"What is it you wanted to tell me about her?"

"Actually, I was thinking she might make a good interview."

"*You'd* be prepared to interview Salli T. Turner?" Victor asked, barely able to conceal his surprise.

"Why not? She's refreshingly honest, and I'm sure she'd be prepared to reveal *plenty* about what goes on in Hollywood if you're a young, gorgeous babe with . . . uh . . . quite remarkable assets. It would definitely be a feminist piece with a twist. What do you think?"

"I think if *you* like the idea, we should give it a shot."

"Good. I can fit it in while I'm sitting around waiting for Mr. Leon."

"For chrissakes, Madison, stop complaining. I'll get back to you A.S.A.P."

"Do that," she said, replacing the receiver with a grin.

"What's up?" Natalie asked, handing her a glass of cold apple juice.

"Victor's got a yen for Salli T. Can you imagine? Victor *never* looks at any woman other than Evelyn."

"And Evelyn is . . . ?"

"His wife, of course. Rules him with an iron fist and a handy riding crop."

Natalie giggled. "You mean he likes to get his powerful little butt whacked?"

"Not so little," Madison answered, smiling back. "Victor's like a big cuddly bear. *Definitely* not an L.A. bod."

Natalie glanced at her watch. "Damn!" she said, grabbing her jacket. "I gotta get to the studio. Anything you need?"

"Don't worry about me," Madison said calmly. "I'm the perfect houseguest. Put me next to a phone and I'm content."

"Cole'll be home soon."

"I haven't seen him in years."

"Then you're in for a shock," Natalie said crisply.

"You probably remember him as a skinny, strung-out hyper teen monster. Right?"

"Right," Madison agreed, remembering how Natalie always used to despair because her younger brother was heavily into rap, gangs and getting high.

"Now he's Mr. Focused. In fact, he's one of the most in-demand fitness trainers in L.A. Oh yeah," Natalie added, as she reached the door. *"And* he came out of the closet. See you later."

*Cole* was in the closet? Funky little Cole with his punk attitude and macho swagger. Madison shook her head . . . who would've guessed? Certainly not she.

Reaching for the phone, she tried the number Salli had given her. No reply, so with nothing else to do, she went in the tiny guest room and unpacked her one suitcase. She could have stayed at a hotel—Victor was quite generous with expenses—but Natalie would have been disappointed. Besides, she *wanted* to stay with her best friend, it was probably the only time they'd get to spend together all year. And they certainly had plenty to catch up on. Madison couldn't wait to get down with some good old girl talk.

At six she clicked on the TV to catch Natalie's entertainment spot on the news. The male news anchor was impossibly handsome, with a dazzling smile. His co-anchor was a young blond Joan Lunden clone. The weatherman was Hispanic. And then on came Natalie with her show-business news, sparkling with her own particular brand of personality and charm.

"I *hate* doing all that gossip crap," Natalie had confided in the car on the way in from the airport.

"But at least it gets my face on TV and it's good experience."

Just as Natalie was finishing her spot, Cole walked in. Or at least Madison assumed it was Cole, although this tall, muscled Denzel Washington look-alike in workout shorts and a Lakers tank bore no resemblance to the lanky teen rebel she'd last seen when she and Natalie graduated college seven years ago.

"Cole?" she questioned.

"Madison?" he answered.

And they grinned at each other, exchanging "You look greats!" and "It's been so long!"

*What a waste,* Madison thought, checking him out. Why were all the truly gorgeous ones gay?

"Got everything you need?" Cole asked, swigging from a plastic bottle of Evian.

"I told your sister—give me a phone and I'm happy."

"You here on business?"

"I write for *Manhattan Style.* Profiles on Power."

"Who're you nailing?"

"Freddie Leon, the agent."

"Cool guy."

"You know him?"

"Gave the dude a private session once when his regular guy was sick. Man, he was into it big time."

"A jock, huh?"

"Competitive, that's the vibe I got." Another swig of Evian. "Y'know, I train his partner, Max Steele."

"You do!" Madison exclaimed, sensing a major break. "Cole! I think I love you!"

"Huh?"

"Max Steele's number one on the list of people I need to talk to. When can you set it up?"

"Hey," Cole said, laughing. "Hold on—I said I train him, I do *not* arrange his schedule."

"All I need is a fast half hour," Madison said, eyes gleaming.

"Max is a busy dude, always runnin' somewhere."

"Of course, I *could* set it up through the magazine," Madison mused. "But if *you* arrange it for me, it'll be so much quicker."

"We run the UCLA track every morning at seven A.M. Whyn't you jog on by an' I'll intro you."

"That's a great idea! I'll be there."

"Yeah . . . an' wear somethin' hot, he's into the femmes."

Now it was Madison's turn to laugh. "I want to *talk* to him, not fuck him!"

Cole grinned. "Hey—you never know . . . he's a real player."

Madison mock frowned. "Behave yourself. I knew you when you were nothing more than a horny delinquent!"

Cole's grin widened. "Yeah, well, nothing much has changed. 'Cept now I'm horny in the opposite direction."

"So Natalie told me."

He grabbed an apple from the counter. "She kinda gets a buzz from it—y'know, her brother, the fruit. When the two of us go out we take bets on which guys are straight an' which ones dance with Dorothy. I fake her out every time, 'cause my instincts *rule!*"

After Cole went off to shower, Madison tried Salli again. This time Salli answered her phone, all breathy-voiced. "Hi," she said. "This is Salli T."

"Remember me?" Madison said. "Your flying coach."

"'*Course* I do," Salli said, sounding pleased. "Wow! You're actually calling me. Didn't think you would."

"I spoke to my editor. He loves the idea of an interview."

"That was quick."

"Very. Can I come by sometime after twelve tomorrow?"

"Well . . ." Salli said hesitantly. "I really *should* tell my publicist. He'll be mad at me if I arrange something on my own."

"Publicists have a habit of screwing everything up," Madison said crisply, trying to discourage her because dealing with publicists was a total pain in the ass. "Do it if you want, but I should warn you, by the time he gets into it, I'll probably be long gone."

"You're right," Salli agreed. "And I *do* want to be in *Manhattan Style*. It will be like a kind of new image thing for me, right?"

"We'll have fun," Madison promised.

"Okay," Salli said, like a little kid planning something naughty. "I'll give you my address and you can come to lunch tomorrow."

"Looking forward to it."

And she was. There was something very appealing about Salli T. Turner. In spite of the obvious sex-bomb presentation—big boobs and clouds of bleached hair—she had a certain sweetness and vulnerability. A kind of early Marilyn Monroe quality.

Madison used her laptop to E-mail New York, requesting a clippings file on Salli. Then she checked out her copious notes on Freddie Leon, and finally relaxed, adding a slug of vodka to her boringly healthy apple juice as she kicked back in front of the TV and waited for Natalie to get home.

L.A. was turning out to be better than she'd thought.

out unconscious form on Freddie Leon, and firmly picked, adding a slug of vodka to her bourbon.

. . . multipurpose juices she kicked back quite a most of the

Freddie waited two minutes to get horse.

. . . was anyone out to be aware that the

# chapter 9

ON IMPULSE FREDDIE
Leon decided to stop by Lucinda Bennett's Bel Air
mansion. He was tired of waiting for the signed
contracts, tired of being prisoner to her capricious
will. He didn't usually make house calls, but since
Lucinda was being so difficult, he felt a little hand-
holding might be in order. *Hold a child's hand and
you can lead them wherever you want*—his father
had told him that when he was thirteen, and he'd
never forgotten. Yes, it was time to put an end to all
this nonsense, as only he could.

Nellie, Lucinda's faithful Bahamian housekeeper,
answered the door. "Why, Mr. Leon, what *you* doin'
here?" Nellie asked, throwing up her massive arms
as if to ward him off. "Madam—she no expectin'
you."

"Correct, she's not," Freddie agreed, handing her
the three dozen red roses he had prudently purchased at Flower Fashions on the way. "Put these in

a vase, Nellie, and give them to her. Tell her I'll be waiting in the living room."

"She be in the middle of a foot massage," Nellie confided.

"I'm sure you can disturb her," Freddie replied, striding into the tastefully decorated living room, overlooking a cool blue infinity pool. Lucinda owned several houses; this one in Bel Air was his favorite. He stood by the window staring out, aware that he might have a long wait. Knowing Lucinda, she'd have to get herself together, check her makeup, hair, clothes. Lucinda was one of the old-fashioned breed of stars, unlike the young actresses today who slumped into his office looking like they'd just stepped out of somebody's bed. Angela Musconni was the hottest young star around, and when Max Steele had encountered her leaving Freddie's office last week, he'd grabbed his partner by the arm and whispered in his ear, "You *gotta* be kidding? I wouldn't fuck her with somebody else's dick." Trust Max to say exactly what everyone else was thinking. Angela looked like a heroin addict on the run, but she was an excellent actress.

After twenty-five minutes Lucinda made her entrance. She was a tall woman with dramatic features and smooth, pale red hair worn in a becoming bob. She was not traditionally beautiful, more striking with her aquiline nose and piercing eyes, but her talent was ferocious and her fans equally so. Lucinda had been a star for almost twenty years.

"And to what do I owe this honor?" Lucinda asked, sweeping into the room, resplendent in a pale beige cashmere pantsuit and extremely high heels.

"I'm playing errand boy today," Freddie said, kissing her on both cheeks.

Her finely penciled eyebrows shot up. "Freddie Leon—errand boy? I can hardly believe it."

"Believe it, sweetheart. I'm well aware of how insecure you get, so I'm here to personally pick up your signed contract."

Lucinda's finely rouged scarlet lips pursed dramatically. "Really?"

"Lucinda, dear, you should know better than anyone, there is *no way* I would push you into anything that wasn't right for you."

Lucinda collapsed into an overstuffed chair, kicking off her shoes like a petulant ten-year-old. "It's not that I'm being difficult, Freddie," she said. "It's simply that I don't want to look . . . foolish."

"How could *you* possibly look foolish?" Freddie asked forcefully.

"Well, Dmitri said—"

"Who's Dmitri?" he interrupted.

"Someone I've been seeing," she said, becoming uncharacteristically coy.

Oh God, now he got it. She had a new man in her life, and like the legions before him, he was putting in his ten cents. "Have I met Dmitri?" he asked.

"No," Lucinda replied, still verging on the coy side. "But you will."

"I'm sure," Freddie said. "Is he around today?"

"He's out by the pool," Lucinda said. "Let's not disturb him, he might be sleeping."

*God, no!* Freddie thought. *Let's not disturb him if he's working on a tan. Jesus! Where do these women find these men?*

"Have I told you that you look incredibly beautiful today?" Freddie said, lightening his strategy.

"No," Lucinda said, slightly flustered. "As a matter of fact you haven't."

"Well, you do. You're my most important client and that's why I'm here." He began pacing. "Sign the contract, Lucinda. Otherwise, this deal is about to fall through, and I wouldn't want that happening to you."

She hesitated. He could sense that she was almost his—not quite. "But Dmitri said that if I was to star opposite Kevin Page, it might make me appear . . . older."

"You—older?" Freddie shook his head. "Every young guy in America will be *wishing* he was in Kevin Page's shoes."

"Yes?"

"Come along, Lucinda, let's go in your office, sign the contract and then I can get on with my day."

"If you're *really* sure . . ."

"Have I ever guided you wrong?"

Fifteen minutes later he was back in his car with the signed contracts on the seat beside him. Sometimes a little personal attention was all that was needed. And for a twelve-million-dollar deal, Freddie didn't mind putting out.


The two men playing racquetball were going at it with a "take no prisoners" attitude. Both men were in their thirties, and very fit; even so the vigorous workout was making them sweat profusely.

Max Steele slammed the final shot, clinching the game. "Fifty bucks!" he yelled triumphantly. "And I want cash."

Howie Powers slumped against the wall. He was a sandy-haired man in his thirties, with crooked features, a stocky build and a permanent tan. "Shit, Max!" he complained, irritated at being beaten. "You gotta win at everything?"

"And what's wrong with that?" Max said cheerfully. "No point in playing if you don't plan on winning."

Howie stood up straight. "I might go to Vegas for the day tomorrow. Wanna come?" he offered. "We can hop a ride on my dad's plane, he's goin' on business."

"Don't you ever work?" Max said, grabbing a towel as they made their way to the locker room.

"Work? What's that?" Howie said, smirking.

Max shook his head. "Beats me why I hang with a bum like you," he grumbled. "You're useless."

"Why would I *wanna* work?" Howie questioned, genuinely puzzled. "I got plenty of bucks."

"Yeah, handouts from your old man."

"You're forgetting my trust fund," Howie said, with another satisfied smirk. "Who needs handouts? I only take 'em 'cause my old man insists."

"Aren't you ever bored?" Max asked, thinking how much he would hate having nothing substantial to do.

"Bored?" Howie said with a manic laugh. "You gotta be shittin' me. There's not enough time in the day to cover all the things I do."

Max nodded knowingly. "Yeah, like uh . . . go to the track, hang with the guys, play poker, smoke some primo grass, pick up girls, gamble, do a little coke, go out and get drunk . . ."

"Sounds like a life to me," Howie said, the smirk creeping back onto his face.

"*I'm* into work," Max said forcefully. "I get off on the power."

"You—you're an overachiever," Howie said. "Me—I'm into getting my rocks off while I can still get it up!"

Max thought to himself that if *he'd* been born with a silver spoon up his ass, he'd probably enjoy the good life, too. But he'd had to work for everything he'd achieved—starting off in the mail room at William Morris, where he'd hooked up with Freddie. A fortunate meeting, for the two of them had risen together, until they'd made their break ten years ago and started their own agency. Now they were one of the top three agencies in town. In fact, right at this moment I.A.A. represented the biggest stars, the hottest screenwriters *and* the best directors and producers in Hollywood.

And yet in spite of their well-earned success, for quite a while now Max had been thinking of making a change. Being an agent was one thing, but running a studio would give him a lot more of the power he craved. Hey, if guys like Jon Peters could do it, he was in like a sailor in a room full of hookers.

The only problem was telling Freddie, who had no idea he was thinking of defecting, and would throw a total shit-fit when he told him of his plans. But that was nothing Max couldn't handle.

Not a word until the deal was done. Only then would he think of the perfect way out.

# chapter 10

NATALIE RUSHED IN FROM the studio all smiles. "Did you catch me on TV?" she asked enthusiastically. "How about the bit I did on Salli T. and Bo Deacon?"

"Must have missed that," Madison said. "What did you say?"

"Oh, I said something like, 'Guess who flew into L.A. together,' you know—provocative inside gossip. The audience loves it."

"They *weren't* together," Madison pointed out.

"Who cares?" Natalie said airily. "They're both publicity hounds. They'll get off hearing their names mentioned."

"If you say so," Madison murmured, not so sure that Salli would be thrilled.

"I *know* so," Natalie said confidently. "You should read some of the letters I get—all they want is the dirt."

"That's sad."

"No. That's just how it is."

"If you say so," Madison murmured.

"C'mon," Natalie said, full of energy. "Move your butt, I'm buying you dinner and hearing all about what happened with you and David."

"It's a short story," Madison said crisply.

"Good. You tell me yours, I'll tell you mine. Oh, did you get to see Cole?"

"I certainly did," Madison said, grabbing her purse. "He came home, jumped in the shower, took off again and told me to tell you he won't be home tonight."

Natalie rolled her eyes disapprovingly. "He met some big showbiz executive—the type who picks a boy of the month. Trouble is Cole won't hear anything against him."

"You're not his mother—don't try to run his life—*especially* his love life."

"Ain't *that* the truth," Natalie sighed, as they headed for the door. "But hey—I'm *way* more street smart than he is; he *should* listen."

"He told me he trains Freddie Leon's partner, Max Steele," Madison said.

"Didn't I mention it?"

"No, you didn't. But Cole said if I'm on the jogging track at UCLA at seven in the morning, he'll introduce me."

"Seven!" Natalie wailed, opening up her car door. "Honey, don't count on *me* to fix you coffee."

They went to Dan Tana's for dinner and sat in a cozy booth.

"Did I tell you I'm doing a piece for the magazine on Salli T.?" Madison said, ordering a vodka martini because she felt like it, and knew it would guarantee a good night's sleep.

"Yes. Didn't old Victor get all excited when you mentioned her name?" Natalie said, requesting a beer.

Madison nodded. "I plan on getting her to talk about the men who run Hollywood—they all seem to have this thing about hookers and strippers with hearts of gold—y'know, Julia what's-her-name in *Pretty Woman*—the one with the big hair. And Demi Moore in *Striptease*. I want to get Salli's take on it."

"Good, you can give me all the leftovers," Natalie said, studying a menu. "I'll use them on my show."

"You're really into your show, huh?"

"Hmm," Natalie said, making a face. "Sometimes I am, sometimes I'm not. It's so predictable. All these people out there plugging books, movies and their goddamn exercise tapes—and *I* have to pretend as if I'm interested."

"What do you *want* to do?"

"Be a network news anchor, of course."

"Sounds like a plan."

"Yeah?" Natalie said ruefully. "How many black news anchors do *you* see?"

"Here's *my* philosophy," Madison said. "If you want something bad enough, you gotta go for it."

"Let's order," Natalie said. *"My* philosophy is— food solves a shitload of problems!"

A few sips of her martini and Madison began talking. "I think I genuinely loved David," she said wistfully. "But the truth is he got scared."

"Typical!" Natalie interrupted.

"Some men say they're okay with strong women, only when they find themselves with one, they can't handle the pressure," Madison continued. Natalie nodded her agreement. "We never talked about marriage," Madison added. "We were happy just being together. Until one day he went out for cigarettes and failed to come back." She paused, remembering, shaking her head because the memories were still painful. "The thing that hurt the most was that after he left, he ran off and married his high-school sweetheart. *That* was a *real* pisser."

"Girl, I know exactly what you mean," Natalie said. "Denzl and I had this great thing going until I woke up one morning and the slippery son of a bitch wasn't there. Nor was my CD collection, which, as you can imagine, *totally* freaked me. Losing him was one thing, but losing Marvin Gaye?"

They stared at each other and suddenly burst out laughing. "Who'd believe *this?*" Natalie exclaimed. "Two smart, hot-looking women like us, and we just got ourselves dumped!"

"At least we can laugh about it now."

"Maybe you can."

*"You* weren't supposed to be with Denzl," Madison said firmly. "And *I* wasn't supposed to be with David. Somebody bigger and better will come along."

"Hmm . . . bigger," Natalie said with a dirty laugh. "I like it!" Then she added a quick *"Not* that I'm interested in getting involved again."

"Me neither," Madison agreed. "All this double-standard crap about how only guys can go out and have sex whenever they want, and it doesn't mean a thing. Women can too. Why should *we* have to be in a relationship?"

"Right on!" Natalie agreed. "Give me a great-looking guy with a great body. We'll have great sex, and don't call me, I'll call you."

"Yes!" Madison said. "As long as you use a condom. Things sure have changed since we were in college."

"Oh, by the way," Natalie said. "The anchorman on my show asked us over to his house for dinner tomorrow night. I said we'd go. Okay with you?"

"You're not fixing me up I hope," Madison said suspiciously.

"He's married."

"In that case, okay. I am *not* into fix-ups."

A waiter hovered by their table. "The gentleman at the bar would like to buy you two ladies a bottle of champagne."

They both looked over. An aging playboy with an ill-fitting black toupee perched on top of his head waved merrily. "Tell the gentleman thanks, but no thanks," Madison said.

"Yeah, suggest he save his money for his old age," Natalie added. The waiter moved away. "That's the oldest pickup line in the world," Natalie said, grimacing. "Surely the poor old dude could come up with something more original?"

"Pickup lines are universal," Madison said wisely. "They go on forever."

"How much you wanna bet he'll come over spouting another corny line?"

Madison shook her head. "No balls," she said.

"Is that a rug he's wearing, or am I seeing things?" Natalie said, stifling a crazed giggle.

"Do *not* make eye contact," Madison warned,

suppressing her own laughter. "Otherwise, he *will* come over, and then we'll be forced to insult him."

Two minutes later he was standing by their table. He was seventy-two and still considered himself a player. "Surely it's not true that two beautiful young women like you do not drink champagne?" he demanded.

"Hello," Natalie said, putting on a sugary sexy voice. "I'm a stripper at the Body Shop on Sunset. Be there at ten tonight. Fifty bucks and I'll perform a special lap dance just for *you!*" The man took a step back. "See you later," Natalie said, barely able to contain her laughter. The would-be player hurriedly returned to the bar. "Guess he doesn't watch TV," Natalie deadpanned.

"I like your line," Madison mused. "Maybe *I* should use it sometime."

"Ha!" Natalie said. "Who'd believe *you* were a stripper? But me, black and pretty—why the hell not?"

"Oh, God! Don't start getting into racial stereotypes. You drove me insane with that crap in college."

"I'm simply saying it the way it is," Natalie said stubbornly. *"You're* a beautiful *white* woman. *I'm* a good-looking *black* woman. Guys *respect* you. They look at me and think—she's black, therefore she's easy."

"You're full of it."

"I live in this world," Natalie said, her voice rising. "I *know* I'm talking truth."

"What do you imagine *I* do—reside in a fairy-tale tower?"

*"You're* not black. *You* don't get it."

"I can't believe we're having this conversation again."

"Anyway," Natalie said. "I'm *glad* you're no longer with David, 'cause if he could run out on you, then he wasn't worth shit."

"The same goes for Denzl."

"What we *should* do is concentrate on our careers and become media moguls. You can *own* your magazine, and *I'll* be the first black Barbara Walters. How's that for a deal?"

"You got it going, girl."

"I love it when you try to talk black," Natalie said, giggling.

"What do you mean?"

"You're too uptight to get into jive talk."

*"Me?* Uptight?"

"You gotta loosen up—get yourself some attitude."

"What *kind* of attitude?"

"Like this, girl," Natalie said, high-fiving her. "Like this."

And they both broke into fits of raucous laughter.

# chapter 11

**K**RISTIN WAS PUTTING THE finishing touches to her appearance when the phone rang. She reached for it. "Hello?"

"A change of plan," Darlene said, all business. "Tomorrow, not tonight."

"You mean Mister X is canceling?"

"Not exactly canceling, merely rescheduling."

"Oh," Kristin said, relieved and yet disappointed because she had wanted the money.

"Tomorrow. Same time, same place," Darlene said. "Which won't interfere with your lunch. You'll have plenty of time to rest up between appointments."

"Thanks so much," Kristin drawled sarcastically.

"I know you don't like seeing Mister X," Darlene continued. "But what's not to like? He doesn't touch you, and he pays more than any other client."

"That's what's so weird," Kristin said. "I'm telling you, Darlene—there's something strange about him."

"Oh, *please,*" Darlene said, dismissing her fears as if they didn't matter. "Guys with fetishes—what's so unusual?"

Kristin put down the phone feeling depressed. She'd wanted to get it over with and done with. She'd psyched herself up for another kinky encounter; now she faced a long evening ahead with nothing planned.

For a moment her mind wandered over the events of the day, and she thought about Jake, the photographer with the tie problem. He had no idea who she was or what she did. "I'd really love to take your picture sometime," he'd said. So why not? It certainly wasn't going to lead to anything. Why couldn't she do something *she* might enjoy for a change?

On impulse she picked up the phone and obtained the number of the Sunset Marquis.

When the hotel operator answered, she realized she had no idea what his surname was. "Uh . . . do you have a Jake staying there?" she said. "He's a photographer. I seem to have forgotten his last name."

"Let me check that out for you," said the operator obligingly, and a few moments later she was put through to his room.

He answered immediately. "Bunny?" he said.

"Not Bunny," she replied, wondering who Bunny was.

"Hey—*Kristin,*" he said, sounding pleased to hear from her. "What a *nice* surprise. Why are you calling?"

Why *was* she calling? "Uh . . . I lied," she said.

"You did?"

"I . . . I don't have a fiancé. What I *do* have is a very jealous husband."

"And you couldn't wait to tell me."

"We're separated."

"That's encouraging."

A long pause, during which neither of them spoke. Kristin finally broke the silence, surprising herself. "Are you free for dinner tonight?"

"Me?" he said, obviously stalling for time.

"No. Mel Gibson," she said shortly, sorry she'd asked.

"Uh . . . are you saying that you *can* have dinner with me?"

"That's exactly what I'm saying."

"What time would you like me to pick you up?"

"I'll meet you," she said quickly, not wanting him to know where she lived.

"Okay," he said slowly. "And where will that be?"

Her mind wouldn't function. She didn't want to meet him where there might be people who knew her. "I'll . . . I'll come to your hotel," she said.

Wrong! Now he would think she was easy. Ha! If he only knew *how* easy. Expensive, but easy all the same.

"If that's what makes you happy," he said. "What time shall I expect you?"

It was so long since she'd gone on a legitimate date that she had no idea what to suggest. "How about seven-thirty?" she said, thinking that would give her plenty of time to change out of her white pristine outfit and get into something more suitable.

"You got it," he said.

"You're sure you can do this?" she asked, half hoping he'd tell her he was busy.

"Would I say yes if I couldn't?"

"No . . ."

"What's your number in case I need to reach you?"

"I'm not at home," she lied, quickly putting down the phone so she wouldn't have to answer his question. Then she was mad at herself. *What are you doing?* she thought. *Why are you going out on a stupid date with a stupid guy that you don't even know?*

*Because I'm entitled to have some fun sometime, aren't I? I'm entitled to behave like a real human being.*

*No, you're not. You chose to be a whore. Stick to what you know.*

She turned up at his hotel on time—punctuality was a prerequisite of the perfect call girl. He was waiting in the lobby, still looking somewhat rumpled in his brown leather jacket and longish hair. She'd changed outfits ten times, finally settling on a simple black dress and a couple of pieces of good jewelry—given to her by an Arab arms dealer. As soon as she saw him she realized she was too dressed up.

"Hey," he said, walking toward her. "This is a really nice surprise."

"It is?" she answered.

"You bet," he said, smiling. She smiled back. "Where do you want to go?" he asked.

"Uh . . . wherever *you* want to go."

"I'm the new boy in town."

She considered the possibilities. Clients took her to all the expensive clubs and restaurants. A few of the maître d's knew her and what she did. "How about . . . Hamburger Hamlet?" she said, thinking fast.

"You look too pretty to hang out at a hamburger joint."

"Don't be silly," she said. "I love hamburgers."

"If that's what you'd like."

*I like you,* a little voice screamed in her head. *I like you because you're normal, because you're not going to pay me. Because you don't know what I do, or anything about me. I like you because you like me just for who I am.*

"My car or yours?" he said, walking her outside the hotel. "Yours is probably better because all I've got is a beat-up old truck, which, I can assure you, has definitely seen better days."

"Let's take yours," she said, thinking that tonight she wanted to feel like an ordinary girl out on an ordinary date. Nothing wrong with that.

"So," he said, as they got into his truck. "What made you change your mind?"

"About what?"

"About going out with me?"

"You never asked."

" 'Cause when you got on that escalator today, you had no intention of ever seeing me again."

"Why do you say that?"

"I can read people."

"See how wrong you were."

"I'm glad."

They went to the Hamburger Hamlet on Doheny and sat in a cozy booth, side by side. Kristin ordered a double cheeseburger and an extra thick chocolate milkshake. She felt like she was back in high school and out on a date.

Jake had plenty to say. He talked about photography and the people he'd met and worked with. He told her about the six months he'd lived in New York and how he'd hated it. She learned that although he was an award-winning photographer with several prestigious exhibitions behind him, he did not take himself too seriously. He made her laugh about his aging father and his father's future bride. She loved listening to him. He was interesting, funny, self-deprecating and undeniably attractive.

"I haven't done this in years," she said, enjoying every decadent minute as she sipped the thick chocolate shake through a straw.

"Done what?"

"Pigged out."

"How come?"

She hesitated for a moment. "My, uh, husband doesn't frequent places like this."

"Let me take a guess," Jake said, peering at her intently. "Your husband is very rich and much older than you—correct?"

She nodded. *Yes, Jake. They're all older than me, and they're all rich and lecherous and disgustingly kinky.* "That's right," she murmured.

"You're too beautiful to stay in an unhappy marriage," he said, his brown eyes genuinely concerned. "You're in a trap, you should get out while you can."

"I know," she said, thinking that marriage was a metaphor for the life she really led.

"Do you have a good lawyer?"

"The best," she answered, summoning up a mental picture of suave Binden Masters, the man who represented all of Darlene's girls.

"Then you should tell him you want out."

"I . . . I plan to," she said, studying his lips, wondering what it would be like to kiss him—a real kiss, not a paid-for performance.

He caught her looking and began asking more questions. She immediately became evasive, not wishing to tell him anything. After a while he realized he was being stonewalled and backed off, calling for the check.

"Come on," he said, getting up. "I'd better take you back to your car. It's been a tough day, and it's rapidly catching up with me."

A tough day? Choosing ties? What was *his* problem?

"Fine," she murmured, pretending to be totally unconcerned. "I'm tired, too."

This was unbelievable. He was in line to get something for free that she usually charged exorbitantly for, and he was *tired!* Or maybe he was meeting Bunny—whoever *she* might be.

Whatever. She didn't care.

Next time she'd think twice before trying to experience life like a normal person.

# chapter 12

T HE RUNNING TRACK AT
UCLA was not crowded. Madison was surprised;
she'd expected it to be packed. But then, of course, it
was quite early. She'd gotten there just before seven
and began jogging in place because it was chilly. She
looked around to see if she could spot Cole and his
client. No sight of them yet.

Cole had suggested that she wear something hot,
but she was not into luring Max with her supposed
sex appeal—she was sure he had all the actresses
and models he could handle. So she'd put on a warm
tracksuit, stuffing her long black hair under a red
baseball cap.

She was busy doing leg stretches when Cole and
Max finally came into view. Cole was certainly an
impressive-looking hunk of male flesh. Max Steele
paled in comparison, although he was still attractive
in a flashy, up-front Hollywood mogul way.

"Hey, Madison—" Cole said, waving at her.
"What're *you* doin' here?"

"What does it look like I'm doing?" she replied, trying not to shiver. "Jogging of course. You think us New Yorkers never get out on the track?"

"Didn't realize you were into it," Cole said, playing his part well.

"Oh, yes," she lied. Truth was she wasn't into physical activities at all, and had to force herself to go to the gym twice a week.

Max was busy checking her out. "Hello," he said, extending his hand. "Max Steele."

*"You're* Max Steele?" Madison said, feigning surprise. "This is such a coincidence."

"How's that?"

"Max Steele of the International Artists Agency?"

"Unless there's another Max Steele lurking around that I don't know about."

"I'm Madison Castelli. I write for *Manhattan Style.* I'm in L.A. to do a piece on your agency."

"Then how come I don't know about you?" Max said, still checking her out and liking what he saw.

"Because I'm supposed to be meeting with Freddie Leon tomorrow. I was told that *he* was the man to talk to."

"Oh, you were told that, were you?" Max said, obviously irritated. "Were you also told that Freddie and I happen to be partners?"

"I understand Freddie Leon runs the agency, but of course I've heard of you."

"That's nice," Max said sarcastically. "Truth is you'll be hearing a lot more about me."

"I will?"

"Bet your pretty ass." She frowned. He didn't appear to notice. "Want to jog with us?" he asked.

"I'd love to." Second lie of the day.

They started out slowly, Cole moving to the front while Madison stayed behind next to Max. "How did you get started in the agency business?" she asked.

He began to talk, telling her all about the mail room at William Morris, and how he and Freddie had made a daring escape and started I.A.A. together.

Within minutes she was out of breath. "You know what?" she gasped. "I haven't done this in a while. Can we go somewhere for breakfast when you're through?"

"I haven't even seen your credentials," Max said, squinting at her. "Maybe I shouldn't be talking to you."

"My credentials?" she said, pretending to be offended. "I write the Profile on Power piece every month. Call my editor if you want. Victor Simons. I'm sure he'll be happy to fill you in."

"I don't have to," Max said. "On account of the fact I've decided to trust you. But I would like to see some pieces you've written."

"I'll have New York E-mail you my interviews with Magic Johnson, John Kennedy, Jr., Henry Kissinger. Oh yes, and there's an interesting piece I did with Castro when I visited Cuba."

"Okay, okay, I'm impressed," Max said, laughing. "You're too attractive to be that serious."

"And you're too smart to come out with tired old lines."

"Did you ever consider a modeling career?"

"Did you?"

He laughed again and turned to Cole. "How do you know this lady?"

"She went to college with my sister."

"What do you say," Madison interrupted. "Can we meet for breakfast when you're through jogging?"

Max nodded, sliding a small cell phone from his jogging pants pocket. "Anna," he said into the phone. "Cancel my nine-o'clock breakfast, and book me a table for two at the Peninsula."

Madison grinned. "I guess that's a yes."

Breakfast with Max went well. He regaled her with stories of all the people he'd discovered whom he claimed he'd then made into enormous stars. Madison listened intently. It was difficult eliciting information about Freddie Leon because all Max really wanted to do was talk about himself and his achievements. She did manage to get some choice quotes; Max was hardly modest.

She knew she was not being up front with him regarding the interview, but she sensed that if he knew the piece was about Freddie Leon, he'd clam up. It was quite clear that Max's only interest was himself.

On their way out he offered to supply her with photographs and also suggested that later in the week she should come up to his office and they'd continue their conversation.

"There's something else," he said, as they stood outside the hotel waiting for valet parking to bring their cars.

"What's that?" she asked.

"I shouldn't be telling you this," he said. "It's strictly confidential, and completely off the record."

"I'm intrigued."

"In the next few weeks I'll be making an announcement that'll blow everyone away."

"How interesting. If I promise not to write it until you give me a green light, can you tell me what it is?"

Max shuffled his feet—quite large in fashionable silver and gray Nikes—then he looked around as though someone might be listening over his shoulder. "I . . . I can't say anything right now."

"Well . . . you know where to reach me. And yes—I'd love to come by your office sometime."

"When are you seeing Freddie?"

"It's being set up right now."

"You want me to put in a word for you?"

"That would be nice."

"Only remember—you need a star for this piece, and baby, you're *lookin'* at him."

"Right," she murmured, not appreciating the "baby" one little bit.

"Good." And he got into his shiny red Maserati and drove off.

# chapter 13

"**D**UNNO WHAT YOU DID, but I gotta say it—you're the freakin' best!"

"Thanks, Sam," Freddie replied, cursing his luck for running into the small-time personal manager in the parking area of his building. The very sight of the short, bearded man aggravated him. "Who are you here to see?"

"You, of course," replied Sam, tugging on his graying beard as he followed Freddie to his private elevator.

"I wasn't aware that we had an appointment," Freddie said, knowing full well they didn't.

"We don't," Sam said. "Took a chance you'd be free for a minute or two."

"I have a very busy morning, Sam," Freddie said, stepping into his elevator. "You'd best make an appointment with my assistant."

"Who needs appointments?" Sam said, trailing him into the elevator. "I can say what I have to on the way up."

*No escape,* Freddie thought sourly. "What's on your mind, Sam?"

"It's like this," Sam announced, quite full of himself. "I'm here t' do you a favor, but if you don't have time to hear what I havta say . . ."

Freddie swallowed his annoyance. "Go ahead," he said shortly.

"I'm givin' you the lowdown," Sam said, speaking out of the side of his mouth like a character in a Damon Runyon movie. "Max Steele's plannin' on takin' a powder an' sellin' his share of I.A.A. to the highest bidder. This I got from someone real close to the source."

Freddie had learned in life to always listen, never volunteer information. So instead of saying, "I already know," he was quiet for a moment. Then he said, "Tell me what you have."

"Well," Sam said, puffed up with his own importance. "Your partner's been havin' closed-door meetings with Billy Cornelius regarding Orpheus Studios. An' from what my *very reliable* source tells me, Billy's plannin' on bringin' in your Maxie boy as head of production, with an eye to him taking over the whole shebang when Billy dumps Ariel Shore."

"Interesting," Freddie said, his poker face giving nothing away.

"Word on the street is that these negotiations are C.I.A. secret," Sam said, digging at his teeth with a dirty fingernail. "So I gotta say to myself I'd better alert Freddie—just in case he don't know."

Freddie gave Sam a long, cold look. "Do you think anything happens in this town that I'm *not* aware of? Do you honestly think that?"

Sam backed down. "Just makin' sure," he said,

fidgeting nervously, because being in Freddie Leon's company was enough to give anyone a case of the hives.

"I appreciate the information," Freddie said evenly.

"An' I 'preciate you gettin' that bitch to sign her contract," Sam grumbled. "What a cooze!"

Freddie froze him with a look. "Don't *ever* call Lucinda names," he said, as the elevator stopped at his private floor. "She's your client, and you should show her nothing but respect. She's made you a lot of money over the years. You'd be wise to remember that."

"I . . . I kiss her goddamn ass," the little man blustered, turning red in the face.

Freddie gave him another long, cold look, strode past Ria's desk, entered his private office and slammed the door. Sam Lowski was the dregs; if he hadn't latched on to Lucinda early in her career, he'd be nowhere now. As it was, without her as a client, he was less than nothing, and Freddie abhorred having to deal with scum. But his information was right on the money—confirming what Freddie already knew.

Ariel Shore was the studio head at Orpheus, and a good friend of Freddie's. He'd observed her swift rise to power and enjoyed her success, because she was a smart woman and knew how to play the game better than most men. Like him she was a killer in business with a charming manner and plenty of style.

Billy Cornelius was another matter. Billy, a tall, red-faced, seventy-two-year-old billionaire, didn't just own Orpheus, he owned a whole slew of entertainment companies and business corporations. A media king—he was also a son of a bitch who'd stab you in the back soon as look at you.

Over the last year Max Steele had formed an alliance with Billy. An unlikely duo, but Freddie had never complained, because having Billy Cornelius on the side of I.A.A. was a definite plus.

Ria buzzed him. "Your wife's on the line."

He picked up the phone. "Yes," he said into the receiver.

"I was wondering," Diana said tentatively. "Would you like me to fax you the seating plan for tonight?"

Damn! He'd forgotten. They were having another one of Diana's boring little dinner parties. "Who's coming?" he said shortly.

"The people you approved last week," Diana answered, sounding uptight. "Remember? We went over the list together."

"Fax me the list and seating. I'll check it."

"I could do a good job if you'd let me," Diana ventured.

"No, Diana, leave it to me," he replied.

"Fine." And she put the phone down hard.

Freddie sat behind his desk quietly for a moment, wondering why he was always so mean to his wife. He knew he treated her in a cold, uncaring fashion, and yet he couldn't help himself. It was as if he resented the fact they were married. Poor Diana. In public she was the perfect wife—never let him down, was always by his side, well dressed, cultured. At home she was available in the bedroom whenever he was in the mood—which wasn't often, because he'd lost interest in sex with his wife. They'd been married for over ten years, and there was no more of that sexual passion he'd felt in the first throes of their relationship. Also, she was the mother of his children; therefore, he could no longer regard her as a sexual object. Besides, sex drained a man's energy, and he needed every ounce of energy for his work. Thank God she had her charity functions and the children to keep her busy.

He considered the fact that news of Max Steele's upcoming defection was out on the street. If Sam Lowski knew, everybody must. Freddie decided the time had come to do something about it. Yes, he would deal with Max as only he knew how.

Ria knocked and entered his office carrying two faxes from Diana, which she handed to him. The guest list and the seating placement. He studied the guest list first. Max Steele was on it; he was bringing Inga Cruelle. Vaguely, Freddie remembered Max telling him about the gorgeous supermodel. "Most fuckable piece of ass you've ever seen" had been Max's description. "We gotta put her in something."

*Yes, we must,* Freddie thought. *We'll put her in the middle of a face-to-face confrontation between you and me, Max. Because if you think you're going to walk without telling me, you have another think coming.*

Freddie continued to study the list. Lucinda and her new boyfriend, Dmitri. That should be interesting. Kevin Page and his current girlfriend, Angela Musconni—nothing like new young talent to give an evening heat. The other guests were a billionaire businessman and his wife, a New York financier and his L.A. mistress, and the head of one of the TV networks. Not a bad mix.

Freddie put down the list. An invitation to the Leons' was a much-sought-after prize—he had to give Diana points for creating evenings that everyone fought to be invited to.

He buzzed Ria. "Get me Ariel Shore," he said abruptly. "And if she's not at the studio—find her. I need to speak to her immediately."

# chapter 14

KRISTIN HAD A REGULAR, once-a-month client who liked to lunch with her before watching her perform with a girl of his choice. Over lunch he made her regale him with tales about her previous month's customers, and he in turn fed her unbelievable dish about Hollywood stars. Not that she was interested—she couldn't care less about who was doing what to whom. As a professional she kept her mouth shut and did her job to the best of her ability. Ratting on a john was a no-no.

So instead of revealing the truth, she made up tales of outrageous sexual goings-on, while her client listened with gleaming eyes and a satisfied smile.

Usually after her session with this particular client, she visited her sister in the nursing home just outside Palm Springs where—as long as Kristin could afford to pay the bills—Cherie resided permanently. Today she couldn't go because Mister X had rescheduled. Damn Mister X! Everything about him made her skin crawl. His disguise, his kinky demands. He was sinister, maybe even dangerous.

She dressed for lunch in a simple, pale beige Armani suit. Underneath the jacket she wore a plunging cream-color blouse and no bra so that the darkness of her nipples showed through the flimsy fabric. Her client enjoyed having other men in the restaurant look and lust. Little did he know that several of them were also clients of hers who knew exactly who she was and what she did.

He liked to lunch at Morton's, where he had a regular table. Kristin arrived first and sat down, wondering, as she always did, what this particular guy's trip was. He was powerful, not unattractive, with a manic if somewhat over-the-top personality—he could probably take his pick of most of the young actresses and models in Hollywood, and yet, he chose to have lunch with her once a month, and then pay for sex. Not so strange really. If she was a date he'd be forced to make small talk, send flowers, buy gifts, build up to the final moment. With her it was a sure thing, he'd pay her and she'd go home. No strings. A simple business deal.

Plus she had no objections to performing with another girl. Why would she? It was her profession. She knew that a lot of the women who did what she did were lesbians, so turned off by men and the way they treated women that they'd switched leagues. Although Kristin knew how to make all the right moves, she had no inclination in that direction.

She watched her client as he made his entrance, smiling and joking with several people as he passed by their tables. He was a nice enough guy, she didn't mind their monthly meetings. It was seeing Mister X later that was freaking her out.

"Hi, Max," she said, as he sat down at the table.

"Hi, doll," Max Steele replied, summoning the waiter and ordering an iced tea. His mind was dodging this way and that. There was so much going on, and yet all he could think about was his date that night with Inga Cruelle. She was giving him a hard time and he liked it. Max considered the chase everything. Once he scored, he was out of there. Which is why he'd never married, and why he enjoyed meeting Kristin once a month. No demands, sensational sex, and the two-girls-together fantasy he'd dreamt about since first drooling over the centerfolds in *Playboy* at thirteen.

"How have you been, Max?" Kristin asked politely.

"Pretty damn good," he replied. "I'm in shape, business is zooming, it's all happenin', babe."

"Still single?" Kristin inquired, not really interested, but she knew he liked her to appear as if she cared.

He roared with laughter. "You know *me*, baby—one woman could never do it for me." He took a couple of healthy swigs of iced tea and leaned eagerly toward her. "So c'mon, honeysuckle, gimme the goods—what's been going on in hooker land?"

"Well," she said, toying with the glass of wine she'd prudently ordered, although she didn't usually drink on appointments. "There was this politician who came into town from Washington, someone *very* high up in the Senate."

Max leaned even closer; this was the kind of stuff he got a buzz from. If only he could get names out of her, but she was adamant about never revealing her clients' identities. In a way it was a good thing—it meant she'd never talk about him. "You wanna give me his name?" he asked, hopeful as ever.

An enigmatic smile. "You know I can't do that."

He ran a hand through his curly brown hair. "You're somethin' else, babe. How come you chose to be a hooker, not an actress or model?"

"You ask me that every time, Max."

"What's the answer?"

"I can *choose* who I sleep with." *Not true,* she thought. *If you can choose, why are you meeting Mister X, when you know he's a sick pervert?* "Models and actresses—they have to cater to people, they're worried about their next magazine cover, their next movie. Me—I never have to worry about the next client, they're lining up."

"You gonna name the politician?" Max asked eagerly, hungry for information.

Kristin shook her head. "You know I'm not."

"Okay, okay," Max said, giving up. "But you can at least tell me what he got up to—or down to—depending on his trip."

"Well . . ." Kristin began, making up a fabulously erotic story that made Max's eyes bug.

Their ritual was always the same. An hour-long lunch, during which she fed him sexy stories which she swore were true, and some of which were. Then she'd follow his car to the Century Plaza Hotel, where he'd rented a penthouse suite. Another girl would be waiting, and after snorting a little coke, the three of them would go in the bedroom. Max would sit in a chair, watching and barking orders, while they did everything he requested. Sometimes he joined in. Sometimes he didn't. Then he would hand out cash and everybody would go home.

She'd repeated this scenario with Max Steele for almost a year now, and the order of events never varied.

Idly she wondered how he'd react if she told him the only reason she was doing this was to support her sister who lay in a coma in a nursing home. Would he offer money and help her to get out of the business? Or would he merely put an end to their monthly meetings because she made him feel guilty? It was difficult to know.

Max glanced at his gold Rolex watch. He'd almost canceled Kristin today, thinking he might save himself for the evening's activities. But then it had occurred to him that it might be better to indulge in some afternoon sex. That way he wouldn't be too anxious with Inga. He'd be in control, so if he *did* manage to get into her sexy little thong, he could give her the great lover treatment he was famous for. Sex with Kristin would keep his appetite at bay. She was very good at what she did.

He studied her face as she sipped her wine. She was quite a knockout, in a totally different way from Inga. Blond, fresh and pretty, the girl-next-door look with a body to die for.

Max had only been in love once, and that was with a girl in high school who'd treated him badly, humiliating him in front of his friends. He'd never forgotten her, never forgiven her either.

It was nice to be with a woman whom he controlled for an hour or so.

It was satisfying to be able to call every shot.

# chapter 15

"**H**I." SALLI T. ANSWERED the door of her huge Pacific Palisades mansion herself. She was barefoot, wearing a skimpy little sundress that barely covered the top of her thighs. What was most evident were her long skinny brown legs, huge silicone boobs, white-blond hair and an abundance of makeup. "It's *so* good to see you," she said, full of enthusiasm. "Come on in."

Madison entered the vast mansion, where she was immediately set upon by two small, fluffy white dogs who jumped all over her ankles, sniffing and barking.

"This is Muff and Snuff," Salli T. said, making no attempt to call them off. "Aren't they adorable? Bobby bought them for me on our wedding day. We took them on our honeymoon, and they crapped all over the bedroom. Boy—was he *furious!* But you know what? Now he loves them as much as I do." She scooped up one of the barking dogs and nuzzled its furry little face into hers. "I'm so *happy* when I'm around animals. Do you have a pet?"

Madison shook her head. "It's not that easy when you live in a New York apartment."

"Tell you what," Salli T. said brightly. "If these two ever have puppies, I'll send you one. I read this thing once where it said you live ten years longer if you own a dog."

"Ten years longer than what?"

Salli T. squealed with laughter. "You're so *funnee!*"

Madison looked around. The front hall was all soft pile carpets and soaring mirrored walls. Directly facing her was a giant portrait of Salli T., bare-assed, lying facedown on a white sheepskin rug.

"That was from my first *Playboy* shoot," Salli said proudly. "I know it's kind of a trip to hang it in the front hall, but it sure gets a lot of attention!" She giggled. "Bobby *loves* it. He brings all his friends by—just to take a peek."

"I bet he does," Madison murmured.

An Asian man in tight orange pants and a white tank top appeared in the hall. "This is Froo," Salli said, waving in his direction. "Anything you want, all you gotta do is ask. He's fixing us lunch. And after, if you want a massage, he does that, too."

"No, thank you," Madison said quickly.

"You *sure?*" Salli said, leading her through the living room, outside to an Olympic-size, brilliant blue pool. "If you let him near your feet, it's totally orgasmic!"

Madison took in the view of the ocean, which shimmered like a glorious picture postcard.

"We can swim after lunch," Salli said. "It's *real*

good for the boobs—keeps 'em up, if you know what I mean!"

"Didn't occur to me to bring my swimsuit," Madison said.

"That's okay, I'll lend you something."

The thought of her slim figure in one of Salli T.'s outrageous black rubber swimsuits brought a smile to Madison's lips.

"We're eating beside the pool," Salli said. *"Sooo* Hollywood. But, y'know, this is what I dreamed about when I was a little girl. I *wished* I'd get to live in a place like this. And my wish came true. Sometimes I have to pinch myself—isn't that crazy?"

"You know," Madison said, sensing that this was going to be a terrific piece. "That's exactly what I'd like to talk about. Your dreams, how you got here, the way the people you met on the way up treated you, the men in Hollywood, all of that stuff."

"Wow!" Salli giggled. "Usually people just wanna know how big my boobs are."

"Well, today," Madison said, "will certainly be different."

# chapter 16

JUST AS KRISTIN HAD FIN-
ished dressing all in white for her meeting with
Mister X, her phone rang. To answer or not to
answer—that was the question. It might be Mister X
canceling again, or perhaps the nursing home with
news of Cherie. She couldn't allow herself the luxury of *not* answering her phone, so she quickly
picked up.

"Is this the hamburger queen?" said a male voice.

"Huh?"

"It's me, Jake. Am I catching you at a bad time?"

On impulse she'd given him her number, but she'd
never thought he'd call. In spite of herself she felt a
tiny buzz of excitement. "Well . . ." she said hesitantly.

He sighed. "Guess I am."

"No, no . . ." she said quickly. "I can talk."

"I realize this is kind of late notice," Jake said,
"but I'm on my way to my brother's house for a
home-cooked meal. Can you come?"

*No, Jake, I will be otherwise engaged with a disgusting perverted freak.*

"I'd love to, only—"

"I know, I know," he said ruefully. "You've probably got guys lined up around the block."

What did he mean by *that?*

"Actually, I have a business appointment," she said stiffly.

"I was thinking," he said. "What with me doing all the talking last night, I never got around to asking what *you* do."

*I'm a call girl, sweetheart. Extremely expensive. Very talented. So if you know what's good for you—stay away.*

"I . . . uh . . . I'm a makeup artist," she lied. "I go to people's homes and give them a professional makeup."

"No kidding?"

"Yes. It's what I do."

"Hey," he said cheerfully. "In that case maybe I can hire you."

"Excuse me?" she said, frowning.

"Photographer. Makeup artist. We should work together."

One part of her wanted to keep talking, but sanity warned her to steer clear of all personal relationships. Getting involved could only lead to big trouble.

*Then why did you give him your phone number? How the hell should I know?*

"Uh . . . I have to go," she said, aware that she sounded flustered. "I'm running late for my appointment."

"How about I give you my brother's address, and maybe you can drop by later when you're through?" A meaningful pause. "I'd very much like to see you again, Kristin."

*And I'd like to see you, too, Jake.*

"Okay," she said, reaching for a piece of paper and a pen.

She had no intention of going—but just in case she changed her mind . . .

On their way to Jimmy Sica's house in the Valley, Madison recounted her afternoon with Salli T. "I never thought I'd say this," she said. "But Salli's adorable. If I was a guy, I'd probably fall in love with her—silicone boobs and all."

"Oh, come *on,*" Natalie said disbelievingly, as she raced her car along the freeway. "Salli T. Turner is the definitive Hollywood cliché. All giant tits and candy-floss hair."

"She *plays* that role," Madison explained. "Which is why she's so successful. But I'm here to tell you that underneath all the dumb gloss and glitter lurks a very nice little kid who's enjoying every moment. Trust me—this woman had it tough getting to the top."

"Sure," Natalie said with a toss of her head. *"I* can tell you about tough."

"Don't be such a mean bitch."

"I'm *not* a bitch," Natalie objected indignantly. "I'm merely voicing the way *everyone* thinks about her."

"No, you're being judgmental. If you got to know her, I promise you—you'd really like her."

"Okay, okay, if you say so," Natalie said, barely missing a huge truck as she skimmed past. "And how about the cute husband? Did you get to meet him?"

"He's in Vegas," Madison said, making sure her seat belt was firmly buckled because Natalie's driving was a trip indeed. "He called ten times, and they had these lovey-dovey conversations. It was quite sweet. They certainly seem to be in love."

Natalie pulled a face. "Think I'm gonna throw up!"

"Will you stop being such a cynic."

"Thing *I'm* surprised at is you," Natalie chided, as she zoomed alongside a Ferrari. "I'd take a bet with you that their marriage will not make it to the end of the year."

"No, Natalie," Madison said, shaking her head. "You're wrong. What they have between them is genuine. Y'see, they both come from small towns, both arrived in L.A. determined to make it big. Now they've got everyone falling all over them to do anything they want, and they're loving it. I'm telling you, I like her a lot, and so would you if you got to know her."

Natalie was still unconvinced. *"Puleeease,"* she said.

"She told me some great stories," Madison offered.

This got Natalie's attention. "Hmm . . ." she said, eyes gleaming. "Tell me every detail."

"No. You'll have to read about them in the magazine like everyone else."

"Oh, come *on,*" Natalie complained, almost rear-

ending a white Toyota. "You wouldn't do that to
me—your best friend."

Madison placed her hands on the dashboard. "Oh,
yes, I would."

"Here's the deal," Natalie said, blithely changing
lanes. *"You* give me all the juicy bits before the
magazine hits the stands, and *I'll* do a whole pro-
gram on it—y'know, give the mag a big plug so
people'll be racing out to buy it."

"I hate to tell you this," Madison said, "but they
race out anyway."

"Why can't you be like everyone else and get
behind plugging something?" Natalie grumbled as
she exited the freeway, cutting off a man in a sports
car who gave her the finger.

"In my next life," Madison joked.

"You're no fun."

"Never said I was."

A few minutes later Natalie pulled her car to a
shuddering stop in front of a modest country-style
house on a quiet side street. "Okay, so I'd better fill
you in on Jimmy Sica."

"What about him?" Madison asked, releasing her
seat belt, relieved they'd arrived in one piece.

"He's incredibly handsome, with a lovely wife—
picture displayed proudly on his desk." A succinct
pause. "And . . . I think he's coming on to me."

Madison raised an eyebrow. "What do you mean,
you *think* he's coming on to you? Either he is or he
isn't."

"Well," Natalie said unsurely. "I *guess* he is, but
somehow I can't believe it 'cause he's married to
such a gorgeous woman."

"Oh, like you're *not* gorgeous. Is that your new trip—putting yourself down?"

"I'm not his type."

"Maybe it's not a *type* he's looking for. Maybe a fast blow job would do it for him."

"Get your mind out of the gutter, girl!"

Laughing, they both got out of the car.

"You know, you're awfully naïve, Nat," Madison said, as they walked toward the house. "Married men are all the same—none of them would say no to a little action on the side."

*"Now* who's sounding cynical."

"Well, it's the truth," Madison said defensively.

"Yeah, yeah, you and your truths."

"Listen, do what you want, but I'm here to tell you that I have absolutely no respect for married men who cheat."

"Get a life, girl. That's major unrealistic."

"I suppose so, especially when we have a president who does it all the time." She shook her head. "What in hell happened to moral values?"

Natalie shrugged as they reached the front door. "Moral values—what's that?"

"Wasn't it something we used to believe in when we were in college?" Madison said dryly. "Remember?"

"That was before all these tell-all books came out revealing every little detail."

Madison frowned. "I find it totally disheartening that every president from Kennedy on was running around the Oval Office with his dick in his hand and WD-forty on his zipper!"

Natalie giggled and pressed the doorbell. "A power hard-on! Tell me—please—where can I find one?"

Madison, sardonically: "Like I said—try the White House."

# chapter 17

KRISTIN WAS EXCITED, and it wasn't at the thought of seeing Mister X again. As she sat behind the wheel of her car, driving toward her destination, she couldn't keep her mind off Jake. It was ridiculous really, because she was too smart to let anyone come between her and her goal of scoring enough money to get out of the call-girl business. And if she allowed herself to get involved, that's exactly what would happen.

*Forget about him,* her cold, calculating side warned her. *He's only another john who doesn't think he has to pay.*

And yet . . . he had a warmth and a laid-back sincerity, friendly eyes and a smile that melted her heart.

For the first time since she'd started in the business she actually felt a deep sexual longing. She *wanted* to sleep with him, she yearned to have long, leisurely, unpaid-for sex, wake up in the morning to find herself safely enclosed in his strong arms.

*Get real.*

*Why should I?*

She pulled up at a stoplight and began drumming her fingers nervously on the steering wheel. Enough thoughts about Jake; she'd better get ready to deal with Mister X and his bound-to-be-kinky demands.

She'd dressed all in white, as instructed, including a short dress and white-framed Christian Dior sunglasses. Darlene had faxed her the address of the motel where she was to meet him, and she was to sit in her parked car outside cabin six until further notice.

A car pulled up next to her, and the male driver leered suggestively through the window. She pretended not to notice and drove quickly off.

The motel—way down Hollywood Boulevard—was a seedy, run-down dump. Automatically she checked that her car door was locked as she pulled into the dilapidated courtyard and drove up to cabin six.

A drunk ambled out of the shadows carrying a half-empty bottle of cheap Scotch. He winked at her, burping loudly as he lurched past her car.

Ten minutes passed. She tried to stay calm, thinking only of the four thousand dollars and how it would pay her sister's hospital bills for a while.

IF ONLY I DIDN'T HAVE TO DO THIS!

*Ah, but you do.*

A gloved hand knocked on her window. A man in a chauffeur's uniform all in black—his peaked cap pulled low over his forehead—opaque wraparound shades completely covering his eyes.

Was it Mister X?

She couldn't tell.

"Leave your car here and come with me," he said in a muffled voice.

She took a deep breath and got out of her car, locking it behind her.

"Over here," the chauffeur muttered, leading her toward a dark-colored limo parked curbside.

He opened the rear door and she obediently climbed inside. He moved to the front of the car and slid behind the wheel.

"Where are we going?" she asked, a certain numbness taking over her mind.

"Mister X requires you to put on a blindfold," the chauffeur said, without turning around. "You will find it on the seat beside you."

She groped on the plush leather seat, found the blindfold and placed it over her eyes.

Four thousand dollars. Cash. It didn't matter. This was the last time she'd do business with Mister X.

# chapter 18

DIANA LEON GREETED HER husband at the front door of their Bel Air mansion. "You're late," she said crossly.

"Didn't realize I was on a time clock," Freddie said, entering the house, which was now full of caterers preparing for their dinner party.

"How can you do this to me?" she said, glaring at him.

"Do what?" he said, distracted and out of breath.

"Invite an extra two guests."

"You can fit 'em in," he said, hurriedly heading for the stairs.

"No, I can't," Diana said, angrily following him. "Our dining table accommodates sixteen people, now you've added two more."

"So we'll squeeze a little. No big deal."

"Why didn't you put them on our original list?"

"Diana," he said irritably. "Do I tell you how to run the house?"

"No."

"Then don't tell me how to run my business," he snapped. "It's extremely important that Ariel is here tonight."

"*And* her husband, whom you can't stand," Diana pointed out, her voice tart.

"Sometimes you have to put up with the guy behind the woman, or *under* the woman, as the case may be."

"Ariel was here last month," Diana said, folding her arms.

"So now we're having her again."

Diana followed him into the bedroom. "Why did you leave it until the last minute?"

"Oh, for God's sake," he snapped, entering his private bathroom. "I have to take a shower. Leave me alone." And with that he slammed the door in her face.

Once rid of Diana, he stood in front of his marble vanity and stared blankly into his shaving mirror. Moments passed before he cleared his mind and began thinking coherently. He still couldn't believe that Max would be stupid enough to attempt to sell out his half of I.A.A. without consulting him first. Surely he had some idea of what it would be like to have Freddie Leon as an enemy?

No, Max Steele probably didn't, because Max thought with his dick most of the time—useful when dealing with female clients—but as any fool knew, the brain has more staying power than the dick any day. The brain is *always* hard.

"Hello, ladies," Jimmy Sica said, throwing open the front door of his house and ushering them inside.

"Hi," Madison replied, as they entered the comfortable house. Natalie was right, Jimmy Sica was incredibly handsome in an *I'm-a-TV-anchorman-with-a-sensational-smile* way.

"Nice to *meet* you," Jimmy said, squeezing her hand a tad too tightly as a chocolate-box-pretty blonde appeared behind him. "And this is my wife, Bunny," he added, putting his arm around Bunny's narrow waist.

"Bunny?" Madison questioned.

"I *know*," Bunny said, with a wide smile that matched her husband's. "It's *such* a silly name, everyone says so. I was nicknamed Bunny as a little girl, and it kind of stuck. I collected bunny rabbits, still do, only Jimmy makes me hide them in a closet."

"Now, now," Jimmy said, patting his wife on the ass. "Mustn't go giving away all our secrets. Madison's likely to write about them. She's a big-time writer from New York."

"I *know*," Bunny said, wriggling away from him. "You already told me, Jimmy pie." She dazzled Madison with a big smile, revealing perfect white Chiclet teeth. "Welcome to our home, Madison. We're *so* excited to meet you. I hope we can all become good friends."

*Oh God,* Madison thought. *Why did I agree to do this? I'm perfectly happy alone. I could be writing my piece on Salli. I don't need to be with people. Especially these people.*

Natalie had gone straight over to the bar, plopping herself down on a velvet-covered barstool.

"What'll you have?" Jimmy said, running over and deftly placing himself behind it.

"Isn't it margarita time?" Natalie replied, flirting in spite of herself. "Can you make one?"

"Can *I* make one?" Jimmy said, as if it was the most ridiculous thing he'd ever heard. *"I* can make anything I put my mind to." He gave her a look that underlined his double entendre.

Natalie quickly glanced around to see if Madison noticed, but Bunny was busy showing her a painting they'd recently bought of two rabbits being chased by a ferocious-looking fox. "The thing I like about this painting," Bunny explained to Madison in a serious voice, "is that the wicked old fox hasn't caught them yet. Isn't that something?"

"Uh-huh," Madison agreed, stifling a yawn.

A toilet flushed somewhere in the distance, then an exceptionally big, black man ambled into the room.

"Say hello to my college buddy, Luther," Jimmy said, steering him in the direction of Natalie. Luther towered over her. "Luther used to play for the Chicago Bears," Jimmy offered. "That is, until he got his shoulder busted."

"Wow!" Natalie said, thinking that this was one big handsome hunk of a guy. "I guess you're okay now, huh?"

"Still alive, sister," Luther said, with a huge grin. "Got me a nice little electrical business. Better than gettin' the crap kicked outta me every weekend— 'scuse my language. Oh, yeah, Jimmy tells me you're on TV with him."

"No," Natalie said. "Jimmy's on TV with me." And she smiled sweetly, realizing that if they ever had sex, she'd probably be crushed to death.

* * *

"Kevin, dear," Lucinda gushed, balancing a martini in one hand and a caviar-loaded toast point in the other. "I'm *thrilled* we're doing a project together. I've seen every one of your movies—three in eighteen months. Poor overworked boy—you must be *exhausted.*"

Kevin straightened up from a terminal slouch. "Thanks," he muttered, considering that a word with his agent might not be a bad thing. Now that he'd seen Lucinda Bennett in the flesh he realized she was too *old* for the part, she'd make him look ridiculous.

"Hey—Freddie," he said, veering in the super-agent's direction. "We gotta talk."

"Later," Freddie said, dismissing him with a wave of his hand. Ariel was at the door, and he needed to speak to her before Max put in an appearance.

Meanwhile, Max was pacing around his penthouse apartment in a fury, having just hung up on Inga. "I will be late, Max," she'd said, in her precise Swedish accent. "Go to the dinner and I will try to join you."

*Try* to join him. Was she totally nuts? Tonight was her big night, an opportunity to meet important people in the industry, and the silly Swedish blonde was blowing it. "Why?" he'd demanded. "What are you doing?"

"It's private," she'd answered curtly.

Bitch! Bitch! Bitch! Just who exactly did she think she was?

"You'd better make it, Inga," he'd said, endeavoring to remain calm. "If you want to be in movies, you'd better make it soon."

"We'll see," she'd said, infuriating him even more with her casual tone.

Now he would have to walk in alone. Shit! If Max Steele got stood up, it would be all over town by noon tomorrow. *Shit!*

# chapter 19

C O V E R

"We'll see," she'd said, infuriating him even more with her casual tone.

Now he would have to walk in alone. Still IfMax hadn't shown up, it would be all their fault, by...

JIMMY SICA WAS RUNNING around playing the perfect host, fixing margaritas, making small talk, flashing his unbelievable smile. While Bunny was busy showing pictures of their kids to the next-door neighbors, who'd dropped by for a drink, an extremely amiable Chinese couple whose grasp of the English language was somewhat elusive.

Madison could see that Natalie was getting along fine with Luther. *I wish I was at home, writing,* she thought for the twentieth time. *What am I doing here? This is not my kind of evening. I have enough casual friends in New York—no need to make new ones. And kiddie talk is not for me.*

She decided that after dinner she'd ask Natalie if she could borrow her car and leave. Luther would probably be only too delighted to drive Natalie home.

"And *this* is a photo of Blackie," Bunny announced proudly. "Blackie was my precious itsy bitsy black poodle who passed away last year." Her lower lip quivered. "I'm *still* grieving."

"Another margarita?" Jimmy suggested. "We're waiting for my brother; he's always late."

"Okay," Madison said, trailing him back to the bar.

"First trip to L.A.?" Jimmy asked, taking her empty glass.

"I've been here several times before."

"I guess you must do a lot of traveling," he said, turning on the blender.

Madison watched the frothy liquid as it spun around in its glass cage. "Natalie tells me you recently moved here from Denver," she remarked.

"Six months ago," he said, refilling her glass and handing it back to her. He paused, giving her a long, lingering look. "You know, Madison, I'm sure you've been told this many times."

"What?"

He flashed his handsome-anchorman smile, favoring her with another intimate look. "You're a powerfully attractive woman. In fact, you remind me of my first real love."

*Oh, get a life, Jimmy Sica. What a tired old line. You'll be telling me your wife doesn't understand you next.*

"Thanks," she murmured, ever polite. "You're not so bad yourself."

That shut him up for a moment.

Bunny ran over. "Where's—" she began.

But before she could finish her sentence, Jimmy's brother walked in. "I'm here," he said with a crooked grin, thrusting a bunch of flowers at her. "Late as usual."

"Thank *goodness!*" Bunny exclaimed, giving him a big hug and a squeeze. "We'd almost given up on you."

"Hey—" he said, still grinning. *"Never* give up on me, you know I always make it in the end."

Madison turned around to check out the new arrival. He was a rumpled version of the perfect TV anchor, only much sexier, with laughing brown eyes and longish brown hair.

"Meet my deadbeat brother, the photographer," Jimmy said with a twist of genuine affection. "Jake, say hello to Madison. You two should have a lot in common—Madison's a big-deal journalist."

"Yeah?" Jake said, giving her a firm handshake. "Big-deal, huh?"

"Not so big," Madison replied lightly, deciding that maybe tonight wasn't going to be such a dead loss after all. Jake had the look. And perhaps a quick fling with no responsibility was exactly what she needed.

"Who do you work for?" he asked.

*"Manhattan Style."*

"Very nice."

"It pays the rent."

"I bet it does."

"And you?" she asked.

"Mostly freelance."

"Really?"

"It pays the rent."

They smiled at each other, and then Natalie bounded over, giving Madison a not-so-subtle wink.

Jimmy put his arm around his brother's shoulders and walked him across the room. "You see how good I am to you," he said in a low voice. "Not one, but *two* beauties. Take your pick, although personally I'd go for the journalist—she's got that icy hot thing going. Very sexy."

"Spoken like a true married man," Jake said, rolling his eyes.

"Don't tell me you're *not* interested?"

"I met somebody."

"Who?"

"Just a girl. Nice. Pretty. Perfect."

"Oh, *shit,*" Jimmy said, bursting out laughing. "You're not in love for chrissake?"

"No . . ." Jake said, hesitating for only a moment. "It's just that there's something special about her—something I can't put into words. Hey—you'll soon see for yourself. I asked her over later."

"Can't wait."

"And *please,* don't hit on her," Jake warned.

Now it was Jimmy's turn to grin. "Like you said, I'm a married man, bro."

"Yeah, *right.*"

And together they returned to the bar.

# Obsession

# Prologue

THE BLONDE FELL WITH A sickening thud—the razor-sharp hunting knife cutting through her carotid artery as if it were slicing butter. Blood pumped from her like oil gushing from an open well.

The woman attempted to scream, her eyes open wide with the fear and knowledge of what was to come next. But when she opened her mouth, blood gurgled out, spilling down her body and soaking her clothes.

Then her assassin struck again—the lethal knife viciously stabbing her breasts.

Once.

Twice.

Three times.

She sighed. A horrible death rattle of a sigh.

And within seconds she was dead.

# chapter 1

she, who seemed to be making an okay wife. Lucky, a nice ex-football player and old college buddy of Jimmy's.

"You're a fool," Natalie said to Jake, shooting Madison a sideways, "why don't you do something

Madison did not respond, she wasn't about to encourage Natalie's, not so subtle matchmaking eyes though she did find Jake extremely attractive.

"I love this!" exclaimed Jimmy, Jimmy's pretty wife, clasping her hands together like an excited little girl, "We used to have such all the time in Detroit. What fun we had."

"We sure did," agreed Jake, looking big, perfect

MADISON CASTELLI'S green eyes regarded Jake Sica with a certain guarded amusement as he entertained his brother's dinner guests with a hilarious story about a recent photo safari he'd been on in Africa. Jake had a kind of deadpan delivery that really caught her attention and attracted her to him, although she had no intention of getting involved again. Not after her last disastrous relationship—absolutely no way.

*I'm twenty-nine, a successful writer for* Manhattan Style *magazine and happily single,* Madison thought, continuing to check Jake out across the dinner table. *So why am I even thinking about this guy? Especially as I only just met him. Plus he doesn't seem at all interested in me—so what's my problem?*

She glanced over at her best friend, Natalie, who'd brought her to the dinner. Natalie and Jimmy were both enjoying their one night off—especially Natalie, who seemed to be making out okay with Luther, a huge ex–football player and old college buddy of Jimmy's.

"You're a hoot," Natalie said to Jake, shooting Madison a sideways "why don't you do something about him?" look.

Madison did not respond; she wasn't about to encourage Natalie's not so subtle matchmaking, even though she did find Jake extremely attractive.

"I love this!" exclaimed Bunny, Jimmy's pretty wife, clapping her hands together like an excited little girl. "We used to entertain all the time in Detroit. What fun we had!"

"We sure did," agreed Jimmy, flashing his perfect smile.

"How about we play charades later?" Bunny suggested, still full of girlish enthusiasm.

"How about *not?*" Jake responded, with a wry grin.

"I'm with you," Madison agreed. She couldn't stand parlor games—probably because she didn't consider herself very good at them.

"Me, too," said Luther, pushing his chair away from the table and stretching. "Man, I do *not* get off on all that goofin' around. Makes me feel like some kind of big old fool."

Bunny pulled a face. "It's *my* party," she said petulantly. "I can do what I want."

"Honey!" Jimmy said, slightly embarrassed. "Whyn't we take a vote?"

"Don't want to," Bunny said, pursing her pink lips, her pretty features contorting into a scowl.

"Sweetheart—" Jimmy started to say.

"Don't nag me all the time!" Bunny shrieked, cutting him off, her baby blue eyes flashing sudden major danger signals.

"Oh, good," Natalie murmured, attempting to lighten things up. "A family fight."

Bunny suddenly jumped up from the table. "I hate you all!" she screeched, before running from the room.

There was a stunned silence.

Jimmy's smile wavered. "She's only kidding," he said, getting up and hurriedly scooting after her.

"Holy *shit!*" Natalie exclaimed as soon as Jimmy was out of earshot. "What was *that* all about?"

Both Luther and Jake appeared unaffected by Bunny's outburst.

"Nothing," Jake said, with a wide, unconcerned grin. "That was simply Bunny being Bunny—no big deal."

"Yeah," Luther agreed, reaching for a bottle of red wine and refilling everyone's glass. "Nothin' changes."

"Does she usually scream at her guests like that?" Madison asked, surprised at their calm reaction.

"She only throws a fit to get Jimmy's attention," Jake explained. "It's her way."

"Good for her," Madison said crisply, pushing her chair away from the table. "Only *I* don't have to stay around to watch."

"No, no," Luther said, chuckling. "You don't get it. This shit's bin goin' on since college. They'll be back in a minute all cozy an' down each other's throats. It's their thing."

"Well, it's not mine," Madison said, standing up. "Besides, I've got work to do." She stared pointedly at Natalie, waiting for her to get up, too.

Natalie didn't budge.

"I guess I'd better call a cab," Madison said irritably, swearing to herself that tomorrow she'd hire her own car—no more being trapped.

"Oh," Natalie said innocently, as if it had only just occurred to her. "You're in my car, aren't you?"

"Yes, Natalie, I am," Madison said, stifling the urge to strangle her.

Natalie was not about to give up on Luther. "Maybe *Jake's* going your way," she suggested.

Now all eyes were on Jake. Madison was furious, especially as Jake was not exactly leaping up to offer her a lift.

"A cab'll be fine," she said stiffly.

"I'll call one," Jake said. "I *would* drive you, but . . . uh . . . I'm kind of expecting someone."

*Oh great,* Madison thought. *He's got a late date, and Natalie's begging him to drive me home. How embarrassing is this?*

"Who?" Luther asked, all interested.

"No one you know," Jake replied, picking up his glass and taking a gulp of wine.

Natalie finally rallied. "I suppose I should be going too," she said, batting her long eyelashes at Luther, waiting for him to stop her.

He got the message. "No, baby," he crooned, giving her a long, slow-burn look. "It's *way* too early for you to leave."

"Gotta get my beauty sleep," she said, doing the eyelash thing again.

"Honey," Luther said, right on cue. "You're so fine you don't *need* beauty sleep."

*Oh, God,* Madison thought, *do I really have to listen to this?*

And then the phone rang, and all hell broke loose.

CONFESSION

"Honey," Lamar said, right on cue. "You're so fine you don't need a tan to sleep."

"Oh, God," Madison thought, "do I really have to listen to this—

...not let Jeff broke loose

# chapter 2

ARIEL SHORE WAS A STAT-
uesque brunette in her late forties with an abundance of charm and a deceptively bland manner.
Beneath the wide and welcoming smile lurked an
astute woman who knew the movie business inside
out, a woman who could sweet-talk like nobody else
and then—if she felt like it—blow a deal right out
the window without a second thought.

Ariel had started her illustrious career in advertis-
ing, moved on to marketing, produced a couple of
low-budget films, then caught the attention of Billy
Cornelius, who had championed her rise to head of
his studio. Some said Ariel and Billy were lovers.
Freddie Leon—the superagent—didn't believe it
for a minute. Ariel was way too smart to sleep with
her boss. Besides, Billy's feisty little wife, Ethel,
watched him like a bird dog—ever since he nearly
left her for a curvaceous starlet with big silicone-
enhanced lips and a talent for latching on to other
women's husbands. Ethel had seen to it that the girl

was run out of Hollywood—forcing her to seek
employment (and other women's husbands) in Europe.

Ariel was career-driven, like Freddie—which was
why the two of them got along so well. They usually
managed to have lunch together a couple of times a
month, at which they exchanged information—a
lunch they both enjoyed, because they genuinely
liked each other.

Freddie greeted her at the door of his house,
hugging her close, whispering in her ear how glad he
was she'd made it.

"This was very short notice, Freddie," she
scolded. "Only for you."

"I know, Ariel," he replied, poker-faced as usual.
"I appreciate it."

"So you should. You owe me, Freddie. And I
*always* collect."

"Like I doubted it," he answered, thinking that
when he told her that Billy Cornelius was planning
on replacing her with his erstwhile partner, Max
Steele, it would be payment enough. "Come on in,"
he added, putting his arm around her broad Armani-
clad shoulders.

Ariel nodded and strode ahead of him. She was an
assertive woman with complete confidence in her
ability to charm and conquer.

As Freddie followed her into the living room, he
wondered how confident she'd feel when she heard
of Billy Cornelius' plans to replace her.

Freddie's wife, Diana, stepped forward, greeting
Ariel with a weak smile. Although Diana rarely
voiced her opinion about any of her husband's
business associates, he knew she couldn't stand

Ariel, whom she considered brash and overbearing. He also knew that Diana suspected he might be attracted to the striking studio head, and had once accused him of just such a thing. He'd laughed off her suspicions; Ariel was too important for him to sully their relationship with sex.

"Hi, Ariel," Diana said with about as much enthusiasm as a dead rattlesnake.

Freddie narrowed his eyes. It infuriated him when Diana exhibited attitude.

"Honey!" Ariel exclaimed, ignoring Diana's coolness. "How *sweet* of you to include me." And before Diana could summon up a reply, Ariel was heading in the direction of hot, sexy young movie star Kevin Page.

"I thought you said she was bringing her husband," Diana hissed.

"She's obviously alone," Freddie replied, too preoccupied to bother with trivia.

"This ruins my table placement," Diana seethed, tight-lipped.

"Get over it," Freddie said, completely unconcerned.

Diana favored him with a hate-filled look, which he ignored.

Later, at the dinner table, all was back on track. Lucinda Bennett, diva supreme, was holding court, telling lurid tales of her early days in Hollywood and how every man on two legs was after her. Kevin joined in with hilarious stories about a particularly stoned director he'd recently worked with. And Ariel added anecdotes of her own early experiences.

Freddie noted that Max was uncustomarily quiet. Either he was contemplating what he considered his rosy future, or he hadn't gotten over the obvious snub from Inga Cruelle, the luscious supermodel who was supposed to be his dinner partner. There had been no telephoned apology; she simply had failed to show.

Earlier Freddie had cornered Ariel and informed her about Max's plans to take over her job, as he knew them. She was genuinely shocked. "I don't think Billy would make a move like that without telling me," she'd said. "Everything's going so well at the studio. We've had two enormous hits this year."

"*And* a couple of flops," Freddie had reminded her.

"The hits make up for the flops," Ariel had replied, not quite as pleasantly as usual.

"I'm merely telling you what I know," Freddie had said. "I'm planning on talking to Max tonight, and I want you involved. After all, you and I are on the same side."

Ariel had nodded, but Freddie knew she was angry, as well she should be.

He glanced around the table. Diana's other guests were doing fine. The billionaire businessman and his wife, and the New York financier and his L.A. mistress, were completely enthralled to be in the company of stars. Good, Freddie thought, now both men would owe him favors—exactly the way he liked things to be.

Brock Martin, the head of one of the TV networks, was also enjoying himself. He had his eye on Kevin Page's date, young actress Angela Musconni— her of the pouting lips and seductive eyes. Angie was only nineteen, but her knowing eyes signaled prom-

ises of wild sensual experience, and Brock felt he
had a chance with her.

"I don't do television," Angie kept on insisting, as
Brock offered her a miniseries, weekly series—or, if
she preferred, a major development deal.

"Not even for me?" Brock finally said, perplexed
by her lack of interest. He considered himself a stud,
having started his career as an actor many years ago,
and he simply couldn't understand why Angie
wasn't reacting with more enthusiasm.

"Tell ya what," Angie said, her New York twang
reverberating along the dinner table. "If I ever *do*
decide t'do TV, it'll *only* be for you. How's that?"

Her pronouncement pacified him, and he gave a
satisfied smirk. She favored him with a seductive
smile, while under the table her child-size hand
groped its way up Kevin's thigh, searching for his
zipper, so she could pull it down and investigate the
possibilities. Angie got off on living dangerously.

Kevin slapped her hand away; he was having a
good time listening to Lucinda Bennett and didn't
need distractions. Freddie had persuaded him to
sign for a movie with Lucinda. He'd almost turned
the deal down, wary that Lucinda was too old. Now
he decided she wasn't too old after all, and he'd
made the right move.

"So, Max," Freddie said quite loudly. "Isn't there
something you've been meaning to tell me?"

Ariel sat up very straight. A silence fell across the
table.

Max jumped to attention. "What would that be?"
he asked, still wondering where the hell Inga Cruelle
was. How dare the Swedish bitch stand him up.

"Come on, Max," Freddie said, playing with him. "You and I have never kept secrets."

"Yes, Max," Ariel said, joining in—her voice sounding ever so slightly strained. "There's a rumor going around."

"A rumor?" Max said warily. Where the fuck was *this* leading?

"That's right," Ariel said, honoring him with one of her most charming smiles. "A rumor that you're after my job."

# chapter 3

ETECTIVE CHUCK TUCCI
hitched up the waistband of his moss green pants,
which were uncomfortably loose due to the fact that
over the last six weeks he'd lost twelve pounds—
thanks to Faye, his wife, who, much against his will,
had put him on a rigid diet. He hadn't wanted to lose
weight; he was forty-nine, six feet tall and perfectly
happy at two hundred and twenty pounds. But Faye
had insisted, nagging him about his heart and cho-
lesterol level, and all other kinds of ominous ail-
ments. He wouldn't have taken any notice of her, but
when she said he felt too heavy lying on top of her
when they made love, he'd decided he'd better
acquiesce. Hence the diet. Hence the loose pants.
Hence his bad mood.

The murdered blonde lay before him in a spreading pool of thick crimson blood. Another dead body.
Another brutal murder. Only this time things were
different. This time the victim lying spread-eagled
on the ground was extremely famous.

Tucci stared down at the once gorgeous woman, her half-naked body vulnerable and exposed, the clothes ripped from her body in a frenzy of violence. Somebody had hacked her to death, almost severing her right breast—viciously stabbing her at least seventeen times.

The white dress she'd been wearing was in blood-splattered shreds around her. No underwear in sight. Blond pubic hair shaved into the shape of a heart. A small tattoo of a colorful bird just below her pierced navel. Fashionable metallic blue polish on her finger- and toenails. She was a beauty.

As he took in the details he let out a deep and weary sigh. This was not his first violent murder—this was his twenty-sixth. However, this was his first famous one.

On his way into the well-appointed living room with its sweeping views from the huge glass windows, he'd passed a portrait of the victim. Young, blond, pretty. Like a top-of-the-line Barbie doll, her youthful body captured in a giant nude painting hanging on the wall.

Now she was dead, gone, her sexy image forever frozen in time.

The police photographer arrived and started setting up his camera and harsh, glaring lights. He nodded at Detective Tucci and soon began his grisly work—photographing the woman's body from every possible angle—while several cops wandered all over the house, sealing off areas.

Tucci was particularly concerned with the security outside the house, for he was well aware that once the news hit the airwaves, the press and TV crews would descend, swarming around like packs of particularly ravenous vultures. Bad enough when the victim wasn't famous. This time it would be a circus, rivaling the Nicole Simpson/Ron Goldman/O.J. debacle.

Salli T. Turner. Pneumatic princess of the small screen. Bountiful blonde with the amazing body and sweet sweet smile. The girl in the black rubber swimsuit.

Adorable girl.

Dead girl.

He continued gazing down at her lifeless, mutilated body and sighed again. Sometimes he thought Faye was right—it was time to retire and get out of the violence business once and for all.

This was one of those times.

# chapter 4

"**I** CAN'T BELIEVE IT!**"** MADison gasped, barely able to absorb the shocking news. "It's impossible. I was with her only a few hours ago. There has to be some mistake."

"No mistake," Jimmy said grimly, his handsome face alive with the scent of a sensational story.

"Our boss never makes a mistake," Natalie agreed, agitated because she hated violence and backed away from covering any stories that even touched on it. Now she was stuck, because she and Jimmy had been summoned to their TV station to get a handle on the case.

Madison shook her head, still trying to get her mind around the horrifying news. Salli T. Turner. So alive and vibrant and sweet. It seemed impossible that she was dead, gone, brutally murdered.

"I'm sorry," Natalie said quietly. "I know you liked her."

"I did," Madison said in a low voice. "How exactly did it happen?"

Jimmy shrugged. "All we know is she was stabbed to death in her house."

"Is it on the news?"

"It will be by the time we get there."

"How did your people find out?"

"Our news director has someone in the police department. We hear everything early." He turned to Natalie. "C'mon, kiddo, we'd better get going."

Reluctantly Natalie picked up her purse, and they all trooped into the front hall.

Bunny emerged from the bedroom and stood with her arms crossed, glaring in sulky silence as everyone prepared to leave.

"You'd better take my car," Natalie said to Madison. "That's if you're okay to drive. I'll go with Jimmy and catch you at home later."

"No," Madison answered quickly. "I should go with you. I'm probably one of the last people to see Salli alive. The detectives will want to talk to me."

"She's right," Jimmy agreed, ignoring his wife's baleful glares.

"Hey—" Luther joined in. "What can *I* do?"

"You can call me later," Natalie said ruefully. "I'll need some kind words. Right now I'm totally freaked."

"Me, too!" Bunny burst out, lower lip quivering. "This stupid murder has completely spoiled our dinner party."

Madison exchanged glances with Natalie. Jake shook his head. Jimmy threw his wife a furious look, grabbed her arm, and marched her back into the bedroom. Everyone could hear his angry growl— "Do you *always* have to sound like the village idiot? Why can't you keep your mouth shut for once?"

The uncomfortable silence in the hall was broken by the sound of the doorbell.

"I'll get it," Jake said, throwing open the front door. And there stood Kristin Carr, a tentative, slightly nervous smile on her glowing girl-next-door face.

"Uh . . . hi," Jake said, genuinely pleased to see the woman he'd only had one date with, but with whom he was definitely enamored. "Didn't think you'd make it."

Kristin glanced past him, taking in the group of people in the hall, immediately noticing two women—a very attractive, dark-haired one, and a pretty black woman who looked familiar. *Oh, God,* she thought, swallowing hard, *I hope they're not women I've partied with. I'll die if they are.* She couldn't stand Jake's surprise and eventual disappointment, for he had no idea she was an extremely successful and much-in-demand call girl. "I guess I'm late," she said, standing awkwardly in the doorway.

"Not at all," Jake replied, blocking her way into the house, thinking that he wanted to get her out of there so he could have her all to himself. "In fact, you're right on time for me to take you for a drink."

"But I thought—" she began, wondering why he didn't invite her in.

"Everything changed," he interrupted, speaking fast. "I'll explain later."

"Fine," she said, feeling as if she'd walked into an uncomfortable situation—exactly what she *didn't* need after her grueling session with Mister X, a particularly demanding client who was into mind trips. She sighed, trying to erase from her memory the experience of stripping naked in the back of his limo and pretending to pleasure herself as per the chauffeur's instructions. Of course, the chauffeur *was* Mister X, no doubt about *that*. He paid exorbitant money, and she had her sister to look after. How else could she manage to pay the enormous hospital bills?

"C'mon, let's go," Jake said.

"Wait up, bro," Luther interrupted, elbowing his way past Jake. "Don't we get to meet this fine lady?"

"Sure you do," Jake said easily, knowing that a fast exit would have been too simple.

Jimmy emerged from the bedroom. "We're outta here," he said brusquely. Then he too noticed Kristin, and stopped short. "He . . . *llo,*" he said, turning on the well-known Sica charm.

Jake moved between them, aware of what a lecherous bastard Jimmy was. "My brother," he said. "Jimmy, say hi to Kristin."

Kristin took a step backward; civilians made her edgy—especially this group.

Jimmy was busy flashing his perfect anchorman smile. "And where has my brother been hiding *you?*"

Kristin recognized the type. She also recognized this man from the TV news, and that made her even more nervous. "Uh . . . away from you I guess," she mumbled, grabbing on to Jake's arm, wishing she were someplace else.

Madison observed the scene. It didn't take a genius to realize Jake was off the market. He definitely only had eyes for this fresh-faced blonde dressed all in white. "Are we leaving or not?" she asked Jimmy impatiently. The journalist in her had kicked in, and she was not interested in anything except finding out what had happened to Salli. She was *certainly* not interested in Jake Sica.

Jimmy took his eyes off Kristin and jumped to attention. "You got it, Madison," he said. "We're on our way."

"Good," she said. And along with Natalie, they left the house.

# chapter 5

THIS WAS NOT AT ALL HOW

THIS WAS NOT AT ALL HOW
Max had planned it. He should have known his
karma was bad when Inga failed to show. Now he
had Ariel on his case with her big phony smile and
faintly Southern accent. Another bitch. Truth was
they were all bitches—the only honest woman he'd
ever encountered was his once-a-month hooker,
Kristin. At least he knew exactly where he stood with
her. Money on the table up front and unbelievable
sex.

He decided to play it dumb. Stonewall both
Freddie and Ariel. Screw it, he didn't have to answer
to anyone.

"What?" he said, quite rudely, so they'd both get
the message they were pissing him off.

"I said," repeated Ariel, refusing to back down,
"there's a rumor going around that you're cam-
paigning for my job."

Shit! Someone had loose lips. Billy Cornelius had

promised him total secrecy until they were ready to make their announcement. Bluff it out, he decided, that was the only way to deal with it.

"I'm flattered that you think I could handle your job," he said calmly. "Truth is—I can barely handle my own." Self-deprecating laugh. Quick glance at Freddie. The ball was now on their side of the court.

Diana, who was totally ignorant of what was happening, did not like the way the conversation was going. She sensed trouble and was not about to let it disrupt her dinner party. "What are you all talking about?" she asked impatiently.

Freddie threw her a look. She caught his displeasure and decided to shut up. Freddie was not pleasant when he was angry; he had a violent, out-of-control temper.

"Beats me," Max said with a casual shrug.

"You know, Max," Ariel said icily, "I always *knew* Freddie was the heart of I.A.A. You were merely the gofer with whom people dealt when they couldn't reach *him.*" A meaningful pause. "How *sad* to always come second."

The guests at the dinner table fell silent. Even Lucinda was quiet, preferring to listen to the drama taking place rather than continue charming everyone with her fascinating stories of Hollywood past.

"Fuck you, Ariel," Max spat out, regretting the words the moment they left his mouth. Cool was everything, and he'd just blown it.

"That's enough," Freddie interjected angrily.

"This is neither the time nor the place to get into this kind of a discussion."

*"What* discussion?" Max blustered, red in the face. "I'm supposed to sit here while Ariel accuses me of all kinds of shit, and then insults me? Oh no, Freddie, it ain't gonna happen."

Freddie rose from the table. It was time to put Max firmly in his place. "Come in the library, Max," he said, his face impassive. "We'll talk in private."

"Got nothing to talk about," Max replied, hating the whiny tone he heard in his own voice.

Diana stood also. Damn Freddie, she thought. He'd planned the whole thing. He'd *wanted* to humiliate Max in front of everyone so that the Hollywood rumor mill would gossip about what an asshole Max Steele was, and how Freddie Leon had caught him with his pants down.

Well, she was not going to stand for it. Max deserved better. He'd always been a good friend to her, and in spite of his appalling taste in the women he dated, she genuinely liked him, and suspected he liked her back. In fact, if she weren't married it was quite possible that she and Max might have gotten together.

The very thought brought a blush to her cheeks. Abruptly she left the dining room and marched into the kitchen, where the help and the caterers were all gathered around the small portable TV.

"What *is* going on?" she demanded, not at all pleased they were slacking off when they should be hard at work.

Ronnie, her regular barman, black and capable— a middle-aged veteran of the more upscale Hollywood parties—stood to attention. "Breaking news, Mrs. L," he said excitedly. "Big murder in the Palisades."

Diana frowned. "I couldn't care less *who's* been murdered," she said tartly. "We have a dinner party in progress. Kindly get back to work immediately. And that's an order."

# chapter 6

DETECTIVE TUCCI WAS
still contemplating the body of the murdered actress when Officer Andy Flanagann sidled up alongside him. Officer Flanagann had been the first
person on the scene—summoned by a neighbor
complaining about barking dogs and loud music.
By the time Tucci had arrived there, the dogs were
locked in the kitchen and the music turned off.
Nothing else had been touched.

Tucci thought Andy Flanagann was young for the
job—still, he had a fresh-faced enthusiasm, and at
least he seemed competent.

"You'd better come with me, Detective," Officer
Flanagann muttered, avoiding looking at Salli T.
Turner's mutilated body.

"What's up now?" Tucci asked, his stomach
rumbling.

"Another victim," Officer Flanagann said flatly.
"Male. Shot in the face. Discovered the body outside the guest house."

"Jeez!" Tucci exploded, thinking, *There goes dinner*. A double homicide was always twice the work and twice the aggravation—especially when both murders were committed by different means. A stabbing and a shooting. Perfect.

"Sorry," Officer Flanagann mumbled, like it was his fault.

Tucci hitched his pants up again, and armed with a heavy-duty flashlight he followed the young officer across the floodlit lush green lawn surrounding an azure blue swimming pool. Salli T. Turner must have worked hard to afford such a palatial spread, he thought. Their path was dotted with giant palm trees, potted bougainvillea and fragrant peach and lemon trees. Some people really knew how to live. Pity they had to die before their time. Especially like this.

Tonight Faye was making turkey meat loaf with her secret salsa sauce—a special treat. Tucci forgot about his diet for a moment and imagined her taking the pan out of the oven and leaving it to cool while she called him into the kitchen to eat. Ah yes, he'd leave his precious Lakers, and race to her side. Faye was a good cook and at forty-two still a most attractive woman. Fiery too. But then, she was half Hispanic, with jet black hair and a pocket Venus body. They'd been married five years; his first wife had died of cancer. He loved Faye very much.

"It looks like one bullet," Officer Flanagann offered. "Seems like the victim might have been on his way to the main house to investigate the noise."

Tucci nodded. Amateur detectives irritated him. It was his case, he'd solve it, he didn't need any help.

The male victim was sprawled on his side, half on

the walkway and half on the grass leading from the guest house. He had no face—just an angry mud-patch of blood and bones.

It was not the first time Tucci had seen someone who'd been shot in the face. It was never a pretty sight. His stomach churned—this time not from hunger—and he wished he were at home.

Carefully aiming his flashlight, he studied the body. Male. Slight and skinny. Clad in psychedelic shorts and a midriff-baring white tank. Pierced navel. Glossy black, shoulder-length hair. Oriental hair.

Tucci leaned closer, his flashlight skimming up and down the lifeless body.

"No weapon," Officer Flanagann said helpfully. "I checked all around."

"Did you go in the guest house?"

"The door was open. I inspected the premises. It does not appear to be a home invasion."

Tucci stared at the body. "Houseman," he said, thinking aloud. "Get the photographer down here. And make sure nothing's touched. Got it?"

"Yes, Detective," Officer Flanagann said, jumping to attention. "Don't you worry. I'll take care of everything."

# chapter 7

KRISTIN SAT NEXT TO JAKE in a booth at the bar in the Beverly Wilshire Hotel. He'd ordered a beer, and she was sipping Evian. Both of them were treading carefully.

"I'm really glad you came by," Jake said, trying hard not to stare, for she was truly gorgeous in a refreshingly wholesome way. "I was beginning to kind of wonder if you'd show."

"Did you think I wouldn't?" she asked, feeling for once like a real girl on a real date and liking the feeling.

He shrugged. "Wasn't sure," he answered honestly.

She smoothed down the skirt of her white dress with the palms of her hands. "Can I ask you something?" she ventured, studying the way his eyes crinkled when he smiled.

"You can ask me anything you like."

She hesitated a moment. "Uh," she began, not

even embarrassed because she was determined to know. "I noticed two attractive women in the hall. Was one of them with you?" *Why am I asking him this?* she thought. *I hardly know him. And yet . . .*

"Oh sure," he said, laughing. "Like I'd invite you over to join me and my family, and there I'd be with a date." His brown eyes were full of amusement. "C'mon, Kristin, what kind of a guy d'you think I am?"

"A nice guy," she answered softly.

He took a swig of beer. "Now you're making me sound boring."

"No, I'm not."

"Yes, you are."

They grinned at each other. He was delighted she'd wanted to know whether he was with Natalie or Madison. It showed that maybe she cared.

"Your brother's on television, isn't he?" Kristin asked, carefully picking a slice of lime out of her drink.

"Jimmy's a news anchor."

"I recognized him."

"He'd like that. His ego's bigger than his brain."

"Do you two hate each other?" she asked curiously.

"Naw. He can be a real jerk, but he's still my brother."

"And so the two of you are going to your father's wedding?"

"Wouldn't miss it. My dad's the character of all time." A beat, then, "Hey—why don't you come?"

She shook her head, natural blond hair swirling around her pretty face. "I don't think so."

"Why not?" he asked, hoping he might persuade her to say yes. "We could have fun."

"I'm not used to having fun," she said quietly.

He looked at her quizzically. "What does *that* mean?"

"I work all the time," she said, tapping her clear polished nails on the table. "My sister was in a bad car accident, and . . . I look after her—pay the bills. She's been in a coma for two years."

Impulsively he took her hand. "You poor kid."

"No," Kristin said fiercely. *"She's* the poor kid. *I'm* the one who's still able to walk around."

"Does that mean you have to support her?"

"I don't *have* to do anything," she said, her voice tightening as she withdrew her hand from his.

"What about your husband? Doesn't he help out?"

A moment of silence. "I . . . uh . . . wasn't quite truthful with you, Jake," she lied, remembering the fictitious rich husband she'd made up to protect herself. "I left my husband six months ago. He doesn't pay me a dime."

"Then you're single?"

"Separated."

He fixed her with a long penetrating gaze. "Glad to hear it."

"Why?"

"Now, isn't that a silly question?" he said teasingly.

She lowered her eyes. His gaze was too intense for comfort.

"So . . . tell me, Kristin," he continued. "Are you currently involved with anyone?"

She was silent again. Was sleeping with a variety of men rich enough to pay for her exclusive services the same as being "involved"?

No. That was business.

*And business and pleasure do not mix.*

A harsh reminder that she shouldn't be sitting here with a man she found undeniably attractive.

"Hey," Jake said, pushing gently. "Do I get an answer?"

"I . . . I don't have time to be involved," she said. "Have to keep working to pay the bills."

"That's *not* a healthy attitude."

She shrugged, studying his lips, wondering what it would be like to kiss them. "I know," she said. "But what can I do?"

"Spend more time with me for a start," he said playfully. "I'm new in town. I need a tour guide, someone to show me what *not* to do."

"I *am* spending time with you."

He took her hand again and she experienced long-lost shivers of desire. "I've never met anyone quite like you, Kristin," he said, his brown eyes sincere and probing. "Are you feeling the same way I am?"

She nodded, unable to stop herself, even though she knew she was venturing into dangerous territory.

"Then why don't we do something about it?" he suggested.

"Like what?" she murmured, knowing full well what he meant.

"My hotel or your place?" he said, deciding to go for it.

Her place was her sanctuary; she never took clients there.

Only Jake *wasn't* a client. He was a man she desperately wanted, and maybe if she slept with him she would get over her overwhelming desire for him, and then normal life could resume.

"My place," she whispered, still flushed with excitement.

He squeezed her hand. "I'll get the check."

# chapter 8

BY THE TIME JIMMY AND
Natalie reached their TV station, news of the Salli T.
Turner murder was spreading across L.A. like an
out-of-control brushfire, which really pissed Jimmy
off because he'd expected to be first to announce the
killing on air.

Madison followed them into the news room, still
dazed by the shocking murder. She kept on thinking
of Salli when they had lunch earlier in the day—so
vibrant and alive. Now Salli was dead, and it didn't
seem possible.

Garth, the news director, a tall man with angular
features and sparse yellow hair plastered to his scalp,
was not pleased either. "What the hell took you so
long?" he screamed at Jimmy, ignoring both Natalie
and Madison.

"I live in the goddamn Valley for chrissakes,"
Jimmy retorted bad-temperedly. "Pay me more
money and I'll move closer."

"Never mind," Garth growled. "You're going on a special news break. Get moving."

"Thanks," Jimmy said sarcastically, taking off for the makeup room.

"As for you, sweetie," Garth said, turning to Natalie. "Prepare me a eulogy for the eleven-o'clock news. Something that'll break everyone's heart *and* keep 'em watching." He licked his thin lips. "We'll use plenty of footage of Salli bouncing along the beach in her sexy black rubber suit. Nothing like T and A and a good murder to guarantee mega-ratings."

"I was thinking," Natalie blurted. "Maybe Madison should do it; she was with Salli today."

Madison threw Natalie an amazed look. *"I'm* not going on TV," she objected. "What's gotten into you?"

Garth took notice of Madison for the first time. "Who're you?" he asked rudely.

"Someone with better manners than you," she shot back, not thrilled by his brusque attitude.

"Madison's my journalist friend from New York," Natalie quickly explained. "She flew out on the same plane as Salli. And today she was at Salli's house having lunch."

Garth's long, thin nose smelled an exclusive. "You *were?*" he asked, practically salivating.

"That's right," Madison replied curtly. "And I can assure you I have absolutely *no* intention of talking about it on TV."

"Why not?" Garth demanded.

Madison frowned. What was wrong with Natalie for suggesting she go on the air? And who was this total *idiot?* "Don't you people care that a beautiful young woman has been *murdered?*" she said furiously. "What is this to you? Nothing more than a ratings race?"

"Now, now," Garth said gently, realizing she could be useful. "Understandable you're upset. But the public has a right to know. As a journalist, you should understand that."

"Sorry," Madison said shortly. "I don't think they have a *right* to anything."

Garth scratched his head. Nothing worse than a stubborn woman—especially a stubborn female journalist. "How much?" he asked wearily, like money could solve any problem.

"How much what?" she said, still frowning.

"Money. For you to get on air."

She gave him an icy glare. "You just don't get it, do you."

"No, honey," he answered patronizingly. "It's *you* who don't get it. News is news, and if you *were* with her today, we're sitting on dynamite. So tell me what it's gonna take to get you in front of the camera?"

Madison couldn't believe what a moron this guy was. "Nothing *you* have to offer," she said, throwing him a dismissive look.

"Drop it, Garth," Natalie said, sensing that Madison was about to lose it. "It was a dumb idea. Sorry, Maddy."

"No, honey," Garth sneered. "For once you got it right."

"Hey—" Madison said, directing her words to Natalie. "I'm out of here. You work for this asshole, *I* don't."

"Who're *you* calling names?" Garth said, a plum red flush spreading up from his neck.

"Forget it," Madison said. "Let's just say it *wasn't* a pleasure."

"Maddy—" Natalie began. But it was too late—Madison was on her way out.

Angrily she made her way to the front desk and requested the young man at reception to order her a cab. Then she used her cell phone to reach her editor, Victor Simons, in New York, where it was now one-thirty in the morning.

"Listen to me, Victor," she said, her words tumbling over each other as she was overcome with a sudden rush of adrenaline.

"What?" Victor mumbled, half asleep and disoriented. "It better be important."

"It is," Madison said, finally realizing that she did have a hot story, and she'd better pursue it. "Salli T. Turner was murdered tonight. Stabbed to death."

"You sure?"

*"Very* sure."

"Weren't you having lunch with her today?" Victor asked, sounding a lot more alert.

"Yes. I was at her house earlier."

"Then it must've—"

"—happened after I left," Madison said, finishing the sentence for him.

"You should—"

"Don't worry, Victor, I'm on it. In fact, I'm heading for the murder site right now. Expect to hear from me later."

# chapter 9

MAX STEELE WAS NOT about to be lectured to by the likes of Freddie Leon—or "the Snake," as everyone referred to him behind his back. Screw Freddie. Screw 'em all. Max was on an "I hate everyone" roll.

The plain truth was that Ariel was right: people always had regarded Freddie as the major partner in I.A.A.; Max Steele always came second. Oh, he knew what they said—"If you can't get to Freddie, settle for good old Max."

Dammit! He'd had enough; he was glad he was splitting. When he was ensconced as studio head he'd be a man to be reckoned with, not some little pissant agent. Then everyone would kiss his ass big time.

Before he'd left, Freddie had made an attempt to edge him into the library. Instead he'd stormed out—he had nothing to say until he'd figured out exactly how he was going to say it.

Now he was in his red Maserati cruising along

Sunset, listening to All Saints on his CD player, wondering what the hell he was going to do to calm down.

He shouldn't have pissed Ariel off—he knew that for sure. She was a cunt—but she was a cunt with connections.

*No bad karma.* That was his new motto.

*I need a snort,* he thought, *a touch of the magic white powder to calm me down and make me feel smooth as velvet.*

Howie would have what he needed. But hadn't Howie mentioned he was going to Vegas with his old man?

Yeah. Maybe. One never knew with Howie—he was a number-one degenerate fuckup, typical son of a rich man. Money no problem, there was always more where that came from. Never kept a job for longer than two weeks. Never met a beautiful woman he didn't want to sleep with. Never encountered a drug he wasn't willing to try. Max reckoned Howie had brain damage from all his excesses.

Still . . . you could relax with a guy like Howie, have some laughs. And sometimes Max needed laughs when business got too intense.

He pulled his Maserati up outside Riptide, on Sunset, and left it with an eager valet. Max was known around town as an excellent tipper.

Riptide was the latest place to hang—a restaurant club with good food, crowded bar, and many beautiful and available women. Not that beautiful, available women were hard to come by in Hollywood. Truth was they were everywhere—would-be models and actresses who flocked into town hoping to become the next Pamela Anderson or Claudia Schiffer, and ended up posing for *Playboy* or getting walk-ons in some horny producer's movie. Then there were the women who'd made it—the television stars with their own series, and the supermodels with their lucrative cosmetic contracts. And above all of them were the megastars like Sharon Stone, Michelle Pfeiffer and Julia Roberts—talented females who'd gotten to the top in spite of the odds.

Max liked to sample all levels. Howie usually settled for the would-be's, claiming they were more grateful.

Bianca, Riptide's shapely Brazilian maître d', greeted him warmly, as well she should—he'd gotten her the job after a night of interesting sex on a friend's yacht in the Marina. Banking favors was Max's specialty.

"Hi, Max—joining Howie's table?" Bianca asked, gold hoop earrings jangling on exceptionally small earlobes.

"Thought he was in Vegas," Max replied, giving her a friendly pat on her black-satin-clad ass.

"He's here," Bianca said, leading him through the crowded restaurant. "You know," she said, over her shoulder, "I can't believe the news about Salli T. Turner. She was in here all the time with that shitheel husband of hers. I wouldn't be surprised if he was the one who did it."

"Did what?" Max asked blankly, waving at various friends and acquaintances as he trailed Bianca through the room.

She stopped short. "Haven't you heard?"

"What?"

"Salli was stabbed to death," Bianca said, lowering her voice to a horrified whisper. "They're saying whoever did it cut off one of her breasts."

Max shuddered. "Jesus!"

"It's so horrible! Did you know her?"

Max nodded, remembering the time Salli T. had come to the office with the intention of seeing Freddie. Naturally Freddie was completely disinterested, so Max had ended up feeling sorry for her, and taken her for a drink in the bar at the Peninsula, where he'd given her career advice. In return she'd offered him a blow job. He'd turned her down. Not his type. Too obvious with the fake boobs and cascades of platinum hair. But sweet with it, almost naïve in a way.

"When did this happen?" he asked.

"Earlier tonight," Bianca answered. "I'm getting myself a gun. If it can happen to her it can happen to anyone."

"Now, don't go getting paranoid," Max said, not mentioning that he'd had a hidden compartment specially built into his Maserati which housed a fully loaded Glock.

"Why not?" Bianca demanded, dark Brazilian eyes flashing. "It's the truth."

"Was it a break-in?"

"Nobody seems to know. It's all over the TV."

And then they were at the booth. And there sat Howie in a three-thousand-dollar Brioni suit, a four-hundred-dollar Lorenzini shirt, and a hundred-and-fifty-dollar Armani tie. There was nothing cheap about Howie—especially when he was spending his old man's money.

On the table in front of him was a half-empty

bottle of Cristal in a silver ice bucket, with two glasses and a large glass dish filled to the brim with the best beluga caviar.

Lounging next to Howie on the comfortable leather banquette was Inga Cruelle, Max's erstwhile date, a blank expression on her perfect, supermodel face.

"Jesus!" Max exploded.

This was not turning out to be his perfect day.

# chapter 10

NGELA MUSCONNI WAS
bored. She'd had enough of watching the goings-on
at the grown-up table. She was nineteen years old,
for chrissakes, too young to sit around with a bunch
of boring old farts.

Kevin Page had talked her into coming with him.
"C'mon, babe," he'd persuaded, still impressed with
his own sudden fame. "It's a movers-and-shakers
deal—we gotta go."

"What do I care?" she'd answered with a couldn't-
care-less shrug. She'd met enough so-called movers
and shakers on her way up. They were no big
surprise, star fucks, every one.

When she'd first come to Hollywood, nobody had
wanted to know her. Oh yeah, a blow job was
acceptable to certain producers who'd promised her
everything and then forgotten her name. Apart from
that, she was treated like a nothing—a dumb little
street kid.

Now they all wanted to suck up to her, including

Brock Martin, who really thought he was hot shit on a plate. Of course Brock didn't remember two years ago when he'd tried to pick her up at the Farmer's Market on a Saturday morning, and offered her money for a hand job. Pervert! Out trolling for teenagers when he had a wife and two kids at home.

She'd been broke at the time and quite tempted; now she could reject him and enjoy watching him beg. But it was amusing for five minutes; after that it was a yawn.

She didn't get it. What fun was there in sitting around a fancy dinner table with waiters serving all kinds of gourmet crap, when she and Kevin could be making out, eating pizza or cruising the clubs?

And what was with Kev brownnosing Lucinda Bennett's saggy ass? She was old enough to be his *grandmother,* for chrissakes.

Angie sighed. Sometimes Kev was so out of it. Even though he was five years older than her, he was not nearly as street-smart. If she was planning on staying with him, she'd have to teach him how to operate.

Restlessly she got up from the table. "Goin' to the john," she mumbled. Like anyone cared. Kev certainly couldn't give a rat's ass.

She wandered through the ornate living room, taking in the silver frames filled with signed photos of presidents and movie stars. Then she checked out the expensive art hanging on the walls—tastefully lit. There was a Picasso here, a Monet there. *Bo . . . ring.*

The only place any sounds were coming from was the kitchen, so she gravitated in that direction.

Peeking around the door, she was amazed at the size of the industrial-looking room. Holy shit! The fucking kitchen was bigger than her entire New York apartment!

A bunch of people were busy, busy, busy. Ah, the staff—her kind of people. She'd grown up in New York, where her mom worked as a maid and her dad drove a union truck. Recently she'd moved them from Brooklyn to a house she'd bought them in Paramus. They'd hated it. Too bad.

"Hi, guys," she said, wandering into the enormous space filled with industrial ovens, several dishwashing machines, thick wood-block cutting boards and two giant center islands. "Can I bum a cigarette?"

Ronnie, the barman, who was stationed in front of the TV, dragged himself away. "Sure, Miss Musconni," he said, groping in his pants pocket for a pack of low-filter Camels. "Only don't smoke it around Mrs. Leon, she don't allow smoking in the house."

"Really?" Angie said with a wicked grin, plucking a cigarette from his crumpled pack. "I'd like to see her try to stop *me!*" She got off on the clout that came with movie-stardom—it gave her a constant high. "Hey," she said, edging nearer the TV. "What's going on?"

"Big murder in Pacific Palisades," Ronnie announced. "Up the street from Steven Spielberg's place. We're watching live coverage from outside the house."

"No shit," Angie said, moving closer to the small screen. "Who got wasted?"

"Salli T. Turner," Ronnie answered, twisting his head to make sure Diana Leon wasn't creeping up on him. Mrs. Leon was the most demanding of Hollywood wives; she had a nasty habit of appearing unexpectedly.

Angie's hand flew to cover her mouth. "God, no!" she gasped. "Not Salli!"

"Did you know her?"

"Yes," Angie whispered, her face ashen.

"That's too bad," Ronnie said.

"Who . . . did . . . it?"

"They don't know, Miss Musconni."

"I do," Angie said fiercely. "He always threatened he was going to kill her. Now the bastard has."

"Who?" Ronnie asked, hoping for some inside scoop he could sell to one of the tabloids.

But Angie was already on her way back into the dining room.

Diana threw Angela a furious look. Wasn't it bad enough that Freddie had tried to ruin her dinner party by fighting with Max? Now this so-called actress had burst back into the room, telling everyone about the murder.

Diana knew exactly what would happen next: they'd all be dying to go home and huddle in front of their televisions. Damn! Why couldn't Salli T. Turner have gotten herself murdered on another night?

Angie announced the news, then immediately dragged Kevin off, barely saying goodbye.

*Good riddance,* Diana thought sourly.

Soon all the remaining guests were talking about the O.J. case—reliving the most notorious murder trial of the century. Everyone who lived in L.A. had an opinion. But the discussion didn't last long, because after Angie and Kevin's abrupt exit—just as

Diana expected—they all wanted out. Brock Martin was first on his feet, anxious to run over to his TV station. Lucinda was next, television junkie that she was. And Ariel couldn't wait to split.

Freddie was not at all fazed by everyone making a fast exit, but Diana was seething, although she put on a good act of saying goodbye graciously.

As soon as the last person left, she turned on Freddie. "I don't ask much of you," she said, tight-lipped. "But one thing I *do* expect is that when we're entertaining, you behave like a gentleman. My dinner parties are important to me, and you ruined tonight."

"What *are* you talking about?" Freddie snapped, in no frame of mind to suffer one of Diana's moods.

"How dare you air your problems with Max in front of my guests," Diana said, her voice rising.

His eyebrows rose. *"Your* guests, Diana?"

She backed down. "Our guests," she conceded.

"I hope you're not telling me how to run my business," Freddie said, grim-faced.

"No . . . But Max is your *partner,* your *friend* . . ."

"Bullshit," Freddie said harshly. "I made him—and let no one forget it. He thinks he's capable of running a studio. Ha! Any moron could run a studio better than him."

"It'll be in Army's column tomorrow," Diana fretted. "It doesn't make *you* look good."

"Diana," Freddie said coldly. "Stay out of my business."

"Fine," she replied, turning her back on him and hurrying upstairs, wondering if any of the staff had overheard their argument. God! That's all she needed. Ronnie, the barman, running around the Bel Air and Beverly Hills circuit telling everyone that the Leons had a big fight. Freddie was as high profile as any movie star. Mr. Superagent. Mr. Power. He was as big as Mike Ovitz had once been, before the debacle at Disney.

Once upstairs, Diana sat at her dressing table and wondered what Max was doing now. She understood why he had to leave the agency; it was because Freddie had always kept him in the background—kind of like the court jester. But she knew the truth. Underneath Max's brash exterior lurked a caring, sensitive man. And one of these days she planned on finding out exactly how caring and sensitive he was.

The intercom buzzed. "I'm going for a drive," Freddie said, his tone cold and flat. "Don't wait up."

*Not to worry,* Diana thought. *I have better things to do with my time.*

# chapter 11

JAKE FOLLOWED KRISTIN IN-
to her apartment, looked around, and let out a long
low whistle. "Some place," he said, admiring the
expensive decor.

"Uh . . . thank you," she answered nervously. He
was right, her apartment *was* nice. And so it should
be; she'd overspent working with a decorator, and
the result was soothing and tasteful, exactly what
she'd been looking for. She considered her apartment her haven, the one place she could be alone.
Now she was bringing Jake—a virtual stranger—
into her private domain.

*Am I insane?* she thought. *Why am I doing this?*
*Because you like him.*

*No, I don't like him. I'm merely lonely. I need the
arms around me of a man who isn't paying me. Is
that a crime?*

*Yes, because you're setting yourself up to get hurt.*

"Would you like a drink?" she asked, still feeling
ridiculously skittish.

"Wouldn't mind a beer." He laughed. "Bet that's something you *don't* have."

"It's not my drink of choice, but I can offer you vodka or wine."

"Not a heavy drinker, huh?"

"I never drink by myself."

"So you're a good girl," he said teasingly.

"Now you're making *me* sound boring," she countered.

"Wouldn't want *that*," he said, coming up behind her and putting his arms lightly around her waist.

She turned in his embrace and began to say something, but he stopped her with his lips, and they were as good as she'd known they'd be.

He kissed her for several long, slow-motion minutes. She couldn't remember the last time she'd been kissed, because paid-for sex did not usually involve that kind of intimacy. The sensation was unbelievably heady and yet fraught with danger.

Finally she forced herself to push him away. "I need a drink," she whispered.

"So do I," he agreed. "We're both nervous."

"You're nervous, Jake?" she asked, surprised. "Of what?"

"*You* make me nervous. In fact," he added with a rueful grin, "you made me nervous the first time I spotted you in Neiman's."

"I did?"

"You certainly did. I mean there I was, minding my own business, searching for a tie. And there *you* were, sitting at the martini bar, looking to break my heart."

"I was not," she objected. "If I might remind you—it was *you* who picked *me* up."

"No. It was *you* who came and sat beside *me.*"

"Liar! Liar!" she said, enjoying the game. "I was already there—*you* sat next to *me.*"

"I did?"

"You did."

"Then I must be smarter than I thought."

She laughed softly. "You're so romantic."

"Was your husband romantic?"

"Please don't talk about him," she said, quickly moving over to a side table where she kept glasses, red and white wine and a bottle of vodka. It was not like she ever entertained—the setup was purely decorative.

Once more, Jake came up behind her. "I'll play barman," he said, taking the bottle of vodka out of her hands.

"If you insist," she said, shivering slightly.

He poured them both a healthy shot. "Where's the ice?"

"In the kitchen."

She watched him as he went into the kitchen. He was very watchable, tall and lean with a long-legged stride that she found irresistibly sexy. She could hear the jangling of ice cubes as he removed them from the freezer. When he returned he handed her a glass. "Okay, this is the deal," he said. "I'm making a toast."

"To what?"

"To you—because you're beautiful—inside and out."

*Oh no, Jake, don't say such things. The truth is that I'm ugly and I never want you to find out.*

"I know this is all happening fast," he continued. "But I feel I've got to tell you."

"Tell me what?" she asked, holding her breath.

He took a long beat, then—"This'll sound like another line—only it's the truth. I . . . uh . . . I guess I've never felt this way before."

*Oh, God! Please don't get carried away, Jake. Take this for what it is, one night of love. One long, leisurely, unpaid-for night of love.*

"How about you?" he demanded, staring at her.

She stalled, pretending she didn't understand. "How about me what?"

"Jeez!" he said, perplexed. "I'm declaring all kinds of true feelings and you're stonewalling me. What's going on, Kris?"

Nobody called her Kris; it felt familiar and endearing. She shrugged. "I . . . I don't know," she murmured. "Something . . ."

"Yeah . . . something," he agreed. And then he was kissing her again, his body pressing hard against hers, his lips insistent and intoxicating.

She felt herself dissolve inside. This was too good to pass up. One night. Didn't she deserve one night of happiness?

Jake's hands slid down her shoulders to her breasts and began fingering her nipples through the flimsy folds of her white dress—causing her to catch her breath. She'd faked sexual excitement for so long that the real thing was almost a surprise. She shivered with anticipation; it was as if she'd never been touched there before.

Slowly he started easing her dress off her shoulders. She leaned back, making it simple for him.

He released her breasts from the thin material and bent to kiss them, rolling his tongue around her nipples in a way that immediately started to drive her slightly crazy. She sighed loudly, knowing for sure that she never wanted him to stop.

"You . . . are . . . so . . . beautiful . . ." he murmured, his tongue continuing to arouse her. "So . . . fucking . . . beautiful."

*I'm a professional, Jake, I have to keep in good shape.*

"Thank you," she whispered, wondering if it would seem too bold if she went for his belt and pushed down his pants.

"I haven't been with a woman in over a year," he admitted. "Unless sex means something, it's not for me."

Words to stop anyone in their tracks. "I . . . uh . . . can understand that," she managed.

"The reason I'm telling you is so that you know you can trust me."

Trust him? What did he mean? And then she got it: he was informing her so that she'd be aware he didn't have AIDS or any other catchable diseases.

Oh God, now he was waiting for her to give him *her* sexual history.

*Well, Jake, it's like this. I'm a whore. But you can feel perfectly safe because if they touch me I always insist they use a condom. And I visit my gynecologist twice a month. And . . . Oh shit, why am I fooling myself? This silly charade of falling in love has nowhere to go.*

*And yet . . .*

"I haven't slept with anyone since my husband," she murmured.

"Well then," he said, obviously pleased with her reply. "You and I are about to make this a night to remember."

# chapter 12

MADISON HAD THE CAB take her to a late-night car-rental place, and now she sat behind the wheel of a green Ford Galaxy driving toward Salli's house in Pacific Palisades. No more depending on other people to get around this town.

Her thoughts were full of Salli, as she tried to dredge up every detail of their lunch together. She remembered walking into Salli's luxurious house— her sense of how unlike New York city living it was with its big, high-ceilinged rooms leading out to lavish gardens, and an enormous swimming pool. The sun was shining and music was playing in the background. It was the radio, because every so often a male disk jockey would announce his last three choices. She remembered the dogs, yappy little things racing all over the place.

"They're my babies," Salli had said, scooping them up in her arms. And then later Salli had confided that she couldn't have kids—something to do with an abortion that had taken place when she was fifteen. "I was dirt poor," she'd said with a rueful laugh. "So I guess I got me the town butcher."

"Is that off the record, or can I use it?" Madison had asked, playing fair because she didn't want to take advantage of Salli's almost naïve openness.

"Go ahead—print the truth for once," Salli had answered boldly. "I'm sick of all the lies." And then she'd *really* started talking.

Good journalist that she was, Madison had made shorthand notes in her head as Salli rambled on— even though her mini-tape machine was recording every word, because nowadays the lawyers wouldn't allow the magazine to print an interview unless there was tape to back it up.

Sitting beside the pool, chewing on carrot sticks, because she was on a constant diet, Salli began peeling back the layers of her life.

*Small-town girl Salli got pregnant, had an abortion, won a local beauty contest at the age of fifteen, fought with her widowed father, dropped out of school and took the bus to Hollywood with exactly one hundred and three dollars in her cracked, white patent-leather purse. She had brown frizzy hair, slightly buck teeth and quite a bit of puppy fat. But she was still pretty enough to make heads turn.*

*She faked her ID and immediately got a job as a waitress in a strip joint out by LAX airport, where she was so impressed by most of the strippers' attributes that she decided she'd better do something about her own modest 34B's. With that goal in mind she began saving her money for just such an event.*

*While she was waiting, a cabdriver boyfriend took a nude Polaroid of her and sent it in to* Playboy. *Eight* weeks later they rejected her as too skinny. This infuriated Salli, who immediately became determined that one day she'd be on the magazine's cover.

New tits became more important than ever. She found herself an agent and started doing extra work. Naturally, the agent, an older man with grown kids, fell in lust with her. Of course he had no clue she was barely sixteen. She held out going to bed with him until he came up with the money for her new boobs. It took a year because—being a nice family man—he was riddled with guilt. Eventually he left his wife, paid for her operation, and on the night they finally slept together, expired on top of her before consummating the act. It was a traumatic experience, one that Salli did not forget in a hurry.

After that she became an expert tease—never letting any man get too close, although they all tried. Instead she concentrated on making herself the best she could be.

The new boobs gave her a head start; they changed her life. Instead of waitressing, she turned to exotic dancing and began making enough money to continue her transformation from small-town beauty queen to Hollywood starlet. First she dyed her brown hair a Marilyn Monroe platinum blond. Then she had her teeth capped and managed to lose a staggering twenty-five pounds. With her new glamorous look— all big boobs, tiny waist and long legs—she soon found a new agent and began getting small roles on TV shows and in films. If she'd wanted to do porno she could've made a killing, but sensibly she opted not to go that route. Instead she specialized in playing dumb blondes with spectacular bodies. An easy task. What wasn't easy was fighting off all the men. They *came on to her in droves—including married famous ones who all had the same excuse: "My wife isn't into sex, so suck my dick." Sometimes she did, sometimes she didn't. She had to like a guy before she did anything.*

*It was a long haul, but Salli finally made it back to* Playboy. *This time they were all over her, and not only did she get the cover, but four pages of photographs inside* and *the centerfold.*

*Fame at last. Her spread was so popular that a year later she did it again. And then her career really started to take off, culminating in her own TV series,* Teach!, *and yet another* Playboy *cover.*

Teach! *became the* Baywatch *of the nineties, and Salli became the heroine of horny teenage boys across the world.*

*Along the way she married an actor, Eddie Stoner, then divorced him two years later. And was currently married to the infamous Bobby Skorch—a man who regularly risked his life for a living.*

Once more Madison wondered what had happened after she'd left. Salli had seemed in such a good mood, upbeat and enthusiastic about her future. She'd told Madison she planned to stay on *Teach!* for one more year, and then take a shot at movie stardom.

Now it was all over. And there had to be a reason why.

Madison drove determinedly toward Salli's house.

# chapter 13

"**I** DON'T BELIEVE THIS," Max said, enraged.

"Howdy, pal," Howie said, oblivious of his friend's anger. "I want you to meet Inga."

Max glared furiously at the exquisite supermodel lounging casually on the leather banquette in a barely there black dress. "What the fuck are *you* doing here?" he exploded.

"You two know each other?" Howie asked, obviously surprised.

"Not only do we know each other," Max blustered, "but Inga was my date tonight, and Inga failed to show."

"Don't be so silly, Max," Inga said in her infuriatingly precise accent. "I was *not* your date. We had a business appointment I could not make. And kindly do not use foul language."

Max's famous smoothness slid away as his face contorted with frustrated rage. This Swedish bitch was dissing *him*, Max Steele. No fucking way! And what the hell was she doing with a lowlife like Howie, his supposed friend?

"Am I in the middle of something here?" Howie asked, all playboy innocence.

"Not at all," Inga answered coolly.

"Did we, or did we not, have an appointment?" Max demanded, dropping the word "date."

"A vague arrangement, nothing definite," Inga said, dipping two fingers into her champagne glass, then delicately licking them in a highly suggestive way.

"Hey," Howie said, sliding out of the booth. "I'll be in the head if anyone needs me."

Max sat down on the leather banquette. "Inga," he said, regaining his composure, "you were supposed to meet me at Freddie Leon's house, remember? It was an important sit-down dinner and it was place-carded. Your absence was embarrassing—not to mention rude. You can't get away with shit like that in this town and expect to work." He glared at her, waiting for a reaction. "Do you understand me?"

Inga regarded him for a long, silent moment. "Inga does what Inga wants," she said at last. "And I can assure you, Max, that when the right project comes along, they will be begging for Inga to appear."

Max was stunned. Just who did this broad think she was?

"Honey," he said. "Keep on believing *that,* and you can watch your movie career *never* take flight." Abruptly he got up from the table. "I'm off the case—find yourself a new agent."

Howie was in the men's room snorting a line of

coke from the dark green marble countertop. The attendant, having been handed a fifty-dollar tip, was looking the other way.

"You're lucky I'm not undercover vice," Max said, stealing a healthy pinch of the white powder and rubbing it into his gums.

"They'd never get in the door," Howie said with a manic chuckle. "This place is protected."

"Protected my ass," Max snapped.

Howie slipped the small plastic straw into his pocket and swiped the tip of his nose, getting rid of any telltale white powder. "What's with you and the babe?" he said. "She really break a date with you?"

"Nobody breaks a date with Max Steele," Max said stiffly. "It was purely business and the stupid bitch blew it."

*"I've* got something I'd like her to blow," Howie chortled, grabbing his crotch in an exaggerated manner.

"Where'd you meet her?" Max asked, still fuming, but hiding it well.

"Cocktail party at Cartier's earlier. She was standing there looking hot, so I bought her a trinket."

"Trinket?" Max questioned.

Howie laughed sheepishly. "So it was a gold tank watch. Big deal. It got me a date, an' you gotta admit—she's the business. Makes Cindy look plain."

"Models are better-looking than actresses," Max admitted, feeling better as the coke began to take effect. "Although—you gotta remember—they're also stupider."

Howie gave a ribald laugh. "I wanna fuck her, not take a lesson in physics."

"I heard a rumor she's got the clap," Max said, his mean streak surfacing.

"No shit?" Howie said, too stoned to care.

By the time they returned to the booth, Inga was gone. "She must be in the john," Howie said.

With a deep sense of satisfaction Max knew better. She'd dumped on Howie just as she'd dumped on him.

Supermodels! Tall and tan and young and dumb. He'd know better than to ever chase after one of *them* again.

# chapter 14

"**W**HY DID WE HAVE to leave?" Kevin whined, as Angie recklessly raced his black Ferrari along Sunset. "I was havin' fun."

"If that's your idea of fun," Angie sneered, "then you like need *major* detox."

"Fuck you!"

"Fuck you, too!" she retorted, screeching the powerful car to a halt at a stoplight. "I'm not into all that phony BS. If you weren't a friggin' movie star, those people wouldn't talk to you."

"So?" Kevin said belligerently. "I *am* a friggin' movie star."

"You're not Leonardo DiCaprio."

"Wouldn't want t'be," Kevin said sulkily, thinking that it was about time he dumped Angie. She was too bossy by far, and now that he had two big box-office successes behind him, he could get any girl he wanted. Angie didn't know it, but she was busy nagging herself out of a gig. "Where we goin'?" he asked, noticing that she'd zoomed past the street where they'd set up house together.

"I need to score," she said, rubbing her forehead. "I'm like totally bummed."

*You need to clean up your act,* he thought. Angie was heavily into drugs and he wasn't. Been there. Done that. He had no desire to become the next Robert Downey Jr. or Charlie Sheen. Those guys were old enough to know better.

"Fuck," he mumbled. "I can't go scorin' drugs with you. It's not good for my image."

"You never do anything for me," she complained.

"It's time you dropped out of the drug scene," he said, thinking about Lucinda Bennett and the movie they were going to make together.

"I don't need a freakin' lecture," Angie snapped. "I just lost a very close friend."

"I never heard you mention Salli."

"That's 'cause we had a big fight before you and I got together."

"Big fight about what?"

"When I was sixteen we used to share an apartment," Angie said. "Until she stole my boyfriend who wasn't even worth stealing. He was a son of a bitch. I bet it was *him* who killed her."

"What're you talking about *now?*"

"Eddie Stoner."

"Eddie Stoner," Kevin repeated. "The actor?"

"You know him?"

"Think I worked with him once."

"Did you or didn't you?"

"Who remembers?"

"Anyway—he was a rough bastard, so I figured if

Salli wanted him so much, she could have him. I moved out, and a couple of weeks later she and Eddie got married in Vegas." Angie sighed her disgust. "Some *dumb* move. All he had going for him was a big dick and a sharp right hand. He used to beat the shit out of me, and as soon as they were married he started on her. I thought 'cause she was older than me she'd be able to handle him. But she couldn't. One night she phoned me, and she was hysterical. I told her, 'Don't come cryin' to me—you wanted the loser, you got him.' And I didn't help her. Then she started to get famous and all that shit. Eventually she divorced him. It was a real drag. I know she had to call the cops on him a few times, and that he threatened to kill her. Hey—he threatened to kill *me* when we were together. I'm surprised he didn't come creeping back when *I* made it, considering I made it bigger than her." She paused, then thoughtfully added, "Maybe I should tell the cops what I know."

"You can't go around accusing people," Kevin said, frowning. "You want us *both* dragged through the tabloids?"

"Okay, Kev," Angie said, her mind on other matters. "Let me score a gram or two an' I'll think it over."

"You gotta get out of the drug scene," Kevin repeated sternly.

"I can," she answered defiantly. "Any time I want."

"Sure."

"Yeah, *sure.*"

"You're difficult, Angie, you never listen."

"I know, you've told me a million times. But what

would you do without me, Kev? You'd be running around this town with your dick in your hand, and they'd all be taking you for the ride of the century. Right?"

"If you say so." And he wondered exactly how he should go about dumping her.

# chapter 15

DETECTIVE TUCCI CALLED his wife, Faye, and told her that, just as he'd expected, the area around Salli T. Turner's house was turning into a media circus. There were TV trucks with their news crews, reporters, and crowds of people milling around outside on the street. Everyone was contained behind police lines, while helicopters hovered overhead, and in the house the phone did not stop ringing. Even though it was late at night, word had spread fast.

Tucci swore softly under his breath. There would definitely be no dinner tonight, not unless it was take-out pizza, and he hated to do that to his stomach.

By midnight the police photographer had finished his grisly task, and the medical examiner was now in charge. Later Salli's mutilated body was put on a stretcher and taken off in an ambulance headed for the morgue where an autopsy would take place and evidence would be gathered.

When the ambulance attendants loaded Salli's body aboard, the crowds went wild, screaming and yelling her name. Tucci couldn't help wondering if the murderer was out there somewhere, watching . . . waiting . . . getting his kicks.

The facts as Tucci knew them were such: There was no sign of a break-in, which meant that Salli had obviously known her killer, and had probably let him into the house. She must have been comfortable with him—if indeed it was a male—because she'd taken him into the living room and out by the pool. In the sink behind the bar Tucci had found two hastily washed glasses. He'd immediately put them into a plastic bag and sent them to the lab to be checked.

So, he decided, whoever the killer was had entered through the front door. Salli had greeted the person, they'd had a drink together, walked out near the patio, and then, for some unknown reason, he or she had worked themselves into a frenzy and stabbed her to death.

The houseman had probably been on his way to the house to see what all the noise was about, because according to neighbors, music had been playing extremely loudly and the dogs were barking nonstop. On his way to the house, Froo, the Asian houseman, had encountered the killer, who'd shot him point-blank in the face—which indicated that Froo would have recognized the man . . . or woman.

For the last two hours Tucci had been trying to contact Salli's husband, Bobby Skorch. Apparently he was in a car somewhere on his way back from a gig in Vegas. His cell phone was turned off, and he appeared to be unreachable.

Tucci wondered if Bobby had murdered his wife. It wouldn't be the first time a husband was responsible. Maybe Bobby Skorch had driven back from his appearance early, fought with Salli, stabbed her to death, then got back in his car, driven away and would turn up later—the distraught husband. It was hardly an uncommon scenario.

Tucci sat at a table in the kitchen making numerous notes. He was known for his detailed accounts and he enjoyed making sure that he didn't miss one single thing.

Somewhere in this puzzle there was an answer, and he fully intended to find out what it was.

# chapter 16

MADISON PARKED A couple of blocks from the house. There were TV camera crews and reporters everywhere, and of course huge crowds of onlookers. The police had already roped off the area around the house and there was a strangely festive atmosphere—as if people were reveling in the action.

She left her car and hurried over to the nearest cop. "Who's the detective in charge of this case?" she asked, flashing her press pass.

"Can't give out any information at this moment," the cop said, barely glancing at her.

"I understand that," she said evenly. "However, I know he'll want to talk to me, so please would you get a message to him. My name's Madison Castelli, I'm a journalist from New York and I spent the day with Ms. Turner in her house."

"Really?" the cop said disbelievingly.

"Yes, really," Madison replied.

"Can you prove that?"

"How am I supposed to prove it?"

"With all due respect, ma'am, there are a lot of people here trying to get into the house. . . ."

"I'm sure there are, but if you tell the detective that I was with her today, I'm certain he'll want to see me."

"I told you, ma'am—I can't do that, there's too much going on."

"Look," Madison said, fast losing patience. "I work for *Manhattan Style,* my editor is Victor Simons." She handed him a card. "This is his number. If you give this to the detective in charge, he can check with my editor and verify my story. Other than that I don't know what I can do, but I *do* know that he'll want to see me."

"Not tonight, ma'am. Maybe he'll interview you tomorrow. Why don't you leave your name and number and go on home."

"Can I be sure he'll get it?" she said, swallowing her aggravation, because she knew it wouldn't do any good to lose her temper.

"Absolutely, ma'am."

"I have an audiotape of Salli at my house. On it she talks about everything that's going on in her life. I'm sure it will be helpful."

The cop took another look at her. Maybe she wasn't handing him a bullshit story, maybe she was legit. "Whyn't you wait here a minute," he said. "I'll go check."

"Thanks."

She watched as the cop made his way into the house. Where were Natalie and Jimmy? They should be here already. She could see quite a few on-the-scene reporters standing on the street doing remotes to their TV stations.

The cop returned after a few minutes. "Detective Tucci says he'll be in touch tomorrow."

"Are you telling me he doesn't want to see me now?"

"That's right, ma'am."

"Then I guess I'll write the story my way, and mention the detective on the case refused to see me. I'm sure the *L.A. Times* will be interested in a firsthand account."

"Whatever you say, ma'am."

"I'm merely telling you what I plan to do, so you can pass it on to Detective Tucci."

"I'll let him know."

She returned to her rented car, drove to the nearest gas station, went into the phone booth and looked up Tucci in the phone book. Then she started making calls. Third time lucky.

"Is Detective Tucci there?" she asked the woman who answered.

"I'm sorry, he's not."

"Is this his wife?"

"Yes. Can I help you?"

"It's most important that I speak to your husband. I have information pertaining to the case he's working on. I talked to an officer in charge of crowd control, and I'm not sure if he gave Detective Tucci my message. I work for *Manhattan Style* magazine."

"Oh, I know that magazine," Mrs. Tucci interrupted. "I read it every month."

"Glad to hear it. Then you might know me— Madison Castelli?"

"Certainly, Miss Castelli—I've read your work. I like it a lot."

"Call me Madison. And your name is?"

"Faye."

"Okay, Faye—well, um . . . tell your husband I had lunch with Salli today, I have an audiotape of our interview, and I'd really like to see him personally."

"Oh, I'll do that," Faye said, impressed. "You can depend on me."

Madison gave Faye her phone number, then, secure in the fact that she'd done her duty, she got in her car and drove back to Natalie's.

Cole, Natalie's brother, was sprawled on the couch in front of the TV staring at the screen. "You heard the news?" he said, as she walked in.

"Yes."

"I used to train Salli, y'know," he said dully.

"You did?"

"A coupla years ago, when she was married to her first husband, Eddie. He was a maniac. She was a peach."

Madison sat down on the edge of the couch. "Tell me about him."

"Salli used to tell me stuff," Cole said. "To everybody else she'd say she got a black eye or all beat up walking into a door. One time he broke her arm and I had to rush her to the hospital. She called the cops on him a couple of times, but he'd always talk them round. She was lucky to get away from him."

"Are you saying you think *he* did it?"

"Wouldn't be surprised," Cole said with a shrug. "He had a way hot temper. That dude was *always* pissed about something."

"Like what?"

"You know the deal. He was a small-time actor—worked plenty, but was never the star. This made him *real* sour. I stopped working out with her when Eddie began getting jealous."

"Of you?"

"Yeah."

"But you're gay."

Cole laughed mirthlessly. "Try telling Eddie. He didn't want her around *any* guy who looked good. He was into control, that's *all* he wanted. I'm kinda surprised she got away from him; it took a lot of strength."

"What was his name again?"

"Eddie Stoner," Cole said grimly.

Madison got up and went to her laptop, where she put in a request to New York for information.

*Eddie Stoner. Let's find out exactly who you are.*

# chapter 17

"OH . . . MY . . . GOD,"
Kristin murmured, stretching luxuriously. "That
was pretty . . . damn . . . good."

Jake pinned her arms above her head, holding her
wrists tightly so she could barely move. "That wasn't
pretty damn good," he said sternly. "That was
sensational, *and* you know it."

"Yes, of course I know it," she said, giggling softly.
"You don't have to torture me to make me talk."

"And what makes you think I'm about to torture
you?" he asked, mock-serious.

"I don't know, maybe you'll make love to me
again."

"Would that be torture?"

"Oh, yes. Beautiful, incredible, fantastic torture."

He laughed. "I guess I'm going to have to make
you beg."

"Really?" she said, attempting to roll out from
under him.

"Yup," he said decisively. "I'm gonna have to do it."

"Okay, how do I beg?" she said, realizing she'd never felt so relaxed and carefree and happy as she did at that very moment.

"You say, 'Please Jake.'"

"Please Jake," she repeated, unable to keep the laughter out of her voice.

"Now say, 'I beg you, Jake, to give me more.'"

"I'm not saying that."

"Don't argue. I'm trying to teach you."

"Dear Jake," she said, smiling. "That was so damn good that I'm *begging* you for more."

He bent his head to her left nipple, teasing it with his tongue. "Keep begging," he said. "I like it."

She felt his hardness against her naked thigh, and sighed with pleasure. "Isn't it time you begged me?" she suggested, after a few moments of utter bliss.

"Huh?"

"I want to hear *you* beg."

"You do?"

"Right now, soldier!"

"Hey—" A big smile spread across his face. "This is like we've been together for years."

She laughed softly. "Well, we haven't."

"Oh, *big* surprise," he said jokingly. "But we're going to be—right?"

*Why did he have to spoil everything?* "Jake," she said, searching for the right words. "I haven't been completely honest with you."

"Don't want to hear about it now. You can be completely honest with me over lunch tomorrow. But right now, let's just enjoy the moment."

She tried to roll away again. He turned her back toward him and began sucking on her lower lip. "I never realized," she gasped, "that kissing could be so erotic."

"Then you've got a lot of learning to do."

"Will you teach me, Jake?"

"You want me to?"

"Yes."

"Well, first you've got to gently caress the lips with your tongue very very slowly. Like this."

"Oh, you're good," she said, shivering.

"So I've been told," he answered confidently.

"And who told you?"

"Huh?"

"Well, you informed me you hadn't been with a woman for over a year," she said curiously. "So who told you?"

A long pause before he spoke. "My wife," he said at last. "She died in a car crash a year ago."

"Oh, God, I'm sorry—I didn't know."

"You know the old cliché—there's nothing like time to heal. Anyway, we were separated when it happened."

"Were you getting a divorce?"

"She was seeing another guy. In fact, she was on her way to visit him when a truck came out of a side street and totaled her car. She had no chance."

"Are you telling me she left you for someone else?"

"Yup, that's exactly right. Which is why there hasn't been anyone since. Because how could I trust anyone after that? Megan was my high-school sweetheart, we were married straight out of school. I thought we had a pretty good marriage, and then . . ." He trailed off.

"Jake, I . . . I'm really sorry."

"When somebody lets you down, it's difficult to trust again. But then I saw you sitting in Neiman Marcus, and you had this great luminous quality, and I *knew* you were special. And now, days later, here we are. God works in mysterious ways, huh?"

She was suffused with guilt. Why did this have to happen? Why did she have to fall in love with a man she could never tell the truth to? And how was she going to extract herself from this situation? Because there was absolutely no way she could ever tell him.

"Hey," Jake said. "This wasn't supposed to turn into a confessional. This is you and me starting out, it's not about either of our pasts. But while we're on the subject, is there anything you want to tell me?"

*Plenty,* she thought, suffused with guilt. *But there's no way I'm doing so.*

She put her arms around him to hide her shame, and hugged him very tight. She was definitely going to make this a night to remember, because after this one night of passion, she'd decided she would never see him again.

"So," Jake said, smiling. "What did I do to deserve such affection?"

"Everything," she murmured.

And then he was kissing her again. And before she knew it they were making love for the second time. And it was so amazing, so different, so satisfying.

And just as she was heading toward another great climax, the phone rang, jangling her back to reality.

"Ignore it," Jake said, still inside her, pinning her beneath his body, the feel of him driving her crazy.

She wondered who it could be, but she didn't have to wonder long, because after three rings her answering machine picked up.

*Oh God,* she thought, panic-stricken, *I forgot to turn the damn machine off.*

Jake was also close to a climax, so there was no way she could escape to turn down the volume.

"Hi, Kristin, sweetie," said Darlene. "Boy, has Mister X got a hot nut for *you*. Talk about obsession. Can you believe he wants to book you again tonight, *and* he's willing to spring for another five thousand big ones for the privilege. Twice in one night. Honey, you've really got it going." A husky giggle. "What's your secret? A mink-lined snatch? Call me back ASAP. The man is waiting."

204

# chapter 18

**M**ADISON WOKE TO NATalie pushing her shoulders. "What's up?" she mumbled.

"There's a Detective Tucci on the phone," Natalie said, already dressed and made up. "Isn't he the detective covering the Salli T. Turner case?"

"That's right," Madison answered, suppressing a yawn.

"Why's he calling you?" Natalie asked curiously.

"Because I phoned his house last night. I couldn't get into the location and I thought I should talk to him about the audiotape I have of Salli." Leaning over, she reached for the phone. "This is Madison Castelli."

"Miss Castelli," Tucci said, his tone slow and measured. "I understand you have some information for me."

"Yes, I do. You see, I was with Salli yesterday. She gave me an in-depth interview for my magazine. In fact, I have the tape if you'd be interested in hearing it."

"Most definitely."

"Shall I come to the station?"

"That's most accommodating of you, Miss Castelli, but I'll be at the Pacific Palisades house all morning. Can you come there?"

"Certainly."

"I'll expect you as soon as possible."

"I'll be there as soon as I can."

"See you then."

She replaced the receiver. "There goes Freddie Leon for the day," she said wryly.

Natalie handed her a well-needed cup of coffee. "What do you mean?"

"If I'm going to meet the detective, how can I get in to Freddie today? I was planning on dropping by the I.A.A. office to visit Max Steele."

"You couldn't anyway," Natalie pointed out. "It's Sunday, they'd be closed."

"Oh, right."

"And regarding Max Steele," Natalie added. "There's a story about him in the *Times*. Seems he's leaving I.A.A. to head up Orpheus Studios."

"You're kidding?"

"It's on the second page."

"Really?"

"Is this a surprise?"

"He told me he had some news, only I didn't realize it was going to be public knowledge so fast. I'd better call him."

"He's probably sleeping."

Madison reached for her robe and got out of bed. "What happened after I left last night?"

"Oh, Garth was his usual un-charming self," Natalie said. "I was at the station all night interviewing anybody who knew her and putting together a retrospective. It's media frenzy time, all anybody's talking about. And once they find out you were with her, *you'll* be a media sensation, too."

"Thanks a lot," Madison said dryly. "If you hadn't told your news director . . ."

"What can *he* do?"

"Tell other people, to punish me for not appearing on his shitty show."

"It's not a shitty show," Natalie said defensively.

"Sorry, I didn't mean that."

"Yes, you did!"

Madison felt bad about insulting her friend. "C'mon, Nat," she said warmly, "let's not start the day off badly. Did they reach Salli's husband yet?"

"Yeah, there's coverage of him going into the house looking wrecked."

"What about the ex, Eddie Stoner? Have they questioned him?"

"They're looking. Nobody seems to know where he's at."

"Is he the prime suspect?"

"Could be. God!" Natalie exclaimed. "Can you imagine what the tabloids are going to do with this story?"

Madison nodded. "It'll turn into another O.J.-and-Nicole circus."

"You got it," Natalie said. "Only this time they won't be able to play the race card. Thank God!"

"No, but you can bet they'll play the sex card," Madison said. "You know, sexy blonde, big boobs, all of that sexist crap—like Salli was asking for it."

"You think so?"

"I *know* so. She was beautiful, rich, sexy *and* a woman. Major strike against getting any kind of fair treatment." Madison sighed. "This whole thing makes me sick. Yesterday she was alive, today she's dead. I simply can't believe it."

"Me neither," said Cole, walking into the room. "I heard on channel five that Salli's dad is flying in from Chicago, and there's a private funeral tomorrow. I'd like to be there."

"That's a tough one," Natalie said. "Salli had so many fans, they'll all want to attend."

"I'd still like to go," Cole said.

"Me, too," Madison agreed. "How can we arrange it?"

"I'll see what I can find out," Natalie said. "Right now I've got to get back to the studio. Then Luther wants to take me to lunch, and girl, I am *not* passing *him* up."

As soon as Natalie left, Madison decided to call Max Steele. She had his home phone number, so she picked up the phone and got through immediately. "Hi, Max," she said. "This is Madison—remember? Breakfast yesterday?"

He sounded groggy. "What's doin'?"

"I read your news."

"News?"

"You told me you had an announcement; however, you didn't tell me it was going to appear today."

"What announcement?" Max said, kicking off his bedcovers, realizing he was suffering from a monster hangover.

"Is it true you're taking over Ariel Shore's job at Orpheus?"

"Shit!" he said, sitting up. "Where'd you hear that?"

"It's in the *Times.*"

"Christ!" he said. And he knew what had happened. Freddie had opened the door before he was ready to leave, and shoved him out. Hard. Now Billy Cornelius would be mad as hell, and there was nothing he could do about it.

"Off the record," Madison said. "Would you mind giving me Freddie Leon's home number?"

"Why?" Max said suspiciously. "You wanna ask him about this?"

"No, it has nothing to do with you. I'm simply looking to find out everything I can about him. That *is* why I'm out here."

"If you want the dirt on Freddie, talk to his secretary—Ria Santiago. She knows things nobody else does."

"Would you happen to have *her* phone number?"

"Yeah, I'll give you both numbers." *Nothing like a little sweet revenge,* Max thought.

Madison hung up and glanced at her watch. It was too early to call anyone else. Waking Max was one thing, but she figured she'd be nice and let the others sleep for an hour or so, although she was sure Freddie Leon was an early riser—he looked the type.

While she was waiting she called Victor in New York, where it was three hours later. "I'm holding the press for your story," Victor said. "I need it like yesterday."

"I'm seeing the detective on the case this morning. As soon as I get back I'll write it up and fax it to you."

"Good," Victor said. "And maybe you can include the name of the killer."

"Yeah, sure, Victor," she drawled. "Why not? Simple."

"No need to be sarcastic, Maddy. I'll talk to you later."

"Yes, Victor, later."

# chapter 19

**A**RIEL SHORE ARRIVED AT Billy Cornelius' house at eight in the morning and insisted upon seeing him. Ethel, his feisty wife, was still asleep. The butler, a prudent man, did not wake Ethel. Instead he ushered Ariel into the living room, where she waited impatiently for ten long minutes.

When Billy finally appeared, she thrust the *L.A. Times* in his face. "What's *this?*" she said through clenched teeth, towering over him.

Billy Cornelius stared bad-temperedly at the newspaper. "What're you talking about?" he snapped, his left eye twitching.

"This ridiculous story about Max Steele getting my job," Ariel said. "Read it."

Billy scanned the story with beady, red-rimmed eyes. "Bullpuddy, hogwash," he said.

"It better be," Ariel said sternly. "Because I'm sure you wouldn't relish Ethel finding out about us."

Billy curled his lip. "You wouldn't do that, Ariel."

"Think again, Billy, I certainly would."

"You promised."

"I *know* what I promised," she said, marching up and down. "And I know what *you* promised. You break yours, I can break mine. What is this crap with Max Steele anyway?"

"I was planning on telling you," Billy said. "I considered bringing him in as head of production. Nothing definite."

She arched an eyebrow in disgust. "Without informing me?"

"Max is a go-getter, he knows everyone."

Ariel planted herself in front of her so-called boss. "Listen to me, Billy, and listen carefully. *I* run the studio. You do not make decisions like that without my input. Max Steele will have nothing to do with Orpheus. *Nothing.* Is that perfectly clear? Because if it's not, I'm sure that Ethel will be able to make it *very* clear to you."

"You have nothing to worry about," Billy said, backing down in the face of Ariel's fury.

"And next time you sneak around behind my back," Ariel said, eyes glittering dangerously, "you'd better be more careful. I want a retraction, and I want to see it in Monday's paper. Do we understand each other, Billy?"

Billy Cornelius nodded. He might be one of the richest men in America, but when Ariel Shore screamed, he jumped.

# chapter 20

**W**HEN DIANA AWOKE ON
Sunday morning, she realized that Freddie had not
returned home the night before. It wasn't the first
time he'd stayed out all night.

Nevertheless, she was livid. How dare he think he
could simply walk out and not return.

And where exactly was he? Not that she was
worried about other women—Freddie had never
been a sexual being. Even in the beginning of their
marriage they'd made love infrequently; then several years ago, their lovemaking had stopped alto-
gether.

No, it wasn't another woman. It was Freddie's way
of hurting her. First he ruined her dinner party, then
he stayed out all night. What a cold bastard he could
be.

The children were away in Connecticut staying
with her mother, so the house was quite peaceful.
She got out of bed and marched downstairs to the

kitchen. The caterers had done a masterly job of cleaning up.

Throwing open the fridge she surveyed the left-overs, wrapped neatly in Saran Wrap. Cold hors d'oeuvres always appealed to her, so she took out an egg roll and wolfed it down without thinking. Then she stomped around the house, making sure everything was in place and that the catering staff hadn't stolen anything. Diana lived in fear that someone was going to rip her off. It could be because she had been brought up by extremely strict parents in Utah who suspected everyone of stealing. She'd never forgotten her stern upbringing.

The Sunday *L.A. Times* was neatly laid out on the kitchen table, alongside the *New York Times*. Usually Freddie got to them first; he was fastidious about his newspapers and did not like anyone else touching them before him. However, today Diana felt it was her duty to mess them up before he got home.

The heading of a story on page two caught her attention.

### *ARIEL OUT, MAX IN.*
### *MAX STEELE TO LEAVE I.A.A.*
### *AND JOIN ORPHEUS.*

How could this have possibly gotten into the newspapers so quickly? Somebody must have leaked it early, long before Freddie and Max's confrontation.

Diana read the story quickly, then rushed to the phone.

Max answered immediately. "Yes?" he snapped, sounding most unfriendly.

"Max, this is Diana. Can we meet?"

"Why?" he asked suspiciously.

"There's something I wish to discuss."

"Is it about Freddie?"

"He mustn't know we're meeting."

"Whatever you say, Diana."

"Nine-thirty at the Four Seasons. The dining room."

"I'll be there," Max said.

"Good," Diana replied. She'd known he wouldn't turn her down.

215

# chapter 21

EDDIE STONER WAS AWAKened from a liquor-induced sleep at six A.M. on Sunday morning by two burly cops, who burst rudely into his apartment and informed him he was under arrest. He was between girlfriends at the time, so there was no one to buffer their entrance.

"What the fuck is *this* about?" Eddie mumbled, as they instructed him to get out of bed.

"Parking tickets," cop number one said. "You got thirty-four of 'em, all unpaid. You're under arrest, bud, so let's go."

"Parking tickets!" Eddie Stoner said, throwing off the sheet, knowing he was naked and not caring. Let the cops get an eyeful and see what they *didn't* have.

"Yeah, unpaid tickets," said cop number two, proceeding to read him his rights.

"Jesus Christ!" Eddie grumbled, reaching for his pants. "Don't you guys have anythin' better t'do?"

"Where'd you get that scratch on your chest?" cop number one asked.

"Didn't realize gettin' a parkin' ticket meant havin' to explain my physical state," Eddie replied, running a hand through his mane of dirty blond hair. "There's one on my ass, too—wanna take a peek? My girlfriend's got long fingernails."

"Get dressed," cop number two said.

Eddie Stoner shrugged, threw on a T-shirt and some sneakers. "Fuck!" he said. "You're haulin' me in for parkin' tickets. Who the fuck'd believe *this?*"

# chapter 22

**M**ADISON PLAYED THE
tape as she drove her rented car on the way to Salli's
house. It was truly heartbreaking to hear Salli explain her life in her own words—exactly as Madison
remembered. She found it particularly interesting
when Salli talked about Eddie Stoner. "Eddie was
basically a good guy," Salli said. "Just frustrated,
'cause like his mom drove him loco. Never left him
alone for a moment, laid a big fat guilt trip on him
'cause his father ran out on them when Eddie was
twelve. So like he always felt kind of responsible for
her. An' she got off on that—telling him he was a
bum and no good. Guess he wanted to prove her
right. She hated me, thought I was a little tramp.
Said so to my face. Well, I guess I gotta confess—
Eddie did beat me up a few times. But it wasn't his
fault, and later, he was always so nice and loving,
begging my forgiveness. I had to escape though,
otherwise he would've dragged me down with him."

Madison listened to her own voice on the tape. "If

I remember correctly, Salli, you told me on the plane that Eddie was a psycho freakazoid asshole actor who sued you for alimony. You also told me that he still thinks you'll take him back one day."

"Wow!" Salli's voice again. *"You've* got a good memory."

"So which is it? Was he a sweetheart? Or a wife beater?"

"A little bit of both," Salli said. And then wistfully—"But I must've loved him at one time."

Madison switched off the tape. She wished she'd asked more questions about Eddie Stoner.

Now it was too late.

"Nice of you to come, Miss Castelli," Detective Tucci said, greeting her at the door. He was a tall, heavyset man with brown hair and faded blue eyes. Not unattractive, Madison thought as he took her arm and led her inside the house. Walking through the hall without Salli there to greet her felt strange. Automatically, she glanced up at the giant portrait. It was still there, smiling down at everybody.

"Merely doing my duty," she replied. "When I leave here I'm writing a piece for my magazine, and I thought I should let you know what I have, in case it could be useful for your investigation."

"That's very thoughtful of you, Miss Castelli."

"On the tape, Salli talks about her ex-husband, Eddie Stoner. When we flew into L.A. a couple of days ago, she was telling me he always expected they'd get back together. Do you think he could've—?"

"Mr. Stoner's already in custody on parking-ticket violations," Tucci said. "Of course, that's official information, not for publication. I can trust you, Miss Castelli, can't I?"

"Please call me Madison," she said, nodding. "I spoke to your wife; she was most charming on the phone."

"Faye's a good woman."

"Salli was a terrific girl," Madison said. "You've only seen the public image, but to know her was to realize that she had a certain sweetness that really came through. I'm so saddened by this horrible tragedy."

"The world seems to be," Tucci said. "There's already several Web sites set up to discuss her murder."

"I can imagine."

"May I listen to the tape back in my office?" Tucci said. "Then maybe I can ask you questions about it later."

"I made a copy for you."

"You're very organized."

"I'm a good journalist."

"My wife said that. She speaks very highly of your work. Faye's the one who has the time to read magazines, I don't."

Madison laughed politely.

"Are you from here?" he asked.

"New York," Madison said. "I'm in L.A. preparing a story on Freddie Leon."

"I'm afraid I don't know who that is."

"Your wife would, I'm sure."

"Oh, yes, Faye—she knows all about show business."

Madison smiled again. She liked this man; he was

warm and seemed to care. "Did you meet the houseman yesterday?" Tucci asked.

"Froo. Yes, I did. I gather he's the other victim."

"We think he heard noises and came to investigate."

"Well, Detective, if there's anything I can do, please don't hesitate to call me."

"You say she had a certain sweetness?"

"That's right."

"I'd like to solve this one."

"Tell me—do you think it could be the ex-husband?"

Tucci shook his head. "I never make random guesses. With DNA today we'll be able to find out in no time."

"Just like they did with Nicole Simpson, right?" Madison said, unable to resist the dig.

"That was a botched case."

"I'm sure you won't botch this one. I trust that you'll do Salli justice."

"It's my intention, Miss Castelli, it's certainly my intention."

# chapter 23

**M**AX COULD NOT BE-
lieve what was happening to him. One moment he
was a partner in the most successful talent agency in
Los Angeles, the next he was about to head up a
studio, and now Billy Cornelius had just got off the
phone, telling him that things had changed, and
there was no way they could work together.

"What do you mean changed?" Max had blustered.

"You should never have leaked it," Billy had said.
"Too late now. The deal's off."

Max was furious. Now he'd have to go crawling
back to Freddie and say, "Let's forget and forgive."
Only Freddie was not the forgiving kind. Everyone
knew that.

Max couldn't help thinking about Inga Cruelle.
He'd always had great success with women. How
dare she treat him like he was simply another guy on
the make.

He glanced at his gold Rolex. It was almost time to

meet Diana. Before he did, however, there was something he had to do. He had a plan.

He went to the phone and called Kristin. To his annoyance her answering machine picked up.

"Hey, baby," he said. "This is Max Steele. I've made a decision. I'm taking you out of the business, honey. Making you exclusive. You tell me what it'll cost to set you up, and I'll do it." He paused for a moment, quite pleased with himself. "I've been thinking about things. I want you to be with me. Y'see, I need somebody like you around, somebody to keep me focused. I can introduce you to people, change your life. Nobody'll know who you are, or what you used to be. This is gonna work out, Kristin. Trust me." Another pause. "I have a breakfast meeting, so call me any time after twelve and we'll work something out. Okay, honey?"

And when he hung up the phone he was convinced he had her. Beautiful Kristin beside him would change his luck.

Diana was about to leave the house when Freddie walked in. He was unshaven, his eyes wild-looking, his clothes crumpled—most out of character for a man as fastidious as Freddie Leon.

"My God!" Diana said, staring at her disheveled husband. "You look as if you slept in your clothes. What hotel took you in looking like that?"

"Diana, leave me alone," Freddie said, pushing past her on his way upstairs. As far as he was concerned, Diana was becoming more trouble than she was worth.

"Yes, Freddie, I will," she called after him. And set off to seal her future with Max Steele.

# chapter 24

ON THE BEACH IN MALibu, two teenagers ran down to the sea. They were wearing black rubber wet suits, their surfboards tucked under their arms.

"Great waves, dude," said one.

"Sweet," agreed the second one.

Just as they were about to enter the water, they noticed a fan of long blond hair and one delicate arm tangled in seaweed.

They glanced at each other. "Holy shit! What's that?"

"Looks like a body."

Together they dragged the lifeless form out of the water and laid it on the sand.

The body was a female. Gorgeous, blond, and very very naked.

Another murder.

Another beautiful day in L.A.

# Murder

# chapter 1

THE MEDIA WERE IN A FRENzy. A beautiful blond sex symbol, Salli T. Turner, star of TV's *Teach!*, had been murdered, and the circus was in full swing. Her luxurious mansion in Pacific Palisades was surrounded on all sides by TV trucks, their crews, reporters, and the general populace held back behind police lines.

The slaying of Salli and her houseman, Froo, was already as high profile as the Nicole Simpson/Ron Goldman killings. The media liked nothing better than a good, juicy, violent murder to hang onto, and Salli T. Turner was the perfect victim. A blond goddess, she was known on every continent as the girl in the black rubber swimsuit, thanks to the worldwide success of her TV show and her many photo spreads in numerous popular magazines—including three *Playboy* covers.

Salli had been married twice. Her current husband was Bobby Skorch, a man whose profession was performing dangerous stunts. When Bobby had returned home from Vegas at three A.M., Tucci had confronted him with the shocking news. Bobby had appeared to be so distraught that he'd locked himself in the master bedroom and refused to come out.

Salli's former husband, Eddie Stoner, a small-time actor, was currently under arrest for parking violations. The arrest, however, was a scam—the police had wanted to get him into custody so they could question him, and thirty-four unpaid tickets had seemed a good way to accomplish it.

Detective Chuck Tucci had only managed two hours of sleep the previous night and was now feeling the effects. He was also aware that very shortly he'd have to give some kind of press conference to satisfy the hordes of media who hovered outside the murdered star's home like hungry vultures waiting for something to be thrown into their gaping mouths. Detective Tucci knew exactly what he'd like to throw—several hand grenades.

Early in the morning his understanding wife, Faye, had packed him a care package—one corned beef, lettuce and tomato sandwich, his favorite, *and* a carton of her homemade coleslaw, which she knew he loved. He'd missed dinner the night before, and when he'd finally arrived home at some ungodly hour, Faye had been asleep. As soon as he'd made enough noise to wake her, though, she got up, and in spite of the fact that he was supposed to be on a diet, she'd hurried down to the kitchen and fixed him a delicious plate of scrambled eggs. Faye was a good woman, also a most attractive one; feisty, with hispanic blood, she was a pocket-sized Venus, with a mass of black hair and kind brown eyes. Detective

Tucci often gave thanks for the day he met her: he'd been investigating a murder in Malibu, and she had been the social worker sent to collect the two children in the house. Three months later they were married.

Last night he'd wolfed down the plate of eggs she'd fixed him and begged for more. "You can't eat anything else this late," Faye had scolded, wagging a disapproving finger at him. "It's bad for your stomach."

Bad for his *stomach?* Given half the chance, he would've devoured everything in sight, in spite of the fact that he'd spent the evening in the company of two dead bodies—Salli T. Turner, hacked to death by her frenzied killer, and Froo, her houseman, shot in the face—two bloodied bodies he'd had to inspect and watch being photographed. Finally, when forensics were finished, he'd observed as the bodies were hauled off to be autopsied, and then he prowled around the house, making copious notes in his worn blue leather notebook. After that he interviewed the neighbors, and now, in the morning sunshine, all that was left were the chalk marks to show exactly where the unfortunate victims had fallen.

Detective Tucci shook his head and tried not to think about food. His care package was sitting in the kitchen where he had left it, and there it would stay until he got desperate. He was now waiting to interview the infamous Bobby Skorch. A few hours ago, Bobby's lawyer, Marty Steiner, arrived at the house and rushed straight to the bedroom, where he'd been huddled with his client for the last two hours. Marty was smoothness personified, with his slicked-back silver hair, smug face and expensive jogging suit. A "dream team" reject, he was a man obviously determined to hit the headlines. One look and Tucci had immediately tagged him "Hollywood lawyer," although he'd promised himself not to make such quick judgments. Faced with Marty Steiner, the temptation proved irresistible.

He glanced at his watch, noting that the brown leather strap was worn and that he needed to buy a new one. Maybe next weekend he and Faye would go shopping. Faye loved wandering along the Third Street promenade, checking out the stores, and as long as they got to stop for a hamburger or a hot dog, he didn't object.

Now that his mind was back on food, his sandwich, tightly packaged in Saran Wrap, sitting quietly in the kitchen, was beckoning him. Finally he gave up and hurried into the kitchen.

Salli T. Turner's plump, middle-aged Filipino maid, Eppie, sat at the end of a long marble counter, crying into a glass of milk and a plate full of cookies. Earlier he had questioned her; between sobs she told him she didn't know anything. According to Eppie, she arrived at the house every morning at eight A.M. and departed at three P.M. When she left yesterday, Missy Salli—as she called her employer—had been happily having lunch out by the pool. He'd asked her about Bobby Skorch. "They very much in love," Eppie had answered tearfully. "Always laughing."

Well Bobby Skorch wasn't laughing now, Tucci thought grimly. And he wasn't talking either. Not that he had any obligation to do so—but if he didn't, it would cast a deep pall of suspicion over him.

Tucci's eyes swiveled to the end of the marble

counter where he'd left his sandwich. It was gone. So was his carton of homemade coleslaw. "I . . . uh . . . had some food I left here," he said, trying to ignore his rumbling stomach.

"What?" Eppie said rudely, like she couldn't believe he was thinking of food at a time like this.

"A sandwich," he said, clearing his throat. "And a carton of coleslaw."

"Oh," Eppie answered vaguely, lowering her swollen and red-rimmed eyes. "I didn't know it was yours. I ate it."

"You *ate* it?" Tucci said incredulously.

"Sorry," Eppie said, stuffing another cookie into her mouth. "It was only an itty bitty *snack.*" And then, noticing that the detective was not pleased, she burst into sobs again, almost choking on her cookie.

"Goddamn it!" Tucci mumbled under his breath, just as his partner, Lee Eccles—summoned back from a fishing trip—arrived.

"Jeez!" Lee exclaimed. "There's a friggin' circus goin' on outside. What in hell happened here?"

231

# chapter 2

**M**ADISON CASTELLI SAT
in front of her laptop at the kitchen table, diligently
attempting to compose a story about Salli T. Turner. When they'd first met, Madison had considered
Salli to be the definitive Hollywood bimbo, but
after a while she'd changed her mind, and they
got along fine. Later on, when Salli had found out
that Madison worked for the high-concept magazine *Manhattan Style,* she'd immediately wanted to
be in it, so they'd arranged to get together for an
interview.

The day of Salli's brutal murder, Madison had
lunched with Salli at her palatial Pacific Palisades
mansion, where they'd acted like a couple of girlfriends, chatting about everyone and everything.
Actually, Salli had done most of the talking, while
Madison listened—but that's what good journalists
did, and Salli certainly had plenty to say.

Now she was dead, and Madison sat at her laptop
staring blankly at the screen. She already had gone

to Salli's house and told the detective in charge of the investigation everything she knew. She also had given him a copy of the audiotape she'd made of her interview with Salli. He'd said he would listen to it later and call her if there was anything he wanted to discuss with her.

Pushing back her long dark hair, she sighed deeply. In a way, it was probably best to get it all out on paper, yet in another way, she was so upset by Salli's death that she wasn't sure she could remain completely unattached.

Drumming her fingers on the table, she wondered what to say about the girl everybody *thought* they knew but didn't really know at all. Salli T. Turner, the sizzling platinum blonde who regularly appeared on *E.T.* and *Hard Copy,* and was a staple in every tabloid—photographed running into parties, emerging from clubs and discos, clad in revealing tight rubber dresses and exceptionally high heels, her bountiful cleavage always on show. She seemed always to be waving and laughing, her megawatt smile lighting up the night.

And yet, beneath the boobs and abundance of blond hair had lurked a very simple girl, a very *nice* girl. And even though they'd only known each other a short time, Madison had liked her a lot, for Salli had possessed a naïveté and freshness which was surprisingly endearing.

Abruptly she closed her laptop. She didn't feel like writing; she felt like crying. This horrific murder was so senseless. *Why* had it taken place? What had Salli done to merit such a frenzy of violence?

Madison knew what she *should* do—forget about the murders and concentrate on Freddie Leon, since he was the main thrust of her trip to L.A., and she'd done virtually nothing about arranging an interview. Of course, the elusive Freddie Leon was notorious for not granting interviews, but Victor Simons had assured her he could set it up.

*Yeah, Victor,* she thought sourly. *When?*

To take her mind off Salli, Madison decided to call Freddie Leon's longtime secretary, Ria Santiago—whose private home number she'd gotten from Max Steele. She had to stop thinking about Salli; it was all too dark and depressing, and she'd been depressed enough when she'd arrived in L.A.—what with David, her live-in love of two years, walking out on her. Damn David! Why couldn't he have been honest with her? The cowardly skunk had gone out for a pack of cigarettes and failed to come back. Oh yes, he'd left her a stupid note about how he couldn't deal with commitment, then five weeks later he'd gotten married!

Men! She'd had it with them. Why couldn't she find one like her father, Michael, who at fifty-eight was the best looking and nicest man she knew? He and her stunningly beautiful mother, Stella, had an idyllic marriage. They'd been together thirty years and hardly ever spent a night apart. Madison missed them since they'd given up their elegant New York apartment and moved to Connecticut. It was far too long since she'd spent a weekend with them, and as soon as she was through in L.A., that's exactly what she planned on doing.

Everyone told Madison she was a female version of her father, which secretly pleased her because she adored her dad—he was powerful and charming, two qualities she greatly admired. Besides, she had no desire to compete with her mother, who was fair haired and deliciously feminine. Madison liked being tall and rangy with smooth olive skin, jet-black hair and direct, almond-shaped eyes. And then there were her lips—men fell in love with her lips, which were full and seductive and ever so slightly pouty. However, Madison was a no-nonsense girl who played her looks down and concentrated on being smart. She loved competing with the boys and coming out on top. *Maybe that's what frightened David away,* she thought ruefully. *Couldn't take the competition.*

Before she could punch out Ria Santiago's number, Cole, Natalie's fitness-trainer brother, came into the room. Cole was gay in a fiercely masculine way and much too good-looking for his own good. Like everyone else in L.A. on this quiet Sunday morning he was thinking about her violent death.

"Hey," he said, reaching for the coffeepot.

"Hey," Madison responded.

"Didja go see the detective?" Cole asked, pouring himself a mug of black coffee.

"I sure did."

"Anythin' new?"

"Nothing that I know of."

"It's shit," Cole mumbled, pulling out a chair and sitting down. "Salli didn't deserve to get taken out like that."

"I know," Madison said in somber agreement.

Cole reached for the TV clicker and tuned into the *E!* channel, where they were already showing a quickly put together retrospective. There was Salli in red. Salli in blue. Salli in skintight. Salli in her famous black rubber swimsuit. And then the male star of *Teach!* appeared, an actor past his prime, who still thought he was a major stud. "Everyone was in love with Salli," the actor said, Hollywood casual in well-fitting linen pants and a chest-baring silk shirt, his capped teeth catching the light. "Salli was a *very* special person."

Commercial break.

"Would you switch to Natalie's channel?" Madison asked.

Cole obliged. There was Natalie on the screen, vibrantly pretty, dressed in a shocking-pink jacket and short white dress.

"The Salli everyone knew and loved came from a little town outside of Chicago," Natalie said. "And we have learned from family and friends that ever since Salli took her first steps, she wanted to be an actress."

Cut to baby pictures of Salli. A fat little cutie. And then on came a "friend of the family"—a stone-faced woman with badly dyed red hair and an eyelid twitch. "I knew Salli since she was two years old," croaked the woman, her voice a gin-soaked rasp. "An' to know her was to love her."

"Jesus!" Madison murmured. "They'll be crawling out from everywhere."

"Who?" Cole asked.

"People who met her once in their lives. It's *their* chance for glory."

"Guess you're right."

"It happens every time somebody famous dies."

"Yeah," Cole agreed.

"Where's her family? Her mother?"

Cole rubbed his faintly stubbled chin. "Didn't she tell you about her mom when you interviewed her?"

"She hedged—I didn't pursue."

Cole took a deep breath, his handsome features deadly serious. "Salli's mom was murdered when she was ten. It was her big secret."

Madison felt a cold chill creeping up her spine. "How do you know this?" she asked.

Cole was silent for a moment before replying. "There was a time Salli an' I were pretty close," he said, refusing to make eye contact. "She kinda viewed me as a challenge—y'know, the good-looking guy who wasn't into having sex with her. It drove her nutty. Salli liked to think she could get any man she zeroed in on. Sex was her big validation, her comfort zone."

Madison raised an eyebrow. "And did she get you?"

"We did it once," Cole admitted sheepishly. "For God's sake, *don't* tell Natalie."

"Of course not."

"It was before she got really famous."

"And that's when her then-husband, Eddie, became jealous of you?"

"He suspected something was goin' on, even

though he knew I was gay. So he made her stop using me as her trainer."

"I don't get it," Madison said, frowning. "If you're totally gay, how did she—"

"Hey," Cole said, throwing up his well-muscled arms. "I'm gay, not dead. And Salli knew exactly what to do to turn me on. She was an expert at sex. It was her game, and man—that girl always played to win."

Madison nodded understandingly. Nothing really surprised her. And Cole was right, Salli *had* gotten off on all the attention.

Cole stood up. "I'm goin' for a hike," he said. "Wanna come?"

She shook her head; everyone was so energetic in L.A. Didn't they know how to relax? "I'll pass," she said. "I'm hoping to interview Freddie Leon's secretary."

*"You,* girl, are missin' out," Cole said, heading for the door. "Nothin' like a good hike in the hills to set your head straight."

"Thanks for the offer," she said, reaching for the coffeepot and refilling her cup. "Maybe some other time."

As soon as he left, Madison called Ria Santiago, identified herself and told the secretary she was writing a piece on Freddie Leon for *Manhattan Style* and would like an opportunity to sit down and talk.

Ria's response was cold. "Does Mr. Leon know about this?"

"I'm hoping to meet with him tomorrow."

Ria: "I doubt it. Mr. Leon does not give interviews."

"I'm sure he'll make an exception."

"I'm sure he won't."

And the bitch hung up.

# chapter 3

KRISTIN CARR SAT IN FRONT of her dressing-table mirror, staring blankly at her blond and beautiful reflection. She knew that at twenty-three she was undeniably gorgeous, but she also knew that what was reflected was merely her outer image. Inside she was a whore, and she was certain that everyone knew it.

*Prostitute, hooker, call girl, whore.* All names that described her profession.

*I sell my body for the almighty dollar,* Kristin thought sadly. *I allow men to use me any way they want. I'm meat. They devour me. And everyone is happy. Everyone except me.*

The sinister Mister X crossed her mind and she shuddered. His sick demands were beyond mere kinky, but he paid well for the privilege of humiliating her. And that's why Darlene had phoned the night before, leaving a message on her machine that Mister X had asked to see her again—even though she'd been with him earlier that same evening.

The problem was that Kristin had taken it upon herself to have a life—much as her inner voice had warned her not to. Instead of listening to her gut feeling, she had gone ahead and fallen in lust with Jake Sica—a laid-back, award-winning photographer, whom she had met in Neiman Marcus. One and a half dates later they were in bed, *her* bed, then last night came the phone call from Darlene—loud and clear on her answering machine.

And lying in bed making love, Kristin had felt Jake shrivel up inside her before he rolled away.

She hadn't known what to say. In fact, neither of them said a word. After a moment or two, Jake got off the bed and hurried into the bathroom.

*Punishment,* Kristin thought. *Punishment for imagining I could have a life.*

She had reached for her silk robe at the end of the bed, sat up and put it on. Jake had stayed in the bathroom a long time. When he came out he was dressed and ready to leave.

"I forgot," he'd said, hardly able to look at her. "I'm expecting an important call."

Disappointment had flooded over her. Wasn't he even going to discuss it?

*So what?* she'd thought defensively. *Maybe this is best. What could he say? Excuse me, Kristin, why didn't you tell me you were a hooker?*

*Sorry, Jake, I forgot.*

"Uh, I'd like to explain," she ventured, hoping for at least a chance to say something—even if it was only an apology.

"No, Kristin, really," he said, anxious to leave. "There's nothing you have to explain to me. Uh—

the truth is—your lifestyle and mine—they uh . . . simply don't mesh."

*Was that it? Was the nonpaying customer leaving?*

"I understand," she said stiffly, thinking that if he didn't want to get into it, he wasn't worth having anyway. "I'll see you around."

"Yeah," he replied. "Guess so." Then he stopped at the door, turned and stared at her accusingly. "I wish you'd told me," he said.

"Why?" she said, filled with hurt.

"Because it's not fair you didn't. I would've used a condom."

The final blow. How *dare* he say that to her, as if she was a common street prostitute. "Fuck you," she'd yelled, suddenly furious. "Fuck *you!*" And she had gotten up, chased after him, slamming the door on his retreating back. Then she went to her dressing table and sat there, staring, staring, staring at her reflection.

When Max Steele, her once-a-month client, phoned in the morning, she had not picked up. Instead she listened to his message as her answering machine recorded it. Max had never done her any harm—in fact, she quite liked him. She didn't know exactly *what* he did, only that he was a big Hollywood player.

"Hey, baby," he said. "This is Max Steele. I've made a decision. I'm taking you out of the business, honey. Making you exclusive. You tell me what it'll cost to set you up, and I'll do it." A long pause, then—"I've been thinking about things. I want you to be with me. Y'see I need somebody like you around, somebody to keep me focused. I can introduce you to people, change your life. Nobody'll

know who you are, or what you used to be. This is
gonna work out, Kristin. Trust me." Another long
pause. "I have a breakfast meeting, so call me any
time after twelve and we'll work something out.
Okay, honey?"

*Okay, honey,* she thought. *I can do that. If you
want to pay me the kind of money Mister X does, you
can have me. Because nobody else wants me. I'm
used goods. So, Max Steele, I am all yours.*

# chapter 4

"**Y**OU'RE LATE," DETECTive Tucci said to his partner, thoroughly grumpy because the maid had devoured his sandwich—not to mention an entire carton of Faye's homemade coleslaw.

"Hey, buddy, *you* try racin' back from a fishin' trip in the middle of nowhere," Detective Lee Eccles complained, frowning. He was a tall, stoop-shouldered man with a weathered face and exceptionally large hands. "It ain't easy," he grumbled. "An' *then,* when I stopped by the station—my freakin' luck—I got sent out on another homicide. Or a suicide—who the fuck knows? Knockout blond babe washed up on the Malibu shore. Legs from here to Cuba. Forensics are runnin' a check on her now."

"You missed the big one here."

"My freakin' luck again. Fill me in. Tell me what we've got."

"Two dead bodies. One female, one male. The female stabbed multiple times. The male shot once in the face. The female's husband arrived home at three A.M. Gave him the news, he shut himself in the bedroom. His lawyer, Marty Steiner, arrived this morning—they've been locked in there together for a couple of hours."

"That piece a shit," Lee spat in disgust.

"You know him?"

"Some freakin' asshole," Lee said, picking at his teeth with a dirty fingernail. "Had dealin's with him before."

Lee Eccles and Detective Tucci had been partners for an uneasy six months. Tucci's previous partner had been a veteran detective, now retired. Lee was smart enough, but too abrasive for Tucci's taste. His favorite off-duty pastime was hanging out in bars and strip clubs, and he constantly talked about women in such graphic terms that he offended Tucci's sensibilities because his remarks were so sexist and derogatory. Tucci had complained once.

"Get yourself to a fuckin' monastery," Lee had responded with a mean scowl.

"What the hell does *that* mean?" Tucci growled, and they almost had gotten into a fistfight.

Since that time they had tolerated each other, but there was no real camaraderie.

"You don't look so good," Lee remarked.

"Didn't get any sleep," Tucci replied. *"And* I'm hungry."

"You're always freakin' hungry," Lee said, impatiently cracking his knuckles. "If you stopped eatin' so damn much, you wouldn't have such a big gut."

"I'm dieting," Tucci admitted, stung by the criticism.

Lee guffawed. "Yeah, until the next donut comes along!"

Tucci didn't bother answering. His gut wasn't *that* bad—Faye said she loved cuddling up to him. "You're huggable," she often said. *Hmm* . . . he thought, it would be nice if she changed that to "fuckable." Not that they had any problems in that department—although she *had* told him he was getting too heavy when he was on top, making love to her. Hence the diet.

"What's the deal?" Lee said impatiently. "We gonna wait 'til the husband decides to come out an' speak to us? Whyn't you go knock on the door an' tell him we need t'interview him *now.*"

Lee was right for once, Tucci thought. He definitely had had enough of sitting in this house of death. Still, he had to do it by the book. "Bobby Skorch doesn't *have* to talk to us," he pointed out. *"You* know that."

"He'll talk. For your info, when I was over at the station I took a gander at the ex. The dumb jerk is sittin' in a cell sweatin' it. Apparently he called his lawyer, who ain't exactly breakin' a leg to bail him."

"Really?" Tucci said.

"Yeah, and you'd better get your fat butt outside an' make some bullshit announcement to the media," Lee said. "The natives are gettin' ornery, nearly pulled me to pieces on my way in. An' while you're out there, take a look at the ass on that little Chinese chick from channel four. Now *she's* a piece! I wouldn't mind reamin' it up *that* juicy rear." Tucci threw him a disapproving look and Lee chuckled heartily. "What's your problem? Don't wanna get it up with anyone 'cept Faye?"

246

"Do me a favor," Tucci said, clenching his teeth and willing himself to remain calm. "Leave my wife out of this conversation."

"Oh, yeah, yeah—your wife," Lee said mockingly. "Faye's too fuckin' good to mention." A ribald laugh. "Face it, Tucci, she's got your balls in a lather an' your dick strapped to her left tit."

"That's enough," Tucci said, his face reddening. He knew that Faye and Lee had a history of sorts. She'd gone on a date with Lee once, long before she met him, and Lee had behaved badly. She wouldn't reveal the details, but suffice to say that whenever Lee's name came up she made a disgusted face.

"Yeah, yeah," Lee said, cracking his knuckles again. "So show me where you found the dead broad. Shit, I'm sorry I missed out on *this* babe. Wouldn't've minded an in-the-flesh close-up of *those* tits."

Tucci decided he'd had enough. As soon as he could, he was making an appointment to see Captain Marsh and requesting a new partner.

# chapter 5

MURDER

**D**IANA LEON PULLED UP
outside the Four Seasons, left her car with a parking
valet and entered the hotel. She felt oddly apprehen-
sive. It was the first time she would be with Max
Steele on her own. And yet, why not? Max and
Freddie had worked together for many years, and
she'd always had a friendly relationship with her
husband's partner—although deep down she knew
it was more than that, and now it was time they both
voiced something that was becoming painfully obvious.

*Yes, Max,* she hoped she had the courage to say.
*I'm married to Freddie, but it's a marriage in name
only. And since you're not attached to anybody right
now, and you're departing I.A.A., I suggest that I
leave Freddie and come with you.*

Diana was forty-three years old and this was the
boldest move she'd ever made. She had been married to Freddie for fifteen years. Now, finally, she

was doing something on her own without getting Freddie's permission.

She giggled nervously to herself, feeling like a silly schoolgirl. If Max was in agreement, *could* she leave Freddie? *Would* she leave? The situation was in Max's hands; she would have to feel her way carefully.

"Mrs. Leon," the maître d' greeted her warmly. "How nice to welcome you again to the Four Seasons. Mr. Steele is waiting."

Oh, God! She was having breakfast with Max Steele, a notorious womanizer. What must people think?

As she approached the table, Max stood up to greet her. She experienced a fleeting moment of sheer panic. Max was so unlike Freddie, who was always in control. Max was an unpredictable wild card and he excited the hell out of her.

"Hi, Diana," Max said.

She noticed that his hair was slightly mussed in a most attractive way, and that his suntan, as usual, was glowing. He was dressed all in white from his pristine pants to his casual summer cashmere sweater.

"Hello, Max," she said, hoping that she'd picked the right outfit. The girls he dated were always outrageously underdressed in flimsy little mini-dresses and barely there tank tops. This morning, after much thought, she had chosen a Calvin Klein blue blazer, worn over a pale-blue silk shirt and beige linen slacks. Casual, elegant and understated—that was her look and she wore it well.

"I was kind of surprised to get your call," Max said.

"Well," she answered, choosing her words carefully as she sat down, "I was surprised and upset about what happened last night."

Max nodded his agreement. "Yeah—that husband of yours," he said, picking up a coffee spoon and tapping it on the table. "Couldn't say what he had to say in private. Had to do it in front of that fucking— I'm sorry, in front of Ariel. She's not my favorite person."

"Nor mine either," Diana said quickly. "In fact, if it was up to me, I wouldn't have her in my house. She's duplicitous. I'm sure she got to where she is by sleeping with Billy Cornelius."

Max laughed. *"C'mon,* Diana," he teased. "I've never heard you talk like that about people. You're always Miss Straightlaced."

"Is that what you think of me, Max?" she said, giving him a bold look.

Max was no fool; he caught the signals. Diana Leon was flirting with him. "Uh . . . never really thought about it," he said, wondering where this was leading. The waiter came over and hovered by their table, order pad in hand. "What'll you have, honey?" Max asked.

She liked the way he called her "honey." It was casual, yet extremely intimate. "Maybe some tea."

"No toast? Eggs? Waffles?"

"No, just tea. Earl Grey," she said, speaking directly to the waiter.

"The lady wants tea," Max said. "And bring me another orange juice, two eggs, sunny-side up, one slice of crisp bacon, three pieces of toast, not too well done, and more coffee."

"Yes, Mr. Steele," said the waiter.

"So," Max said, leaning back and surveying the room. "What can I do for you, Diana?"

*You can ravish me,* she longed to say. *You can take me to bed and do all the things to me that you do to your numerous girlfriends. And I will love you, care for you and be the faithful woman forever by your side.*

"I wanted to say, Max, that whatever happens, you have my full support."

"That's good to know," he said, his wandering eyes checking out a pretty brunette with long tanned legs on her way out of the dining room. "The truth is, Diana, I changed my mind."

"You changed your mind?" she repeated, not sure what he'd changed his mind about.

"Freddie and I have been through so much together; there's no way I can leave the firm. I simply can't do it to him."

The waiter returned and refilled Max's coffee cup.

Diana waited until he had left before speaking. "I'm sure you're aware that in the *Times* today there's a story about you taking over at Orpheus Studios," she said.

"It's all bullshit," Max said sharply. "They write these stories before anything's signed. I spoke to Billy Cornelius this morning and told him the deal is off."

"You *did?*"

"Yes, honey. Y'know, on reflection, I reckon I was going through some kind of midlife crisis thing. Freddie'll understand."

"But, Max, if you feel you can do better elsewhere, then you *should* move," she said, a slight tinge of desperation creeping into her voice.

"Hey, hey—" Max said, with a half smile. "Don't encourage me."

"I'm encouraging you to be yourself," Diana said, her expression earnest.

"Did Freddie send you?" he asked curiously.

"No, he didn't," she responded indignantly. "As a matter of fact, Freddie failed to come home last night. I have no idea where he was. He walked in when I was leaving this morning, looking dishevelled."

Max stared at her disbelievingly. "Freddie, dishevelled?"

"Yes, Freddie."

"Don't tell me he's got a broad . . . I mean, no disrespect to you, Diana."

"There's no one else, Max," she said confidently.

"If you say so . . ."

"The truth is," she leaned toward him, lowering her voice to a whisper, "Freddie doesn't like sex."

"Doesn't like sex, huh?" Max said, storing that little piece of information away for future use.

"I can speak to you in the strictest confidence, can't I?"

"Sure, baby," Max said agreeably. Hey, bonding with Freddie's wife was a kick. This way he could get the inside track on everything.

Diana wondered if she had said too much. No. Why *shouldn't* she confide in Max? He would never betray her. "Freddie's not a sexual being," she said. A long, meaningful pause. "But *I* am . . ."

Oh, Jesus. Was she coming on to him? Freddie's uptight wife? No way. And yet . . . she had that predatory look, a look Max knew only too well. Women on the make . . . he'd had more of those than he cared to remember. Usually actresses. Hey, it wasn't *his* fault if he was irresistible to women.

"Diana," he said carefully. "I'm not sure you should be here with me."

Her slate gray eyes stared boldly into his. "Why not?"

"Because . . . uh . . ." he began, thinking fast, it wouldn't do to insult her by telling her he wasn't interested. "Because I . . . uh . . . well, I guess I'm very attracted to you," he lied.

Her face lit up. He had said the right thing. "You *are?*"

"Yes, Diana, honey. But, believe me, this is not the time for either of us to do anything about it."

"Why not?" she demanded, bedroom eyes materializing out of nowhere.

Oh, shit! She wasn't going to give up easy.

"Trust me. It's not."

Tentatively she reached across the table, placing her hand gently over his. "I've waited so long for this moment, Max. Something told me it was inevitable."

He slid his hand out from under hers, indicating the approaching waiter with his eyebrows. "Be cool, Diana," he said in a low voice. "The tabs have spies everywhere. You're an important Hollywood wife—you're news. So am I right now. We shouldn't even be seen together like this."

"I know," she said. "But for once I don't want to do the right thing. I want to do what makes me happy."

Freddie's wife was on a roll. *Jesus!* What had he done to deserve *this?*

"Diana," he said, attempting a serious voice. "I

have too much regard and respect for you to allow you to jeopardize your future."

"What do you mean?"

"We all know Freddie has a vindictive streak. If he even suspected you had eyes for another man . . ."

"I don't care," she said stubbornly.

"*I* do. I'm trying to protect you here."

"When I'm with you, Max, I don't need protecting."

This kind of response was exactly what he *didn't* need. "You might *think* you don't," he said sternly. "But trust me, you do."

He imagined Freddie's face if Diana went to him and informed her husband she was running off with Max Steele. The shit wouldn't just hit the fan, it would explode all the way from Beverly Hills to Bel Air. Christ! How to get out of this one?

Then it came to him. The perfect solution. "Diana," he said, with a perfectly straight face. "I think you should be the first to know. Last night I got engaged."

# chapter 6

**F**REDDIE LEON THOUGHT OF himself as an in-control and reasonable man, but in view of what had happened over the last twenty-four hours, he could not remain calm. His faithful partner Max Steele had betrayed him, and it infuriated Freddie that Max had manipulated him in such a way. The disloyal son-of-a-bitch.

Freddie stood under the powerful jets of his shower, soaking his body. After a night away from home he felt the need to thoroughly cleanse himself. Hotel rooms disgusted him—however luxurious. The late Howard Hughes had had the right idea, covering his shoes with Kleenex and walking around with a hospital mask over half his face.

Last night Freddie had known he had to get out of the house. He had no desire to lie in bed beside Diana, listening to her nag about how he had ruined her dinner party.

Through the noise of the shower he heard the phone ring, and to his annoyance no one picked up.

He stepped out of the shower and answered it himself. It was Ria. "Yes?" he snapped, wondering why his secretary was bothering him on a Sunday.

"Mr. Leon," Ria said. "Are you aware there's a woman from *Manhattan Style* magazine in town? She's been sent out here from New York to write a piece on you. In fact, she fully expects you to grant her an interview."

"Excuse me?" Freddie said irritably.

"Madison Castelli. She's here to conduct an exclusive interview with you."

"Why me?" Freddie said, frowning.

"You're very high profile, Mr. Leon." As if she had to explain it to him. Freddie Leon knew exactly how important and powerful he was. "So I'm to presume you don't know anything about this?"

"No, I don't," he said, annoyed she'd seen fit to disturb him at home. "How do *you* know?"

"Ms. Castelli called me herself."

"Where did she get your number?"

"I didn't ask. I merely informed her you would not be interested."

"Right. She'll get no cooperation from me, so if she's smart she'd better quit now."

"With all due respect, Mr. Leon, you cannot tell the press what they can and can't do."

"I can tell them what I like," Freddie snapped and put the phone down. "Diana," he yelled. "Diana!" There was no response, so wrapping a towel around his waist, he walked from his bathroom into the bedroom. Then he remembered; Diana had gone out. "Damn!" he mumbled under his breath. He hated it when his wife exhibited attitude and wasn't around to attend to his needs. He sat on the edge of the bed and decided to give Ariel Shore a call.

When Ariel came to the phone she was suitably cool, which annoyed him even more. He had a good relationship with Ariel and did not want anything spoiling it.

"I guess we're the last to know," Ariel said, her tone icy.

"What do you mean?" Freddie asked.

"Didn't you see the *L.A. Times* this morning?"

"I haven't read the papers yet."

"Take a look. Your partner made an announcement, or somebody made an announcement for him."

"How could that happen?"

"*Exactly,* Freddie," Ariel said triumphantly, as if she'd caught him cheating at cards. "How *could* it happen without either of us knowing about it? *We're* supposed to be Hollywood insiders. *We're* supposed to know everything weeks before anything takes place."

"Ariel, I—"

"Anyway," she rudely interrupted. "I went to see Billy this morning."

"You did?"

"I thought it was time I settled this nonsense."

"What happened?"

"I told Billy he could not hire *anyone* without asking me. And if you're as clever as I *know* you are, when Max comes crawling back, you'll immediately terminate your partnership."

"You don't have to tell me what to do, Ariel," Freddie said, pissed that she would even try. "That was already my plan."

"Good, because my studio does not care to conduct business with anyone who has anything at all to do with Max Steele."

"Point taken, Ariel," Freddie said. And as far as he was concerned, that was the end of Max Steele.

# chapter 7

**M**ADISON HAD FIN-
ished writing her piece on Salli T. Turner. She didn't
consider it up to her usual standard, but she knew
that she was too emotionally involved to be able to
do any better. She faxed a copy of the article to
Victor in New York, then immediately wished she
hadn't. Victor responded quickly. He phoned and
told her it was good.

"Not good enough," she answered, an expert at
putting herself down. "Do I have time to do a
rewrite?"

"No," Victor said firmly. "The piece is excellent.
Stop being so critical."

When Cole returned from his hike, he suggested to
Madison that he take her out for lunch. "We'll grab a
Neil McCarthy salad at the Beverly Hills Hotel," he
said persuasively.

"I don't know," she demurred, feeling guilty at the
thought of going out to lunch while Salli lay brutally
murdered. "I'm not in the mood."

"C'mon," Cole urged. "It'd make *me* feel better to get out. An' if Natalie's around, I'll even take her."

She stood up and stretched. "Natalie's having lunch with Luther."

"Who's Luther?"

"An ex-football player she met at Jimmy's house last night."

"Straight?"

"Of course."

Cole grinned. "Shame!"

Madison couldn't help laughing. "Okay," she said, deciding it might be good to get out after all. "We're on for lunch. You talked me into it."

"Didn't have to do much talkin'," Cole said with a friendly wink.

"So what did you do?" Jimmy Sica asked his brother, who had just gotten through telling him what had happened between him and Kristin the night before.

"I left," Jake said. "What would *you* have done under those circumstances?"

"Jesus!" Jimmy said, shaking his head. "It would've shocked the crap outta me. And she seemed so . . . gorgeous."

"She was gorgeous all right," Jake said grimly. "Five-thousand-a-night gorgeous."

They were standing in the middle of their father's bungalow at the Beverly Hills Hotel, waiting for him to emerge from the bedroom so they could escort him to his wedding ceremony, which was to take place in the lavish gardens.

"What a scam!" Jimmy exclaimed. "D'you think she was planning on charging *you*?"

"Of course not," Jake said sharply, already regretting telling his brother. "We had a good thing going."

"So you think if the phone deal hadn't happened, you wouldn't have found out?"

"That's exactly right."

"Did you use a—"

"Nope."

"Well, buddy, *you* had better get yourself tested pronto."

"I plan to."

Jimmy flopped down on the couch, legs splayed. "There's no way you could've known. The hookers in L.A. are the best-looking broads in town."

"How would *you* know?"

"I get around, little bro."

Jake couldn't stop pacing up and down. "She seemed like such a sweetheart," he said. "Innocent . . . clean-cut . . ."

"Where exactly did you meet her?"

"In the men's department at Neiman Marcus."

"Ha!" Jimmy exclaimed. "That should've given you a clue. What was she doing *there?*"

"Sitting at the martini bar. *I* picked *her* up, it wasn't as if *she* was coming on to *me.*"

"That's what *you* thought," Jimmy muttered darkly.

"D'you think I overreacted?" Jake asked.

"Are you shitting me?" Jimmy said, making a face. "She's a *hooker* for crissake."

"I hope you're not speaking about my future bride," their father, Cosmos, said, emerging from the bedroom clad in a John Travolta *Saturday Night Fever* three-piece white suit and a screamingly bright red tie. He was a handsome man, but at least sixty pounds overweight, which caused his three-piece suit to bulge in all the wrong places.

"No way, Dad," Jimmy said, attempting to conceal his amusement at his father's outrageous outfit.

Cosmos Sica was sixty-two years old with a shock of silver hair, matching moustache and a wily grin. The woman he was about to marry was a twenty-year-old manicurist from San Diego who was to be his fourth wife. Jimmy and Jake were used to their high-living dad, and as far as they were concerned, the old guy could do what he liked—and typically he did. Cosmos was smart enough in business that it was okay for him to be stupid about women. And if he could afford them, why not?

"You look good, Dad," Jake lied, knowing his father craved compliments.

"An' you don't look so bad yourself, son," Cosmos said, admiring himself in a wall mirror. "Isn't it about time you found yourself a regular girl?"

"He did," Jimmy said with a slight smirk.

"Good," Cosmos said loudly. "It's not healthy for a man to be by himself. You need a warm body to snuggle up with at night."

"She's not exactly someone I'm planning on spending the rest of my life with," Jake said, throwing Jimmy a warning look.

"Shall I tell him?" Jimmy said, starting to laugh.

"No way," Jake objected.

"Tell me what?" Cosmos asked, brushing the edge of his moustache with his fingers. "This is my wedding day—you can tell me anything."

"He fell in love with a hooker," Jimmy announced, unable to stop himself.

"He did *what?*" Cosmos yelled.

"He thought she was a nice girl," Jimmy said. "It turned out she was a nice girl all right—the kinda nice girl you *pay.*"

Cosmos roared with hearty laughter. "Nothing wrong with a pretty girl making an honest living. That's what I say."

Jake glared at his brother. "Quit making my business public knowledge."

"I'm your father, for crissake," Cosmos boomed. "What's with the public knowledge? You know you can trust me; it'll go no further."

*Sure,* Jake thought glumly, *knowing Dad, everyone will be in on the joke by the end of the wedding. Damn Jimmy and his big mouth.*

Jimmy hauled himself off the couch. "We ready?" he said.

Cosmos nodded vigorously. "You bet!" he said, almost popping a button on his vest. "Fourth time lucky, huh? Come on, boys, I'm impatient to get to my wedding night!"

In spite of a huge and expensive face-lift there was something about the lobby of the Beverly Hills Hotel that screamed old Hollywood. "I keep on expecting to bump into Clark Gable or Lana Turner," Madison joked, glancing around.

"I know what you mean," Cole said. "This place has history."

"It sure does," she agreed.

"C'mon," he said, taking her arm. "We're eating on the terrace of the Polo Lounge. You ever had a Neil McCarthy salad?"

"Sounds vaguely communistic."

"The best chopped salad you'll ever have."

"You're so knowledgeable," she teased. "And to think—Natalie and I were both under the impression you'd end up being a gang member."

"Right," Cole drawled. "Instead, I'm a politically incorrect gay guy who knows everyone's secrets."

"You do?"

"I sure do."

"Are there any more secrets about Salli?"

"Maybe," he said mysteriously.

Madison let it drop; she knew when to push and when not to. "So, Cole," she said lightly. "What's *your* love life like? You seeing anyone special?"

"Haven't gotten that lucky—yet," he said ruefully. "So I keep playing the field. 'Course it drives Natalie insane. She's convinced I'll get AIDS and then she'll have to look after me. And you know how *that* would piss her off."

"She's always adored you, Cole. When we were at college together she was always talking about you and worrying that you were okay."

"Yeah," he laughed. "I know, I know. She sure loves her baby brother."

"How did she take it when you told her you were gay?"

"Y'know, she was kinda cool. It was my parents who freaked. An' it was Nat who talked 'em around."

As they continued walking through the lobby, Madison spotted two vaguely familiar faces coming toward her. She thought about taking evasive action, but it was too late. Jimmy Sica had seen her.

"Madison!" he said, flashing his perfect anchorman smile. "What are *you* doing here?"

"I could ask *you* the same question."

"It's our dad's wedding," Jimmy explained, gesturing toward Cosmos. "Allow me to introduce you to the man himself. We're on our way to his execution—fourth one."

Cosmos took her hand, squeezing it tightly. "Delighted to meet such a lovely woman," he said, oozing charm before turning to Jake and inquiring *sotto voce,* "Is this the young lady you were telling us about?"

"No," Jake said quickly. "Madison's a journalist from New York."

"I love it when I get billing," Madison said, with a nod in his direction. "Do you all know Cole, Natalie's brother?"

"So *you're* the famous fitness guru," Jimmy said, shaking Cole's hand. "Natalie keeps on telling me you're the best in town."

"The best what?" Cole said, grinning cheekily.

"The best guy to get my pathetic abs in shape," Jimmy said, grinning back.

"I can do that," Cole said.

"Stop flirting," Madison scolded. "They're both straight, or at least I *think* they are." Her eyes met Jake's. "How was your date last night?"

"Casual," he answered. "Nothing serious."

"Why don't you two drop by the wedding?" Jimmy suggested.

"We're on our way to lunch," Madison explained. "Besides, we're not exactly dressed for a wedding."

"You look great to me," Jake said.

Jimmy's attention was taken by a woman in a blue jogging outfit who wanted his autograph. He loved being recognized, especially in front of his father, who was duly impressed.

"Hey, I'm sorry last night kind of, uh . . . ended abruptly," Jake said.

"That's all right," Madison answered, thinking that her first impression from last night had not been wrong; he was very attractive in a sexy, laid-back way. "It was abrupt for all of us."

"Bad news about Salli. You knew her, didn't you?"

"Yes, it's so sad. She was a sweet person. You might not realize it from her public image, but she was."

"You wouldn't be free for dinner tonight, would you?" Jake asked impulsively.

"Uh . . ." She tried to think of an excuse, but none came to mind.

"She's free," Cole said, answering for her.

"Well, yes, I guess I am," she said, shooting Cole a "mind-your-own-business" look.

"Pick you up at seven?" Jake said.

"Let's go," Cosmos boomed. "I got a wedding to attend. An' a bride to make happy!"

"Lots of luck, Mr. Sica," Madison said.

"It's not luck I need, pretty lady," Cosmos said, roaring with laughter again. "It's stamina. An' plenty of it!"

The three of them walked off.

"That's *you* settled for tonight," Cole said, pleased with himself for interfering.

"What made you think I *wanted* to go out with him?" she asked irritably.

"He seems like a cool dude—go for it."

"*What?*"

"Hey—if I can't have him, why shouldn't you?"

"Cole," she said sternly. "You railroaded me into that."

"No way."

"You did," she said accusingly. "I'm not sure he even *wanted* to ask me out."

"Then how come he did?"

"Oh, God! How do I know?"

"Maddy," Cole interrupted. *"You* are *totally* fine. So go—have yourself a good time, an' stop worryin'."

"Now you sound like Natalie."

He arched an amused eyebrow. "Somethin' wrong with that?"

She took his arm. "Okay, matchmaker, let's go get lunch. I'm starving!"

# chapter 8

AT EXACTLY NOON KRIStin picked up the phone and called Max.

He answered immediately. "Perfect timing," he said, sounding excessively cheery. "You're an engaged woman."

"Excuse me?" she said, wondering what he was up to now.

"Don't worry," he said. "It's a paying job. You'll be my fiancée for a while. What do you think of *that?*"

"I think you're crazy, Max," she said with a sigh. "But then that's nothing new."

"Don't you like my idea?"

"I'll repeat what I just said. You're crazy."

"Can you come over?"

She'd never been to his house, and yet, if he wanted her to move in, she certainly had to check it out. "Where do you live?"

"I'll give you the address. Be here in an hour."

"I can't do that," she said quickly. "I have somewhere to go first. I could be there around four."

"Where are you going?"

"We haven't done the deal yet, Max," she said sharply. "So don't question me."

"Okay, okay," he answered, soothing her with his voice. "But, honey, believe me—this is gonna be a cool situation."

She was resigned to her fate—whatever it might be. "If you say so."

"I *know* so," he assured her, and then he gave her his address in Bel Air. She replaced the receiver and sighed deeply, wondering if she was making the right move. What did she really know about Max Steele? He was just another client, that's all. Why was she even considering such a radical move?

All she could think about was Jake. They'd had such a strong connection, or so she'd thought. And then her stupid answering machine and Darlene's message had ruined everything.

She had known she would get screwed by Mister X, one way or another.

She went to her closet and picked out the simplest clothes she possessed. Then she pulled her long blond hair back into a ponytail and did not bother putting on makeup.

It was time to visit her sister.

The drive to the nursing home took about an hour. Kristin liked to play books on tape, usually biographies; it gave her something to talk about with clients who were into conversation. Right now she was listening to Robert Evans' *The Kid Stays in the*

*Picture.* He had led a fascinating life—businessman, movie star, head of a studio, grand producer in the great Hollywood tradition. Recently she read that he'd had a stroke and then a few weeks later had gotten married for the fourth time. Then had *that* marriage annulled! Hollywood survivors—they were a breed unto themselves!

She wondered what Jake was doing. He must be at his father's wedding by now, wearing the tie she'd picked out and having such a good time that he'd probably forgotten all about her. She couldn't help remembering his final words: *I wish you'd told me. . . . I would've used a condom.*

How could he say something so hurtful? As if she would ever have put him at risk!

She found it impossible to concentrate on Bob Evans, so she put on the radio instead. A newscaster was talking about the murder of Salli T. Turner. Kristin had never met her, although she'd had several encounters with her wild husband, Bobby Skorch. Bobby was a notorious womanizer, and loved call girls. She had attended several parties where he'd performed quite publicly—even though everyone knew he had a famous wife at home. Bobby was into showing it off, and he had plenty to show: he was one of the most well-endowed men Kristin had ever seen. So well-endowed, in fact, that several of the girls refused to have sex with him— Kristin being one of them.

She remembered after one particular party Darlene had lectured her the next day. *"Never* turn down a client," Darlene had said, practically tut-tutting her annoyance. "It's bad for business."

"He's a tattooed freak," Kristin had replied. "And I don't ever have to do anything I don't want to."

Kristin could not stomach hearing about Salli T. Turner's particularly brutal murder, so she switched stations. A newscaster was speaking about President Clinton, Kenneth Starr and all the goings-on in Washington.

Hollywood and Washington—the men in both cities were beyond horny. Kristin was well aware it was all about power and control. Politicians and movie stars—these men had so much that sometimes the only way they could get off was relinquishing both.

She switched stations again. A news reporter droned on about another murder.

"The body of a young woman was washed up on the Malibu shore this morning. Identity unknown. The only description so far is that the victim was Caucasian and blond. Detectives are investigating."

Two murders. Two blondes.

Another normal Sunday in L.A.

When Kristin arrived at the nursing home, she was greeted warmly by the nurses at the desk. "How's Cherie doing?" she asked, handing over a large bag filled with candy, all the current magazines and a couple of best-selling novels. It was good to keep the nurses happy—that way they'd be sure to give Cherie special attention.

"Same as ever," Mariah, the fat, black, friendly nurse, replied. "No change."

"You never know," Kristin said hopefully. "One of these days she might open her eyes, like Sleeping Beauty."

"Yeah, baby—keep on thinking that way," Mariah said, oozing her large frame out from behind the desk.

"That's why I come here every week," Kristin said. "My voice gets through to her—I know it does. She has to realize *someone* cares."

"You're lookin' pale today," Mariah said, crinkling her eyes. "Everything okay with you, hon?"

"I'm fine," she said quickly. "Too many patients this week." Early on she had told all the nurses that she worked as a dental assistant.

"Ugh! Dunno how you do it," Mariah said. "Staring into all those sloppy mouths. It'd drive *me* loco."

"Somebody's got to do it," Kristin said, anxious to see Cherie.

"Bet all your patients fall in love with you," Mariah said with a saucy wink. "You sure are pretty 'nuff."

"I'm there to do a job, that's all," Kristin said, thinking, *Ain't that the truth.*

"Yeah, yeah," Mariah said disbelievingly. "Didja catch *Lethal Weapon 4* yet? What a movie! I'm hot for that Chris Rock. Skinny an' sexy! Wouldn't mind spendin' a night in *his* company."

Kristin summoned up a laugh. "Yes, he is cute," she said. Actually she had no idea who Chris Rock was.

"Cute?" Mariah exclaimed. "Honey bun, he's a *horny* hound dog!"

Kristin followed Mariah into her sister's private room and stared down at Cherie—a shadow of the beauty she once had been, kept alive on a machine. It broke her heart every time she saw her.

"Hi, baby," she said, sitting on the edge of the

hospital bed and taking her sister's hand, which was ice cold. "It's Kristin. How are you today?"

No response. There was never any response. But she'd stay for an hour and keep talking.

Maybe one day she would get a reaction. She had to keep trying.

If she gave up, all hope would be lost.

# chapter 9

MARTY STEINER EMERGED from Bobby Skorch's bedroom at noon, made his way downstairs and confronted the two detectives in the front hall.

"We're ready to ask Mr. Skorch a few questions," Detective Tucci said, asserting himself.

"I'm sure," Marty Steiner replied, smooth as a one-eyed snake. "Fact is, he's too upset to talk to you right now. And I'm requesting that you vacate the premises."

"We still have things to do here," Tucci pointed out. "This *is* a crime scene."

"I think you've had enough time to collect all the evidence you need," Marty Steiner said. "Mr. Skorch would like you and your partner to leave immediately. This is an extremely difficult time, and Mr. Skorch does not need to deal with having his house invaded."

"I'll remind you again—this *is* a crime scene,"

Tucci said, hating the sleek lawyer and everything he represented.

"Yeah," Lee said, joining in. "It's a goddamn crime scene, for crissake. You think we *wanna* be here?"

Marty Steiner's face gave not a flicker of recognition in Lee's direction. "If you wish to stay, you'll need a warrant," he said calmly. "The bodies have been removed. As I said before, you've had ample time to collect your evidence. Now I want you people out of here."

"Are you telling me that Mr. Skorch has nothing to say to us?" Lee said, belligerent as ever.

"That's correct, Detective."

"Where was he last night?" Lee asked, getting right in the lawyer's face.

"On his way back from Vegas."

"He didn't arrive here 'til three," Lee said accusingly.

"I'm sure you're aware that it's a four- or five-hour drive."

"His *wife* was murdered," Tucci said. "Doesn't he have any questions for *us?*"

"Mr. Skorch has a funeral to prepare for," Marty Steiner said, his voice hardening. "Now unless you have a warrant, I insist you vacate at once."

Tucci and Lee exchanged glances. "I knew he was an asshole," Lee mumbled under his breath.

"Nothing we can do," Tucci said.

"Why *wouldn't* Skorch talk to us?" Lee muttered. "I'm gonna check on his alibi. I wanna know exactly what time he left the hotel in Vegas, an' who was in the car with him. He probably got back here early, found his wife with a guy an' lost it."

"If that was the case," Tucci said, ever the voice of reason, "where's the other man? Why hasn't he come forward?"

"Would *you* under these circumstances? The jerk must've run for his life."

"We'd better go," Tucci said, thinking to himself that maybe on the way back to the station he could stop by a diner and grab a bite to eat.

Lee shrugged. "Fine with me. I came to this case late. If *I'd* gotten to the prick when he arrived back from Vegas, I'd have questioned him then and there."

"He knew his rights," Tucci said, choosing to ignore the fact that Lee was criticizing him. "He was aware he didn't have to talk to me."

"The asshole's guilty," Lee muttered. "Fuckin' guilty."

On his way back to the station, Tucci stopped at Fatburger and devoured a couple of hamburgers with everything. Then he indulged himself with a side order of French fries and onions. There was no way he would confess to Faye that he ate all that food—she'd be too angry. He'd lie, tell her he grabbed a salad.

Back at the station he remembered Madison Castelli's tape and decided to give it a listen. He found it most informative, hearing Salli T. Turner tell about her life. She had a lovely voice—young and vibrant.

Tucci's thoughts kept flashing on her dead body, the vicious cuts and lacerations, the sheer fury the murderer had wreaked upon his victim.

Ah, the price of fame, he thought. Was it worth it? Not for Salli T. Turner.

Later in the day he went down to the morgue to inspect the body of the "Mystery Malibu blonde" as the media were calling the latest victim. The media were having a field day. First the celebrated Salli T. Turner, and now an unknown beautiful blonde washed up on the Malibu shore. Movie star territory. Two murders in as many days. Ratings were zooming.

The mystery blonde was young and lovely. Probably no more than nineteen or twenty, Tucci figured. What happened to her that she ended up dead?

"We're tracking her dental records," Lee informed him. "Should have something by tomorrow."

Tucci shook his head. There was so much violence in the world, so much anger. He picked up the phone and called Faye. "I'll be home late tonight, sweetheart," he said.

"I'm not surprised," she said. "Salli T. Turner is all over the television. What a terrible tragedy. They're comparing her death to the Nicole Simpson murder."

"They would."

"Don't think about it," Faye said. "Solve it."

"I plan to," Tucci answered.

"Did you enjoy the sandwich?"

He didn't have the heart to tell her that the maid had eaten it. "Delicious," he lied.

"How about the coleslaw?"

"Even more delicious. Almost as delicious as you."

"You're such a flatterer," she said, chuckling happily. "Did you meet with that woman from *Manhattan Style*—Madison Castelli?"

"Yes. She brought me an audiotape of her interview with Salli."

"Have you played it?"

"I was listening to it now."

"Anything useful?"

"It sounds to me like Salli had a real problem with her ex. I'll question him shortly."

"Has he been arrested?"

"Yes. We brought him in on parking violations."

"I miss you," Faye said wistfully.

"Miss you, too," Tucci replied.

"I could make you your favorite pasta tonight," she said, playing the temptress. "Special treat 'cause you've been so good."

The two burgers had made him uncomfortably full, not to mention totally guilty. "That'd be nice," he said, not quite as enthusiastic as she expected him to be. "I'll call you later."

Lee appeared, eating a jelly donut, the jam dribbling down his pointed chin. "The captain wants to see us," he said, wiping his sugary hands on his pants. "Like pronto."

Tucci got up from behind his desk and followed Lee into their captain's office.

Captain Marsh was exceptionally tall, black and bad tempered. He smoked cheap cigars, sported a halfhearted Afro and needed immediate dental work. "The chief of police called—he'd just heard from the mayor's office," he said, getting straight to the point. "This Salli Turner murder. They need an arrest, an' they need it *now*. Forget about everything else an' work this case hard. I promised the chief we'd have someone in custody within twenty-four hours. If you need extra help—let me know. I'm expectin' immediate results."

*There goes dinner,* Tucci thought. *Nothing like a little pressure to get you through the day.*

# chapter 10

"**I** CAN'T BELIEVE YOU'RE
going out with that Jake guy," Natalie said, rolling
her eyes in a disapproving way.

"Last night you thought he was cute," Madison
pointed out.

"I also thought he was *available*," Natalie said
crisply. "Available and cute is one thing. Available
and taken is another."

"Who *says* he's taken?"

"Oh, come *on*, girl!" Natalie said. "Did you *see*
the way he hustled that blonde out of sight last night.
He was hot for her. I mean *steamin'*."

"Apparently not *that* hot," Madison retorted.
"Anyway—wasn't it you who said I should get out
and have fun? Take my mind off David the jerk?"

"Yeah, but not if you're jumpin' from one jerk to
another," Natalie replied. "That'd be too sad."

"It's a date," Madison said patiently. "I'm not
moving in with him."

"Praise the Lord!"

"Don't go getting religious on me."

"If Jake's anything like his brother . . ."

"I thought you *liked* his brother; you dragged me over there for dinner last night."

"That's only 'cause Jimmy and I work together."

"Anyway, I'm seeing him. Big deal. One lousy date."

Natalie threw up her hands. "Okay, okay. I'm only trying to watch out for you."

"How was your lunch with Luther?"

Natalie's pretty face broke into a wide smile. "He is *some* hunk."

"You like him, huh?"

"Understatement, girl. He's big and damn sexy. Makes me feel protected."

"Now it's my turn to wave a warning flag in your face. Don't forget, you, too, are coming out of a lousy relationship. Denzl—remember? So don't get carried away."

Natalie giggled. "This is *such* a buzz!" she said. "I feel like we're back in college, sitting around talking about guys. I mean, aren't we a little *old* for this crap?"

"Yes," Madison agreed, smiling.

"One of these days," Natalie said, "I'd like to be married with a couple of kids, live in a nice little house by the sea, have a great husband who comes home every night at the same time, *and* watch Oprah!"

"Dream world, Nat," Madison said. "You'd *hate* missing out on the action. You *love* what you do."

"True. But I want to do more than cover the entertainment beat. I am *so* sick of talking about Salli T. Turner. Yeah, she was a big TV star and great looking—if you like silicone. But the girl got herself murdered, and now *I* gotta go on and on eulogizing her. It's enough already. I want to report real news, not sensational Hollywood murders."

"I understand," Madison said. "But, remember, it wasn't Salli's fault she got killed."

"Yeah, I know, it's a tragedy. Truth is—it brings back too many bad memories for me."

Madison nodded sympathetically, remembering the night in college when Natalie had been attacked and raped by a man who turned out to be a serial killer. They caught the guy, but it had taken Natalie a year to get over it and stop shaking.

"What're you gonna wear tonight?" Natalie asked, hurriedly changing the subject. "Something sexy, I hope."

"I don't do sexy," Madison said straight-faced.

"You know what would be *really* good for you?"

"What brilliant idea have you come up with now?"

"Use *him* like guys are always using *us*. Throw some condoms in your bag and have a night of wild sex."

"What're you *talking* about?"

"Guys do it all the time. And my personal opinion is you need one night of mind-blowing sex. Kind of like a revenge fuck."

"Revenge for what?" Madison asked patiently.

"For the way David treated you."

"He did what made him happy. Besides, one-nighters are not my style."

"*Make* it your style. And you're *not* wearing one of your laid-back outfits. Have I got a dress for you!"

"Don't do dresses either," Madison objected.

Natalie wasn't listening. "It's red, short and *veree* sexy. I was saving it for your birthday—but since you're here, it's perfect! Oh yeah, an' you gotta wear your hair down."

"Why are you trying to make me into something I'm not?" Madison asked, exasperated.

"Treat tonight like an adventure. What's to lose?"

Later, both Cole and Natalie sat around watching Madison get ready for the date. She tried to argue, but instead, couldn't help dissolving into laughter as they instructed her. Cole was a whiz with the makeup brushes; he worked on her eyes and lips, then stood back to admire his handiwork. "Kevyn Aucoin—drop dead!" he crowed.

"It's the Madison makeover!" Natalie yelled. "You're like one of those secretaries with the bun and glasses."

"I don't wear glasses."

"You know what I'm saying. Remove the glasses, let the hair down and *voilà*—you're Sharon Stone!"

"I'm not even blond, Natalie. And I feel ridiculous in this dress."

"But you *look* hot, girl!"

Cole handed her a packet of condoms. "No, thank you," Madison said, shoving them back at him.

"Just in case," Natalie urged. "Maybe Jake'll take you dancing, and you're in his arms, and then there's that wild moment of no return. If that happens you'll be so damn sorry you don't have them with you. 'Cause no glove—no love."

"Now I *really* feel like I'm back in college," Madison said, laughing. "You two are unbelievable."

"Yeah, we're a fun couple, aren't we," Natalie

said, impulsively hugging Cole. "Get used to us, 'cause, girl, we're takin' our act on the road!"

"What's *your* plan tonight, Cole?" Madison asked.

"Got a *hot* date."

"Who with?" Natalie demanded.

"Your favorite," Cole said. "Mr. Mogul."

"Oh, God," Natalie groaned. "Don't you *get* it yet—those power guys are into using and abusing buff young things like you. They're worse than playboys who try to get one over on women."

"I wish you'd meet him. He's a nice guy."

"Nice guy, my ass," Natalie snorted. "He's a billionaire gay caballero who'll use you big time."

"You're prejudiced," Cole said, narrowing his eyes. "You'd sooner see me settle in with a nice boring accountant."

"I don't care what you do. Your lifestyle doesn't bother me."

"Liar! You wish I was straight."

"Can you two quit fighting," Madison said, placing her hands on her slender hips, wishing she could get out of tonight's date with Jake.

Too late. The doorbell rang, and both Cole and Natalie began shoving her toward the door.

No backing out now.

# chapter 11

"**W**HAT ARE *YOU* IN such a bad mood about?" Freddie asked irritably.

"I'm not," Diana replied, although she obviously was.

"And where *were* you this morning?" he added, annoyed that she hadn't been around to tend to his every need.

"Why do you care?" Diana said, her face flushed. "I didn't ask where *you* were last night."

He threw her a warning look. "Don't get pissy with me, Diana."

"Why *did* you leave?" she continued, determined not to be intimidated. "You know I'm not happy alone in the house."

"You weren't alone. You had dozens of caterers around."

"Oh, *please.*"

"Do you have any idea how much these dinner parties of yours cost me?"

"As if you care," Diana said, exasperated. "It's all

285

tax deductible." She stalked into the kitchen and poured herself a cup of coffee. It was difficult for her to get over the shock of Max's engagement. Unbearable timing, yet she *still* couldn't stop thinking about him. Freddie followed her into the kitchen. She turned and faced him. "What are you doing about Max?" she demanded.

"Breaking all ties with him as soon as possible," Freddie answered, as unemotional as ever. "I'll buy him out."

"You can't do that. He's your partner," she said, reminding him of something he knew only too well.

"True. However, I have fifty-one percent, he has forty-nine. He's history."

"You might be making a mistake."

"How many times have I told you not to interfere in my business?"

"You're so insulting," she said, her face reddening. "Who was right beside you when you were building the business up? Who went out with boring movie stars and made them feel like a million dollars so they'd sign with you? I was with you every step, and don't you forget it."

"What the hell's gotten into you today?" he asked, his voice rising.

She took a gulp of coffee and let her frustration rip. "When was the last time you touched me, Freddie?"

"Oh, God!" he groaned. "Not that again."

"You don't care, do you?"

"Of course I do."

"No, Freddie, you never liked sex much anyway, and now in the last few years . . ." She trailed off.

"Enough of this nonsense," Freddie said harshly. "I have more important matters to deal with."

Diana's anger and frustration continued to surface. "I want a man who loves me," she blurted. "In every way."

Freddie's response was completely devoid of emotion. "What are you after, a divorce?" he asked coldly.

She shook her head, frightened to tell him that yes—that's exactly what she wanted. "I . . . I don't know," she stammered.

"Pull yourself together, Diana," he said, leaving the kitchen.

She trailed him into the library. "Are you aware that Max got engaged?"

"What are you going on about now?"

"He's engaged."

"To the model who stood him up last night?"

"No, to someone called Kristin—I have no idea who she is."

"How do you know?"

"Max phoned this morning."

"Oh, did he? Abject with apology no doubt. Dying to slither back into my good graces."

"He merely told me he was engaged."

"Why didn't he announce it last night?"

"He hardly had an opportunity, the way you and Ariel ganged up on him."

"I don't intend to keep repeating myself, Diana—stay *out* of my business."

She glared at him. "If that's the way you want it. And by the way, if I *do* decide to divorce you, Freddie—how *would* you feel?"

He looked at her in astonishment that she would consider such a rash move. "Don't even think about it. We're perfectly happy. Everyone knows that."

She stomped out of the room. Freddie shook his head. What the hell was going on with her? She must be going through the change of life early. God! Poor hard-done-by Diana. Didn't she realize how lucky she was? After all, she was married to one of the most important men in town.

# chapter 12

**M**AX PROWLED AROUND
his house with plenty of time to spare before Kristin
arrived. He didn't want to waste it doing nothing, so
he called Howie to see if he was around. Howie's
service picked up. Max left his name, and then
decided to take a swim in his luxurious pool and
maybe work on his tan for an hour or so. Might as
well catch some rays, he thought, grimly acknowl-
edging that he had nothing else to do.

Tomorrow he would face Freddie; no way was he
dealing with that little problem today. He knew
Freddie too well. In fact, he knew him better than
anyone—which, he realized, wasn't saying a lot
because nobody really knew Freddie. He was a man
of mystery—impossible to bond with on a man-to-
man level. He wasn't into ball games, poker, horses
*or* women. Just work.

Max wandered outside, stripped off his shirt and
pants and dropped into a lounge chair. He was

happy in his brief white Calvins—the snug style—
which emphasized his considerable assets.

As he stretched out, his mind drifted briefly to
Inga Cruelle, the woman who'd stood him up last
night. Supermodel bitch! She'd dumped him to go
on a date with Howie Powers, whom she'd picked up
at a cocktail party. How dumb could a girl get?
Howie was his friend, but everyone knew the man
was an idiot, a rich playboy with nothing going for
him except his father's money.

Yes, Inga had really blown it. No way would he
help her with her so-called movie career now; she
could find herself another agent.

When he'd had enough sun, he jumped in the pool
and swam, as usual overdoing it. Max never did
things by halves, he always had to excel—probably
because when he was a kid, his father beat the crap
out of him if he wasn't the best at everything he
tried. After swimming, he decided he had an appetite. Lunch at The Ivy didn't seem like a bad idea;
the only problem was that eating alone was not on
his agenda—too loser-like.

Maybe he'd give Inga one last chance.

No, he decided. Screw her! Nobody dumped on
Max Steele and got away with it.

Of course, there was a long list of other lovelies he
could call, but he wasn't in the mood to make
conversation, and all most of them talked about
were their careers.

Actresses. He'd had it with actresses. How nice it
would be to have Kristin in his life. A natural beauty
with no ambitions. And no more clients except him.

Idly he wondered how much it would cost a week
to keep her. Hmm . . . she probably didn't come

cheap. But what did he care? He owned half of I.A.A. and whatever happened between him and Freddie, he'd still end up with a bundle of money.

Instead of lunch he decided to go to Jhama Juice and grab a health drink. Jumping in his Maserati, he set off. The sun was shining; things weren't so bad; tomorrow he'd make everything okay with Freddie.

As he drove along San Vicente he thought about Diana Leon and how bizarre it was that she had come on to him. If Freddie ever found out, he'd choke on his own surprise.

Depending on what happened between him and Freddie, he wondered if maybe he *should* have an affair with Diana, simply to keep her on his side.

No, she was too old. He couldn't remember the last time he'd had a girl over thirty. Did they even exist in L.A.? Not in *his* mind.

He parked in the underground structure below the health-juice bar, locked his car and began walking out of the tunnel-like structure.

"Gimme your fuckin' money, mothafucker."

*Oh, Jesus!* Before he could spin around he felt a gun sticking in his back. *Oh, Jesus!*

"An' take that fuckin' Rolex off, or I'll blow your mothafuckin' head off."

# chapter 13

**V**AN MORRISON WAS SING-
ing "Have I Told You Lately That I Love You." As
Kristin listened to the touching lyrics she felt like
bursting into tears. Whenever she left Cherie, she
was always in a highly emotional state. The doctor
who looked in on Cherie a couple of times a week
had long ago told her she should pull the plug, but
she couldn't bring herself to do it. While her sister
was still breathing, there was always the possibility
of a miracle.

Deep down, however, she knew it wasn't realistic.
Deep down she knew her precious sister already was
dead.

The heartfelt lyrics enveloped her as she raced her
car along the freeway. Should she tell Max about
Cherie? That was the question. Maybe if he knew, he
wouldn't want her. Too bad. She had a new policy—
the truth above all else. If she'd been truthful with
Jake she wouldn't be so miserable now.

What was Max up to anyway? She was anxious to

find out. First she had to go home and change and return Darlene's call. Darlene was probably mad that she hadn't responded to last night's phone message. What did she care? She was through worrying what other people thought.

Her apartment was delightfully cool and welcoming. She'd left the air conditioning on full blast because it was one of those muggy days that L.A. denizens always said screamed earthquake weather. She'd never experienced an earthquake herself, having arrived in L.A. after the big Northridge one of '94. It seemed impossible that it could be as bad as people said, but all the same she kept a special earthquake cupboard filled with canned goods, bottled water and flashlights. If there was ever another major quake, she'd get in her car and drive straight to the nursing home. It worried her that they probably wouldn't look after Cherie properly in an emergency situation. That's why she visited every week, taking the nurses presents and candy, making sure they paid attention.

The first thing she did when she walked through the door was check her answering machine to see if Jake had called. Not that she expected him to, of course, and quite frankly, she didn't care if she ever heard from him again.

So why was her heart beating so fast as she approached her machine? Why was she willing the red message light to be flashing?

The red light *was* flashing. One flash. One message.

Probably Darlene wanting to know why she hadn't responded regarding Mister X.

She pressed down the rewind button. "Kristin,"

said a muffled male voice, not Jake's. "Why didn't you come last night? I do not appreciate being ignored. It is not good for either of us. Tonight. Eight. The end of Santa Monica Pier. I'll pay you double. Be there."

She was shocked. How had Mister X gotten her home number? Had Darlene given it to him? This was absolutely unacceptable.

In a fury, she picked up the phone to complain to Darlene, but Darlene's housekeeper informed her she was out. Kristin left a message for a callback and hung up, still outraged. Mister X being in possession of her home number made her feel totally vulnerable and somewhat uneasy. Having her number was only one step away from getting her address. She shivered at the thought.

Maybe Max's timing was right on target. At least if she was living with *him* she'd be protected. The more she thought about it, the more she knew it was the only sensible move.

Hurrying to her closet, she changed into a simple yellow sundress and high-heeled sandals. Then she applied some makeup and set off to close the deal with Max.

# chapter 14

AS HE DROVE HIS TRUCK to pick up Madison, Jake had a strong urge to call Kristin. He'd had a few drinks at his father's wedding and also time to think things over. Why *hadn't* he demanded to know what was going on? It was a puzzle he couldn't quite solve. What was Kristin doing in bed with him anyway? It wasn't like she'd asked him for money. What was her motive? And how long had she planned on keeping her profession a secret from him?

He'd seriously thought they had something together, so when he heard that woman's voice on her answering machine, he'd gone into shock. As for Kristin, she'd lain there, not saying a word in her defense. God, she must've thought he was a gullible fool.

Now he was depressed and a little bit drunk, and sorry that he'd asked Madison out to dinner. She was an attractive woman, but she wasn't Kristin.

Was he supposed to stop caring about somebody simply because she turned out to be a hooker?

*But how can I care for someone I don't even know?* he asked himself glumly. He'd seen her three times and fallen in love. How dumb was *that?*

He parked his truck outside Natalie's house, got out and walked slowly to the front door. Jimmy had booked him a table at The Palm. "Take her there, order the steak and lobster, get her drunk, fuck her and forget about Kristin," his brother had told him.

"Is that all you think about with women? Getting laid?"

"If *you* were married to Bunny, that's all *you'd* think about. She nags me to death."

"She always did. You knew that before you married her."

"I've been meaning to tell you," Jimmy had confided. "You do know that I see other women on the side?"

Jake had no desire to listen to Jimmy's sexcapades. "What is this, confession time?" he'd said abruptly. "I don't want to hear about it."

"I'm your brother," Jimmy had said indignantly. "If I can't tell *you*, who can I tell?"

"Dad—he's the philanderer in the family. At least he marries *his* conquests."

Jake had not wanted to hear any more about his brother's extracurricular love life. Bunny might be a pain—but it didn't seem fair that Jimmy used that as an excuse to be unfaithful.

He rang the doorbell of Natalie's house.

Cole answered. "Hey, man," he said. "How was the wedding?"

"Predictable," Jake answered, entering the small house. "My dad's sixty-two, his bride's twenty. I guess that says it all."

"You gonna call her Mommy?" Cole joked, leading him into the living room.

"I'm not going to call her, period," Jake said dryly. "I went to the wedding; I've done my duty for the year."

"You and your dad tight?"

"Is Madison around?" Jake asked, not comfortable with Cole firing questions at him.

"Yeah, I'll call her. Hey, Maddie!" Cole yelled. "Your knight in tarnished armor is here."

"Very funny," Jake said. "Can I get some water?"

"Sure." Cole left the room, returning moments later with a bottle of Evian, which he handed over.

"Thanks," Jake said, swigging from the bottle.

A few moments later Madison walked in. Jake did a slow double take. He'd known she was an attractive woman, but he hadn't realized she had such a great body and was so devastatingly beautiful. Her oval face was surrounded by a cloud of dark hair, which up until this time he'd only seen pulled back. Her seductive lips were emphasized with a brownish gold lipstick, matching the subtle shadow above her elongated eyes. She wore a red dress which took his breath away—low-cut, short, with little spaghetti straps. She looked amazing.

"Hi," she said, unaware of the effect she was having on him.

He'd gone back to his hotel after the wedding and changed out of his one and only suit into khaki pants and a denim shirt with no tie. "I feel underdressed," he said, and then he realized he had said almost the same thing to Kristin on their first date.

"Shall I go change?" Madison asked. "*I* feel half naked."

"You *look* sensational, and if you're comfortable like that . . ."

"No," she laughed, delighted to see he hadn't bothered to dress up. "I'm certainly *not*. Getting all done up was Cole and Natalie's idea. They were in a make-over mood, and I went along with them. Do you *mind* if I go change?"

"Whatever makes you happy."

She smiled. "That'll make me happy."

Two hours later they were engrossed in deep conversation. Madison had put on a loose sweater, black jeans and a casual jacket. But she had left her hair down and not removed her makeup. Men's heads turned. She was a striking woman.

Jake found her fascinating because he could talk to her in a way he couldn't talk to most women. She was sharp and savvy and knew everything that was going on, yet she wasn't a know-it-all. She listened intently to what he had to say and had a throaty laugh he found quite enticing. They'd already discussed politics, religion, the state of the movie industry, publishing, pornography on the Internet and his favorite subject—photography. Madison was a stimulating conversationalist.

"Where are you from originally?" he asked, taking a bite of one of the best steaks he'd ever tasted.

"I'm a true New Yorker," she said. "In fact, my

parents still live there. Well actually, they don't—they moved to Connecticut."

"What does your dad do?"

She was silent for a moment. "Uh . . . he's in commodities."

"Commodities," Jake said. "The stock market?"

"Kind of."

"I don't get the stock market," Jake said. "It's like legalized gambling to me."

"Have you ever been to Vegas?"

"Haven't been. Don't want to go."

"Damn!" Madison said with a low sexy laugh. "There goes my plan of taking you there for a long weekend of unbridled lust."

Jake sat up very straight. "Huh?"

"Just joking," she said with a tantalizing smile.

He was confused; under virtually any other circumstances he would have found this woman completely irresistible. But he had to be honest with himself and admit that his mind was still on Kristin. All night he kept on wondering what she was doing and if she was thinking about him.

"Why don't you tell me about her," Madison said, leaning forward, her eyes bright with genuine interest. "I'm an excellent listener. In fact, it's part of my job."

"Tell you about whom?"

"Listen," she said, matter-of-factly. "Three months ago I broke up with my boyfriend. Or rather *he* broke up with *me*. Now believe me, I *know* it takes time to get over something like that. I'm almost there; you're obviously just starting."

He considered denying it, then thought—why not be honest? She was too smart and too nice to try and fake it. So he began telling her his story, while she listened attentively—interjecting an occasional wise comment.

"That's it," he said when he'd finished his sorry tale. "And like an idiot, I told my asshole brother, who announced it to everyone at our dad's wedding. Now I feel like the world's biggest jerk."

"Don't," she said, shaking her head. "Your reaction was perfectly understandable. You felt out of control and betrayed."

"That's exactly it!" he said excitedly. "Hey—were you ever a shrink?"

"No—but I write stories, so I know people. My father taught me how to analyze situations and sum up the players. He's a brilliant man."

"So . . . what's my next move?"

"You call her up, apologize for bolting like a frightened rabbit and make a date for lunch on neutral territory."

"Are you sure?"

"Yes. You have to give her a chance to explain why she didn't tell you."

"Good," he said, relieved. "I can't wait to hear what she has to say."

"Remember," Madison said sternly. "No accusations. Simply hear her out."

"I'll do it," he said, finishing off his steak.

"You won't be sorry," she said, taking a quick peek at her watch. "Now, do you mind if we leave? I want to catch the ten o'clock news, see if there's anything new on Salli's murder."

"No problem," he said, calling for the check. Then he looked at her long and hard. "Y'know, if this was another time, another place—"

"I know," she said softly. "You don't have to say a word. We'll get together again when we're both feeling a little less vulnerable. How's that?"

He grinned. "You're a great lady."

She grinned back. "And you're a great guy. So let's get the hell out of here!"

# chapter 15

$S$INCE CAPTAIN MARSH was demanding an arrest in the murder of Salli T. Turner within twenty-four hours, Detective Tucci knew that he had to put the rest of the day to good use. The fact that Bobby Skorch had summoned his lawyer and refused to talk to them had aroused Tucci's suspicions. If Bobby had nothing to hide, then why wouldn't he allow himself to be questioned? he wondered. And why wasn't he anxious to find out the details of his wife's brutal murder?

After their meeting with Captain Marsh, Lee decided he should get on the next plane to Vegas so he could thoroughly check up on Bobby Skorch's every move from the previous day.

While Lee was taking care of things in Vegas, Tucci interviewed Eddie Stoner, Salli's ex. The good news was that Eddie's lawyer had not arrived to bail him out. The bad news was that Eddie was in a vile mood.

"What the fuck am I bein' held for?" Eddie

demanded, wild bloodshot eyes bulging with fury as he sat at the interview table.

"Parking tickets," Tucci said, pulling up a chair. "Too many of 'em."

"So where the *fuck* is my lawyer?"

"You had your phone call, Eddie."

"Well," Eddie said truculently. "I want another goddamn phone call."

"You know the rules—one call."

"This is a joke," Eddie snarled. "I'm tellin' my fuckin' union 'bout this shit."

"What union?"

"The Screen Actors Guild, that's who. No way they'll let their members be treated like this."

"Where were you last night, Eddie?"

"I want a lawyer present before I answer any questions."

"Why? You got something to hide?"

"I need a cigarette."

"Sure, Eddie. Let me get you one."

Tucci got up and left the room. He could see that Eddie Stoner was a nervous wreck, and it wasn't just for the want of a cigarette—he was obviously hooked on something stronger than nicotine, and he was starting to miss it badly.

Tucci bummed a cigarette from the desk sergeant and reentered the interview room. "Here you go."

"Thanks," Eddie said, grabbing the cigarette and lighting up.

Tucci took a moment to study him. Eddie was good-looking in a dissolute way. Although only thirty, he had bags under his eyes that you could take on a trip, a long mane of dirty blond hair, flat blue eyes and a mean scowl. He was wearing an old Nike

T-shirt, jeans that had seen better days and scuffed sneakers.

"I'd like to see you go home today," Tucci said. "So let's make this easy on everybody and you tell me where you were last night."

"Let me ask you somethin'," Eddie said, dragging hungrily on his cigarette. "What's so important about where I was last night? You hauled me in on parking tickets, not a fuckin' murder."

Tucci studied him. From that remark, it would appear that he didn't know about Salli T. Turner's murder. Or maybe he was playing it smart. "What's preventing you from answering?" the detective asked.

"'Cause I don't 'preciate bein' dragged outta bed in the middle of the night. You guys have fuckin' balls of steel."

"Just doing our job."

"Yeah, well, when I do *my* fuckin' job, I don't hassle people in the middle of the night."

"Y'know," Tucci said. "Unrelated to this little mess, you're a very good actor. I've seen you in a couple of movies. Shame you never got that big break."

"You bet your ass it's a shame," Eddie said excitedly. "I look at the assholes who make it an' I gotta say to myself—why the *hell* isn't it me? Jean-Claude Van Damme: what the fuck's *he* got that I haven't? I'm better lookin', an' I'm *certainly* a better actor."

"Right, Eddie," Tucci agreed. "You're also an American."

"You bet your ass."

"So, I'll tell you what I'll do, Eddie. Since your

lawyer hasn't responded, I'll let you make another call if you tell me where you were last night."

Eddie ran a hand through his long hair. "Let me think," he said. "I picked up a coupla chicks at a club on Sunset. Went back to their place 'round midnight, got crazy outta my skull. I musta got home around three."

"Who were the girls?"

Eddie laughed dryly. "You think I ask their names?"

"You mean you spent the night with two women, and you don't know who they are?" Tucci asked, knowing he must sound like some out-of-touch old fogy.

"This is Hollywood, man—chicks are every-where. Who gives a shit what they're called?"

"Try to remember, Eddie."

"Hey—you're not *listenin'* to me," Eddie said irritably. "I dunno who they were. Picked 'em up in a club. *They* were horny—*I* was horny. We all got off."

"Do you remember what club it was?"

"I was in the Viper Room earlier. Maybe it was a place called The Boss."

"Does The Boss have a doorman?"

"They got a bouncer."

"Would he know who the girls are?"

"Hey, man, he's not lookin' to identify no one. All he's lookin' for is a big, fat tip."

"Okay, Eddie."

"Do I get my call?"

"Yes. Only I don't want you leaving town. Oh, and by the way—"

"What?"

"Your ex-wife—"

"Salli?"

"She was murdered last night."

"Oh, *fuck!*" Eddie said, his upper body slumping onto the table. "Oh, fuck! Now you're gonna tell me you think I have somethin' t'do with it?"

"I'm not saying anything," Tucci said. "But don't leave the city. Is that clear?"

"How'd it happen?" Eddie asked, sitting up. "Was it that moron she married? I warned her he was trouble."

"When did you last see her?" Tucci asked.

"Hey, man," Eddie said, throwing up his hands. "I may *look* stupid—but I know when it's time for no more questions. I need a lawyer."

Tucci got up and headed for the door, where he stopped for a brief moment studying Eddie's expression. "She was stabbed to death," he said. "Multiple times. I'll make sure you get your phone call."

# chapter 16

**A**S SHE DROVE TO MAX'S house in Bel Air, Kristin made another attempt to listen to the Bob Evans biography on tape. Once again she couldn't concentrate and turned it off. She tried to steer her thoughts away from Jake, thinking instead of Cherie and the nursing home. Her sister had looked paler than usual today. The doctor who took care of her had left a message with one of the nurses that he wished to speak with her. Since Dr. Raine was never at the nursing home on Sundays, her only real day off, she knew she had to call him, but she kept putting it off; whatever he had to say she was certain it would not be good. Dr. Raine was a nice man, but he didn't understand about miracles.

She often thought about the day she and Cherie had gotten in their battered old car and set off for Los Angeles. Cherie had been so excited; in fact, it was she who had instigated the trip. "We're going to be famous actresses," Cherie had promised, her pretty face glowing with anticipation. "Both of us. And we'll *never* be jealous of each other. We'll *never* have any of that stupid sibling rivalry."

Three months after they left home, their parents were killed in a train wreck, so there was no going back. The tragedy had drawn them even closer, since they then had no one except each other—at least until Howie Powers entered their lives, a man Kristin hated with a burning intensity. She'd neither seen nor heard from him since the accident. He obviously couldn't have cared less whether Cherie lived or died.

Kristin wondered what Cherie would think of what she was doing now to make a living. There was no doubt that her sister would disapprove, but what choice did she have? The nursing home bills had to be paid, and she couldn't make a living as an actress—too tough a profession by far. Besides, she'd never studied, nor ever had any ambition in that direction. Cherie had been the ambitious one. Cherie had envisioned stardom for both of them.

The gates to Max's house were closed. Strange how in the affluent neighborhoods of L.A. everyone surrounded themselves with iron gates, guard dogs and elaborate alarm systems, Kristin thought. They lived in fortresses. Who did they expect was coming to get them?

She got out of her car and rang the outside buzzer. No reply. She rang it again, then glanced at her watch. It was almost five o'clock, and she'd told him she would be here at four. Had he not bothered to wait?

She rang again and again. Nothing.

After ten minutes of trying she realized nobody was home. Had Max Steele changed his mind? Was that it? He'd invited a hooker to move in, and then he'd reconsidered.

Angrily she got back into her car. Why was it that every man she met let her down? How come they were all a bunch of selfish, sex-crazed, perverted bastards?

Then it occurred to her. If she was going to deal with bastards, she may as well get paid for it.

Mister X's words ran through her head. *I'll pay you double.*

*Double was good. In Mister X's case, double meant a great deal of money.*

*Who needs you, Max Steele? You couldn't even leave a note for me. Whatever happened to common courtesy?*

Backing her car out of the driveway and into the winding street, she drove home.

When the bullet hit Max it was like a sharp blinding jolt from hell. He felt as if his shoulder was being torn away from his body, and he screamed out in pure agony. This wasn't a movie. This was the real thing. And he could not believe it was happening to him.

He had given the bastard his Rolex, much as he hated doing so. He had handed over his money as well—all twenty bucks of it—which was every dollar he had on him.

The meager sum clearly had made the guy mad. "You're drivin' a freakin' Maserati," the robber snarled, ski mask concealing his face. "A cocksuck-in' Maserati, an' you're walkin' around with twenty pissin' bucks. Don't jack me off, mothafucker."

"That's all I have," Max had responded with a shrug.

"Fuck you, you rich bastard!" the robber screamed. And then he had fired a shot—just like that.

Max fell to the ground. The robber didn't seem to care whether he died or not. He kicked him in the groin with the sharp tip of his cowboy boot before he grabbed the keys of the Maserati and drove off, leaving Max lying there in a pool of blood.

He lost consciousness almost immediately, until somewhere in the distance he heard a child's voice yelling, "Mommy! Mommy! There's a man lying down. Mommy! Mommy!"

And the worried mother's voice answering, "Don't look, darling. Stay away from him. Get in the car and lock your door."

Oh Jesus! What did they think he was—some falling down drunk bum? He tried to speak, his voice weak as he managed to croak, "Somebody . . . gotta help me."

The woman said, "You should be ashamed of yourself!" Then she must have noticed the ever widening pool of blood, because she suddenly gasped, "Oh, my God! You've been shot!"

"Get . . . the . . . police . . ." he mumbled. "Go for help. . . ." And he slumped back, wondering if he was dying.

The woman jumped in her car and phoned the police on her cell phone. She even waited until they arrived.

The next thing Max remembered was lying in an ambulance as it raced him to an emergency room, sirens screaming.

He couldn't believe it. He, Max Steele, had gotten himself shot.

Then everything went black.

LUCINDA'S CALL CAUGHT Freddie by surprise. He was in his study, contemplating Diana's foul mood and Max's unconscionable behavior when she phoned. "Darling," she drawled, as only a superstar of Lucinda's caliber could. "I desperately need a favor."

"What?" he asked, suspicious as always of movie stars courting favors.

*Manhattan Style* is doing a cover story on me," she informed him. "The editor, Victor Simons, is an old friend, so I know it'll be a positive piece. However, Victor has asked me to do him a personal favor which involves you." A dramatic pause. "Darling, the magazine wants to profile *you.*"

"Lucinda, you know I don't do publicity," he said, keeping his voice pleasant and even.

"Yes, Freddie, darling, I do know that. But if you did this for me, they'd give you full copy approval, so what's to lose?"

"My privacy," he said grimly.

*"What* privacy?" she retorted, as if it was the most amusing thing she'd ever heard. "You're acknowledged to be the most famous agent in Hollywood. You *should* do it, Freddie. After all, Sumner Redstone is in all the media; so is Michael Eisner."

"Sumner owns the world, Michael runs a studio," Freddie pointed out.

"Who knows," Lucinda said. "Perhaps that's what *you'll* do one of these days."

"Mike Ovitz already made that mistake," he said, annoyed because he knew he was going to have to say yes. Recently he'd persuaded Lucinda to sign for a movie she really didn't want to do. It was a twelve-million-dollar deal—which meant almost a two-million-dollar commission for the agency. How *could* he turn her down?

"Well, anyway," Lucinda said, bored with the conversation. "I *would* like to tell Victor yes, that you'll meet his reporter tomorrow at eleven. Can you accommodate me, Freddie—please? I hardly *ever* ask favors. Please?"

"What's the name of the reporter?" he asked resignedly.

"Madison something or other. Apparently she's very good."

"Is she aware I get copy approval?"

"It doesn't matter whether she knows or not. Victor Simons is the editor."

"Only for you, Lucinda," Freddie said, sighing. "Have Victor send me a fax confirming I have copy *and* headline approval."

"Thank you, darling," she cooed. "I knew you wouldn't let me down."

When she hung up, it occurred to him that the woman she'd mentioned must be the same journalist Ria had told him about. That's all he needed—an interview with some nosy journalist prying into his life.

The phone rang again. "Yes?" he said impatiently.

"Mr. Leon?"

"Who's this?"

"I'm phoning from Cedar Sinai."

Freddie felt his stomach turn. Why was he getting a phone call from a hospital? "What is it?"

"Max Steele was recently admitted. We thought you should be informed immediately."

"Admitted for what?"

"Mr. Steele was shot during a robbery."

Freddie was silent. He didn't know how to digest this piece of information; it seemed so unreal. "How bad is he?" he asked at last.

"It's critical. We have him in intensive care."

"I'll be right there," Freddie said, slamming the phone down and jumping up from his desk. "Diana!" he yelled. "Diana!"

She was sitting in the living room reading a book on Oriental art, studiously pretending to ignore him.

"You won't believe this one," he said. "We have to get over to Cedar's immediately. Max has been shot."

Diana leaped out of her chair. "What!" she exclaimed, the color draining from her face. "How? Where?"

"Apparently it was a robbery."

"How serious is it?" she asked.

"I don't know. Let's go."

314

"Oh, my God!" she said, her face crumpling. "Oh, my God!" And suddenly she burst into tears.

"Pull yourself together," Freddie said tersely. "Hysterics aren't going to help anyone."

And even though he was mad at Max and felt he'd been betrayed, Freddie was panicked at the thought of anything happening to him.

# chapter 18

"**H**OW WAS IT?" COLE asked the moment Madison walked in.

"What are *you* doing here?" she said, surprised to see him. "I thought you had a hot date."

"Got canceled," he answered.

"That must've pleased Natalie," she said, shrugging off her jacket.

"You could say she's thrilled. There's no way she approves of me seein' Mr. Mogul." He indicated his dinner laid out on the coffee table. Pizza, a carton of French fries and a large-size Diet Coke. "Hey— wanna piece of pizza?"

"What happened to your health foods?"

He grinned, patting his finely muscled stomach. "Sometimes you gotta give it up."

She settled on the couch. "What was his reason for canceling?" she asked, stealing a French fry.

Cole made a "how would I know" gesture. "Dunno. Don't care," he said vaguely.

She could see he was hurt. "I'm sure it was a good one."

"Who knows," he said, picking up another piece of pizza. "Oh, by the way, some dude called Victor wants you to call him."

"My editor," she said, reaching for the phone and waking Victor up in New York—which seemed to be becoming a habit. "What's going on, Victor?" she asked.

"You have your interview with Freddie Leon," he said, sounding pleased with himself. "Tomorrow, eleven o'clock, his office. *Be* there!"

"I'm impressed," she said, delighted that he'd finally delivered on his promise. "How did you arrange it?"

"Let's just say my connection came through."

"How long will he give me?"

"Use your charm, Madison. I'm sure you'll get as long as you want."

"Thanks, Victor—I love it when you deliver."

"Good news?" Cole asked when she hung up the phone.

"Excellent," Madison said. "I've got my interview with the elusive Mr. Leon."

"So, c'mon," Cole said. "Tell me all about your date."

"Actually, it was very nice," she said, curling her legs under her. "Jake's a terrific guy. He's also completely enamored with someone else, but that doesn't make him a bad guy. We had a great time, talked about everything. Then I gave him advice on his love life. How's that?"

"Doesn't sound too romantic to me."

"It's not supposed to," she said. "Can we switch channels and watch the news? I'd like to see if there's any new developments in the Salli T. Turner murder."

"They identified the blonde those two surfers pulled out of the ocean today."

"They did? Who is she?"

"Some girl from Idaho."

"Really?"

"What they're saying is she was drowned in a swimming pool, *then* dumped in the ocean. How about *that?*"

"God, there's some sickos out there," Madison said, shivering. "Anything new on Salli?"

"The same old crap. One moment she's the Virgin Mary, the next she's the biggest slut who ever walked, depending on what channel you're watching."

Madison really wanted to get into bed and watch TV there, but she had a strong suspicion Cole felt like having company. "Is Natalie back?" she asked.

"If I know my sister, she will *not* be comin' home tonight," Cole said with a big grin. "I took a look at Luther when he came to pick her up. Boy, he's a big one."

"Yeah—just the way Natalie likes 'em."

They both giggled. "Hey, Maddie," Cole said. "It's cool you had a good time."

"Jake's an interesting man," she said. "However, I can promise you this—I am *not* in the frame of mind to get involved with anybody right now. And since he's already involved, no problem."

"Not into one-nighters, huh?" Cole said teasingly.

"No," she answered firmly. "And you shouldn't be either—too dangerous."

"I often wonder what it must've been like in the sixties—when sex wasn't gonna get you zapped. When you could do anything and not have to pay with your life."

"Yeah," she said. "It must have been pretty nice then. That's when my mom and dad got together."

"You talk about your dad a lot. You're real tight with him, huh?"

"I certainly am. He's a wonderful man."

"And your mom?"

"She's great, too, but I've always been closer to Michael. He taught me how to get out in the world and go after what I wanted. He taught me to be fair, and, most of all, he taught me to follow my dreams."

"Michael sounds like quite a guy."

"He is."

Luther was a romantic. He took Natalie to a small restaurant in Santa Monica overlooking the ocean. It happened to be located in the hotel he was staying at—Shutters on the Beach. Of course, he omitted to tell her this vital piece of information as he plied her with red wine and compliments.

"Y'know, baby," he crooned in a low-down, smoky voice. "I feel like you an' I—well—like we was an accident waitin' to happen."

Natalie leaned across the table. It wasn't exactly how she would've put it, but he had a point. And she was quite ready to jump into bed with him and start what she was sure would be a more-than-satisfying sexual relationship. Even though Luther lived in

Chicago, he could visit on a regular basis, and that would make seeing him all the more exciting.

He reached for her hand, pressing his strong fingers up against hers. She felt the heat and smiled to herself. Oh, baby, this was going to be finger-licking good!

And then her cell phone went off. "Damn!" she exclaimed, scrambling in her purse to answer the stupid thing. It was Garth, her station manager.

"We need you here immediately," Garth said tersely. "We got a lead on the Malibu blonde. Turns out she might be part of a high-priced call girl ring. I want you to come in right now and put together a story on her."

"Now?" Natalie objected. "I'm in the middle of a date."

"You can get laid anytime," Garth said rudely. "This is important."

"How important?"

"You're always whining that you want to get into real news. If you do a good job, this could be the start of a whole other direction for you."

"News anchor?" she questioned breathlessly.

"Don't get carried away."

"I'll be there," she said, clicking off her phone. Suddenly Luther's luster dimmed. He was big and sexy, but he was, after all, only a guy. "Uh . . . Luther," she said.

"Yeah, baby?"

"I know you're a real understanding guy, so if I told you I had to go to work . . . could we pick this up where we left off—say tomorrow night?"

"But baby—"

320

"I know, I know," she said softly. "It's a real bummer, an' I'll miss you like crazy—"

He shook his head like he couldn't quite believe this was happening to him. He was a man *definitely* not used to a woman putting work before him.

"Go with me on this, Luther," she murmured sweetly. "And I promise, tomorrow we'll make it a night to remember."

Before he could object, she was on her feet and out the door.

# chapter 19

ANGELA MUSCONNI, THE hot nineteen-year-old movie star with a bad drug habit, was in bed with her current boyfriend, Kevin Page, another hot young movie star, with *no* bad drug habit, when the phone rang.

They'd been in bed all day as they'd partied all night and not gotten to sleep until five in the morning.

Angie stretched out a long naked arm, wearily groping for the receiver. "Yes," she mumbled. "Who's wakin' me up?"

"Angelina," said a voice, echoing from her past.

"Who's this?" she asked suspiciously, although a familiar gnawing in the pit of her stomach told her exactly who it was.

"You know I'm the only one who calls you Angelina."

"Eddie?" she questioned sharply. "Is that you?"

"Yep, it's the man himself."

"Wadda *you* want?"

"I want you to bail me outta jail."

"What *are* you talking about?" she said, struggling to sit up.

"I'm in deep shit, Angie. Can't reach my lawyer, an' I dunno who else to call who'd have the money to bail me. I gotta get outta here *now*. The cops told me Salli's bin murdered, an' they got their eye on me."

"I haven't spoken to you in three freakin' years," she said accusingly, finally becoming fully alert. "Ever since you ran out on me and married Salli."

"I know, babe, but if old friendships mean anythin', you gotta come and get me. I can't take it here."

"Jeez!" Angie said, completely amazed that he had the nerve to call her. "Is *that* why they've arrested you? *Did* you do it, you bastard?"

"No fuckin' way," he said indignantly. "I'm here 'cause of some crap about unpaid parking tickets."

"You were always threatening us, Eddie," she said, remembering the past. "Me *and* her."

Kevin rolled over in his sleep. "Whoissit?"

"Nobody."

"You gonna come?" Eddie demanded.

"Why should I?"

"Oh Christ! I need you, Angelina."

Angie was torn; on one hand she was outraged that after all this time Eddie had called her, and on the other her natural curiosity was fast getting the better of her. "Maybe," she said grudgingly.

"What does 'maybe' mean?" Eddie blustered. "You comin' or not?"

"I'll see," she said, putting the phone down and breaking the connection. She stared at Kevin, who didn't stir. Carefully she edged her way out of bed.

Kevin grabbed her bare leg, startling her. "Where you goin'," he mumbled.

"I gotta go out," she said briskly. "Emergency."

"Bring food," he said, as he rolled over and promptly went back to sleep.

She ran to the bathroom and pulled on a pair of tight jeans and a midriff-baring sweater. She knew Kevin always kept a stack of bills stashed beneath his pile of T-shirts, so she went to his dresser drawer and helped herself to a bundle.

*Why am I doing this?* she asked herself. *Sure, I loved Eddie once, but the asshole dumped on me big time. Now he's probably hacked up Salli, and I'm the one springing him from jail. What's wrong with me?*

But Angie always *had* gotten off on excitement, and this was the most exciting thing to have happened to her in a long time. Being a movie star was way too safe and predictable. Living on the edge— that's the way she liked it.

And there was nobody better than Eddie Stoner for taking you on a trip to the wild side, and then right to the very edge.

# chapter 20

FROM HER CHIC, UPSWEPT, dark blond hair, to the tips of her finely manicured, blood red, inch-long nails, Darlene La Porte was one of the best-groomed women in Beverly Hills. It took a lot of money to look like Darlene—plenty of big bucks, considering she kept a team of professionals always on call to attend to her grooming needs. She had a hairdresser who came to her house every morning. Then there was her manicurist, dietitian, makeup artist, clothes stylist, yoga instructor and personal trainer. They were all on Darlene's payroll. She was no movie star, but she took better care of herself than most of them did.

The payoff was worth it. She looked thirty. She was actually forty-one.

A youthful appearance was extremely important to Darlene. She needed to interact and relate to the young girls who worked for her. Every month there was a new batch of pretty girls who arrived in Hollywood hoping to become actresses or models.

When their dreams faded—which invariably happened fast—Darlene was there to lead them on to another path. She offered them glamour and excitement and big money. She offered them movie stars and moguls and intimacy with all the men they'd have no chance of getting anywhere near in real life. Once they were thoroughly initiated, she then had them service the rest of her client list—those men with unspoken demands and demented perversions. Men such as Mister X.

Darlene had no idea who Mister X was. She only knew that he grossly overpaid, and that was enough to keep her perfectly happy. The only interaction she'd ever had with him was over the phone. Last night he had called to book a repeat performance with Kristin. When he phoned back an hour later, she had to tell him that she had been unable to reach Kristin. He'd sounded angry. She had asked him if he wanted another girl. He said no. Then five minutes later he called back again and said yes—but only if she had someone fresh and new. Darlene immediately thought of Hildie, a pretty blonde from the Midwest who'd only been a working girl for two months. She and Mister X had arranged a meeting place, and Darlene had called to tell Hildie. "This guy's a tiny bit weird," she'd warned her, thinking of Kristin's complaints. "But he's not dangerous, and here's the good news—he pays *really big!*"

"Sounds like fun!" Hildie had said with all the confidence of youth.

Now Darlene sat in front of her television staring at a picture of Hildie on the news, taken at her high school prom. Hildie at sixteen with braces on her teeth and brown frizzy hair. Hardly the same girl Darlene had sent out on a date with death. The Hildie that she knew was blond and sleek. Hollywood and four years of experience had given her a totally new image.

Now she was dead.

Drowned.

Not in the ocean where she was found. In a swimming pool.

And Darlene remembered another of her girls who'd ended up fished out of the ocean. A year ago. Kimberly. By the time Kimberly's body was discovered, there was not much left to identify.

Three weeks prior to her body washing up on the beach, Kimberly also had gone on a date with Mister X.

Darlene had chosen not to connect the two events. Kimberly had been a wild party girl—into coke and heroin. Darlene imagined that she'd died under unfortunate circumstances—maybe partying with friends after her appointment with Mister X. Darlene had not called the police.

Now Hildie.

And Darlene knew that if she went to the police this time the publicity would be so overwhelming that in no time she would become public property like Heidi Fleiss. After that, her lucrative call girl business would be over.

There was only one way to deal with such a terrible event. Never send any of her girls out with Mister X again.

Yes, she decided, even though it meant giving up a healthy amount of commission, that's exactly what she would do.

Conscience assuaged, she began switching channels until she found an old Ava Gardner movie.

Ah . . . she thought. Whatever happened to Hollywood glamour?

Darlene settled comfortably into her couch, and within minutes was totally engrossed in the movie.

## chapter 21

$S$INCE MISTER X HAD NOT stipulated that she wear any particular outfit or color, Kristin chose to go with scarlet. She felt bold and bad and vengeful—while deep inside she felt hurt and abandoned and useless.

Jake didn't want her.

Even Max Steele had rejected her.

And Cherie lay in the nursing home—never showing any improvement—simply lying there, wasting away—waiting for her to pull the plug.

Once in a while Kristin did a little cocaine to take away the pain. Tonight she indulged, snorting the insidious white powder, all the while hating herself for doing so. And yet she knew it would make her feel better, set her up for her date with Mister X. After all, he deserved the best, didn't he? Because her mystery man was the only one who seemed to care about her.

Two sharp, final snorts and she was done.

Every time she did cocaine she vowed it would be

the last. Yet, when her supply ran out, she'd always call Darlene and set up another delivery.

She stared at her reflection in the mirror. *Kristin. Call girl supreme. Worthless whore.*

The scarlet dress looked sensational on her. Her blond hair swirled around her fresh gorgeous face.

She took a deep breath, grabbed her purse and left her apartment.

*Mister X . . . here I come. . . .*

*And I promise—you will not be disappointed.*

# Revenge

# chapter 1

THE GIRL WAS BARELY MORE than sixteen. The pupils of her large hazel eyes were enormous. So was her sexual appetite.

Bobby Skorch had picked her up on Sunset as soon as he'd been able to get out of the house, which had been a hassle due to all the fuss over his wife— superstar sex symbol Salli T. Turner—who had gotten herself murdered the night before.

*That Salli,* Bobby thought, his mind mired in a drugged-out haze, *you never knew what she was going to do next, always full of surprises.*

Finally he'd managed to sneak out of the house by lying on the floor in the back of his maid's car. She'd dropped him off at a hotel where he kept a permanent penthouse suite in his manager's name.

Later he'd taken a cruise along Sunset in the black Ferrari he kept in the basement parking area of the hotel—also registered in his manager's name.

The girl had been hanging around outside a club, and she'd willingly accompanied him back to his hotel. Now she was riding his dick like she was competing in some kind of equestrian event. He didn't have to do a thing except lie back and tolerate the ride, because he certainly wasn't enjoying it. This girl wasn't Salli. *Nobody* was Salli. She was one of a kind. The others were all slags and sluts and whores.

He had no idea what the girl's name was, or whether she had AIDS or the clap—he didn't care.

Bobby was into taking risks. He'd taken a big risk marrying Salli, whom many people had considered a joke with her large fake tits and cascades of dyed platinum hair.

But hey, a lot of *her* friends had considered *him* a risk. Bobby Skorch, the original danger man, with tattoos from here to Cuba, including one on his famous dick.

All he knew was that together they were an awesome sight. *S'long, Pammy and Tommy, Heather and Richie. The Skorches ruled.*

And he'd loved her with a burning passion. Now she was gone.

The girl spread her legs even wider, practically balancing her mothlike weight on his dick. Then she moaned—a prelude to ecstasy.

He wasn't there. Not even close. He was hard and angry and stoned and in the worst pain of his life.

When the girl's moans turned to orgasmic cries and he felt her coming, he screamed his anguish so loud that two maids working on the penthouse floor came running to hover outside the door of Suite 206, their eyes bulging with fear and curiosity.

Satisfied and more than a tiny bit alarmed, the young girl rolled off him, quickly scurrying to get into her clothes. When she reached the door, she looked back at the man, still spread-eagled on the bed, still erect.

There *was* no release for Bobby Skorch. He was in hell.

And there was absolutely nothing he could do about it.

# chapter 2

"T HE GUY HAS PUSSY FOR
breakfast," Detective Lee Eccles said, chewing on a
ragged toothpick.

"What?" said Detective Tucci, distracted as he
pored over his copious notes on the Salli T. Turner
murder.

"Salli's old man, Bobby Skorch. His cock is bigger
than the Empire State Building—an' every broad in
Vegas has had herself a slice."

Tucci removed his glasses, glanced up at his partner—whom he didn't particularly like—and nodded. "I know. He has quite a reputation."

Tucci's wife, Faye, had informed him last night—
when he'd gotten home after midnight—that Bobby
Skorch was the king of the tabloids. "Not that I read
those rags," she'd quickly assured him. "Only sometimes I can't help it when I'm waiting in the checkout line at the market."

*Sure, Faye,* he'd thought affectionately. *Why don't*

*you admit that it's your secret vice? You're like a teenage boy hiding his* Playboy *magazines.*

But then he had his secret vices too, food being one of them. Especially since Faye had put him on a rigid diet. No fats. No sugars. Life was hardly worth living.

He'd already checked out Bobby Skorch. It turned out that Salli's husband had quite a rap sheet. Two arrests for drunken driving; assault with a deadly weapon—the weapon being a broken vodka bottle with which he'd made an unprovoked attack on a photographer; unlawful possession of a firearm; driving with a suspended license; and sexual battery of a teenage girl. The usual celebrity list of misdemeanors.

Tucci sighed and looked up at Lee, who was now perched on the edge of his desk, cleaning his dirty fingernails with the wooden toothpick. "What else did you find out in Vegas?" he asked.

"Plenty," Lee said, digging deep. "Saturday afternoon our boy performed a motorcycle stunt, jumpin' over like a hundred and three cars—some kind of crazy shit. Came out of it without a scratch. After that, he took himself to a lap-dancin' joint, where he picked up three strippers an' ferried 'em back to his hotel. Then I guess he partied for a coupla hours, an' when he finally left, the doorman told me he still had two of the girls with him."

"You mean he brought them back to L.A.?" Tucci asked, considering the possibilities.

"They were in his limo when he left the hotel." Lee paused for dramatic effect. "But here's the kicker. Bobby didn't *drive* back to L.A. like Marty

Steiner said. He took a private plane. So *why* is his asshole lawyer tellin' us he was in the car for five hours? The fucker *flew* back. I already questioned the pilot—he told me they arrived in L.A. at eight— which just *might* have given him time to get to the house, kill his wife, an' who knows what else."

"The strippers were on the plane?"

"Yeah."

"Who met them at the airport?"

"A limo. I'm tryin' to locate the driver. The jerk's taken off on vacation. Limo company's trackin' him for me."

"And the strippers?"

"I'm on it."

*I bet you are,* Tucci thought. When it came to women, Lee was a disrespectful dog, given to making sexist and derogatory remarks. It was one of the reasons Tucci couldn't stand him. That and the fact that Lee had once had a date with Tucci's wife— long before they'd met—but it still bothered him, especially since Faye refused to discuss it.

He'd already decided that as soon as this case was put to bed he was requesting a new partner.

"Any action on the lab reports?" Lee asked.

"She had consensual sex shortly before her death. Put up quite a struggle when the stabbing frenzy began. The lab is analyzing the skin under her fingernails and fibers found on her body. There's also blood that isn't hers."

Lee nodded, hitched himself off Tucci's desk and strolled over to the coffee machine. Tucci watched him go. All day long he'd had a weird feeling. He'd investigated twenty-six murders and this one was giving him the most trouble. He couldn't help picturing Salli's hacked-up body, lying in a pool of blood. Salli T. Turner. So young and vibrant and pretty. So horribly butchered.

Salli T. Turner was headline news, and not just in the tabloids. Her image was everywhere. The blonde of the day. Little Miss Murdered TV Sex Symbol. The girl in the black rubber swimsuit. Star of the hit TV show *Teach!* and a hundred magazine covers.

Who'd killed her in such a vicious and unconscionable way? he wondered. The public wanted answers. So did Tucci's captain—not to mention the mayor. And Tucci wouldn't mind knowing himself.

The two chief suspects were her current husband, Bobby Skorch, and her recent ex, Eddie Stoner. Both men had a proclivity toward violent behavior—especially concerning women.

Eddie had his own rap sheet—which included getting busted for possession of cocaine, assaulting a police officer, and several domestic abuse arrests. Salli had certainly picked herself a couple of charmers.

Tucci bent over his desk, concentrating on his closely written notes. He had always found that when investigating a murder, it was of major importance to write even the smallest thing down while the evidence was still fresh. Not that he had much evidence to work with: No fingerprints. No witnesses. No murder weapon.

Where was he supposed to start? Ah yes, the bullet extracted from the wall near Froo the houseman's residence. The unfortunate man had been in the wrong place at the wrong time. Probably alarmed by the loud music and the frantic barking of Salli's two small dogs, he'd gone to investigate. Maybe he'd

even heard her screams, although none of the neighbors had mentioned hearing screaming—only the
music and the dogs. Of course, in Salli's neighbor-
hood the houses were so goddamn big he was
surprised they'd heard anything at all. The bullet
that had obliterated Froo's face had embedded itself
in the wall. Tucci was checking on any guns registered to Bobby or Eddie.

He'd already decided to interview the neighbors
again. Sometimes a twenty-four-hour break would
give people time to remember things they hadn't
considered important.

Details—that's what solving a murder case was all
about. Details.

Detective Tucci was known for his detail work.

# chapter 3

THE OFFICE BUILDING THAT housed I.A.A. was impressive. Designed by the premier modern architect, Richard Meier, the man who was also responsible for the splendid new Getty Museum, the clean lines were superb. Acres of Italian marble and pristine white walls with just the right amount of glass block. Dominating everything was a huge David Hockney painting of a swimming pool hanging in the massive lobby.

Madison Castelli took all this in as she approached the front desk. "I'm here to see Mr. Leon," she announced.

The Asian woman at the reception desk glanced up. "Do you have an appointment?"

"I certainly do," Madison replied.

"Please take a seat," the woman said.

Instead of going straight to the seating area, Madison strolled across the lobby and stood under the Hockney painting, gazing up at the impressive work of art. As a journalist she loved observing visual images. Capture those and you had your reader hooked. She found Hockney's work to be arresting and very Californian—which was interesting considering he was from England.

*Well, here I am in the lobby of I.A.A.*, she thought, her mind working overtime. She glanced at her watch, noting that it was exactly eleven o'clock, the time of her appointment. She wondered how much time Freddie would grant her, and if he was as intimidating as his reputation.

Freddie Leon was known as the most important agent in town. He was also known as the most reclusive, and it had been tough arranging this interview. Finally, Victor Simons had called in a favor, and now here she was. She was intrigued at the prospect of meeting him, but also anxious to get on with it. She wanted to get out of there in time to attend Salli T. Turner's funeral this afternoon.

She glanced over at the reception desk. The Asian woman was busy on the phone. Hmm . . . It was her experience that the more important the subject, the less they kept you waiting. She made a mental bet that Freddie would summon her to his office within five minutes, and she was right. "Miss Castelli," the woman called out less than two minutes later. "Somebody's on their way down to fetch you."

"Thanks," Madison said.

Moments later a young black man in a spiffy suit and expensive horn-rimmed glasses appeared at her side. "Miss Castelli?" he asked politely.

"That's right," she said.

"Please come with me."

She followed him to a glass-enclosed elevator. They traveled up three floors, then walked down a long corridor flanked with many open door offices. Finally they reached the desk of Ria Santiago, Freddie Leon's executive assistant and sentinel.

"Good morning, Miss Castelli," Ria said. She was an attractive Hispanic woman in her mid-forties with a stern expression.

"Good morning, Ms. Santiago," Madison responded. "I'm sorry I disturbed you by calling you at home yesterday. I was under the impression that everyone knew about my visit here."

"Apparently they do now," Ria said, with a thin smile. "Mr. Leon's expecting you. Please come with me."

Madison followed her into a spacious office with an incredible view of Century City. The room was decorated more like a library than a working office; there were large couches on either side and expensive art on the walls. In the middle of the room was the great Freddie Leon, seated behind a magnificent steel and glass desk, poring over papers. He did not look up when she entered.

"Take a seat," Ria Santiago said, indicating a Biedermeier chair to the side of his desk.

Madison had a feeling that if she didn't exert herself immediately she would be hustled out within fifteen minutes.

"Mr. Leon," Ria said, all business. "Your eleven-thirty called to say they'll be five minutes late. I'll alert you three minutes before they're due."

*Hmm . . .* Madison thought. *Does he really think I'll be satisfied with half an hour? No way.*

Ria left the office. Freddie continued to study the papers on his desk.

"Good morning, Mr. Leon," Madison said, determined to make her presence felt. "I'm delighted you agreed to see me."

Freddie put down his pen and looked up at her for the first time. He saw a beautiful, slender woman in her twenties, with jet hair pulled back, large eyes and full lips.

She stared right back at him, taking in *his* appearance. She saw a poker-faced man in his forties, with cordial features, straight brown hair and a quick bland smile, which she noticed was not reflected in his eyes.

"Good morning, Miss Castelli," he said. "As I'm sure you've been told, I'm seeing you as a favor. I don't normally give interviews."

"I understand, Mr. Leon. I've sat down with a lot of people who don't normally give interviews. Sometimes my subjects find it an enjoyable experience, sometimes they hate it." She smiled. "Let's hope you find it enjoyable."

He smiled back—once again the smile not quite reaching his eyes. "I'm really extremely boring and very dull," he said, tapping his index finger on his chin.

"Isn't that for *me* to say?" she said, slightly amused.

"It depends. What kind of a journalist are you?"

"Maybe you should ask some of my other subjects," she answered calmly. "Henry Kissinger, Fidel Castro, Margaret Thatcher, Sean Connery. Take your pick."

"Quite an eclectic group," he said. "I'm duly impressed."

"Perhaps you wouldn't be if you read the pieces."

"I'd like to read them."

"Then I'll make sure they're faxed to you this afternoon."

He was summing her up, trying to decide what he thought of her. "Now," he said, "before you start bombarding me with questions, I should tell you that I do *not* discuss the money my clients make. In fact, I do *not* discuss my clients period. I don't talk about my family, politics, sex, or my personal opinions on anything."

Madison laughed politely. "Wow! This is going to be some story!"

He liked the fact that she didn't seem to be in awe of him; it made for a refreshing change. "You don't seem to understand, Miss Castelli—I do not *want* to *be* a story in your magazine."

"Mr. Leon," she said patiently. "There's a great amount of public interest in what goes on in Hollywood, and you are the absolute power broker. People have heard about you, you have a famous name. Sometimes, when we achieve greatness in our lives, we have to give up our privacy."

"I don't have to give up anything, Miss Castelli."

"I wish you'd call me Madison."

There was something in her eyes that drew him in. She was not the normal pushy journalist he was used to encountering at openings and parties. This was an intelligent woman who knew what she wanted and had no fear of pursuing it. For a moment he forgot she was the enemy. "Can I offer you a drink? Apple juice, Diet Coke . . ."

"How about I buy *you* a coffee, somewhere other than your office."

He raised his eyebrows. "Excuse me?"

"Oh, please," she said lightly, playing with him. "I know the game. Your eleven-thirty is running five minutes late—I don't think so. Why don't we get out of here, drive somewhere, grab a coffee and talk about how you got into this business? People would kill to know how you got started."

"Now let's not get dramatic."

"I promise I won't pry into your personal life. I merely wish to portray you as an ordinary human being who has achieved great power, not as some ice-cold Hollywood mogul—which is the impression everyone has of you."

He couldn't help laughing, which he found to be a relief after the stress of the last twenty-four hours. "You're very persuasive . . . Madison. To tell the truth, I wouldn't mind getting out of here, it's been one of those mornings."

*"Can* I buy you a coffee then?" she asked, fixing him with a strong gaze.

She was a beautiful, smart woman, and smartness had always intrigued him. "Why not?" he said, surprising himself. "I suppose I can live dangerously for once."

He got up from behind his desk, and together they walked out of his office.

Ria gave him a stony stare. "Mr. Leon," she said, her voice full of disapproval. "What about your eleven-thirty?"

"Postpone it," he said easily. "I'll be back in an hour. Miss Castelli has persuaded me to play hooky."

Ria frowned. It was unlike Freddie Leon to be so lighthearted. "Very well," she said, tight-lipped. "If you're absolutely sure."

"Yes, I'm sure, Ria."

"And if the hospital calls—"

"You have my numbers."

REVENGE

But Bonnar, it was unlike Freddie Leon to be so flustered. "Very well," she said, tight-lipped. "If you're absolutely sure."

"Yes, I'm sure. Just—"

"You have my number—"

"You have my number."

# chapter 4

KRISTIN COULDN'T STOP shivering. She was naked and alone, locked in some funky little beach house where she'd been held captive all night.

She was not afraid. She refused to be afraid. This was another one of Mister X's sick sex games, and now that it was light outside, she was confident he would soon come back to release her.

Last night she'd met him at the end of the Santa Monica Pier, as arranged. As usual he was dressed as a chauffeur—all in black with a baseball cap pulled down low over his forehead, and oblique wrap-around shades hiding his eyes.

"Where are we going?" she asked, as he gripped her arm and led her back to his car—a limo.

"You'll know when we get there," he said.

Mister X was a man of mystery, and for her sins she was getting used to his odd ways.

Kristin had climbed into the back of the limo, thinking that however bad her life was, at least she was luckier than her sister, Cherie, who was lying in a coma in a private nursing home because she'd chosen the wrong guy to get engaged to. Howie Powers—a no-good playboy with too much of his daddy's money.

"Put on the blindfold," Mister X commanded.

She'd done as he asked, covering her eyes with the soft velvet mask that was lying on the backseat. As she did it, she told herself, *I'm a paid whore, I deserve everything I get.*

Mister X had then driven along the Pacific Coast Highway at great speed for about twenty minutes, turning off at what felt like a bumpy dirt road. When the car had finally come to a halt he'd thrown open the rear door and almost dragged her out.

She could hear the roar of the sea and smell the cold night air, and for a moment she'd felt fear. "Can I take off the blindfold?"

"No," he replied, roughly gripping her arm and proceeding to take her on a trip down perilous steps to what she assumed was a house. Several times she nearly fell, but he yanked her up. Finally they entered the house, which smelled musty and damp. He led her to a bed, pushed her onto it and said, "Strip."

"What?"

"You heard me."

This was her worst experience with him yet. The man was a true pervert—getting his kicks from frightening people.

"First I want my money," she said, berating herself for not asking earlier.

"Spoken like a true whore," he said, shoving an envelope stuffed with cash at her. She felt the stack of bills with her hands and was instantly reassured. This much money would pay her sister's nursing home bills for months.

"Strip," he repeated in a flat monotone. "Slowly."

She stood up and did as he asked. Hating him. Hating herself.

Standing there naked, she felt vulnerable and exposed. This man who had asked her to do a variety of perverted deeds had never once touched her sexually. Was he finally going to make love to her?

Suddenly she heard the door slam, followed by the click of a heavy lock. Next she heard wild laughter from outside. Then silence.

She waited a few minutes before ripping off the blindfold. The room was pitch black—she couldn't see a thing, there was no light coming in at all.

It was then she realized she was totally alone.

She didn't panic. This was only another way Mister X had of getting his sick kicks.

After a while she began groping around for her clothes, only to discover the perverted freak had taken them.

She edged her way slowly around the small room, feeling ahead of her with her hands. First she tried the door; it was firmly locked. Next to it was a window, which on examination appeared to be boarded up. No getting out of there until he chose to come back, so she settled on the narrow bed, covered herself with the one thin sheet and attempted to sleep.

Now it was morning, light was creeping through

the small gaps in the sturdy boards covering the window, and soon Mister X would be back to release her.

No matter how much money he offered in the future, this encounter was definitely the final one. She would *never* do business with him again.

# chapter 5

ANGELA MUSCONNI, HOT young actress, knew she was doing the wrong thing, but then Angie had not gotten where she was today by doing the right thing. So against her better judgment, she bailed out her old boyfriend, Eddie Stoner, who might or might not be a suspect in the violent murder of his ex-wife, Salli T. Turner.

Eddie had gotten himself arrested for unpaid parking tickets and his lawyer had vanished on him—so he'd called Angie and asked *her* to put up his bail. She threw down the appropriate money, and had him out of there in no time.

Eddie was delighted to see her, and so he *should* be. It had been three years since he'd left her, and in those three years she'd become a bankable movie star.

Obviously Angie still harbored feelings for Eddie—even though she lived with Kevin Page, another hot young movie star—otherwise she never would have agreed to bail him out.

352

"You look amazin', Angelina," Eddie said, seated in her Ferrari as she drove him to his apartment.

"I *should* look great," she boasted, thinking that he didn't look as hot as she remembered. "Like I'm a big movie star now."

"Glad it happened for one of us," he said, scratching his stubbled chin.

"It could still happen for you," she said, driving recklessly. "You're not too old. What are you—twenty-nine?"

"Thirty," he said grimly. "Thirty and fucked."

"Can't be all bad," she said lightly.

"Get *this* shit," he said, outraged. "Those filthy pigs dragged me out of bed in the middle of the night an' threw me in jail. They freakin' think *I* did it."

"Did what?" she asked innocently.

"Killed Salli."

"Did you?" she asked, throwing him a sly sideways glance.

"No freakin' way," he said vehemently. "How could you even *think* I'd do somethin' like that?"

"You used to beat the shit out of us, Eddie," she reminded him. "Me *and* Salli. You can't deny it."

"So once in a while I got a little carried away," he said with a careless shrug.

Angie remembered him getting more than a little carried away. Eddie in a rage with his eyes bulging was not a pretty sight. Before Salli had stolen him from her, he'd been a violent bastard, prone to beating her up whenever he felt like it.

"Did you get carried away with Salli on Saturday night?" she asked boldly, secure that now she was famous he wouldn't dare touch her.

"What're *you?*" he said, scowling. "A freakin' cop?"

"Just askin'. No need to go nuts."

"I'm gonna tell you who did it," Eddie said, nodding his head. "Her moron husband, Bobby, *that's* who."

"How do *you* know?" Angie questioned. "It was probably some crazy stalker. I've got a ton of 'em. I'm sure Salli did, too."

"It was Bobby," Eddie repeated. "He's a stoned psycho—I've seen him in action."

"Doing what?"

"Anythin' he can," Eddie said ominously. "Drive faster," he added. "I wanna get to the TV, see what's goin' on. The cops told me she was hacked to death. What else are they sayin'?"

"Not a lot."

When they reached his apartment one thing led to another, and before she knew it, Angie found herself back in his bed. Sex with Eddie was everything she remembered—and more. Eddie might not be a star on the screen, but he was certainly an above-the-line performer between the sheets. A sexual box-office hit.

When they were finished, she knew she should dress and go home to Kevin—who was in bed waiting for her, expecting her to bring food. But Eddie was back in her life, and Eddie was her addiction—an addiction she'd thought she was over. Apparently not.

"Why'd you dump me and marry Salli?" she asked, leaning on one elbow and staring at him accusingly as they lay in bed. "I was only a baby. *You* treated me like I was nothin'."

"You're *still* a baby," Eddie said, grinning, because he was well aware he was the greatest cocksman that ever lived. Women were so damn easy, give 'em head for ten minutes and they were his forever. "An' rich, too, I bet."

"You got *that* right," she said, giggling.

"What're you doin' with all your loot?" he asked, reaching for a cigarette on the bedside table.

"Whatever I want," she answered cheekily.

"You goin' with anybody?" he asked, keeping his tone deliberately casual.

"Don't you read the fan magazines?"

"Oh, yeah," he said sarcastically. "Like I'm freakin' *glued* to the fan magazines."

"I'm living with Kevin Page."

"Kevin Page?" he snorted. *"That* fairy."

"He's not a fairy," she said defensively.

"Get a life, sweetheart," Eddie said, blowing smoke in her face. "He's gay as a two-cent piece."

"Kevin is *not* gay."

"Yeah?" he said, tweaking her left breast. "I bet he doesn't do it to you like I do."

This was true. Kevin might be on the cover of every teenage girl's fan magazine, but as a lover, he had a lot to learn. "You're *sooo* conceited," she said with a sigh, longing for his hands all over her, not to mention his tongue where it would do her the most good.

Eddie laughed confidently. "So what else is new?"

# chapter 6

"WHAT WAS THAT ABOUT a hospital?" Madison asked, as she settled next to Freddie Leon in the passenger seat of his gleaming maroon Rolls-Royce.

"Off the record?" he said briskly.

"Of course."

"My partner was shot last night."

"Max Steele?"

"You know him?"

"Yes, we went jogging together a couple of days ago."

"You get around."

"Is he okay?"

"It hasn't hit the news yet," Freddie said, gazing straight ahead as he drove along Santa Monica Boulevard. "Right now he's in intensive care. My wife is sitting vigil at his bedside."

"This is terrible news."

"It's the reason I agreed to get out of the office today, couldn't concentrate. You see, as of last week . . . well, Max and I were not exactly on good terms."

"God! I hope he'll be okay."

"So do I," Freddie said dryly. "Because if Max dies, everyone will say I put a hit on him. That would go nicely with my reputation. Right?"

"How can you be so cynical?" she said, wondering why he would even say such a thing.

"Let's make a deal, Madison. Unless I signal that you can put your tape on, *anything* I say is completely off the record. Agreed?"

"I'll go with that."

"Excellent decision."

She shook her head. "This is a very violent town."

"Where are *you* from?"

"New York."

"And I suppose New York isn't violent?"

"I've been here three days, and already Salli T. Turner's been murdered, and now Max Steele has been shot."

"Read the papers, something happens every day."

"Was he at home?"

"No, the police say it was a robbery in a parking lot. Apparently somebody wanted his Rolex." Freddie sighed. "Do you *know* how many times I've warned him not to walk around with a seventeen-thousand-dollar gold watch on his wrist?"

Madison wanted to respond, "How about you in your two-hundred-and-fifty-thousand-dollar car?" But she did the prudent thing and resisted. "Will you be able to *keep* it out of the news?" she asked.

"I doubt it."

"And you say your wife is at the hospital with him?"

"Diana took it badly. I never realized they were so close."

*Hmm,* Madison thought, *there's a telling remark.*

"You'll have to excuse me," Freddie continued. "My head's not in a good place right now. When I left the hospital last night I took a ride to the beach. We have a small house there which nobody ever uses. It's the only place I can relax. I enjoy solitude."

"So do I."

"I'll lend you the keys one day."

"I'll take you up on that. I love the beach," Madison said, thinking that Freddie Leon was not at all like his reputation. This titan of the big deal seemed lonely and almost vulnerable.

They rode in silence for a while.

"Y'know," Madison said. "The last thing I want is to hassle you. So if this isn't a good time, we don't *have* to talk today—we could get together next week."

"I like you," Freddie said, ignoring her offer. "I knew that the moment you walked into my office. Believe me—I don't say that to many people."

"I'm flattered."

"Madison—interesting name."

"My parents met on Madison Avenue," she said lightly. "My mother was shopping, and I guess my father was looking."

"Your parents still alive?"

"They live in Connecticut, moved out of the city last year."

"Smart. That's exactly what I plan on doing eventually—buy myself an old farmhouse in France and give all this up."

"You'd relinquish all your power and leave L.A.?"

"In a moment," he said, making a sharp turn onto Melrose.

"Where are we going?" she asked, peering out the window.

"My secret place," he said. "Only it's not so secret with the tourists. It's somewhere I don't have other agents and producers begging for favors. Also, they serve the best Danish in the city."

"Where's that?"

"Farmer's Market on Fairfax."

Her eyebrows rose. "Farmer's Market?"

"You'll love it," he assured her.

"I will?"

"Yes, Madison, you will."

She settled back in the passenger seat. This meeting was turning out to be much more interesting than she'd expected.

# chapter 7

DIANA SAT BESIDE MAX Steele's hospital bed. He was still unconscious and in intensive care, but the doctors had told her he had a good chance of making it. She hoped and prayed it was true, because if he survived, she definitely had decided to tell Freddie she was leaving him.

Of course, there was one small snag. When she and Max had met for breakfast, he'd revealed that he had just gotten engaged, and she—like a fool—had later shared the news with Freddie. When Freddie left the hospital last night, he'd instructed her to contact Max's fiancée immediately.

She had not done so. Why should she? It seemed unnecessary. She was perfectly happy sitting next to Max, watching over him. The last thing she needed was a stupid fiancée getting in her way. For a brief moment she'd considered calling Max's secretary at home to get the girl's number, but then it had seemed more sensible to wait until the next day.

Now it was Monday morning and she finally

realized she'd better call the girl or Freddie would throw a fit. He was a stickler for getting his own way. It irked her, but there seemed to be no other choice.

She called Max's secretary, Meg, who sounded completely devastated. "When can I come to the hospital?" Meg asked, choking back tears.

"Not yet, dear," Diana responded.

"Everyone at the office is so concerned," Meg continued. "Mr. Leon called a staff meeting this morning and told us all. Oh, Mrs. Leon, it's such a shock. What can I do?"

"I need the number of a friend of Mr. Steele's," Diana said crisply, unable to bring herself to say "fiancée."

"Of course, Mrs. Leon—who would that be?"

"Her name's Kristin something. I don't have a last name."

"Hold on a moment, I'll look in the book."

Diana held on impatiently. It was obvious Meg knew nothing about a fiancée. Good.

Finally Meg returned. "I can't seem to find a listing in the business book for a Kristin. However, his personal phone book is on his desk. Would you like me to take a look in that?"

For a moment Diana was tempted to say no. If she was unable to get the girl's number she couldn't inform her. "Very well," she said at last.

Meg left her hanging again and returned a moment later. "Since we have no last name I'll look under the K's," she said. "Ah yes, there *is* a Kristin listed. Kristin, and in brackets, Darlene, then there's a number."

"Give it to me," Diana said impatiently.

"Yes, Mrs. Leon. Is there anything else I can do?

Maybe bring some of his clothes to the hospital? Or drop by his house?"

"Good idea, Meg. Go to his house and warn the housekeeper that if anyone comes to the door, not to say a word. We're trying to keep this quiet."

"There're spies in all the hospitals, Mrs. Leon," Meg said. She was an avid reader of the tabloids.

"I know, dear. Which is exactly why we've hired security."

Diana did not call immediately, but waited another half hour before reluctantly dialing the number Meg had given her.

An uptight-sounding woman answered.

"Is this Kristin?" Diana said, equally uptight.

"Who *is* this?" the woman demanded, her voice shrill and angry.

"Mrs. Freddie Leon," Diana said haughtily.

"There's no Kristin here."

"Is this Darlene?"

"Are you from the media?"

"Ex*cuse* me?"

"Don't bother me at home again," the woman shrieked. "Call my lawyer. I'm suing every one of you. You people make me *sick.*"

And with that the woman slammed the phone down, leaving Diana stunned.

# chapter 8

NOW THAT HIS FATHER WAS safely married for the fourth time, Jake Sica decided he'd done his duty by attending the wedding, and now it was time to start getting *his* life together. Since arriving in L.A. from his home base in Arizona barely a week ago, so much had happened, and he'd been so preoccupied that he'd done nothing about finding an apartment, let alone checking in with the magazine he was about to start taking pictures for. Which was kind of stupid, because until he let them know he was in L.A. and ready to work, there would be no weekly paycheck coming his way. And although he was an award-winning photographer, he was not exactly rolling in bucks. Which is one of the reasons he'd decided to take the highly paid magazine job in L.A.

He sat in a coffee shop on Sunset toying with a late breakfast of bacon and eggs, ruminating his fate, and wondering why it was his luck to have met a gorgeous, delectable woman—with whom he'd fallen instantly in love, not to mention lust—who then turned out to be an extremely highly paid call girl. Goddamn it! The whole scenario was like a bad movie.

Last night he'd had dinner with his new best friend, Madison, and she'd advised him to call Kristin and hear her side of things. He'd done so, but Kristin was out, so he'd left a long message on her answering machine. So far she hadn't responded.

He had a feeling she might have been sitting beside her machine listening to him and hating him because he'd walked out on her when he'd found out the shattering truth.

Fuck! He'd blown it. He should at least have stayed around long enough to listen to what she had to say. Instead he'd marched out like an insulted virgin, yelling something like, "Why didn't you tell me? I would've worn a condom."

Jesus! Talk about bad behavior.

After brooding over his coffee, he finally went to a pay phone and tried again to reach Kristin.

This time a female voice answered, only it wasn't Kristin—it sounded more like a foreign maid. "Kristin?" he asked hopefully, even though he knew it wasn't her.

"No, this Chiew. I take message?"

"Uh . . . I need to talk to the lady you work for. Will she be back soon?"

"Don't know. Madam not come home last night."

Oh, that was great. She was probably out with a big-bucks client having wild, paid-for sex.

"What time *will* she be home?"

"No, sorry."

He gave her his number at the hotel, impressing

upon her that it was urgent Kristin call him the moment she came in. He didn't know what else to do, but he *did* know it was imperative that he talk to her as soon as possible so that he could try to straighten things out.

He went back to his table, finished his coffee, paid the check and strode out into the hot noon sun.

In her office at the TV station, Natalie De Barge was busy working on what could turn out to be the biggest story of her career, and it wasn't about Salli T. Turner. The lead had been handed to her by her news director, Garth, who had a loyal spy in the police department. She'd taken the small amount of information he'd given her and run with it.

Natalie was well aware that this was her big opportunity to get out of boring show-business gossip and into hard news. This was her chance to shine with a *real* story. She, Natalie De Barge, was about to become famous.

She'd been working on her story all night, and now she had it together in time for the noon news.

As she sat at her computer finishing up, Jimmy Sica, the good-looking news anchor with the dazzling smile, wandered over and stood behind her. "I hear you got a hot deal goin', babe," he said, rubbing her shoulders.

"That's right, Jimmy," she replied, shrugging his hands off her back.

"Y'know," he said casually, "Garth and I were talking, and although your story's kind of showbiz-related, he thought *I* should be the one to break it."

She turned around and stared up at him. "You've *gotta* be kidding. This is *my* story, Jimmy. *Mine*. I worked on this all damn night and all morning, and I am *not* giving it up to *anyone*."

"But it'll be stronger coming from me," Jimmy pointed out.

"What's *wrong* with Garth?" Natalie snapped, her eyes flashing major danger signals. "He didn't have the balls to tell me himself?"

"Guess he knew you'd be mad," Jimmy said weakly.

"Fuck him and fuck you, Jimmy," she said furiously. "I'm on air with this. Don't mess with me."

"No need to get nasty," he said, backing off, a hurt expression on his handsome face.

"If *you* had a great exclusive, wouldn't *you* be angry?"

"I'm only trying to be helpful."

She narrowed her eyes. "In what way?"

"You're not used to presenting hard news. You do the trivia—who's sleeping with whom—the Leonardo DiCaprio and Gwyneth Paltrow shit."

"Yes. And that's *exactly* what I'm trying to get away from. *This* is my opportunity."

"Okay, okay, don't get your panties caught up your butt," Jimmy said, rapidly backing off. "I'll tell Garth."

"Yeah, and while you're doing that, tell him the *next* time he has something to say to me, he can do it himself."

Jimmy mock-saluted. "Got it."

Natalie was fuming. She should've known that Garth wanted *her* to do the work, while Jimmy took all the glory. It was always that way.

But they weren't getting away with it this time. This story was *definitely* hers.

# chapter 9

"**I**'M COMPLETELY DIS-
armed," Madison said, brushing a lock of dark hair
out of her eyes.

They were sitting outside at Farmer's Market
eating Danish and sipping iced tea.

Freddie leaned across the small table. "What was
that?" he said.

She laughed, "I *said,* I'm completely disarmed by
you. You're nothing at all like your public image."

"Yes, but we'll keep that between us, won't we?"

"In everything I've read about you, you come
across as a cold power broker with a heart of stone.
A man who's only interested in mega deals. Are you
aware that everybody's scared of you? Yet here *I* am,
a journalist of all people, sitting here with you
having an exceptionally pleasant time."

"Glad to hear it," he said, sipping his iced tea. "As
I told you before, you caught me on a strange day."
For a moment he paused, staring reflectively into the
distance. "You see, yesterday I thought I wanted

nothing more to do with Max Steele. And today I keep thinking about how we both started out together, our close friendship, the way we built our agency from nothing. Max was the personality, I was the brains. Not that I'm saying Max doesn't have brains. He's a hard worker and street smart—qualities I admire."

"I only met him briefly," Madison said, remembering Max climbing into his pristine red Maserati with a big smile on his face. "However, I must say I liked him. He's a complete egomaniac, but an unabashed one—which gives him a certain amount of charm."

"How did you meet him?" Freddie asked curiously.

"My girlfriend's brother, Cole, arranged it so that we bumped into each other jogging. He knew I wanted to ask Max about you."

"And how does Cole know Max?"

"Cole's a personal trainer. In fact, I think he's worked *you* out a couple of times. Black guy, very good-looking."

"Diana hires the trainers."

"I get the picture. Your wife runs your personal life. You run the business."

He threw her one of his cold looks. "I can assure you, Madison, my personal life is all mine."

*Hmm,* she thought, *mustn't go too far; this is an interesting, complex man, and I should hold back.* "So far you haven't allowed me to put on my tape recorder," she said, hoping he might acquiesce. "Which means I have no interview."

"That's all right," Freddie said, taking another sip of iced tea. "As I told you before, we must get to know each other first before I subject myself."

"But this would be so perfect to write about," she said enthusiastically. "The real Freddie Leon. The man who actually bleeds if he's cut."

"Maybe it's the perfect interview for *you,*" he said evenly. "However, it is not quite the image *I* wish to present to the world."

She fixed him with a long look. "When *do* I get to put on my tape?"

"Maybe later in the week I'll take you to lunch and give you the official interview, the one I've never given before."

"Sounds good to me."

He offered a glimmer of a smile. "I'll tell you how Max and I started out, all about our first clients, the people we've dealt with over the years. I'll give you a good interview. But today I feel like forgetting about everything. You can understand that, can't you?"

"As a matter of fact, I *do* know how you feel," she said, nodding vigorously. "When Salli Turner got murdered I was in shock, and it's only been a couple of days."

"Was she a friend of yours?"

"An acquaintance. I'm going to her funeral later. Did *you* know her?"

He shook his head. "No."

She remembered Salli telling her about how she'd met Freddie in the underground garage of his building. Probably he was stalked by so many would-be actresses that he genuinely didn't remember.

"Where's the funeral?" he asked.

"Westwood," she replied. "Cole's taking me, he knew Salli pretty well."

"It seems Cole knows everyone."

"He does. And all their secrets, too. Sort of like you, although on a different level." She took a big bite of Danish; Freddie was right, it was delicious. "Who do *you* think murdered Salli?"

Freddie paused before answering. "Difficult to know with these girls," he said slowly. "They arrive in town with nothing but their looks and a whole lot of ambition. Then, if they're lucky, they make a little money, get a touch of fame, and that's when they all pick the wrong man. They're incapable of dating anyone with substance. I've seen it happen a thousand times. We have a girl at our agency, Angela Musconni. She's a wonderful young actress, yet there's something about her—something I know will eventually destroy her—one way or the other."

"Must be tough for you to watch. Can we talk about that?"

"Don't push it, Madison," he said shortly.

She pushed it anyway. "I was thinking of interviewing your secretary, maybe your wife, and some of your friends," she said. "Would that bother you?"

"When I'm ready, I'll give you the list of who you can talk to," he said abruptly.

"You're very controlling, Freddie."

"The secret of my success, Madison."

"Okay," she said, sighing. "The rules are yours, so I guess I'm going to have to play the game your way."

"Good. Because otherwise you'd be out of the ballpark."

An hour later he dropped her off in the underground parking garage at his building. "Call me tomorrow," he said.

"Will I get past the dreaded Ria?"

"If you're persistent."

"Gee, thanks."

She collected her car from the valet and drove home.

"Am I glad you're here," Cole said, greeting her at the door. "Natalie called—she's breakin' a big story on the noon news, wants me to tape it. You got any idea how to work this goddamn machine?"

"Put in a tape, and press Record."

"I don't have to set it?"

"C'mon, Cole—of course not. When you play it back, you merely fast-forward to where you want to go."

"Hey—very smart."

"What's Nat's story about?" Madison asked, opening the fridge and taking out a bottle of Evian.

"The Malibu blonde deal. She's been working it all night."

"What happened with Luther?" Madison asked, swigging from the bottle.

"She gave him up for her story."

"Natalie putting work before a guy? Now *that's* progress." They both laughed. "What time should we leave for Salli's funeral?"

"Soon as we've watched big Sis. We should get there early."

"Good."

"How'd it go with Freddie?"

"He's quite an amazing man," Madison said thoughtfully. "With a great deal of personal integrity."

Cole raised an eyebrow. "Never heard *that* about Freddie Leon. Around town they call him the Snake—y'know, he'll bite you soon as look at you."

"You're a cynic, Cole."

"Takes one to know one," he said, turning on the TV and fiddling with the tape machine.

"I have bad news," Madison said, flopping down on the couch. "The story hasn't broken yet, but Max Steele was shot in a robbery yesterday."

*"Whaaat?"*

"He's in intensive care. *Don't* spread the news; I was told in confidence."

"Anythin' we can do?"

"Guess not."

Cole shook his head and turned the sound up on the TV as Jimmy Sica appeared on screen and began reading the current news.

"Jimmy's one good-lookin' dude," he commented.

"And straight, too," Madison murmured dryly.

"A guy can fantasize, can't he?"

"Personally I think his brother Jake's more attractive. Jake doesn't realize how sexy and handsome he is. Jimmy does. He probably spends most of his life admiring himself in front of a mirror."

"That's 'cause he's on TV," Cole pointed out. "The dude *has* t'look good."

"Jake would get *my* vote any day."

"Gotta feelin' you're into him, huh?" Cole teased.

"We're friends, that's all," Madison said defensively. "As I told you last night, the man is taken."

"That, sugar pie, would *never* stop me," Cole said with a wicked grin.

"Hey, if a guy is bagged, it's okay with me—I can walk away."

Natalie appeared on screen. "The sister's lookin' fine!" Cole exclaimed proudly.

"She sure is," Madison agreed, impressed with Natalie's businesslike image: a black Armani suit with a white silk shirt, and no outrageous jewelry—Natalie's usual trademark.

"Good evening," Natalie said, poised and in control. "Natalie De Barge reporting." A short dramatic pause. "Hollywood. Land of dreams. A fantasy paradise where anything can happen, and sometimes does. Yesterday a young girl's body washed up on the Malibu shore. We were all quick to christen her the Malibu Mystery Blonde—after all, this *is* L.A., land of the instant sound bite, and we—the media—go with it every time. What could be better? A beautiful young blond female to titillate our thirst for the latest headline. But *our* Mystery Malibu Blonde has a name. She was nineteen-year-old Hildie Jane Livins from Idaho. Hildie came to L.A. three years ago, just like thousands of other young hopefuls with starry eyes and Hollywood dreams."

The camera cut to a medium shot of a plain-faced woman in a print dress standing outside a remote farmhouse. "Hilda was a good girl," the woman said. "I lived next door to her family going on thirteen years. She was a pretty little thing. Never gave no one no trouble. Minded her own business an' helped her mom around the house."

The camera cut back to Natalie. "In Hollywood Hildie tried to make it in show business. She got a job working as a checkout girl in a supermarket, attended acting class, and hung out with her friends who were also trying to make it. Mavis Ann Fenwick was Hildie's roommate for two years."

Cut to shot of a skinny brunette with a big ass. She was standing on a Hollywood street, dressed in shorts and a T-shirt. "Hildie was the coolest," Mavis Ann said, blinking nervously. "We always had fun, and when things weren't going good, she *never* complained." A manic giggle. "Once we lived on Campbell's soup for three solid weeks 'cause we couldn't afford nothin' else."

Camera back to Natalie in the studio. "Eventually the temptations of Hollywood lured Hildie into a life of decadence," Natalie continued. "This innocent young girl met a sophisticated worldly-wise woman who goes by the name of Darlene La Porte. Darlene's real name is Pat Smithins—a former convicted prostitute who has also been arrested several times for pandering. According to Mavis Ann and other friends of Hildie's, Darlene promised Hildie money and acting opportunities if she agreed to sleep with movie stars and rich men. Darlene, in fact, became Hildie's madam." A long pause. "Now Hildie is dead, murdered by drowning and dumped in the ocean to make it look like an accident. When we tried to reach Darlene La Porte for her comments, we were informed she had nothing to say. Tell *that* to Hildie's grieving parents."

*"Jesus!"* Cole exclaimed, leaping up. "Whaddya think?"

"I think it's damn good investigative reporting," Madison said. "I only hope she has plenty of hard facts to back up her story, because Darlene whatever her name is will have her lawyers crawling all over everyone."

Cole grabbed his jacket. "Come on," he said. "We got a funeral to attend."

# chapter 10

KRISTIN WAS DESPERATELY
trying to keep it together, but it was getting difficult.
She was naked and alone, locked in a boarded-up
room with no bathroom, she had no food or water,
and although she was desperately trying not to
panic, it had already occurred to her that maybe
Mister X might *not* return.

The thought sent tingles of fear up and down her
spine. Nobody knew where she was or with whom
she'd had a date. Mister X had booked her directly,
and like a fool—because she was upset and disappointed about the Jake situation and Max not keeping their appointment—she'd gone.

*Stupid little whore. You're getting what you deserve.*

She attempted to shut off the inner voice that
screamed in her head. The voice that always spoke
the painful truth.

The light seeping through the boarded-up window

was stronger now. It must be at least noon, she thought, and still there was no Mister X.

The sick degenerate son of a bitch. Her greed had led her to him. Her greed would be her downfall. And yet all she'd really wanted to do was make sure Cherie was taken care of. Was that so terrible?

Cherie. What would happen to her if Kristin wasn't there to pay the bills? Oh God! They'd switch off the machines keeping her alive. Oh God!

With a sudden burst of strength Kristin hurled herself against the door like she'd seen heroes do in movies.

It didn't budge. She wasn't a hero. She wasn't even a heroine. She was just a lonely whore locked in a room with an envelope filled with cash.

*I'm going to die in this room.* The thought seemed to hover over her like a black shroud.

She slumped to the floor. And then she screamed—a long, piercing wail of a scream.

But there was no one around to hear.

# chapter 11

CAPTAIN MARSH WAS yelling about the news story on the Mystery Malibu Blonde. "Where'd they get their information?" he shouted. "We only just identified the girl. How come they're on air with a full story before we gave out an official statement?"

Tucci shrugged. "I got a funeral to go to, Captain. Can we get into this when I come back?"

"No!" Marsh snarled. "Where's this Darlene woman? I want her questioned pronto."

"We've already contacted her lawyer. He's agreed to bring her in later to answer some questions. We had to put on the pressure. She apparently has . . . connections."

"Fuck this shit!" Marsh stormed. "Salli T. Turner. Now, this. I need some fuckin' arrests around here."

Tucci stifled a yawn. "Yes, sir."

"Where's Eccles?"

"Questioning the lap-dancers who flew back with Bobby Skorch."

"He would be," Captain Marsh growled.

Tucci glanced at his watch. "I don't want to be late—"

"Get the fuck outta here."

Tucci was only too glad to leave. He felt like crap. Hungry. Tired. Overworked. There'd been a spate of murders over the last month. He'd been lucky enough not to have pulled duty on any of them—but now this.

Faye said it was a good thing. "You'll solve them," she'd told him in a quietly confident voice. "You're the best."

It was nice to have a woman who believed in him all the way.

On his way to Salli T. Turner's funeral, he stopped at a Winchell's and bought three glazed chocolate donuts. Faye's disapproving face flashed into his brain. Jesus! It wasn't as if he'd had time for lunch. The donuts were in *place* of lunch—a poor substitute, but certainly better than nothing.

Meanwhile, in a luxury hotel on Sunset, Lee Eccles knocked on the door of Suite 300 and prepared to interview the two lap-dancers/strippers who'd flown to L.A. with Bobby Skorch. He'd tracked the limo driver, who told him where he'd deposited Bobby and the girls.

The two women answered the door together. Lee flashed his badge and informed them he was there on official business. They mentioned they were about to take off on a shopping spree, but at his insistence they reluctantly backed into the untidy suite and he followed them in.

Their names were Gospel and Tuscany, both

blondes, both stacked. Gospel, who was clad in a red cat suit with several gold crosses hanging round her neck and two giant crosses hanging from her ears, had long, straight hair down to her waist. She was stoned.

Tuscany, pneumatic body poured into a crotch-skimming leopard skin dress and hooker heels, had short bubble-cut hair.

"This won't take long," Lee said, checking out the spacious suite which was costing *somebody* a buck or two. "I only have a few questions."

"Don't you need a warrant t'do this?" Tuscany said, obviously the brighter of the two.

"Want me to get one?" Lee countered, shooting her his best "I'm a cop—get outta my face" look.

"If it's about that old guy in Vegas," Gospel interrupted, feigning outrage. "Wasn't *my* fault he had a heart attack. Dunno *why* his old cow of a wife is suing me. You from the insurance company?"

"No, he's not from the insurance company," Tuscany said irritably. "He's a cop. Didn't you see his badge?"

"Cop, insurance company—all the same to me," Gospel said, absentmindedly stroking her left nipple through the thin material of her cat suit.

"What do you want anyway?" Tuscany demanded, staring him in the eye.

Lee didn't answer for a moment. He was fantasizing about how they'd be girl on girl. Pretty raunchy if he knew his women. Yes, this was definitely a dynamic duo. "You flew into L.A. Saturday night with Bobby Skorch, is that right?" he asked, eyeballing Gospel's ample cleavage.

"Who told you that?" Tuscany said suspiciously, tugging down her leopard skirt.

"The Secret Service," Lee drawled sarcastically.

"Bobby said we weren't supposed to tell anybody," Gospel whined.

"Why you wanna know?" Tuscany demanded.

"Routine," Lee said. "Did Bobby give you money?"

"Whaddya think we are—hookers?" Gospel said, clearly insulted.

"Not at all," Lee said with a smirk. "I know you're two nice young ladies who simply happen to strip for a living—right? You make a buck here, a buck there. Why not? If you've got it, show it."

"We're good at what we do," Gospel said defensively. "That's why Bobby chose to fly *us* to L.A. with him, and not any of those other bitches."

"After you got off the plane Saturday night, what happened?" Lee asked. The limo driver had already told him he'd driven all three of them to the hotel, but he wanted to hear their version.

Gospel giggled. "What *didn't* happen?"

"You came directly to the hotel?"

"Yeah, we came straight here," Tuscany said. "So what?"

"Can you recall what time you arrived?"

"Dunno," Gospel said with a careless shrug. "Maybe seven or eight. We had a coupla shots, then Bobby hadda go out."

Tuscany shot her a warning look.

"He told us not to tell anybody that either," Gospel added lamely. "Said we was to say we were with him all night."

"Aren't you supposed to give us a warning or something?" Tuscany said. "You know, like one of those 'anything you say may be used as evidence against you' kinds of deals. That's what cops do in the movies."

"That's only if I'm planning on arresting you," Lee said. "Which I'm not."

"Ooh, good, I'm so relieved," Tuscany said sarcastically.

It was as if neither of them knew what was going on. "You *do* know about the murder?" he said, exasperated.

"What murder?" Gospel said, her eyes widening.

"Salli T. Turner."

"Horrible!" Gospel squeaked. "We watched some of the coverage stuff on TV."

"And you *do* know that Salli was Bobby Skorch's wife?"

Both girls went into dumb overdrive.

"Didn't know that," Tuscany said.

"Me neither," Gospel said.

"Didn't even know he was married," Tuscany added.

These girls were plain stupid, but then he hadn't expected a couple of Einsteins. "So, ladies," he said, "you'd better think *very* carefully about what you're about to tell me and be completely honest about it. Because otherwise, you girls could find yourself in a shit-load of trouble. Get it?"

# chapter 12

OUTSIDE PIERCE BROTHers cemetery in Westwood there was a line of limos and cars stretching for blocks. It was always that way at a celebrity funeral. In Hollywood, celebrity funerals were regarded as an event—people attended them to be seen; it validated their very existence.

Tucci bypassed the line, showing his badge to security, who waved him by. He'd devoured all three donuts on the way there, and now he felt bloated and guilty. If Faye knew what he'd eaten for lunch she'd kill him. *Maybe death's better than deprivation,* he thought with the shadow of a smile.

He fell in with the other guests entering the already overcrowded chapel. Although he was early, there were only a few places left. He recognized the journalist who had brought him the audiotape of Salli. She was sitting near the back, so he quickly slid in beside her.

"Good afternoon, Detective Tucci," Madison said, turning to give him a quick once-over.

He acknowledged her with a nod, unable to recall her name—which infuriated him because he was good at remembering names, although in the last few months this had happened to him several times. A couple of weeks ago he'd complained to Faye. His wife had prodded him gently in the stomach and said teasingly, or so he'd thought, "Alzheimer's. You're nearly fifty, you know."

Screw nearly fifty. He was forty-nine years old, he had another ten months to go before he was fifty. Sometimes Faye exhibited an uncharacteristic mean streak.

"Miss Castelli—Madison," he almost shouted, so happy was he to suddenly remember her name.

"Yes?" she said, startled.

"Uh . . . how did the piece you were about to write on Salli turn out?"

"I've done better," she said wryly.

"I'm sure it was excellent," he responded. "My wife raves about your work. Reads your magazine every month."

"Thank you," she said with a pleased smile.

Tucci considered Madison Castelli to be a very beautiful woman with her dark hair and almond-shaped eyes—not to mention her lips, which gave "seductive" a whole new meaning. Not that he was interested in other women, but he could look and admire, couldn't he?

He leaned forward to see who she was with.

"Hey, man," Cole said, noticing he was getting checked out. "How ya doin'?"

Tucci nodded briefly and leaned back. Then he began surveying the room, noting one famous face after the other. Faye would have a great time here; she loved stars and gossip, her one failing.

"This is so very sad," Madison sighed, shaking her head. "I still can't believe it."

"I know," he agreed.

"Do you have any leads?"

"We'll be making a statement soon."

"Was my tape helpful?"

"Yes, ma'am."

All of a sudden raucous, old-fashioned rock and roll began blaring through the speakers, silencing any further conversation. Mick Jagger. Metallica. Rod Stewart. Kiss.

Tucci thought his eardrums might burst. Funerals today—you couldn't trust 'em.

Eddie Stoner insisted they attend Salli's funeral, and Angie didn't argue. After all, she was in his bed again, why shouldn't she go along with what he wanted to do? If she'd been working, it might have saved her from falling back into his life, but her new movie didn't start shooting for six weeks so she had plenty of time to play.

Her immediate problem was Kevin. What to do about Kevin? By this time he must have realized something was amiss since she'd run out in the middle of the night. She knew she had to call him eventually, and she did so reluctantly when she was in the car on the way to the funeral. "Uh . . . listen, Kev," she said cheerfully when he answered. "Somethin' came up."

"Where the *fuck* have you been?" Kevin exploded; he sounded like he'd been waiting by the phone.

"I bumped into an old friend, and, uh . . . I won't be back 'til later."

"Later when?"

"Dunno," she said evasively.

"Hey—" he said furiously. "How about not bothering to come back at all?"

"Go screw yourself," she said, her temper rising. "It's my house, too. I paid half the money."

"Y'know, Angie, this isn't working for me," Kevin said grimly.

"Not working for *you,*" she said indignantly. *"I'm* the one who's checking out."

"Oh, you're leaving? Good. *I'll* keep the house."

"No freakin' way," she objected, her voice getting shriller by the minute. "We bought the house together, remember?"

"Tell you what," Kevin said, relieved to have this sudden escape hatch. "I'll call *my* lawyer, you call *yours*—let *them* work it out. Right now I don't want to see you here."

"You don't get it," Angie yelled. *"I* don't want to see *you* there. Anyway," she added, lowering her voice, suddenly remembering that Eddie was sitting right beside her. "I can't talk about it now. I'm on my way to Salli's funeral."

"Oh, your good friend Salli," Kevin jeered. "Isn't that the girl you used to nonstop trash?"

"Can't you speak well of the dead?" Angie said contemptuously.

"Goodbye," Kevin said, and hung up.

Eddie, who was pretending to concentrate on driving her Ferrari, stared straight ahead. "Problems?" he said, casually patting her on the knee.

"I was plannin' on dumpin' him anyway," Angie muttered. "His ego's bustin' out all over. The asshole's startin' to believe his own publicity. Jerk! Some people can't handle stardom."

"Not like you, huh?" Eddie said, tossing back his luxuriant mane of dirty blond hair.

"I handle it, ace," Angie boasted. "All these sexcrazed producers tryin' to jump me. Not that I'm exactly Miss Sex Symbol 1998, but they're horny dogs—they all wanna know if they can still get it up. Ha! Dumb old cockers—they pop Viagra with their morning coffee. Think gettin' a boner makes 'em more of a man."

"Now, now," Eddie said, laughing to himself. "Don't go gettin' bitter on me."

When the car turned off Wilshire Boulevard, Eddie immediately noticed a long line of limos ahead of them. "We should've taken a car and driver," he moaned. "This is gonna be a rat fuck."

"Thought you *wanted* to drive the Ferrari," Angie retorted, her mind still half focused on Kevin.

"I did," he said, opening the window, leaning out, and attracting the attention of a young Hispanic traffic cop. "Hey, excuse me, friend. I've got Angela Musconni in the car. She's tryin' to avoid gettin' mobbed or set upon by the photographers. Anything you can do for us?"

"Sure, man," the cop said, attempting to peer into the passenger seat and take a good look at Angie, whom he'd recently seen in a movie where she'd strutted around half naked. "Leave your car. I'll get a parking valet to take it. You can sneak her in through the back."

" 'Preciate it," Eddie said.

"Very smooth," Angie said, jumping out of the car.

"Yeah, well, don't see why my darling should wait around," said Eddie. Then he leaned over and gave her a long, slow French kiss.

Angie surfaced with a stupid grin on her face.

It was great being back with Eddie, especially now that *she* was in the boss position.

# chapter 13

"I'M SUING EVERY SINGLE stinking one of them. I'm suing that black bitch, *and* the TV station, and anyone else who dares cross me."

"Calm down," said Darlene La Porte's lawyer, Linden Masters, a tall man with piercing blue eyes and a distinguished white beard. Linden had an air of respectability about him, which went down well with judges, considering he represented some of the most notorious people in Hollywood, including Darlene, who'd come to him when she'd grown tired of using cut-price lawyers, and had realized that paying for the best got her the services she required.

"That bitch practically accused me of *killing* Hildie," Darlene fumed. "I know *nothing* about it."

"Which is exactly why we're visiting the police station later today," Linden said in an irritatingly calm voice. "You'll tell them you don't know anything, after which they'll leave you alone. Cooperation is the key. If you avoid speaking to them, Darlene, they'll think you have something to hide."

"What do you mean?" she asked crossly.

Linden pulled on his beard. *"Did* you send Hildie out to meet a client?"

"No," Darlene said, pacing up and down the thick pile carpet in her luxurious living room.

"You're sure? Because if you did, you'd better tell *me.* As your lawyer I'm here to protect you. And if you're concealing any evidence at all . . ."

"Oh, God, Linden," she said, collapsing into an overstuffed armchair. "Of course I'm not." What she really wanted to say was "Yes, I sent her out with the one client I know nothing about. He calls himself Mister X. I hear from him only occasionally. He pays big bucks. All cash. The girls think he's weird, but he's never done any of them harm." But, of course, she said no such thing.

"Good," Linden said.

Darlene jumped up and walked over to the large picture window overlooking Wilshire Boulevard. She gazed out, watching the cars race by at great speed. For a moment her mind drifted back to a year ago and Kimberly. She'd fixed Kimberly up with a client. That client was Mister X. A week later the girl's body was fished out of the ocean.

In her mind Darlene had always refused to connect the two, imagining Kimberly had gone off with her friends *after* her appointment with Mister X, and died or been murdered at one of the drug parties she always hung out at. Now this.

"I *help* these girls," she said, speaking rapidly. "If I wasn't around to supervise their lives they'd be out on the street or mud wrestling in some seedy place by the freeway. *I* save them from themselves. Thanks to me they live in nice apartments, wear beautiful clothes. I'm *good* for them."

"You don't have to tell me," Linden said, sure that Darlene believed her own lies. But as long as she paid his exorbitant bills, what did *he* care?

"What will this do to my reputation?" she wailed, turning toward him. *"Can* I sue? I have no desire to become another Heidi Fleiss."

"There's not much chance of that," Linden said. "They caught Heidi on alleged tax evasion. You *pay* your taxes."

"Yes, yes, I'm a good citizen," Darlene said, convincing herself that she was. "I own a successful flower shop, which is where my income comes from. And I pay plenty of taxes. *Plenty.* Now my reputation has been besmirched and I want retribution."

"Don't worry," Linden said. "We'll get it. But you've got to remember, Darlene, you *do* have a record, and that's *not* in your favor."

"Dammit, Linden," she snapped. "I pay you a lot of money to keep my reputation clean."

"I'll be back to fetch you in two hours," Linden said, anxious to escape her bad mood. "In the meantime, don't speak to anyone. No public comments. Tell your service to handle all calls."

"Very well."

Darlene saw Linden to the door and went into her bedroom. Hildie had been such a sweet, fun-loving girl, almost innocent in a way. *Why* had she sent her out with Mister X? She knew the man was a pervert. Why hadn't she chosen one of her more sophisticated girls? Then she remembered, it was Kristin he'd wanted.

Impulsively she went to the phone and dialed Kristin's number. The maid informed her she was out. "I need to speak to her urgently, Chiew," Darlene said.

"I sorry," Chiew replied. "Miss Kristin no come home last night. I worried. No message, nothing."

"Didn't come home?" Darlene said, panic suddenly rising. It wasn't like Kristin to vanish without leaving word where she was—she always made sure she was reachable in case there was an emergency concerning her sister. "Do you know where she went?" Darlene asked, attempting to remain unruffled.

"No, ma'am. A gentleman called. Jake Sica. When she come back, he want her to phone him at hotel."

"Give me his number," Darlene said abruptly. "And when she does come home, have her call me immediately."

Darlene looked at the number as she put down the phone. She had a bad feeling, a very bad feeling. Who was this Jake? Kristin didn't go out unless it was business. She'd confided to Darlene that she had no need of a personal life, all that concerned her was making enough money to take care of her sister.

Picking up the phone, Darlene quickly called the number. It was a hotel. "Jake Sica," she said, trying to get her mind around the name which sounded vaguely familiar.

He answered on the first ring.

"I understand you're looking for Kristin," Darlene said.

Jake immediately recognized the woman's distinctive voice from Kristin's answering machine. "Who's this?" he asked.

"It doesn't matter who I am. Do you know where Kristin is?"

"You're her madam, aren't you?"

*"Excuse* me?"

"I was there when you called on her machine. You wanted her to meet a Mister X. You said he'd pay her a lot of money."

"Who the hell are you?" Darlene screeched, blowing her usual cool.

"Somebody who cares about her."

"If you care about her so much, how come you don't know where she spent last night?"

"Not that it's any of your business, but we got into a fight because of your message. Now I'm looking for her, too."

Darlene slammed the phone down. She wasn't about to get involved. This could only lead to trouble.

Lurking outside the bedroom, Junia Ladd, Darlene's significant other, had been listening to the conversation with her ear pressed close to the door. Junia, a pointy-faced girl of eighteen, with delicate ivory skin and wispy fair hair, had been Darlene's live-in lover for eighteen months, ever since Darlene had rescued her from a juvenile detention center.

Junia enjoyed the luxury of living with Darlene, but sometimes she had to break free, and when she did, she needed extra money. Making something on the side was most desirable, because although Darlene was generous, she always had to know exactly how Junia spent her money. Junia could go into Sak's or Neiman's and charge whatever she wished, but if Darlene suspected she was out spending her money on grass or coke, she threw a nasty fit.

Sometimes Junia stole the odd hundred from Darlene's Prada purse when she thought she could get away with it. Other times she tried to do people favors in return for cash. Giving Mister X Kristin's number was a favor for which she'd gotten paid five hundred bucks. Luckily Darlene had been in the bathroom when she'd answered the phone. It was Mister X tracking Kristin. He must have sensed Junia was someone he could manipulate, because the first thing he'd said was "Give me Kristin's home number and I'll pay *you* five hundred bucks."

"How do I know you'll do that?" Junia had said, glancing at the bathroom door, making sure that Darlene was not about to emerge.

"Go downstairs in an hour. The hall porter will have an envelope with your name on it. The money will be there. Leave another envelope with Kristin's number for me. Mark it 'Mr. Smith.' "

"Okay," Junia had said. "Only don't you *dare* tell Darlene."

The deal had taken place on Saturday. Now with all this stuff going on about Hildie getting murdered and Mister X being involved and Kristin not coming home all night, Junia had the shakes. She wondered if she should confess to Darlene what she'd done.

No, she couldn't. She was too scared. Darlene had a vicious temper, and Junia didn't want to get thrown back onto the streets. She liked her setup. She even liked the dyke action, although that wasn't to say she was totally gay. Junia swung both ways, considering it prudent to keep one's options open.

Then she thought again about Kristin, whom she really liked because Kristin was a genuinely nice person, unlike Darlene's other girls, who were mostly stuck-up pieces of work Junia didn't get along with at all.

She could hear Darlene banging about in the bedroom. This was probably not a good time to tell her about Mister X's phone call, but Junia realized she'd better do something.

She ventured into the bedroom.

"Goddamn it!" Darlene screeched. "How *dare* the cunt drag me into this murder investigation. I'm suing her black ass right off television. You'll *never* see *her* again."

Darlene was on one of her rants. Once she got going there was no stopping her until she'd gotten satisfaction one way or another. Darlene, who presented a calm and sophisticated public image, was actually a raving bitch. However, over the eighteen months they'd been together, Junia had learned how to handle her moods.

"I am *not* happy," Darlene said ominously. "And I look like shit. I'm going to change." She stalked into her dressing room.

Junia hurried over to the notepad next to the phone. Darlene had a habit of writing everything down, and sure enough, there was the name of the guy she'd been talking to about Kristin—Jake Sica—and a number.

Junia didn't know what to do. It wasn't like she was a Good Samaritan or anything, but how could she sit back and do nothing? Hildie had been murdered, and indirectly it was probably Darlene's fault.

She was sure Darlene didn't remember, but one night about six months ago she'd gotten drunk on a bottle of Cristal, and under the covers she'd confided to Junia the story of Kimberly and her connection to Mister X.

Junia had listened and said nothing. The next morning Darlene seemed completely oblivious to her ramblings of the previous night, and it was never mentioned again.

If Darlene went to jail, did that mean that she, Junia, would be left in the apartment with all the money and clothes and stuff?

Yes! She'd be the official custodian while Darlene was locked away. Wow! Not too bad a job.

Then reality hit. That's not the way it would work. No, she'd be thrown out quick as shit. She'd have nothing.

Surreptitiously she copied down Jake's phone number and slid it into the pocket of her jeans.

"Hey, Darl," she yelled through to the dressing room. "Want me to go to the cop station with you?"

"Are you *serious?*" Darlene said, marching back into the bedroom wearing a La Perla bronze lace slip on her well-toned body. "*You,* my dear, will stay out of this. Let us not forget where I found you. So I suggest for the next few weeks you keep a very low profile indeed. In fact, I don't even want you answering the phone. Let the service pick up."

"It's not like I have anybody calling me," Junia grumbled. "You don't allow me any friends."

"That's not fair," Darlene said sharply. "We live a different kind of lifestyle than other people. You're happy just to be with me, aren't you?"

Junia wanted to say, "No, you're twenty-three years older than me, and we've got nothing in common."

But she didn't. She knew she was living a cushy life, and she wasn't about to blow it.

At least not until she was good and ready.

# chapter 14

$T$HE FAMILY ENTERED FROM
a private room in the back and filed into the first
pew. They were led by the bereaved husband,
Bobby Skorch, who was heavily sedated or maybe
stoned—he could barely keep his balance. Bobby
was clad in an ankle-length black leather coat and
dark shades; his long, greasy, black hair was pulled
back in a tight ponytail. He was smoking a cigarette.

Behind him came Salli's father, a short stout man
with a carrot-color crew cut and a nervous tic. And
then followed two very young, fair-haired girls—
pretty in an unsophisticated way. They were Salli's
half sisters. Their mother, an overweight woman
wearing too much makeup and an unsuitable shiny
blue satin cocktail dress, trailed closely behind
them. And finally Grandpa, an old man with a wily
gait, wearing a shabby, ill-fitting brown suit.

Tucci's attention was on Bobby, the grieving husband, who'd been spotted last night picking up a girl

on Sunset and taking her to a hotel. *Some grieving husband,* he thought. Hmm . . . he couldn't wait to hear Lee's report on the two strippers.

The more he thought about it, the more he was beginning to target Bobby Skorch as his prime suspect.

"That's Angela Musconni with Salli's ex," Cole said, nudging Madison.

She took a peek at the exquisite young woman who was walking in from the side door accompanied by a wild-looking guy with a mass of dirty blond hair. Salli had obviously harbored a penchant for guys who resembled out-of-control rock-'n'-rollers.

"So that's Eddie," Madison said in a low voice. "Salli talked about him on the tape, said he used to beat her."

"I told you that," Cole said. "Hadda make the hospital run a coupla times myself. In fact, Eddie and I duked it out one day."

"You did?"

"Yeah. I kinda got on him 'bout the way he was treatin' Salli, an' he called me a fag. So I beat the crap outta him." Cole laughed at the memory. "The dude deserved it. Treats women like shit."

"Do you think he could've murdered her?" Madison asked.

"Wouldn't surprise me."

She watched as Eddie and Angela sat down, noticing that as soon as they were settled, Angela began running her hands through the back of Eddie's hair and cooing in his ear. Obviously they were a couple.

Then Madison's attention was drawn to talk show host Bo Deacon, whom she'd met on the flight to L.A. It was only a few days ago, but it seemed like months had passed. Bo made a noisy entrance, demanding seats in front. He was with a zaftig redhead in her forties who clung to his arm as if she expected him to make a daring escape at any moment.

"Bo was coming on to Salli on the plane—or trying to," she whispered to Cole. "Only Salli wasn't buying his bullshit."

"Another slimeball," Cole said.

"You know everybody."

"In my job—sure. I'm kinda like a shrink or a barman—my clients spill the goods."

"You trained Bo?"

"For about three months. He's a lazy son-of-a-bitch. Didn't wanna work it, then blamed me 'cause he continued to put on the pounds. So he fired me. *That* was the luckiest day of my life. He had hot and cold running women *and* a wife—a jealous wife."

"Charming."

"I used to work him out in his dressing room at the studio. There were all these little interns running in and out. His deal was to fuck 'em an' fire 'em."

Madison sighed. "Aren't there *any* nice guys in Hollywood?"

"Me."

"I mean nice *straight* guys."

"Hey—didn't you know?" Cole said with a big grin. "Straight guys are a dying breed."

"Thanks!"

* * *

"Why are we here?" Mrs. Bo Deacon demanded. Her name was Olive, and she was a former show-girl.

"Out of respect," Bo growled, wishing his wife would shut up. She was drunk as usual; he'd caught her slurping straight Scotch behind the bar at their house before they'd left for the funeral. "If I *wasn't* here, people would talk. Salli was on my show countless times."

*I bet that wasn't all she was on,* Olive thought with a hidden scowl. Did her cheating no-good husband think she didn't know what he was up to? If it wasn't for the children, and the glory of being married to a famous man, she would have left him years ago.

"I hope you don't expect me to go to the recep-tion," Olive said, her overly glossed lips turning down at the corners. "Salli T. Turner was nothing more than a cheap tramp."

"How can you say that at her funeral for cris-sakes?" Bo objected, glancing around to make sure no one had heard.

"Because it's true," Olive hissed. "And I for one am not turning her into a saint now that she's dead."

"You're a real bitch, Olive," he said, getting a strong whiff of the Scotch on her breath.

"Yes, and don't you love it. *That's* why you married me."

*No,* he thought, *I married you because you had big tits and you were sexy as all get-out, and like a dumb schmuck I thought you'd stay that way.*

Unfortunately, now Olive was about as sexy as a

sack of old beans. Plus she was a true lush, and however many times she promised him she'd stop drinking, it never happened. Two stays at the Betty Ford Clinic and it *still* didn't happen.

She muttered something to him. He wasn't listening; he was too busy waving at everyone in sight. He'd found, over the fifteen years that he and Olive had been married, that the only way to deal with her when she'd been drinking was to ignore her. Sometimes it actually worked.

By the time Natalie arrived in Westwood it was too late to get anywhere near the funeral. The crowds were huge. She located her camera crew and took up a position with them behind the ropes. The trick was to catch the celebrities on their way back to their cars. Some would speak to her. Some wouldn't. After all, this wasn't exactly a big movie premiere. This was a funeral—a hot funeral.

Natalie was on a high. Her story had gone over big; even Garth was pleased. This could be the start of a whole new direction for her, and it was about time. She was ready. She'd been ready since college.

The widower in the black leather coat leaned back on the hard wooden bench and let his tears flow as he listened to Mick Jagger screaming out "Satisfaction." He'd personally picked every track. They were not Salli's favorite songs, they were his. *He* was the one who'd been left behind. *He* was the goddamn survivor, so *he* could choose the music.

Nobody could see his tears, because his heavy black Ray-Bans concealed the action.

He swiped a hand across his cheeks, destroying

any evidence of vulnerability. On the back of his hand there were two words tattooed through a blazing heart. *Salli Forever.*

And while Mick Jagger continued to yell out "Satisfaction," Bobby continued to wail his silent scream of unbearable pain.

# chapter 15

STRUGGLING TO KEEP IT together, Kristin decided that lying on the floor and feeling sorry for herself was not going to help her situation. She was trapped—that much was obvious. She was naked, which made her even more vulnerable. And she was determined to survive this ordeal. She had to, for Cherie's sake.

She got up and took a long, deep breath. Then she went over to the small bed and frantically ripped off the one sheet. Holding it taut, she punched a hole in it with her fist, and then forced her head through the opening. Next she punched out two more holes for her arms and ripped off the bottom. Now she was wearing some kind of tentlike poncho, but at least she wasn't naked.

Next she inspected the wooden bed, dragging the sagging mattress onto the ground. The bed frame stood several inches off the floor, supported by four sturdy legs. Using all her strength she managed to tip the frame sideways. She inspected the legs closely. Yes! They screwed into the base. If she could dismantle the legs, she would have several formidable weapons to use on Mister X when he came back.

She needed a screwdriver—but where was she going to get *that?*

Easy. She still had her jewelry. A ring. Small stud earrings. A Saint Christopher medal that she never took off.

Unclasping the chain on her pendant, she worked with the small gold circle, slowly but surely loosening the first leg.

The feeling of triumph when it finally came off was intoxicating.

After a few minutes of rest, armed with the small but lethal weapon, she made a pass at the window, giving it a hearty whack. The glass shattered—which really got her adrenaline going, so much so that she hardly felt the shard of glass which cut across her arm. The pain meant nothing. Determination meant everything.

Brushing the broken glass out of her way, she went to work on the boards covering the window. Using the wooden leg as a battering ram, she attacked the middle board, using every ounce of strength she could muster. For a while she thought it wasn't going to give, but after half an hour of solid slamming, the board finally began to sag in the middle, causing her to strengthen her attack, even though she was dripping with perspiration and quite exhausted.

The small room was like a sweatbox with very

little air. Outside she could hear the pounding of the ocean. Where was she? she wondered.

And where was Mister X?

What was his devious plan? Was it murder?

Because if it was, he'd chosen the wrong victim.

# chapter 16

THE FUNERAL SERVICE seemed never-ending. Many people insisted on speaking, including Salli's agent, her manager, her publicist, her female and male costars from the television series, and finally her father—who mumbled a few almost unintelligible words, so intense was his grief. Bobby Skorch said nothing.

After the ceremony there was an air of frenzy. Everyone was up and socializing. The crowds outside were enormous, and as the celebrities filed out of the chapel, screams from nearby fans filled the air. Three or four helicopters hovered overhead, photographers were balanced in trees with telephoto lenses, while the cops went crazy trying to get everyone safely into their cars and limos and out of there.

Madison stood outside with Cole, getting jostled on all sides. "This is quite a scene," she commented, looking around in amazement.

"It sure is," Cole agreed. "And I want out."

That was easier said than done, though, since they

were caught in human gridlock as everyone vied to get their cars first.

Somebody accidentally shoved Madison in the back. She turned around to object and came face-to-face with Bo Deacon. He looked at her as if he knew her, but couldn't quite remember from where.

"Mr. Deacon," she said. "Madison Castelli. Remember—we met on the plane a few days ago? You, me and Salli."

"What's that?" he said, attempting to back away, which was impossible because of the mass of people.

"On the plane, flying in from New York."

He moved backward, his wife moved forward. "I'm Mrs. Deacon," Olive announced coldly. "Who did you say you are, dear?"

"Madison Castelli. Your husband and I flew in from New York together. He wanted to sit next to Salli, so I changed seats. It's such a terrible tragedy, isn't it?"

Olive shot her husband a filthy look. "You wanted to sit next to Salli, huh?" she sneered as if she'd caught him jerking off in Times Square.

"For five minutes," Bo blustered. "I had some business to discuss with her."

"What kind of business?"

"Nothing important."

"You make me *sick.*"

"Be quiet, Olive," Bo said, desperately gesturing to the valet. "Bring me my damn car at once. Don't you know who I am?"

Madison wondered what was going on with Bo and his wife. He appeared to be extremely agitated. And she was quite obviously drunk. A delightful couple.

Before she could wonder any further, Bobby emerged, surrounded by Salli's family. People fell back, making a path for him through the crowds. Salli's two little half sisters were crying, overcome with emotion. Their mother kept on urging them to be quiet.

"They shouldn't bring kids to something like this," Cole muttered. "Look at 'em, they're all confused. Probably never been out of Idaho before."

Salli's father was openly sobbing, tears rolling down his face.

A lone photographer managed to dart through security and started snapping pictures of the family.

Two guards leaped forward and grabbed him by the shoulder, smashing his camera to the ground. "You fuckers!" the photographer shouted. "I'm only doing my job."

Madison turned away in time to see Eddie Stoner pushing his way through the mob, dragging Angela Musconni behind him. Eddie was heading directly for Bobby, a purposeful look in his eye. "You did it, didn't you?" he yelled belligerently as he drew closer. "You . . . freakin' . . . did it."

Bobby refused to acknowledge him, but everyone else turned to gape unashamedly.

"C'mon—admit it! You motherfuckin' hypocrite," Eddie screeched. "You killed my Salli."

Bobby finally focused. "You talking to me?" he snapped. "You cowardly piece of dog shit."

"Yeah, it's *you* I'm talkin' to," Eddie responded, thrusting out his jaw.

The two little girls clung to their mother, terrified by the two angry men.

"Don't do this," Salli's father begged, tears

streaming down his weathered cheeks. "Please don't make a scene."

"Make a scene?" Eddie shouted bitterly. "I'm gonna bash his freakin' face in."

Angie grabbed his arm. "Let's get out of here, Eddie," she urged. "This isn't doing you any good."

Eddie was on a roll. He shrugged her off, almost causing her to lose her balance. Then he threw a wild punch, cutting Bobby above the eye with his pinkie ring, and knocking off his dark glasses, which fell to the ground and shattered.

Bobby let out a roar of pain and fury and swung back. Before anyone could intervene, the two of them were embroiled in a vicious fistfight.

Paparazzi sprung out from everywhere, flashing away with their cameras, elbowing each other for the best position. The helicopters overhead hovered even lower. Several security guards leaped forward, intent on separating the two men—so intent that they forgot about controlling the media.

"Oh, God! I can't stand it. This is turning into a circus," Madison gasped.

"We'd better get our asses outta here," Cole responded, taking her by the arm. "We'll pick up the car later."

Half of her wanted to go, and the other half wanted to stay. There was a big story taking place right in front of her and she knew she had to cover it. "No," she said. "I have to see what happens."

"Somebody's gonna get hurt, that's what'll happen," Cole said, still attempting to pull her away.

Two of the guards had Eddie in a lock, with both his arms twisted behind him.

Bobby took the opportunity to smash his fist into

Eddie's face. There followed the sound of teeth breaking and then blood began spurting.

"Leave him alone, you crazoid freak!" Angie screamed, jumping on Bobby and pummeling him with her fists. Bobby hauled back, shaking her off and then hitting her on the jaw. She dropped like a stone.

"Jesus!" Cole groaned. "Now I *gotta* get into it." And he went for Bobby, wrestling him to the ground.

Pandemonium reigned. Women were screaming. Men shouting and swearing. Like a swarm of mosquitoes the photographers were everywhere. And the TV news crews, sensing blood, broke ranks and added to the chaos.

In his struggle to get out of the way, Bo Deacon was accidentally hit in the face by a security guard. "My nose," he yelled. "You idiot! You've broken my fucking nose."

"Serves you right for coming here," Olive muttered.

"Get me to a fucking plastic surgeon," Bo screamed. "And shut the fuck up!"

There was not enough security to control what was going on. The entire aftermath of the funeral was turning into some kind of crazed celebrity riot.

And there was absolutely nothing anyone could do.

By the time Tucci made it to the scene, everybody was involved. Quickly taking in the situation, he shoved his way through the crowds, grabbing Cole off Bobby—who now had a bloody nose as well as a gash over his left eye. Tucci summoned the help of a couple of cops.

Angie staggered to her feet. "I want that man arrested!" she screamed, pointing an accusing finger at Bobby. "The prick assaulted me. I want him arrested."

"Go fuck yourself, cunt!" Bobby responded.

"You *dumb* asshole!" Angie screamed. "Look what you've done to Eddie. Look at him!"

Eddie could hardly talk. He was sitting on the ground with blood gushing from his mouth; two of his front teeth were missing.

Tucci took control of the situation. "You'd all better come to the station," he said. "We'll sort it out there."

"You bet!" Angie yelled, pointing at Bobby. "I'm suing his ass! We're pressing charges."

Meanwhile the cameras captured every exquisite, celebrity moment.

# chapter 17

"**A**RE YOU JAKE?" JUNIA said.

"Who wants to know?" Jake asked, cradling the phone.

"You interested in hearing about Kristin?"

"Where is she?" he asked, jumping to attention.

"You got money?"

"What is this—a shakedown?"

"I know stuff about Kristin you'll want to hear. But I gotta get paid for my information, 'cause if I give it up, I'll have to scoot outta town."

"How *much* money?"

"How much you got?"

"This conversation is dumb—I don't even know who you are."

"Your girlfriend could be in danger."

"What kind of danger?"

"You read about that blonde found dead in the ocean? It could've been Kristin."

"Who *are* you?"

"If you've got ten thousand dollars, we can meet. If you don't, forget it."

"Where am *I* going to come up with ten thousand dollars?"

"Not my problem."

"You sound like a crazy person."

"Insults make me want to hang up."

"Okay, okay, I'll meet you," he said, deciding that the smart thing to do was to find out what this was about. After all, if Kristin was in trouble, he wanted to help.

"And you'll bring cash?"

"Yes," he lied impatiently. "Where do we meet?"

"There's a restaurant, Chin Chin, on Sunset Plaza. I'll be at a table outside. Be there in an hour."

"How will I know you?"

"I'm wearing an orange sweater. And don't blow it—if you want Kristin safe, you'd better bring the money."

Jake put down the phone, his mind in turmoil. What in hell was going on here? And what could *he* do?

First of all, he'd hardly brought any money to L.A. with him—six or seven hundred dollars at the most. His bank was in Arizona, and there was no way he could make a withdrawal that size today. And who was the mystery person on the phone? It certainly wasn't the woman who'd called Kristin's answering machine—this woman sounded much younger.

Quickly realizing he needed help, he picked up the phone and called his brother at the TV station. Jimmy wasn't there, so he tried him at home and got his wife.

"Jakie—we miss you," Bunny cooed. "When are you coming to dinner again?" She'd obviously forgotten the petulant fit she'd thrown the last time he was there.

"Tell Jimmy to call me as soon as possible," he said, hanging up and pacing furiously around the room.

What next? he wondered. Suddenly he thought of Madison. She was an intelligent woman and a journalist. She was also the only friend he had in L.A. Hoping that she'd have some ideas, he called her.

"Hi, Jake," Madison said breathlessly. "I just walked in. You're not going to *believe* what happened at Salli's funeral. Put on your TV, I'm sure it'll be all over the four-o'clock news."

"There's something urgent I have to discuss with you," he said. "Can I come by?"

"Of course."

"See you in a minute," he said, grabbing his leather jacket and racing downstairs, stopping at the desk to tell them where he'd be. Then he jumped in his truck and drove over.

Madison greeted him at the door. "You sounded like it's something important."

"It is," he said grimly.

"Come in and tell me everything. You remember Cole, don't you?"

"Yeah—hi, Cole," he said. "Uh . . . Madison, this is kind of private. Can we talk somewhere quiet?"

"Hey, man, you caught me on my way out," Cole said. "I got appointments backed up, an' they're all gettin' pissed at me, 'cause since *this* lady hit town I never get anythin' done. It's more of a kick hangin' with her."

"Didn't mean to be rude," Jake said.

"No sweat," Cole said, kissing Madison on the cheek. "She'll tell you all about our insane funeral experience. It's a story, man."

"Can I get you anything to drink?" Madison asked as soon as Cole left. "Seven-Up? Evian? Pellegrino? We've got it all."

He shook his head and sat down. Madison looked great as usual, and she seemed to be free of complications. Why couldn't he have met *her* first? "Remember I told you about a woman I was seeing?"

"Kristin, wasn't that her name?"

"Yeah, well . . . I did what you suggested and tried calling her. She wasn't there, and, according to her maid, she didn't come home last night. Which I guess, considering the business she's in, is not unusual. However, she *still* hasn't gotten home, and a short while ago I got a weird call from some girl who informs me Kristin's in danger, and if I meet her and hand over ten thousand bucks, she'll fill me in."

"You're kidding?"

He shrugged. "No, although I thought *she* was. That's exactly how I felt. I mean I know L.A.'s got a crazy reputation, but this has to be a bad joke, right?"

"Let me get this straight," Madison said, frowning. "Kristin didn't come home last night. You haven't spoken since you walked out on her. Now you've got this person calling, demanding money."

"That's about it. She mumbled something about a dead blonde in the ocean."

"Oh, God!"

"What?"

"Did you happen to watch Natalie on the news today?"

"No."

"She had a story on the blonde. She was a call girl—worked for a madam called Darlene. Does that name mean anything to you?"

"Darlene? No."

"Wait a minute," Madison said, thinking fast. "Do you have Kristin's number?"

"Yeah."

"Give it to me, I've got an idea."

"Hey, listen, we don't have time. I'm supposed to meet my mystery caller at Chin Chin in an hour—which," he said, glancing at his watch, "is now in about half an hour."

"Let me try this first," Madison said, punching out the number. Chiew answered the phone. "I'm looking for Kristin," Madison said.

"Madam not here," Chiew said.

"Is she at Darlene's?"

"No," Chiew said. "Don't know where."

"Damn!" Madison said. "I owe her money. What's Darlene's number? I'm in my car and don't have it with me."

Chiew gave her the number.

Madison hung up. "I want you to take a look at something," she said to Jake.

"I gotta get going," he said impatiently.

Madison pushed Natalie's videotape into the VCR and began playing it for him. "I think Darlene could be your girlfriend's madam, too," she said.

"And I have a feeling that whoever you're supposed to meet is right. Kristin might be in trouble."

"Shit!"

Madison jumped up. "C'mon, Jake," she said firmly. "I'll go with you. Between us, we'll find out exactly what's going on."

# chapter 18

LATER IN THE DAY, WHEN Max showed definite signs of improvement, Diana had him moved out of intensive care and into a private suite. He was conscious and well aware of the fact that she was sitting beside him, holding his hand.

"How are you feeling?" she asked anxiously.

"Like I had a battle with a rhinoceros," he groaned. "What happened to me?"

"You got shot."

"Shot?" he said, managing a laugh. "Who did it— a dissatisfied actress?"

"The police would like you to try and identify some mug shots when you're ready."

He sighed. "Oh, yeah, yeah, I *really* feel like doin' that. Y'know, identify some gang member who's gonna come back and cream my ass. I think not." He struggled to sit up, wincing with pain. "Hey, how come *you're* here?"

419

"I came as soon as I heard. I stayed with you all night."

"That's nice of you."

"It's more than nice, Max. I think you must know how I—"

Before she could finish her sentence, the door opened and Freddie strode in. "Well," Freddie said. "What kind of a situation did you get yourself into this time?"

"I've done worse, haven't I?" Max said, grinning weakly.

Freddie gave a dry laugh. "A lot worse. The good thing is that you're okay. Has Diana been looking after you?"

"She's the best," Max said. "Thanks for the loan."

"With my compliments," Freddie said, infuriating Diana.

An attractive black nurse entered the room. "Everything all right, Mr. Steele?"

"Perfect."

"Ring if you need me."

"Not bad," Max said as the pretty nurse retreated.

"Congratulations," Freddie said. "Diana told me you're engaged. Who's the unlucky lady?"

Max struggled to figure out what Freddie was talking about, then it started to come back to him. Kristin. Hadn't he told her to come to his house? Oh God, was she going to laugh when she heard *this* one. Maybe an engagement wasn't such a good idea after all, although it might stop Diana, who had been about to say something intimate when Freddie arrived. Yes, he'd be wise to keep the story going. "I'm engaged to a beautiful girl called Kristin," he said. "You haven't met her, but you will."

"Where is she?" Freddie said, turning to Diana with a questioning expression.

"I tried calling her," Diana explained. "The phone was answered by a woman called Darlene who was extremely rude."

Max knew exactly what must have happened—Diana had connected with Kristin's madam. He choked back a laugh. Thank God she hadn't put it together. "Oh, yeah," he mumbled. "Darlene's her cousin. Sometimes she stays there."

"Give me Kristin's number and I'll phone her personally," Freddie said. "Can't wait to see the woman who's hooked *you.*"

"Don't want to worry her," Max said.

"She must be worried anyway," Freddie said. "Not hearing from you."

"To tell you the truth," Max lied, "she was so happy we got engaged that she went to visit her family in San Diego. I guess that's why you couldn't reach her, Diana. She'll be back in a few days, so let's not worry her for now."

"If that's the way you want it," Freddie said.

"That's the way . . ." Max said, feeling sleep creeping up on him.

"Is there anything I can do?" Freddie asked.

"Yeah," Max said, grimacing. "Tell me all is forgiven. I was a schmuck."

"I think we've both realized we're a team," Freddie said gravely. "I'm taking the rest of the day off. If you need anything, Ria can reach me."

"Where are you going?" Diana asked.

"I need to be alone for a while," Freddie said. "I'm driving to the beach house."

"What time will you be home?"

"Maybe I'll stay overnight," he said abruptly. "I'll call you later."

"Whyn't you take Diana with you?" Max mumbled. "I'm sure there's a bunch of gorgeous nurses on call, an' your wife's been here all night."

"No," Diana said stubbornly. "I want to stay."

"You look tired, Diana," Freddie said. "Max is well taken care of. I'll drop you at home."

Diana realized this was neither the time nor the place to take a stand. First she'd better deal with the fiancée situation; then, when Max was out of the hospital, they could talk about their future together. "Very well," she said, deeply disappointed. "I'll come back later if you like, Max."

"Don't like," he slurred, almost out. "You've been great, but, please, I gotta sleep."

"Then I'll be here first thing in the morning."

"Whatever."

"Can I bring you anything?"

"Yeah, a stack of *Playboys* to cheer me up." Her mouth slid into a tight, disapproving line. "Only kidding," he said. "What's the problem? You don't approve of *Playboy?*"

"The name says it all," Diana said primly. "You're not a boy and you don't play."

*"C'mon,"* Max said. "Lighten up." He gave them both a weak wave, waited until they were out of the room, then rang for the nurse and requested a phone.

"You're not allowed any calls, Mr. Steele," the nurse said. "Don't forget, you're only just out of intensive care. Rest and sleep—that's all you're supposed to do."

422

"Anybody ever told you you've got a great—" He yawned and settled back on the pillow. "Nah—forget it."

"A great what, Mr. Steele?"

"I'm changing my ways," he mumbled, and fell into a deep sleep.

"Anybody ever told you you've got a great—" He
yawned and settled back on the pillow, then—

"Come on, Mr. Stanley."

"—never get tired—" he mumbled, and fell
into a deep sleep.

# chapter 19

LEE ECCLES STOPPED TUCCI
as soon as he entered the station. "What in hell's
going on?" he asked, falling into step beside him.

"Big brawl at the funeral," Tucci said, hitching up
his pants. "I've got 'em all coming in. Everyone
wants to press charges."

"Who're you talkin' about?"

"Bobby Skorch, Eddie Stoner—those are the only
two that matter. If we move fast, we can throw a few
questions at 'em before their lawyers arrive."

"Got it," Lee said. "Let *me* take Bobby."

"What's the story with the strippers?"

"They flew in with him, he checked 'em into a
hotel, then he split a coupla times—which gives him
the opportunity. As an alibi they're less than zero."

"The more I see him, the more I think he could've
done it," Tucci said. "I got a blood sample—one
from Eddie, too."

"How'd you manage that?"

"They're both bleeding. I did a little mopping up

with my handkerchief and jacket. Bobby's the handkerchief, Eddie's the jacket. Faye'll kill me when she
sees I've ruined her favorite jacket."

"Oh yeah, Faye," Lee said with a knowing smirk.
"Mustn't piss *her* off."

Tucci shot him a look. He didn't want to hear
Faye's name coming out of Lee's mouth. If there
wasn't so much going on he would've gotten into
exactly what Lee meant every time he mentioned his
wife.

As it was, there was no time for anything. Eddie
and Angie came rolling into the station, Angie still
screaming about assault charges. They were followed
closely by Bobby, who wanted Eddie arrested. And
then came Bo Deacon with his wife.

Trailing closely behind them were hordes of media, but they had to stay outside, jockeying for
position, waiting for when the principals emerged.

Captain Marsh poked his head out of his office.
"What in *hell* is going on here?" he demanded.

It was at that exact moment that Darlene and her
lawyer chose to arrive.


"Why'd you do it, Bobby?"

Slouched on a chair in the interview room, determined to get Eddie Stoner's ass slung in jail, upset
from the funeral, depressed and suicidal about Salli,
Bobby Skorch stared blankly at the tall, stoop-
shouldered detective with the weather-beaten face
and exceptionally large hands.

"What?" he said, his eyes blank and red-rimmed,
with no shades to hide his pain or his worsening
black eye from the world.

"Why'd you kill her?" Lee Eccles demanded,

leaning over the table and eyeballing Bobby with a ferocious glare.

Bobby's head snapped back. "Who the fuck d'you think you're *talkin'* to?" he said in a low, angry voice. "What the fuck is *this* shit?"

"Your two little scum-buckets from Vegas blew your alibi out the window," Lee said, scrambling for a used toothpick in his jacket pocket.

"Hey—" Bobby said, reality hitting home through his conflicted haze of self-hatred and drug-induced euphoria. "Get me my fucking lawyer."

"Your fucking lawyer ain't here," Lee said, not trying to hide his loathing for the famous person sitting before him. Loathing him because he had everything Lee didn't—including a sex-symbol wife who any red-blooded American male would give his left ball to fuck. *Excuse me*, Lee thought, angrily chewing on his newly found toothpick. *Dead wife. Murdered wife. Hacked-to-pieces wife.*

"You're outta line," Bobby said harshly. "I came here to straighten out a situation. You can't accuse me of shit."

"I'm only askin', Bobby. Thought you might wanna make a confession."

"Go fuck yourself in the ass. You wanna know who killed Salli? It was Eddie Stoner, an' you got him here now—so do somethin' about it."

"Where *did* you go Saturday night when you got back? Didja go to your house an' catch Salli with another guy? Was that what happened?"

"Jesus!" Bobby screamed. "Don't you understand English? *Eddie Stoner murdered my wife,* and I want him in jail. Got it, moron?"

\* \* \*

Oblivious to the scene going on in the next room, Tucci was attempting to calm Angela Musconni. Eddie Stoner slumped in a chair beside her, clutching a blood-soaked wad of Kleenex to his mouth. It was almost as if he'd lost his balls along with his two front teeth.

Angie, however, more than made up for his silence. She was acting like a wildcat, jumping up and down, pummeling the air with her fists to get her point across. "You gotta arrest the prick," she yelled. "Eddie said Bobby did it, an' Eddie knows what he's talkin' about. An' if you *can't* arrest him for the murder, you can sure as crap arrest him for personal assault. He knocked Eddie's *teeth* out and hit me too. I was lying on the ground *unconscious!* I'm pressin' charges. Arrest the prick! I demand it!"

"If we arrest him, Miss Musconni," Tucci said candidly, "it won't look good for you *or* us. The man was leaving his wife's funeral. He was provoked into a fight. There are dozens of witnesses who saw exactly what took place. His lawyer will bail him immediately, and then there'll be a long, drawn-out court battle with all the attendant publicity. Are you sure you want that?"

"No!" Eddie managed to say, spitting out more blood.

"Yes!" Angie insisted.

Tucci regarded the two of them, trying to decide who had the power in the relationship. Right now it was probably Angie—she was certainly the more vocal. But if she pressed charges against Bobby at this particular moment, it would complicate things. When the time came, they'd nail Bobby Skorch, but it would be for murder, not this petty stuff.

"Can I be frank with you both?" Tucci said. "Can I trust you?"

"Huh?" Angie said, suspicion narrowing her eyes.

"Mr. Skorch is indeed a suspect in the murder of Salli T. Turner, so an arrest at this time for assault would do nothing but hamper our investigation."

"Why?" Angie demanded.

"Because if we arrest him on a minor charge, it would not help us." He watched her carefully; she seemed to be listening, which was a good thing. "This is what I'd like you to do," he said.

"What?"

"I'd like you to go home, think about it, and if you still wish to press charges you can do so tomorrow. Is that fair?"

Eddie nodded vigorously. Angie was still not convinced.

"Miss Musconni," Tucci said in his most persuasive voice. "Do the smart thing. I promise, you won't regret it."

"Get me to a plastic surgeon," Bo Deacon whimpered as Olive drove their Rolls erratically down Wilshire Boulevard.

"I'm taking you to the emergency room," Olive said, not at all upset at her famous husband's predicament.

"Don't wanna go to emergency," he groaned. "I want a plastic surgeon."

"Shame your little sweetie is dead," Olive said, weaving erratically from one lane to the other. "I'm sure she was an expert when it comes to plastic surgeons. Let's see, she had silicone tits, pumped-up lips, false cheekbones, a new chin—probably a brand-new pussy after all the action the old one got."

"Jesus, you're a bitch," Bo said, wishing he was anywhere else. "She was twenty-two years old for God's sake. And she's dead."

"Good," Olive said.

"Good?" Bo repeated, not quite able to believe she'd said such a thing.

"Did you fuck her?" Olive inquired, tossing back her red hair.

*"What?"*

"Did you?"

"You're crazy," he said, disgusted.

"Did you do her on the plane, Bo Bo, did you?"

"Jesus, Olive, I can't even talk to you anymore."

"You went to her house, I know you did."

"Are you *insane?"*

"Oh, yes. Saturday. You were there, sniffing around while her husband was away."

"You've lost it."

"Have I?"

"I'm in pain."

"I don't care," she said with a drunken smile, nearly smashing his precious Rolls into the back of a truck.

"You're drunk," he said, stating the obvious. "Stop the car and let me drive."

"I'm drunk," she singsonged. "And you've been fucking around on me. Who's the baddest, Bo Bo?"

"Come on, Olive, not now."

"When?" she demanded, taking her eyes off the road and giving him a long, pained look. "When's *my* time?"

"My nose is broken!" he screamed. "I'm warning you, Olive, don't get into this now!"

"I hate you!" she bellowed, her face contorted with drunken fury as she hit the gas even harder. "Hate you! Hate you! Hate you!"

"For God's sake, Olive!"

And before he could do anything to stop her, she swung the wheel of the powerful car toward the oncoming traffic, and smashed head-on into a gold Mercedes.

# chapter 20

IT HAD TAKEN HER HOURS, but Kristin had finally managed to remove the middle board in the window. Unfortunately the space was only four inches high and two feet across, not big enough for her to squeeze through, but at least she could get some idea of where she was. As far as she could tell she was in some kind of guardhouse halfway down a cliff. The undergrowth on the cliff was unkempt and wild, which made her think that nobody ever came to this building. Several hundred feet below her was the ocean, and there seemed to be no other properties in sight.

She'd tried desperately to pry the rest of the window boards loose, but after a while she'd given up. It was impossible. Her hands were cut and bleeding, and there was a gash on her arm. She was lucky to have gotten the middle board out of there without breaking a bone.

Being able to look out and get some idea of where she was struck her as a major triumph.

What she couldn't figure out was *why* she'd allowed herself to be led down a dangerous cliffside blindfolded. She must have been crazy. One false step and she could've fallen hundreds of feet to her death.

*Little lamb goes quietly to the slaughter.*

What kind of a monster was Mister X anyway? she asked herself. Did he get a sexual kick out of this? Whatever. Clearly his motives were evil. *He* was evil.

The good thing was that she no longer felt like a victim. She had a plan and a weapon, and even though she was hungry and thirsty, she was determined to remain strong.

Now that she had some light, she could explore the room properly. Not that there was much to explore—bare floorboards, the bed, one sheet that she was now wearing, and nothing else.

She'd thought long and hard about what she would do if and when Mister X returned, and she'd finally decided her only move was to take him by surprise, try to knock him out, and escape. If she could do that and make it to the highway, she'd be able to summon help.

The thought of Cherie depending on her gave her strength.

Her inner voice had stopped screaming vile things in her head. Now it urged her to be strong.

*Don't be frightened. You can do it. You're a survivor.*

Yes. She was. And she *would* survive.

Of that she was sure.

# chapter 21

"**T**HAT'S HER," MADISON said, striding confidently toward the open-air restaurant.

"How do you know?" Jake said, squinting at the fair-haired girl sitting at a table by herself leafing through a copy of *Movieline*.

"One, she's alone. Two, she's wearing an orange sweater. Pretty easy to be smart under these circumstances. Did you get her name?"

"Nope."

"Well, okay, let's go over."

Jake put his hand on her arm, stopping her. "She's expecting me to be by myself. She's also expecting ten grand, which I don't have."

"We'll suss the situation out," Madison said. "Let *me* do the talking."

He wasn't sure if he liked Madison's new take-charge attitude. "You can be incredibly bossy," he remarked.

"You wanted help, didn't you?" she fired back. "Come on, let's do it."

Together they approached the girl in the orange sweater. She was busy reading an article on Vince Vaughn, and did not look up until Madison said, "Hi."

"Yes?" Junia said, her eyes darting this way and that.

"Meet Jake Sica," Madison said. "I'm his sister."

"Sister?"

"We're twins. We do everything together."

Junia wrinkled her forehead. What kind of a kinky scene was *this?* "Where's my money?" she said, putting down the magazine.

"Safe," Madison said matter-of-factly. "But of course, as I'm sure you're aware, we can't hand it over without knowing what we're paying for."

"I *told* him to bring the money," Junia said, slamming her delicate fist on the table.

"He did," Madison said calmly, pulling out a chair and sitting down—gesturing for Jake to do the same. "Here's the deal. Why settle for ten grand when you can make a lot more?"

"How?" Junia asked suspiciously.

"Did you ever hear of Watergate?"

"What's that, a bridge?"

"No. Watergate was an event in history. People with the right information made plenty of money out of Watergate."

"I don't get it," Junia said, intrigued in spite of herself, and starting to feel quite important.

"Do you work for Darlene?" Madison asked, thinking that this waif of a girl was the least likely looking call girl she'd ever seen.

"Work for her?" Junia snorted as if it was the most ridiculous thing she'd ever heard. "No way! S'matter of fact, I live with her." As soon as she'd said it, she regretted her words. She wasn't supposed to tell them anything about *her*. No way. Her plan was to get the money and take off.

"You mean you're her girlfriend?"

"S'right," Junia said, nodding vigorously.

"Platonic or otherwise?"

"What d'*you* think?" Junia said with a sly smile.

"Where's Kristin?" Jake said, getting impatient.

Junia ignored him, more interested in what the woman had to say. "What do you mean I can make more money?" she questioned.

"I'm sure you have a very interesting story to tell," Madison said. "And if you're prepared to reveal details about Darlene and exactly how she runs her business, well, I think we could be talking about a *lot* of money."

Junia's eyes popped. "A lotta money, huh?"

"Right," Madison continued, silencing Jake with a warning look. "I work for *Manhattan Style* magazine. If you agree to give us an exclusive, I'm sure I can get my editor to pay you twenty thousand dollars."

"Wow!" Junia exclaimed reverently.

"Here's my card," Madison said, fishing in her purse.

Junia took the engraved card and studied it. "How do I know this isn't a fake?" she asked.

"Why would I go to that kind of trouble?" Madison replied. "You see, we've been planning on writing an exposé on the call-girl industry for quite some time. My brother Jake's a photographer, that's his involvement. He was about to take some photos of Kristin for the magazine."

"Was she cooperating with you?" Junia asked.

"She certainly was," Jake said, getting Madison's drift and joining in. "Which is why it's so disturbing that she's vanished."

"I'm glad you're smart enough to get out now, while you can," Madison said, speaking fast. "We can put you in a hotel for your own protection. I'll have a contract from the magazine FedExed here immediately. Only thing is—you *have* to tell us how to find Kristin."

"Dunno where she is," Junia said. "But I do know that Mister X got her home number, and *he's* the client who had a date with Hildie. And . . ." She stopped, realizing she might be saying too much. "There's more about him, but I need t'see money first."

"Who's Mister X?" Jake asked with a distinct note of urgency.

Junia shrugged. "Nobody knows, not even Darlene. He calls every so often, whenever he wants a girl."

"The phone company," Jake said. "If he called Kristin, maybe they'll have a record of his number."

"I don't think it works that way," Madison said.

"We can give it a shot. It's better than doing nothing."

Madison turned to Junia. "Listen," she said. "You shouldn't go home. We'll check you into a hotel, all expenses paid."

"Why *can't* I go home?" Junia whined. "Darlene doesn't know I'm meeting you."

"Darlene's in trouble," Madison said. "She's all

over the TV. You'll be better off in hiding until we get your story. And remember, it's exclusive, or no big check."

"Well, okay," Junia said reluctantly. "But I'd better get paid tomorrow, otherwise the deal's off."

"Done," Madison said.

There was nothing that excited her more than a hot story. And she could tell this was going to be a good one.

# chapter 22

"**I**'VE BEEN KEPT WAITING
for forty-five minutes," Darlene said, although Linden had warned her it was not smart to complain.
"Forty-five minutes," she repeated icily, not particularly caring whether it was smart or not.

"Sorry, ma'am," Tucci said politely, sitting down
across from the well-groomed, extremely attractive
woman and her Beverly Hills lawyer. "Emergency
situation arose."

"I was forced to rush my lunch to be here on
time," Darlene said, pushing her point home.

Christ! *She* was complaining. All *he'd* had to eat
all day was three lousy donuts, and the way things
were going he'd be working straight through dinner.
Hopefully Faye would save him something. Lately
he'd been daydreaming about her pot roast. The
good thing was that over the last few days he must
have lost at least ten pounds. Goodbye diet. Hello
food.

"We understand you have some questions you'd

like to ask Ms. La Porte," Linden said. "Can we kindly proceed."

"Certainly," Tucci said. It had taken him a while, but he'd finally convinced Angela Musconni not to press charges against Bobby Skorch. She'd left with Eddie—reluctantly.

Meanwhile, Lee had managed to upset Bobby, who'd stalked out of the station just as his lawyer arrived. Marty Steiner was not a happy camper, furious that they'd had Bobby to themselves for an hour. Marty would be even more furious if he knew that even now the lab was running blood-sample tests which could possibly connect his client to Salli's murder.

Tucci was in no mood to conduct an interview with some Hollywood madam, who probably had more connections than a multi-purpose vacuum. He knew the way these things worked. These women always had clients in high places who eventually put on the pressure to get the charges dropped. Not that they had anything to charge Darlene La Porte with. She was a known madam, but right now they had no concrete proof. Her girls wouldn't talk, nor would her rich and famous clients. To nail Darlene they'd have to put some kind of entrapment plan in the works. And now was not the time.

"We appreciate you coming in," Tucci said.

"Appreciate away," Darlene said, shooting him a haughty look. "The sooner I'm out of here, the better."

"Yes, ma'am."

"And *don't* call me ma'am."

* * *

Madison was on a roll. In her mind she visualized the story she was going to write about L.A. and it had her adrenaline pumping. For the time being she forgot about Freddie Leon, because right now she was into investigating the call-girl business. It had all the ingredients for a killer story. Power. Obsession. Murder. Revenge. Her kind of deal.

And Junia—Darlene La Porte's almost underage lesbian lover—was set to spill everything.

They'd stashed Junia in a room in Jake's hotel, made sure she had Spectravision and room service; then they'd gone to Jake's room, where Madison sat on his bed and called Victor in New York.

"Have I got a story for you!" she bragged.

"Freddie Leon was *that* interesting?" Victor boomed in his annoyingly loud voice.

"Not Freddie," she said excitedly. "Bigger and better. Only you've got to come up with a check for twenty grand pronto."

"Excuse me?"

"I have a songbird from the inside of an exclusive call-girl operation. And she's ready to Whitney Houston it."

"You know, sometimes I don't understand a word you say."

"That's okay," she said breezily. "Make the check out to cash and FedEx it to me at once. We'll have a story that'll blow the magazine off the stands."

"Now wait a minute—"

"No waiting, Victor. And I want to work with a great photographer who just *might* be available." She winked at Jake, who couldn't believe this was the same Madison he'd gotten used to. "He's expensive, but you should definitely consider signing him.

His name's Jake Sica. I'll let you know if we can get him."

"Madison—"

"Bye, Victor." She hung up and turned to Jake. "Why work for some popular crap mag when I can get you a gig on *Manhattan Style?*"

"What happened to you?" he said, shaking his head at her metamorphosis. "You're all fired up."

She beamed. "I feel good. In fact, I feel *great*. I'm back in action. This story's going to be *sensational*. Let's go tell Junia the good news."

"I need to find Kristin," he said. "That's the only important thing to me."

For a moment she felt a shiver of disappointment. Just when she'd thought she and Jake were a great team . . .

"Sorry," she said quickly. "You're right, and I have an idea."

"What?"

"We should go by her apartment, see what we can find."

"The maid'll never let us in."

"Jake," she bragged. "Doncha know? You're working with *me* now, and when I'm into it, *I* can do anything."

# chapter 23

**P**ROPPED UP IN BED, WATCHing the unbelievable goings-on at Salli T. Turner's funeral on the TV news, Max Steele was completely comfortable and out of pain thanks to the miracle of modern drugs. The nurses were all fans. Well, how often was it that they got their hands on a genuine eligible Bel Air bachelor? They kept on popping into his room, two at a time, to take a peek at him and ask a question or two, such as did he know Matt Damon? And was Anne Heche really gay or was she just going with Ellen for the publicity? Normal questions the general public liked to ask.

Max got off on being the center of attention. He had his eye on the pretty black nurse—she had a Halle Berry quality about her, and he liked her personality, not to mention her perky tits.

Yes, all in all, it wasn't *that* bad getting shot, and now Freddie wasn't mad at him anymore, which was a good thing, and as soon as he recovered and recuperated at say—the Four Seasons in Maui—it would be back to business as usual.

He kept on drifting in and out of sleep, which was quite pleasant. *Gotta call Kristin,* he thought. *She must've wondered what happened to me. Gotta call her . . .*

Boom. His eyes closed. He was asleep again, which is how Inga Cruelle and Howie Powers found him when they burst into his room.

"Jesus, man," Howie exclaimed, waking him up. "You frightened the shit outta us."

Us? Did that mean the delectable Inga and his erstwhile friend—the brain-dead playboy—were an us?

"How'd you find out?" he mumbled.

"Your maid told me when I dropped by your house," Howie said, picking at a bunch of grapes on the bedstand. "What a bummer!"

"When was that?"

"'Bout an hour ago, soon as we got back from Vegas."

"Didja win?"

Howie beamed, and put his arm around Inga's waist, pulling the exquisite Swedish supermodel close. "I won the prize of all time. Inga did me the honor of becoming my wife."

*"Whaaat?"* Max tried to sit up, but sharp stabs of pain prevented him from doing so. "You got *married?*"

Inga gave a supermodel sneer—the one she'd perfected on runways all over the world. "That is right, Max dear. Howard and I are joined in matrimony."

Max could not believe what he was hearing.

Howie Powers and Inga Cruelle married? Impossible. He, Max Steele, hadn't even fucked her, and she'd married a major jerk like Howie. What was going on in the world? This was insanity.

"Show him the ring, honey," Howie urged.

Inga waved her hand under his nose. On her engagement finger was an enormous diamond, at least ten carats.

"Congratulations," Max managed, the words almost sticking in his throat. "What happened to your fiancé, Inga? The Swedish guy you told me you've been with since high school?"

She shrugged. "Howie is very sweet," she said. "And persuasive. He came to see me last night at midnight. So touching."

"With the ring?"

"Naturally."

"Yup," Howie said happily. "I got to thinkin', I've been a bachelor long enough. We flew to Vegas this morning, did it, and the first person we came to tell was you, 'cause you're my best friend, buddy."

*Yeah, sure,* Max thought. *You came to show me your prize. Because for once in your life, you rich little asshole, you got a girl before me. Well, good luck, 'cause this one's gonna take you for a lot more than a diamond ring. And you're such a schmuck, I bet you never had her sign a pre-nup.*

"I couldn't be happier for you," Max said, full of insincerity.

"Howard," Inga said, glancing at her Patek Phillipe diamond watch—a wedding present Howie had presented to her on the flight home. "I have to go."

"Gotta get my bride to the airport," Howie said. "She's off to Milan for the collections."

*"You're* not going?"

"Havta take care of some business first. I'll join her in a coupla days."

As if Howie, the playboy jerk, had any business to take care of. All Howie did was watch his trust funds grow, that was about it.

"Well . . ." Max said. "Thanks for dropping by."

"Your turn next," Howie said, winking.

*Ha!* Max thought. *Wait until he sees Kristin. She makes Inga look like a skinny version of truly gorgeous. No contest.*

"I'll see you guys," he said.

Inga blew him a kiss. Nice of her. Howie winked again and mouthed, "Somethin', huh?"

And then they were gone.

Max waited a minute and summoned Halle Berry. Life wasn't all that bad.

# chapter 24

TUCCI WAS SITTING AT HIS desk when he got the call that Bo Deacon had been killed in a horrendous car accident on Wilshire. His wife, Olive, who had been driving at the time, had been rushed to Cedars with multiple cuts and bruises, but nothing life-threatening.

She was conscious, hysterical and insisting on seeing one of the detectives in charge of the Salli T. Turner murder investigation.

Since Lee had gone off to re-interview several of Salli's neighbors, Tucci guessed he was it. What a day this was turning out to be. Bo Deacon killed in a car wreck. Talk about bad karma. You leave a funeral and run right into your own death.

Fate. The twists and turns of life. Never predictable.

Tucci left the station and drove to the hospital, calling Faye from the car. "Do you miss me?" he asked wistfully.

"Yes, I miss you," she answered. "When will you be home?"

"Not soon enough."

"How was the funeral?"

"Hectic. Did you see the news?"

"I'll turn it on."

"Faye?"

"Yes."

"I don't want to do this diet thing anymore."

"Why?"

"Life's too short." A beat. "Are we too old to have a baby instead?"

She laughed softly. "What's a baby got to do with dieting?"

"Thought we could get fat together."

"Yes."

"Yes?"

"Yes."

"I love you. Can I have pot roast for dinner?"

"You can have anything you want."

By the time he reached the hospital he had a big smile on his face. Sometimes it was nice to goof off, have nonsensical conversations, fall in love with his wife all over again.

There was a uniformed cop stationed outside Olive Deacon's room. "What's going on?" Tucci asked.

The cop spoke out of the side of his mouth like he didn't want anyone to hear. "She's hysterical, Detective, and drunk."

"So?"

"So she's confessing to Salli Turner's murder."

* * *

"Hi," said Madison, standing at Kristin's front door. "I spoke with Kristin and she asked me to tell you that she'll be home shortly."

Chiew, Kristin's maid, stared at her blankly, guarding the entrance to her boss's apartment with her sturdy body.

"She also asked me to wait for her here, but if you're not comfortable with me coming inside . . ." Madison shrugged, as if it didn't matter one way or the other.

Chiew stared at her for a few more seconds, and then decided that she looked perfectly honest, so surely access to Kristin's apartment was in order? Especially as Chiew needed to take off early to visit her boyfriend in prison.

As soon as the maid left, Madison called Jake in the car and he came right up from the underground garage. The first thing they did was play back Kristin's answering machine. Right away they hit pay dirt: the second recorded message was from Mister X, requesting that Kristin meet him at the end of Santa Monica Pier on Sunday night.

"Let's go," Jake said.

"Where?" Madison said. "If she *did* meet him, it's highly unlikely they're still there."

"Maybe somebody saw them together."

"Then we need a picture of her. Did you take any?"

"No, but there's one of her with her sister in a frame in the living room."

"Get it," Madison said, still in her bossy mode, but now just as anxious as Jake to find out what had happened to Kristin. She kept on hoping they wouldn't turn on the TV and hear about another body washed up on the beach.

While he was getting the photo, she took a quick look around. Nothing unusual. No clues. No jotted-down notes that might tell them more.

Jake brought her the photo. Kristin was indeed a dazzler—Madison had gotten a brief glimpse of her when she'd stopped by Jimmy Sica's to meet Jake for their date, but she'd honestly not appreciated how gorgeous the girl was. Fresh and natural with cascades of golden hair and a glowing smile. Nobody in their wildest dreams would tag her as a call girl.

"Whadda we do now?" Jake asked.

"Call Darlene," Madison said. "Let's see what it'll take to get her to cooperate."

# chapter 25

***H**E'S NOT COMING BACK and there is no way I can escape from this room where I'm being held a prisoner.*

The words ran through Kristin's head as she lay on the mattress in the small space, which was now like an oven. She was trying to reserve her strength.

*I'm tired, hungry, thirsty, hot, dispirited, exhausted. And yet, I'm still alive. And so is Cherie. For her sake I have to get out.*

*But if he doesn't come back . . .*

*If he's left me to rot . . .*

How long could a person last without food or water? Was it days, weeks, months? How long?

She wanted to scream and cry out. Yell for help.

But no. She couldn't do that. Had to stay strong for when HE came.

Mister X.

And he *would* come.

She knew he would.

# chapter 26

"**B**YE, HONEY DOLL."

"Goodbye, Howard."

"Take good care of the ring."

"Of course."

"Give me two days an' I'll be there all ready to fuck your brains out."

"Such a romantic," Inga said with a superior smile. The only one getting fucked in this relationship was Howie. She'd put her true fiancé on hold while she collected as much jewelry as possible in as short a time as possible. Then she'd have the marriage annulled. Howie was an obvious playboy—she was merely getting revenge for all the women he'd used and abused.

Howie made an attempt to kiss his new wife on the lips. She not so gently shoved him away. "Please, Howard, not in public," she scolded. "People are always watching me."

He lifted up her hand where the ten-carat diamond ring sparkled. Ten carats of cubic zirconia. When they'd been married a year and she presented him with a child, he'd buy her the real thing. People thought he was Howie Powers, schmucko playboy. They were wrong. There was much more to Howie than that.

He left the airport and drove back to town. The traffic was deadly, but Howie didn't care, he had the rest of the day all planned out.

Freddie Leon headed for Malibu, cursing the heavy traffic. He'd dropped Diana home first. There was something going on with her; she wasn't acting like herself. And what was this sudden attachment she had toward Max?

Maybe he should consider giving her more attention. He always put business first and she knew it.

And when he wanted to relax . . . well, it wasn't Diana he turned to. No. There was somebody else.

And today he desperately needed to relax.

Olive Deacon clutched Tucci's hand. "I killed him!" she wailed. "He's dead because of me!"

Her alcohol-drenched breath caused him to take a step back. "Who?" he asked.

"My husband, that's who!" she sobbed.

"Mrs. Deacon, I'm going to read you your rights. Anything you say may be used in evidence against you. You have the right to a lawyer. If—"

As he droned on she disintegrated before his very eyes. Her face crumpled, mascara coursed down her cheeks, lipstick stained her teeth.

"Mrs. Deacon," he said quietly, feeling sorry for her. "Do you want to contact your lawyer before we talk?"

"No lawyer," she said between sobs. "It's my fault Bo's dead. I've been punished, and I have to tell you everything."

"You wish to make a formal statement?"

"Yes, I do."

"Very well."

And before he could get his pen out, she began talking.

# chapter 27

T HE MOMENT SHE HEARD THE
click of the lock, Kristin was ready. She raced to
the door, positioning herself behind it, so that
when he opened it, there would be an element of
surprise. Her heart was pounding, but she knew
that if she didn't seize the opportunity all would be
lost.

She was filled with anger as she crouched in
position. Anger would make her strong. Anger
would help her gain her freedom.

Mister X pushed open the door.

She braced herself, holding the bed leg poised
above her head—ready to smash him with it—
ready to run.

Light flooded the dusty little room. He stepped
inside.

For a moment she was paralyzed, unable to move
or think. And then, as if in slow motion, she sprang
forward, sideswiping the figure in black with all her

might—hitting him as hard as she could with the wooden bed leg.

To her amazement he didn't fall. In movies when you saw someone get hit they always fell. Instead he staggered, letting out a furious cry of surprise.

Before he had a chance to react further, she bashed him again.

This time he almost went down. His baseball cap fell to the ground, and his sunglasses hit the floor and cracked. Seizing her opportunity, she ran past him, through the door, out into the unknown, frantically trying to figure out the best way to freedom.

She found herself on a narrow, overgrown path. To her left, hundreds of feet below, was the ocean. Ahead of her there were steps hewn into the rock leading up to a big house perched high above.

The steps were her only way out. She raced toward them, concentrating on survival, not looking back.

As she reached the first step she could hear him behind her. He grabbed her leg. She kicked out blindly.

"Bitch!" he snarled.

"Leave me alone, you sick bastard!" she screamed, scrambling desperately up the hazardous steps.

He grabbed her again, this time getting hold of her makeshift dress. The sheet tore. Half naked, she continued to claw her way up, determined that he was not going to stop her. Nobody was. She was heading for freedom in every way—not just from this man, but this life.

"Don't you get it?" he yelled. "I own you. I always

have. You're *my* whore. My very own personal whore."

There was something about his voice . . . something she almost recognized. It wasn't the Mister X voice, the disguised growl. This was the real man talking, and it was . . . Oh God, SHE KNEW WHO HE WAS!

For a moment she could barely breathe. Then, as if in a trance, she stopped climbing and turned around.

The monster was two steps behind her, baseball cap gone along with the dark glasses. A trickle of blood rolled slowly down the side of his face.

She stared into his eyes.

He knew she recognized him.

They were both still, like two big cats in the wild, watching each other, waiting to see who would pounce first.

"Okay," he said at last. "So now you know. And there's *nothing* you can do." And he laughed, that self-loving cackle she remembered so well. "You and your dumb sister—you're exactly alike," he continued. "She was a whore, too. She didn't deserve to live. Neither do you."

In perfect slow motion she rose from her defensive position, brought her leg back and kicked out with such force that when her leg connected with his chest he had no chance to correct his balance.

He fell back, his hands clutching the air as he tumbled over himself twice, and then disappeared over the edge of the cliff with a long, bloodcurdling scream.

Kristin watched him fall, heard the sound of his

body as it struck a tree on its way to the rocks and ocean below.

She wasn't sorry. She had finally avenged her sister. And it felt completely satisfying, as if it was meant to be.

Howie Powers would *never* laugh at anyone again.

# Epilogue

# Nine Months Later

**D**ETECTIVE TUCCI AGITAT-
edly paced the corridors of Cedars Sinai. Faye was
giving birth and although he'd tried to stay in the
room holding her hand, the sight of blood—his
wife's blood—had sent him running.

His new partner, Wanda O'Donahue, had stopped
by to keep him company. She'd also brought a box of
donuts and a flask of Starbucks coffee. There were
many advantages to having a female partner, although Faye didn't seem to think so.

"How's it going in the delivery room?" Wanda
asked, biting into a donut.

"It's a war zone," he said, grimacing. "A lot of
blood and guts and screaming."

"You'll live," Wanda said, giving him a friendly
pat on the back.

Yeah, he'd live.

It had been some year. The murder of Salli T.
Turner had garnered the most headlines, especially

when Mrs. Bo Deacon had confessed, right after the terrible car accident which killed her husband.

Tucci had not felt that her confession rang true—although his superiors were in "we've caught the murderer" heaven, and the press went into headline overdrive. Olive simply didn't have the details the killer would have possessed, although she *was* able to produce the gun used to kill Froo. It was registered to Bo Deacon.

Tucci stayed on the case, establishing that Bobby Skorch had gone to his house earlier in the evening, made love to his wife, fought with her, and left, forever feeling guilty that he hadn't stayed around.

Bo Deacon had then arrived, unaware that Olive was following him. He'd come on to Salli, she'd told him he had no chance with her. A fight had ensued and he'd killed her in a frenzy of frustration. Then he'd shot the houseman and fled. Olive had observed everything from her hiding place in the bushes next to the pool.

When Olive had killed Bo in the car wreck, she'd been so overcome with guilt that she'd decided to take the blame for the murders and protect her husband's not-so-spotless reputation. At least in death, he would be her hero.

If it wasn't for Tucci and his concern for detail, she would have been incarcerated for life. As it was, she was soon back in her Bel Air mansion with a twenty-five-year-old boyfriend, a lucrative book deal, and a new passion for life.

Tucci took a swig of coffee. It tasted fine. For the last six months he'd taken up spinning—an exhausting form of aerobic exercise on a stationary bike. It worked for him, and it had meant no more dieting, since he'd lost twenty-five pounds.

Faye's doctor approached him, a gentle Asian woman with the most captivating smile. "Your wife would like to see you now, Detective."

"Is it over?"

"Yes, it is."

"And?"

"You're the proud father of a beautiful baby girl."

His grin practically lit up the entire hospital.

The Freddie Leon divorce was one of the most expensive L.A. divorces in recent years. Diana received half of everything—and everything was a lot. Freddie decided it was worth it. He had his freedom and no price was too high to obtain *that*. Besides, business was fine; he could afford to pay Diana off.

A discreet six months after the final decree, Ria Santiago moved into Freddie's beach house—he'd given the Bel Air mausoleum to Diana. After a seven-year affair, he and Ria were finally able to be seen together in public. Freddie felt it was the least he could do for the most loyal woman he'd ever met.

Out of the hospital and fitter than ever, Max Steele eschewed a lot of his material possessions. He traded in his Maserati for a Hummer. Sold his house and moved into the Wilshire high-rise he'd been leasing out. Did not replace his gold Rolex, and after trying to contact Kristin a couple of times and getting no response, he'd fallen in lust with Angela Musconni, even though it was against policy since the agency represented her. Of course, he'd had to persuade Angie to dump the loser she was living with, but that hadn't been too difficult, since shortly after they got together, Eddie Stoner scored a TV series that shot in Hawaii.

It was amazing what could be accomplished when you were one of the most powerful agents in town.

Blaming himself for Salli's death, Bobby Skorch lost all sense of concentration. While attempting a record-breaking motorcycle jump between skyscrapers in New York, he faltered and fell to his death.

Natalie De Barge got the anchor job she'd been yearning for. Sitting beside Jimmy Sica every night, they made a fine couple. When the cameras weren't rolling, she practically had to beat him off with a stick, but that was just one of the hazards of being an anchorwoman.

She put her love life on hold and enjoyed every second of her new, invigorating career.

Her brother, Cole, moved in with Mister Mogul— who so far was treating him like a prince. However, to Natalie's eternal relief, Cole was smart enough not to give up his day job.

Junia took the twenty thousand dollars she received for revealing all of Darlene's dark secrets, and moved to Nashville, where she met a blond and bubbly country singing star with enormous breasts. They soon became a couple. Junia took up singing. She wasn't half bad.

\* \* \*

Darlene was finally nailed on that good old stand-by—tax evasion. Her lawyer, Linden Masters, was so livid to discover she'd kept things from him that he refused to represent her anymore. She hired a new lawyer with even more savvy than Linden, and because of her powerful connections, she got off with an extremely short jail term.

After she got out, she threw all caution out the window and found a ghostwriter to collaborate on a book, naming names. Her book—dramatically enti-tled *Madam*—was due out shortly.

Hollywood waited in a state of paranoid fascina-tion.

Kristin took stock of her life, and her sister's too. She met with Cherie's doctor and finally listened to exactly what he had to say. He was a nice man with brown hair and kindly eyes. "There are no miracles, Kristin," he informed her. "Cherie is brain-dead. The only reason she's still alive is because you won't allow us to pull the plug."

"Pull it," she said quietly. "I understand."

"You're sure?"

"Yes, I'm sure."

After escaping from the beach house, she'd come home and anonymously called the police—telling them all she knew about Mister X, including his death and where they'd find him.

Jake had been frantic to see her, so she had agreed to have lunch with him and to listen to everything he had to say. It wasn't enough though—there was no going back. He was part of her past now, and she was moving forward.

He told her about the story his friend Madison Castelli was working on.

"Do me this one favor, Jake, leave my name out of it."

"It's done," he assured her.

A week later she moved out of her luxurious apartment into a simpler place.

A few weeks later the doctor called and invited her to dinner. "What are you going to do now that you no longer have to pay your sister's bills?" he asked.

"I'm going back to school," she said. "I want to get my degree in child psychology and maybe— sometime in the future—work with children."

"Sounds like an excellent idea."

The doctor didn't lead a glamorous life or drive a flashy car. He was a hardworking professional who really cared for people, and he genuinely liked her for herself. Kristin found a great deal of comfort in his presence. So much so that they were married three months later.

Jake Sica stayed in L.A. for several months, photographing movie and sports stars, singers and moguls. Working for *Manhattan Style* was an interesting gig, and very highly paid, but after a while he began to yearn for the wide-open spaces of Arizona.

One morning he woke up, looked out his window at the hovering smog, and decided that was it.

By noon he was packed and on his way.

Madison wrote the best story of her career, all about the call-girl business in Hollywood. It was so good that Hollywood shelled out, bought the movie rights for an astronomical sum, and asked her to work on the script.

She stayed in touch with her good friend Jake. He was a great guy, but they never quite connected romantically. Wrong timing.

She took a weekend off with her parents in Connecticut. They were delighted to see her, especially her handsome father, Michael.

Then she flew to Hollywood and met Alex Woods, an edgy, incredibly talented writer/producer/director with a penchant for making powerful Oscar-nominated movies. He wanted to make *her* movie.

So Madison entered the next phase of her life with her eyes open and an appetite for excitement.

Things were looking up.